THE SLEEP SPECIALIST

also by Kitty Burns Florey

Sister Bernadette's Barking Dog
Solos
Souvenir of Cold Springs
Vigil for a Stranger
Five Questions
Duet
Real Life
The Garden Path
Chez Cordelia
Family Matters

THE SLEEP SPECIALIST

a novel

Kitty Burns Florey

Raven's Eye Publishing

ISBN: 978-0-6151-4880-9

For Turi and Bruce MacCombie,
dear friends

PROLOGUE

San Miguel de Allende, Mexico
1990

Hana sent me this clipping, Darnell. Cut from the *Times*, tucked into a sympathy card. What a way to find out. *May Munro, Film Actress, 85.* That's the headline. Found dead.

May. I haven't seen her since she ran out on me – how many? Fifty-some years ago. Seen her in the flesh, I mean. I've seen her in the movies, of course. Who hasn't? Died in her sleep, it says, according to her daughter. Whatever that means: *died in her sleep.* And this photograph of her from the sixties, one of her last publicity shots: bruised-looking face, spiky eyelashes, and her smile – almost amused but not quite.

I remember that smile, those soft pink lips, her little teeth. We weren't married long, but how could I forget all that, and her small eager hands, and her huge blue eyes. Her hair spread out over the pillow like some precious metal while she slept. I remember her sleeping.

She could always sleep, and I always had trouble. Even then, when I was young and healthy, sleep came rarely, with difficulty. It was like a distant land, Darnell, the Land of Oblivion – a place in a dream, beautiful and green, life-giving, where you long to go, that you glimpse far off and can never quite reach. I would approach it, I would climb the hills and descend into the valleys, with that blessed, blissful place always before me – and then wake with a start, my eyes staring wide into the dark, thrust back into the barren Land of Insomnia.

I'd struggled with this on and off all my life, but it was especially bad that first summer in New York. Many nights I would give up and go out, walking the streets of the city, thinking about my play, making up dialogue, until I was tired enough to go home.

I walked up Broadway into Harlem. I walked downtown to the Brooklyn Bridge and over it. I walked back from Brooklyn once when the dawn was breaking over my shoulder, up the river where Queens was, the sky smeared with rose and blue. But usually I just walked up Fifth Avenue, maybe up into the 90s, and down again by way of Park, past all those dark and shuttered mansions where people slept the sleep of the rich and where, one foggy morning before dawn, I stood at Park and 81st and watched two thieves break into a building from a second story balcony. I did nothing – watched them fiddle with the lock in perfect silence by the gray light from a lamp and let themselves in – and then I walked on. Another night I saw one man stick a knife into another and leave him for dead. Once I saw what I thought was a brown river running in the gutter and it turned out to be rats, an army of them, slinking along in the dark. I saw whores in fur coats, whores in diamonds, getting into taxis. And once, twice, I saw men with their arms around each other, men kissing, and one night a man dressed as a woman, long-legged and broad-shouldered, with thick black hair pinned back with diamond combs. And once I saw the police arrest a man, slamming him against the paddy wagon and hitting him in the stomach until he slumped over, then fell to the ground. A black man, Darnell. They picked him up and threw him into the back of the wagon, slammed the doors, and when I went over to where they had been I saw his blood bright as paint on the pavement.

On those nights I would get home at dawn or just before, sleeping three or four hours until it was time to get up. I was tired a lot of the time, but I was young, full of energy, and I had things to do. I was writing my first play, and it was going to redeem me. I thought much of myself; I believed in my future. I was probably somewhat ridiculous – wearing confidence like I wore my father's old Panama hat. That old hat had a strange fate – I'll tell you someday, maybe. But even, at times, when my body was exhausted and would have liked to stretch out on the bed those hot afternoons, my brain was full of schemes. And on most nights, when May and I had fallen into bed, whether or not we had performed our peculiar kind of lovemaking, I would fit myself into the groove of her back and her bent knees, and while she sank into sleep I would come irretrievably awake – as if she took the sleepiness from me and added it to her own.

Now I think my difficulty with sleep is nothing but a habit: insomnia has worn its grooves into me and there's no smoothing them out. But in those days my brain just kept burning along no matter what I did to my body. It was as if I had to stay awake for some reason – like a vigil. And maybe that's what it was, after all. I was keeping watch over the last summer of my youth.

■ ■ ■

"Look at this, Darnell. May died. My wife, May Munro."
"I'm sorry to hear that, Mr. Sinclair."
"I don't know if I ever told you I was married to her."

"I think you did mention that one time, if I recall."

"They give me one sentence, which is probably more than I deserve. Listen: *In the thirties, she was briefly married to playwright Robert Sinclair* (Fish Out of Water, Afternoon Coffee, The Monkey Tree, *on which the 1964 hit musical was based); they divorced in 1936, when she married Howard Mackenzie.*"

"Says she was 85 years old. Older than you."

"Oh yes. By five years. It was mortifying to her. She used to say: *When I'm thirty, I'll start lying about my age.* Of course, when she was thirty she had already left me and gone out to Hollywood."

 "I saw some of her movies on TV. Mighty pretty lady."

"Yes. Pretty. She was indeed."

Pretty was always the word. Not beautiful, but that blander, more comfortable adjective: *pretty.* So pretty: everything round, soft, eager. The kind of prettiness that doesn't wear well, that doesn't come from the bones, it's all in the flesh. Maybe that's what makes women like that so sweet, so sad: it can't last, so gobble it up now before it spoils.

"It don't say what she died of. Died in her sleep is all."

"I guess it was just old age, Darnell. Heart, probably."

It's not what I would want for myself: to slip away in the middle of a dream. And how would it happen, really? Would death enter the dream? Would you dream your death and then – just stop? Brain, breath, blood: shut down. The dream I had, once, of climbing out of a pit, or a well, something deep and dark, when I tried to climb out and kept falling back, trying and falling back, and I could see the light up above but could never reach it, until I finally woke up. Sweating, my breath coming short. Would dying in your sleep be like that? To fall back one last time to darkness, silence, nothing. How strange, how unimaginable. And to miss that experience, to sleep through it. It doesn't seem right. Because it has to be – doesn't it, Darnell? – an important one. As important as being born. It doesn't seem fair that you miss your birth. But death – that's something you can be awake for if you're lucky. Awake, following it to the end: that seems the right way. But merciful for May, I think, who loved to sleep, who loved her dreams so much. *I dreamed the room was full of owls, I dreamed I was floating above the city in the night and I could see all the lights, I dreamed Carlotta and I were walking two little black dogs up Second Avenue.* I remember how her hair, spread out on the pillow, seemed to gather up the light and hold it, so that when I went in to wake her, those hot evenings, at suppertime, the room would be nearly dark but her hair would gleam golden, the hair on her head and the hair between her pale white legs, everything gold and white. I can see her as if these fifty-some years have been given back to me, as if she's asleep in the next room. She didn't need that sleep: she just wanted it, loved it, craved it like a bottle or a drug.

■ ■ ■

"What do you think, Darnell? Would you want to die in your sleep?"

"I don't like to think about dying, Mr. Sinclair."

"Well, you're young enough not to have to."

"Ain't nobody that young."

■ ■ ■

Hana dear. Thanks for the card, and the clipping. It's sad, I suppose, though I have to say I don't feel much. It was a long time ago. (I was gratified to see my name on the list of husbands.) I hope you are keeping well. Will you get down here this year? You know I would like to see you, any time you can come.

"If you'd mail this in the morning, I'd appreciate it."

"Will do, Mr. Sinclair."

I love these evenings when we have dinner in the courtyard, when you push my chair out here and light the candles. I love the sounds of the night. The cicadas' dry rasping. A cat complaining or in heat. Music, always: church bells, the cantina band competing with somebody's radio, Pepita singing in the courtyard next door when she waters the plants. Almost nothing has changed since I used to visit this town with Arthur, all those years ago. I wish I hadn't waited until I was in my seventies to come here to live. How often have I thought that? The alien sweetness of the life throbbing here, the endless music, the warmth that gets into my bones. And you, Darnell, so silent, sitting on the stone bench across from me. Do you like this quiet? Hate it? Do you even notice it?

"You going over tonight, then?"

"I don't think so, Mr. Sinclair. Not tonight."

I try to get you to talk, Darnell, because I love to watch your mouth: like two smooth slices of a peach. Then the night grows slowly darker, and you blend into it, you become almost invisible. You absorb the darkness the way May used to absorb the light, and when you light a cigar I watch the glow, the way it pulses slightly in the darkness. The sweet burning smell. Your strong white teeth that look so strangely thick and solid. The sound of your breath as you inhale, exhale. I can hear how much you enjoy this one small daily cigar. How young you are. And how did it happen, finally, that they accepted you down at the cantina? I know that, for months, no one talked to you, or acknowledged your presence except to shut up when you went in. Gradually, it got better. That's all you would say. *It's better now.* You don't tell me why, or how. Did you, silent Darnell, actually talk to the men in the cantina? Did you ever challenge them? Did anyone call you names? Is there a Spanish word for nigger? In Spanish, *Negro* seems harmless – just a word, a color. But I can't stretch my imagination into the cantina, and all you say is that gradually people quit staring at you, started being friendlier. *It's better.*

"When you think about it, Darnell, nobody really knows that for a fact. Do they? That someone died in their sleep. Just because you wake up in the morning and find them dead, looking peaceful. They could have been wide awake when it happened."

"I suppose that's true, Mr. Sinclair."

I wonder if you are thinking about this. But you don't like to think about dying.

Eventually you put your cigar out, carefully, in the little painted tin ashtray you bought down at the *mercado* for six pesos, and, as I knew you would, you say, "Maybe I'll be going across the street, after all, Mr. Sinclair. Just for a few minutes, if it's okay with you."

"Of course. I'm quite comfortable here."

"Be back in half an hour."

"That would be good."

I'm here with the night sounds, the night music.

I don't mind thinking about dying. I think about my own death, which is coming to me soon, it's chasing me, it's at my back. *Time's winged chariot.* I think about May's death, and then about her life. If I could write a play about that summer at the Alhambra Gardens with May, with Orson Price, I might do it – but knowing, the whole time I was writing, that real life – for me, anyway – can never be as sacred and true as what's invented. And, inevitably, it would be a sad, dirty little play, more like one of Joe Orton's than one of mine, but I think it would have a certain compelling dramatic tension, and if I could figure out the ending, Darnell, if I knew what the hell happened to me that summer and could put it into a play, there wouldn't be a dry eye in the house.

ONE

New York City
1934-1935

When Mr. Gant agreed to hire us, he asked me only if I was handy.

"Handy," I said, not exactly questioning but in a reflective tone, as if it was a puzzling word I'd come across in a book. This bought a little time while I looked at Mr. Gant's thicket of eyebrows and the long wrinkle in each gaunt cheek that appeared to be scored cleanly by some sharp instrument that didn't draw blood. He was a big, pale-faced man, taller than I, and shaped oddly: wide and substantial from the front, leaner from the side. His thinning hair lay in stripes across his skull. Instinctively, I disliked him. But May and I were down to our last few dollars. We were living on milk and apples and day-old doughnuts.

"Handy. Unclog a toilet, change a lock, clean out the gutters." A humorless grin twisted the lower half of his face and turned his eyes to slits. "You know what I'm talking about."

"Ah." The sweat of desperation trickled down from my armpits. "Is that all? I thought you meant something difficult, like –" I had to struggle. "Like pumping out the septic system. Or sewing up a new pair of drapes for the lobby."

Mr. Gant laughed, one high-pitched yelp: *Hah!* His teeth were long and yellow, stained with brown from forty years of cigarettes. "We'll leave that one to your pretty wife. As for the plumbing, I think we'll call in the professionals if it gives us any big problems." He shook my hand, hard; I made sure I clenched his with energy. "You're going to be just fine. Any friend of Myra Kramer's."

"She's my wife's aunt, actually."

"Quite a woman."

"Yes," I agreed. "She is." Wondering what he meant. I had a vision of May's Aunt Myra's bleached upsweep, her formidable cleavage as she frowned over her poker hand.

"Well. Glad I found the pair of you. Twelve bucks a week and the basement apartment." He gestured with his chin over his shoulder to where the Alhambra Gardens loomed behind us in all its glory. "See if I can't do a little something for you at Christmas. Assuming Mr. Roosevelt's New Deal works out, of course. Better days are coming, all that socialist doubletalk." He interrupted himself with a jerk of his head. "Hey! You two ain't night owls, are you?"

I had no idea why he was asking, but I knew the right answer. "No, sir. Homebodies, that's us," I said, relieved that May wasn't there to hear me.

"I'm darned glad to hear that. I expect you to be around here most nights. In case of emergency. After ten or so, they're on their own. Maybe eight or nine on Saturdays. Rest of the time, people like to know there's a problem, there's somebody around." He paused. "You're a writer, you say."

I shrugged. "I'm working on a play. But of course that won't interfere with my chores. My work around the building."

He raised his eyebrows. "Damn right it won't," he said, and yelped again, showing his dog's teeth.

May and I retrieved our things from the rooming house on Bedford Street in a taxi – May's two bags and her three-way mirror, four wooden crates of books, my portable typewriter, a carton of odds and ends, and the ancient leather suitcase I inherited from my father. I paid off the taxi with one of our dollar bills, and we carried everything down the short flight of stairs and dumped it inside the door.

"Leave it," May said. "Leave it, Robert. I can't face it yet." We sat down on the sagging couch. May pushed back her hair with both hands, rubbed her forehead hard. "I feel a little dazed. One minute we're on the skids, and next thing you know – this."

"It's going to be okay." I smiled at her. "Hey, May – I tried out for the role of the building superintendent, and I got the part."

She didn't laugh. "Oh, Robert. I hope you can do it. I hope we – I don't know. This basement. It's so strange here." She sighed deeply. "Isn't it strange?"

"Strange? Well, I suppose it is, yes."

The dark unfamiliarity of that little apartment, furnished with other people's cast-offs, seemed romantic and beautiful to me. Dusty gold light from two small, high windows showed a hooked rug under our feet faded to a striated mushroom color, white plaster walls cold and almost damp to the touch, a couch and chair of brown plush. The lamp base was brass, a rearing horse, and the shade was red fringed with black. There was a bookcase, an ashtray shaped like cupped hands, a table painted yellow, a brown Motorola radio. We had a living room, a bedroom, a kitchenette with a hot plate and an ice box, a tiny bathroom with a tub. On the other side of the green front door a brass plaque read

SUPERINTENDENT in script so elegant it was almost unreadable. In spite of the cold shabbiness, the place felt warm and safe.

"I like it here," I said.

I looked down at May and saw that she had fallen into a quick doze. I watched her breasts rise with her calm breathing, and as I watched she shivered. In that powdery light I could just make out the delicate fans of wrinkles that were beginning around her eyes: as always, they made me feel tender toward her, and I wanted to take her in my arms. But I let her sleep. The apartment was cool, but airless. I covered her with a light blanket I found in the other room, and went quietly out the apartment door.

Ahead of me was the furnace room, the boilers, the padlocked storage areas. The walls at that level were painted a sort of khaki, but up a short flight of steps was the marble lobby, with the heavy brocade drapes Mr. Gant and I had joked about, two potted palms turning brown at their tips, and the staircase with its fancy newel post: a polished oak sphere caught in a woven cage of wrought iron vines. We would keep the woodwork polished, Mr. Gant had said, and the palms watered – how often, he didn't say – and the marble floor swept, mopped down every morning, more often if necessary. I stood in the lobby for a few minutes, imagining myself and May doing these small chores, working together, chatting – imagining how it would all become a routine: we would be up early, get the chores done, then she would spend the rest of the day at rehearsals or at an acting class – she had high hopes of getting into a good acting class if we could ever afford it. Or sitting in the Automat with Carlotta drinking nickel cups of coffee and comparing notes on producers, nail polish, hair styles. I loved to think of them together – the girls – talking their inconsequential female talk. While I finished my play in the soft afternoon light of our basement apartment. For the moment, I couldn't imagine a better life.

I crossed the marble floor – it needed mopping now, I noticed, but surely that could wait – and went out the front door. The apartment building was at the corner of Second Avenue and 21st Street – stucco-over-brick painted a light, peeling gray, and dwarfing the buildings around it. It perched on its corner like an elephant on a footstool, with a patch of grass in front, and a scraggly hedge. May had made fun of these bits of green, called them pathetic, but I didn't agree. One thing I loved about the city was the way people made a life for themselves against all odds: they grew flowers in window boxes, they stood patiently in lines, they rode the packed subways, they stepped out into the street smiling, wearing bright colors as if the air was clean and fresh, as if the city just by its existence made them somehow rich. I was glad our building had grass and bushes, and I had no trouble imagining geraniums in pots, maybe a row of tulips next spring.

Pathetic. No, it was Rochester that had been pathetic: no money, no work, and my mother's endless grief, not so much for my father, who had dropped dead suddenly as he watched his ball soar into the air at the fifteenth hole, as for the way of life that had disappeared with his death. The bitterness of her sorrow twisted her face, her small body, even the new way she hugged me: with a sad, clutching desperation, her fingers like claws. And my sister Joan with her petty concerns: kids, house, bridge game, her melancholy husband Bernie hanging on to a job he hated. Rochester was a place to leave.

New York was a place to go to. I stood on the sidewalk with my hands in my pockets, and looked up with satisfaction at the apartment building. Above the front door, ALHAMBRA GARDENS was incised into the stone. I wondered if there had once actually been a garden, maybe a long border of flowers where now there was only scruffy grass. The stucco of the building itself was set with random squares of mosaic; some of the chips were mirrors that sparkled in the summer light. The first floor windows and the double front door were topped with Moorish arches; the wrought-iron grid across the glass made a tangle of stylized leaves and branches. The front steps spread out on either side in a curve like a long, sinuous skirt, at each side a chipped mosaic-covered pot in which a spindly box tree grew. It all seemed wonderful to me: the eccentric building, the hot New York street, the roar of the El rushing by over on Third Avenue, and my beautiful wife sleeping peacefully in the gray light of our basement apartment.

May and I had been married six months, but this was our first real time alone. In Rochester, without jobs, we lived at my mother's until she needed our room for a lodger, then with May's Aunt Myra – an awkward few months marked by shared bathrooms and embarrassed sex and hardly any time alone together. Then those desperate weeks on Bedford Street, Verna Quiller's rooming house, with its paper-thin walls and both of us getting more and more anxious while I tried to find work and our small store of money melted and, when I touched her, May just sighed and said, "When will all this end?"

I met May when we both waited tables at McGreevey's Steak House, once one of the best restaurants in Rochester, now a boarded-up shell. Just after May and I were married, at the end of 1933, I passed by it on the streetcar and had to turn away: the planks across the windows had weathered to silver, the faded FOR RENT was crooked, hanging pink and rakish from a nail – one final irreverence.

I'd known McGreevey's since I was a boy, had eaten many a steak in that red plush dining room – the place where my family had celebrated holidays and birthdays, Joan's high school graduation, my acceptance at Harvard, my parents' twentieth wedding anniversary. May had worked there for years, off and on, whenever she was between acting roles, and Joe McGreevey gave me a job because he had been a friend of my father: he had been part of the foursome, in fact, when my father played his last game of golf. "It was a beautiful shot, Robert," he said. He had tired blue eyes, red-rimmed, and they filled with tears. "Straight and true."

I was a waiter there for nearly a year, until Joe went broke and had to close it down. I first kissed May in the little garden out back, one midnight after we got off work: we kissed and then stood in the near-dark looking at each other, holding hands, hoping no one else would come out the back door but not really caring. "I think you're the first genuinely nice man I've ever met," May said. I could remember that moment, the green twilight and the way a short gust of wind blew back her hair so that I saw her face, her skull, naked and lovely. My heart pounded in my temples, and there was an urgent pause before I took her in my arms and kissed her again, clinging to her as if I was going under and she was a life preserver. Over a year later, the thought of that first night could make me short of breath, weak with excitement.

I strolled around the corner to Second Avenue. Studded between the boarded-up storefronts was a cigar store, a barber shop, a Chinese laundry, a small grocery. The fat Greek sandwich man was on the corner, and a man selling what looked like small lizards from a cardboard box. A peanut-vendor passed, and the scent of roasting peanuts filled the air, smelling like childhood, comfort. From the river, I heard the hooting blast of a passing ship – a romantic sound, faint against the noise of the streets. I continued around the block. It was early evening – rush hour, I realized, seeing the crowds coming from the looming El on Third Avenue, women in summer dresses and men in straw hats. Going around our corner again to the Alhambra Gardens, I had a moment of panic. Jesus, it was huge. Five stories high and full of things I knew nothing about: plumbing and wiring, crumbling plaster, difficult people, nameless emergencies. What in hell did I think I was doing? I thought for a moment of my father's funeral, when I stood with my mother at the grave, and she collapsed into my arms weeping. The same panic: a rip, a void opening.

But this time the moment passed. I took a deep breath. We would be all right. I had faith in my own instincts, in my luck. And, as always, I was cheered simply by the look of things: the vast bones of the El against the sky, our dusty street as it headed east to the river, a skinny black dog nosing in the gutter, the yellow taxis, the women with their smooth bare legs, a flock of pigeons flying in formation above the building across the street.

It was then, as I stood watching, that the man I would come to know as Orson Price appeared around the corner, stopped, and said, "Good evening."

I saw a wiry, deeply tanned man, about my height, hatless, with hair that gleamed reddish-brown in the sun. He was dressed in white linen trousers and a white shirt; the effect was dapper until, on a closer look, you could see that both garments were wrinkled and grimy, and that the cloth case he carried was battered, held together with clothesline rope. He seemed only a few years older than I was – twenty-eight or so, thirty at the most.

"Good evening."

"I've often admired this building. Do you live in it?"

"I do now. I just moved in. I'm the new superintendent."

"Is that the truth." He looked up at the building again. "It seems a decent place to live." He set down the case – it was shaped like a large doctor's bag, scuffed beige canvas with brass and leather fittings – and rummaged in his pants pocket for a pack of cigarettes. He found it, shook one out, reached in another pocket for matches. "You look happy about it."

"I am happy, of course. I've been out of work for a while, and it feels good to have a job."

"I'll bet."

I looked up at the sky. The day was darkening; the moon had just appeared, a yellowish smile in the blue sky. I wondered if

May had awakened. I imagined going in and waking her gently, carrying her into the bedroom, kissing her. I imagined our lovemaking.

"Well, I'll be going in," I said, and turned to go back inside.

"Cigarette?" He held out the pack: one left.

Later, going over this unremarkable first conversation in my mind, as I would do half a dozen times, probing for its meaning, pondering its nuances, I pinpointed this as the decisive moment. Everything could have ended there. I could have said, *No, thanks. Got too much to do.* I could have said nothing, just shook my head, smiled a little, and gone back inside. The future that that moment contained, the rushing railroad train that was my life from then on, could have been diverted into some other track. I could have said or done any number of things, it was painful to think of all the alternatives, but what I said was, "Ah. Yes," and I turned, took the cigarette, stuck it in my mouth. Even unlit, it was wonderful: the dryness of the paper between my lips, the smell of tobacco. I hadn't smoked in nearly a month; it had been one of our necessary economies. Now we could probably take it up again. Twelve a week wasn't a fortune, but it should keep us in Luckies. "Thanks," I said. "My brand."

He found the matches, and we lit up. When he cupped his hand around the match, I noticed a row of satiny white scars across the back of his right hand, as if small, sharp teeth had pressed there, and bitten deep.

"So." He blew out smoke as he talked. "You been in the city long?"

"Probably sticks out all over me, doesn't it? Only a month or so. My wife and I came down from Rochester."

"Rochester. I've never been up there. What's it like?"

"It's not so hot. Pretty quiet. Hard winters." I inhaled; the cigarette was tasting wonderful, and I sucked the smoke deep into my lungs. "I was born there. We both were. Then all of a sudden one day we'd had enough. My wife is an actress," I added, as if that explained it. No need to tell him about the restaurant closing, our lost jobs. Or back even further: my return from Cambridge in the middle of a semester to lie awake listening to my father's old dog howling and my mother weeping softly in the next room. "And I'm writing a play."

"Then this is the place to be."

He had a narrow, ruddy face, and his eyes were an unnerving light blue, bleached like an old shirt. His gaze was direct and friendly. There was an easiness in the way he talked to me, in the way he had set his case down and pulled out his cigarettes, as if he took for granted a vague good will between the two of us based on a connection that had yet to be revealed: we'd been in the third grade together, or had talked years ago in a bar or on a bus. For a moment I wondered if I'd known him at Harvard.

We stood in silence for a moment, smoking. I found myself trying to get another look at his scars. "How about you?" I asked. "You from around here?"

"In a sense, yes." He paused, looking down at the glowing ember of his cigarette; the scars shone white against his tan, curiously beautiful in that light, like bits of pearl. There was a silence, and I was about to break it when he said, "I'm looking for work at the moment."

"Like everybody else in this city," I said. Then, thinking this was a callous, unfeeling thing to say in return for the cigarette, I asked, "What kind of work do you do?"

"Oh, a little bit of everything. At this point, carpentry. Odd jobs. You name it. I suppose you could say I'm just generally handy."

I had to laugh.

"I didn't mean to be funny."

"No. It's just – handy. Sorry, but that word really gets me. When he hired me, the landlord here asked me if I was handy. I don't know a hammer from a – from a what? I don't even know. From a pickaxe!"

He laughed too. "Well, you must have done something right if he hired you."

"I'm damned if I know what it was. He's somebody my wife's Aunt Myra used to know."

"Piece of luck for you, times like these."

"Don't I know it."

We stood for another minute, smoking in silence. He squinted up at the sky and said, "Maybe I'd better be getting on. It's later than I thought."

I wondered where he was going, where he had to be. I said, "Thanks for the cigarette. I'm sorry I took your last one."

"Quite all right. My pleasure."

"My name's Robert Sinclair, by the way."

We shook hands. "Orson Price." His palm felt calloused, sandpapery.

"Are you living around here now?"

"Normally – whatever that means – this is my neighborhood, yes. The park. The avenues. Irving Place. This quiet little corner of New York." His smile was rueful, and I wondered if he too had come down in the world, if our stories were similar. Maybe Orson had once lived a Henry James kind of existence in one of the bay-windowed houses that had their own private keys to Gramercy Park. I wondered if he'd grown up in a place like the big old house in Rochester where my mother insisted on remaining, renting rooms to itinerant men who cheated her, caring for the aging, incontinent dog who still waited at the front door every day at six, as if my father would come through it. Just thinking about it all made my head ache. Orson picked up his shabby case. "I feel at home here," he said. "I hope you folks will, too."

"Thanks. Stop by some time."

"All right. I will."

"I mean it."

Orson grinned. "So do I."

"And good luck finding a job. You'll get something. You know what they say – an able-bodied man can always find work."

"Is that what they say?"

"Something like that." I shrugged, afraid I'd sounded disapproving. "As if it's that easy."

"Well, all I need is one good break."

"Yeah. That's all anybody needs."

I wasn't sure what to say next. Later I remembered, bringing back the scene, reconstructing it bit by bit as I might reconstruct dialogue from a page of a script I had accidentally burned, that at that point I had taken one last puff of the cigarette and thrown it down, ground it out, had been about to speak, when Orson said, "Guess I'll be on my way. It was good talking to you, Robert."

He began to walk briskly up Second Avenue. I thought about calling after him but decided against it. I wasn't sure what I wanted to say, or why I wanted to say anything at all. I went to the corner and watched him until, after several blocks, he turned right, down toward the river, a white figure in the dusk. As I stood there, a woman passed, in a ragged satin skirt that trailed on the sidewalk, with a filthy child of indeterminate sex who stared at me blankly. Somewhere a church bell struck seven. I turned and went back into the Alhambra Gardens lobby and down the steps to the apartment, where May was just waking up.

Her yellow hair was tousled, and she had the faraway, moony look that she always wore when she emerged from one of her naps, her very wide-set blue eyes looking rather stupid. It always made me smile, that look. And she was different in other ways when she awakened, as if she still lived in that dream world where she was another person entirely: more romantic, less brash and smart-alecky. She pushed her hair back from her face and held out her arms. "Oh Robert! I dreamed the apartment was full of baby owls, and we opened a window and let them all go free."

I put my arms around her, kissing her warm face, her soft lips, and we went into the bedroom together, to the iron bed with its bare striped mattress, and May knelt between my legs, and quickly, too quickly, I heard myself moan, it had never been so good, it would never be so good again, and yet it was always good, the way she took me in her mouth, taking me so deep I could feel the back of her throat, her tongue moving, the soft sucking, until I cried out, shivering, my soul trembling with the joy of it, as she sucked and swallowed, and I thought I would die of that agony, that bliss.

We had been married since Christmastime, but our lovemaking still seemed new to me, I could never get used to it, every time was as exciting as the first, when slowly, exquisitely, voluptuously, she had brought me to the edge of what I knew would be heaven, and then to the headlong rush over it, when I lay collapsed in her arms, feeling her teeth bared against my shoulder while she did it to herself – once, twice, maybe again, while I held her – her fingers splayed against the blonde fur between her legs, her gasping breath on my skin. She would not let me penetrate her. *I'm so afraid of having a baby*, she had said that first night in her aunt's house back in Rochester, pushing me away. She had done it to me at first with her wet hand, now with her mouth; then it was her turn to do it to herself while I kissed her lips or sucked at her breasts. At first it had put me off, that this was the way she preferred it – that she wouldn't even consider what I thought of as regular sex, even though I had never experienced it. But it was May I wanted, however she wanted to give herself to me, and oddly, I got to like it, too, her way. We were both used to it. And her virginity moved me strangely; I felt I was not just her husband but her protector, her guardian against the world.

"Oh God, May, I love you."

She whispered, "And I love you, dearest Robert." She was, as always, vaguely distant after sex, even though she whispered words of love, and absently stroked my head, the back of my neck, my chest, until, almost, I wanted to do it all over again, to bring her back from the dreamy distraction that, if I let myself think about it, was both a worry and an annoyance. But she dozed off again in the midst of my languid desire, her head pillowed on my shoulder, and I roused myself and got to work.

There was a table in a corner of the living room, with a bookcase: that was my office. I took my typewriter out of its leather case – the old Remington Noiseless I'd received as a high school graduation present – and removed the striped dust cover my mother had made for me in Rochester: a *typewriter cozy*, I always joked. Then I turned on the lamp and sat down to type. I was revising Act II of my play, *Fish Out of Water*, which starred my hero, Oliver Templeton, the *bon vivant* and man about town I had invented when I was still at Harvard.

I loved Oliver like a brother. He was loosely based on men I had known in college, the ones who always knew what to do and say, what to wear, who could hold their liquor and were up on all the latest dances and could do things like play the mandolin or fish for trout or speak Chinese. Oliver was like them, but nicer – he was never snobbish or cruel, he was a friend to everyone, and, most of all, he was a wit. He made people laugh: at least, I hoped he would. He made me laugh, and he made May laugh, and I had high hopes for him.

I rolled in a clean page and began to type out a revision of the very end of the scene. I could write under any conditions: standing up on the subway, sitting on the toilet, waiting for May to try on clothes in a store, in the notebook I carried in my back pocket, on the backs of menus and, more than once, on my pocket handkerchief. Within minutes of sitting down to it, I was completely absorbed, the typewriter or my notebook or just a pencil and a piece of paper creating a kind of fortress against the world. The new apartment could have been anywhere. It faded from my consciousness, the street noises ceased, and I was in the smart penthouse, all chrome and satin, where Act II was set: Thomasina stretched out on the couch that I always saw as made of leather, Alec coming in to seduce her, then Oliver enters the room in a chef's hat and apron. Oliver, in addition to his other offbeat virtues, is a top-notch cook.

As I worked, the apartment turned dark except for my lit-up corner, and eventually May stumbled out of the bedroom, saying, "Why did you let me sleep so long? What time is it? My God! We've got to get this place in shape!"

I pulled myself back from that world, quickly as I had learned to, and stacked two good pages on top of the pile of typescript, and covered the typewriter. The room seemed different – alien and gloomy, and there was a smell we hadn't noticed before, of damp or (I thought this and then dismissed it as fanciful) of death, perhaps of small animals expiring quietly behind the walls. We lit all the lamps and turned on the radio: Kay Keyser. May said, "That's better," humming along. She looked blowsy to me, as she sometimes did; with her hair uncombed and her make-up rubbed away, she had the slatternly look of her aunt. I wondered what she would be like in ten years, twenty, and imagined her heavier, perpetually untidy, her hair in need of washing. I smiled to think of it – the two of us old – because I knew that the way she looked would always make my heart turn over with love.

She unpacked her clothes and hung them fussily on wire hangers in the wardrobe while I put books in the bookcase. Her things nearly filled the narrow wardrobe, and I had to hang some of my own clothes on hooks or fold them into the drawers of the dresser. Most I just left in the old leather suitcase. I didn't mind. I had become used to the fact that May's makeup and clothes – the blue shadow on her eyelids, the clinging dresses and high heels, her stockings and garter belts and hats – were all components of May, as necessary to who she was as her broad nose and small white teeth. I had become used to the time she spent doing things to her face in front of the mirror. At night she performed sit-ups on the floor to keep her tummy flat. Once I woke to find her sobbing over a tiny pimple on her chin.

May chatted while she straightened the place. We would need to buy a clock, she said. A kettle, a potholder, a plant. Could a plant grow in this light? I ripped a sheet of paper out of a notebook and made a list. Aside from our clothes, my old Remington, the crates of books and May's big three-way mirror, we didn't have much: an unused set of pink wine goblets, a pewter coffee pot, a green glass vase – all wedding presents – and a carved jade cat I had given May for her last birthday. We had put together a photograph album, with pictures of ourselves and various friends and family stuck on the black pages and identified in white ink. The last picture was of the two of us getting off the Broadway Limited; Carlotta had met us at Penn Station and snapped it before we even spotted her. The photograph was slightly out of focus, and you couldn't see the cinders in May's hair and the soot on our clothes, but it caught our confusion and excitement: we would look at it when we were old, thinking back to those days. *These days.* I propped the album up on the bookcase.

Would we ever be able to afford a telephone, she wondered. We needed a couple of washcloths, a knife, a set of hooks for the bathroom door. Should we get a breadbox?

When the apartment was neat, May did her makeup, raising her face to her mirror image like a woman in a trance. She dusted her cheeks with powder, dotted on rouge, painted her eyes and lips. I thought, as I often did: *How she loves herself,* and I noted with pleasure – also as I often did – that her lips were slightly too prominent above her small pointed chin, an incongruity I found perfect. When she was done, she smiled at herself in the mirror, and I smiled to see her do it.

May put on her gypsy skirt, and I wore my father's Panama hat. Mr. Gant couldn't begrudge us our first evening out, to celebrate. We took a few of our last dollars and headed downtown. The streets were crowded with people out for a breath of air on a summer night. May said, "Look at the sky" – a deep turquoise, with ragged clouds turning purple at the edges as the sun sank – and clutched my arm with excitement.

As we passed the wrought iron fence around Gramercy Park, I found myself looking for Orson Price – half-expecting him to descend the steps of one of the gracious old mansions, whistling, his rumpled whites traded in for a seersucker jacket and trousers with a crease, maybe a red bow tie. The ragman was coming down 18th Street, idly whipping his horse; the horse wore a battered straw hat, and strings of drool hung from its lips. A little girl, crying her heart out, was being pulled in a wagon by a bigger boy. A group of men on the corner suddenly laughed in unison, putting their heads back and filling the air with their noise. The door of the neighborhood tavern hung open, revealing brown darkness.

We walked through Union Square where, even at this hour, the armies of people with no place else to go were preparing to sleep – long scraggly rows of them on the rough grass at the north end, away from the turmoil of 14th Street. Near the statue of Lincoln, the Communists were passing out leaflets; the end-of-the-world woman was there, standing on a platform across from Klein's, screaming over the heads of the crowd about salvation. A beggar had his pantleg rolled up to show a suppurating yellow sore. A black man with a harmonica always drew a crowd; that evening he was playing an old spiritual I didn't know, but May sang along, softly, while we stood listening:

I am going far away,
Far away to leave you now,
To the Mississippi River I am going...

The restaurant we liked was further down, off Seventh
Avenue in Greenwich Village – the Mercury Café, friendly and
crowded, with a motherly waitress. We ordered a celebration
dinner: cube steaks, fried potatoes, green beans, a glass each of red
wine, and strawberry-rhubarb pie for dessert, with coffee. A
dollar and twenty cents, with three more nickels for a tip.

"We shouldn't have spent so much," May said over the
coffee, but she smiled as she spoke. We both felt better.

"We'll get our first pay next Friday. We'll be all right now,
May."

"I guess we will."

"And look." I took a pack of Luckies from my shirt pocket. "I
bought them while you were in the ladies' room."

Her smile widened. Under the table, her knee was between
mine. Someone played the jukebox: "I Only Have Eyes for You."
When it was done, I took a nickel and chose "We're in the
Money." We sat back with our cigarettes and drank coffee.

"A rather odd thing happened earlier this evening," I said.
"While you were asleep."

"What?" She reached over and clasped my hand tight. "Tell
me."

I smiled at her eager face. This was what – besides her kisses –
had made me fall in love with her: her hungry, bright-eyed love
for the world. I adored it in her, but it could also frighten me, it
was so indiscriminate. *Let's just leave,* she had said, grasping my
hand in that same way. *Let's just get the hell out of this town, Robert.*
We belong in New York, and you know it. Let's just go!

"I tucked you in and went outside, just because the evening
was so beautiful."

"And?"

I hesitated, and tapped ashes into the ashtray, frowning. Now that I had opened the subject, I didn't know what to say. *What was the big deal: I met this man, he gave me a cigarette, he had scars on his hand.* I said, "Well, I got talking to this fellow from the neighborhood. He was nice, I think you'd like him. Kind of a quiet guy, the kind who would rather listen than talk."

"A rare bird," she said, wryly.

"That's what I thought. I liked him. His name was Orson."

"Orson what?"

Something made me say, "I don't remember. Orson Something," even though I remembered perfectly well: *Orson Price.*

May said, "So? What was so odd about this character?"

"Well – " I hesitated. "The odd part was that I felt as if I knew him already – he seemed familiar. And yet I didn't, really."

"Maybe you saw him on the subway, or he waited on you in a store. Sometimes – doesn't this happen to you? I can still remember a woman I saw on a bus – oh, maybe ten years ago. This woman with huge teeth and eyes the color of pennies. People's faces haunt me. An old man I served in McGreevey's once, a very pink old man with thick, thick white hair! I can still remember his shirt, striped blue and white. Isn't that strange? So maybe that's where you know this Orson person from. A chance encounter that for some reason has – what? Has burnt itself into your soul, Robert." She smiled as she said it, but that was, in fact, exactly how it was. I looked toward the door, almost as if I expected Orson to walk in, as if our lives were a bad play. Through the restaurant window I could see a shabby man holding out a cup: not Orson Price, of course.

I said, "Maybe we'll run into him again."

"That would be nice. Wouldn't it? We don't know many people in New York."

This was a new theme of hers, the contrast between Rochester, where, it often seemed, we knew virtually everyone in town, and New York City, where we knew almost no one. The difference meant nothing to me – I had May, I had my work – and at first she had liked it, found it exciting to be anonymous, but lately it had started to bother her.

"I walk down the street, and not one soul knows my face, not one person speaks to me," she said. "If I fell down a manhole or was carried away to the moon by little green men, no one would notice."

"I'd notice," I told her.

"Oh, you. You might notice if you weren't thinking about your play."

"It wouldn't take more than a day or two. I'd look up from the typewriter and think: Wait a minute! I had a wife somewhere around here!"

She smiled and squeezed my hand, let it go, puffed on her cigarette. "Seriously," she said. "Don't you wish we had a regular circle, Robert? A group of friends that we see all the time, that we can count on. A *crowd*. Now wouldn't that be swell?"

I said it would, but absently, because, first of all, I didn't think it would be swell at all. And secondly, I had meant to say more about Orson Price. I wanted to bring up the brilliant idea I had concocted, that I could hire him to work for us, be our handyman – I wanted May's opinion about whether we could get away with that, and how. I wanted to make a joke about that set of Russian dolls we had seen in a shop down on First Avenue: each doll progressively smaller, one fitting inside the other, until the last one was like a little bean, but painted just as gaudily as the largest: *Mr. Gant hires us, and then we hire Orson, and then what if Orson hired someone else...* But I didn't know how to bring Orson's name up again without sounding – sounding what? I couldn't say.

"We could all get together on Friday nights, have a few drinks, go out dancing or to the movies."

"Yes, it sounds like a lot of fun." I pictured this crowd, an evening in some bar, all the men wanting to dance with May, and me – not a great dancer, not so good at small talk – sitting and making conversation with the dull girlfriend of the man who was draped over my wife. Imaginary scenes like that could become so real to me that I could almost feel myself getting angry. I hoped it was the mark of the artist. Shakespeare, I thought, must have had those visions, kings and soldiers and madmen and lovers striding across a room, speaking, gesturing: seen their faces, heard the tramp of their boots. Had he walked the streets at night, unable to sleep for excitement? And had he also, from time to time, lost heart? Even Shakespeare? Did he sometimes want to just give up? I liked to think of him, wandering around Stratford, standing by the river at two in the morning, trying to understand Hamlet – how to dramatize tortured inaction? Or thinking up puns, rejecting this, trying that. Or composing splendid speeches that, perhaps, he doubted.

> *We're in the money,*
> *We're in the money...*

May said, "I want our life to begin, Robert."

I gave her my attention then, and smiled at her across the table. How deeply blue her eyes were. How soft the rosy blush of her cheeks. I thought: *This is my life, this is enough for me.* But I said, "It will, May. Let me get the play done, show it to Rex Mason or that other guy – Harper. Let a producer show some faith in it. Then things will start to happen."

"I hope so."

"And you've got to start going to really good auditions. It's you I'm counting on to make us rich and famous, honey, not me."

I was rewarded with her smile, the gleam of her perfect teeth, the deepening of the fine wrinkles around her eyes. "Oh, come on."

"I mean it. With your looks? It won't be long."

She loved it when I said those things, and I only wished I believed them. Because I didn't, I leaned across the table and kissed her cheek.

When we left the restaurant, the sky was a bruised, blunted blue, the clouds had sunk to the horizon, and in Union Square the screwballs had all gone away, it was empty even of pigeons, and there were only the sleeping hordes, the beggar with the sore leg, and a few couples like us walking close together in the warm dark. I gave the beggar a nickel, and he mumbled something. I saw that he was young, maybe as young as I was. I stopped and reached in my pocket, found another nickel and dropped it in his cup. May pulled on my arm and said, "Robert."

As we turned down 21st Street, I said, "It's good to have a real home to go back to, May. Isn't it?"

"As long as it's you I'm going home with," she said, and I was pierced by happiness.

"Price," I said suddenly, as if the name were a gift I was giving her. "Orson Price. That was that guy's name."

That night was one of the many on which I couldn't get to sleep no matter what I did: deep breathing, relaxation exercises, reciting poetry in my head, getting up to read. We had no milk, so I couldn't try my warm-milk cure, but it never seemed to work anyway. I lay there for a couple of hours with my eyes wide open, and then I slipped out of bed, dressed, and let myself out of the apartment.

Since we arrived in New York, I had been sleeping worse, probably, than ever before in my intermittently insomniac life, except for the anxious weeks after my father died. I dreaded getting into bed to face the yearning for the sleep that wouldn't come, and so I had begun walking in the night, miles and miles, from the rooming house on Bedford Street up into Harlem or across the East River to Brooklyn, learning the city, wearing myself out with simple physical fatigue that somehow reached my brain, quieted it, and eventually shut it down entirely so that I would fall into bed exhausted when I got home and – almost always – sleep immediately, without dreams, or at least none that I recalled.

One of the best parts about writing, for me, has always been the time spent walking, looking, thinking – even forgetting that I was a writer at all, becoming someone who lived in the world and looked at it. I drank the city in. This is no idle metaphor: in those days, it really did seem to me that the endless streets full of tiny individual lives, the jumble of buildings and windows and shops and cars, the city's fast-beating heart and racing blood, the sweet night air, were an intoxicating cocktail mixed just for me. I would start walking, worrying about the play – I was always worried about the play, which I saw as my only link to another, better life for May and me. The play was always with me, like an illness or an addiction, or a crucial exam on which everything depended: it was hard for me to let it go. As I walked, I played and replayed dialogue, whispering it to myself, stumped by the characters I had created, unable to think their thoughts – until, bit by bit, the dimmed streets and the sleeping buildings that rose up around me, bursting with the press of other lives, would somehow bring the curtain down and leave that playwriting part of my brain comfortable and happy, dozing in the last row, and finally exiting the theatre altogether, humming along in the glow of the city's fizzy champagne, seeing only the wide avenues, the night people, the lights of cars and cabs, the jeweled streets. Meanwhile, the play went on. And the next time I sat down to it things magically made sense again.

I intended to head down to Canal Street and the Manhattan Bridge. I chose my route carefully: I had learned not to walk down the Bowery, which I knew was swarming both night and day with hopeless, often desperate men. Instead I went south on Broadway, strolling slowly, enjoying the cooler air, the lights, the life around me. The streets of the city, I had found, were never entirely deserted, even at one in the morning. There were always revelers, always vagrants and derelicts; they sometimes mingled on the same block, with muttering men in overalls and caps nearly colliding with a high-spirited party in gowns and tuxedos. The all-night cafeterias were lit up and hopeful, surprisingly busy, though half the customers, it seemed, had their heads down on the table, asleep. I saw people sleeping in doorways, on the steps of churches, in any patch of park. Even the spidery fire escapes were populated: whole families went out there to escape the heat, and somewhere you could always hear a child crying.

I don't know exactly why these displays of human desolation – of poverty and displacement and fear – exhilarated me more than they depressed me, but I think that what I found in the streets of the city was not unlike what I found in the theatre: the drama of life, the thrill of observing it go on. I thought of all the deaths in Shakespeare, the blood, the betrayals and furies and cruelty. I thought of the bleakness of Chekhov, of Ibsen. I often thought that it didn't matter whether or not plays presented happy pictures, only that they be real, and that they move us, and offer some kind of hope. Life never seemed hopeless to me as I strolled the streets, observing the drunks, the homeless, the wanderers whose minds were gone, the crying children, the beggars. The very presence of all those people, the richness of the worlds they represented, the way they went on, most of them, went on no matter what, persisting in the face of suffering, made it impossible to despair.

That evening, as I turned off Broadway onto Bleecker Street, I saw two figures across the street embracing in a doorway – and not just embracing, it seemed clear after a moment, but actually having intercourse. Half-ashamed, I stood watching: the man's body slamming rhythmically against the woman's with a kind of rhythmic groan. Then he drew away, and I saw that it was two men, and that it hadn't been sex at all – it had been a beating, not a love scene. The man in the doorway slumped to the ground, and in the streetlight I could see the quick gleam of a knife. As I stood watching, the attacker turned and ran down Bleecker.

I'm not sure what I would have done if a police car hadn't pulled up just then, brakes squealing. I like to think I would have gone to the victim's aid, taken charge, hailed a passing car and insisted that the driver bring the police. Or, better yet, taken off after the guy on foot, shouting "Stop that man!" Pursuing him until he could run no further, then collaring him, knife or no knife.

As it was, the police arrived – by chance or design, I never knew – and I turned quietly away before they could stop me and ask questions. There was nothing I could tell them. I had seen nothing, only a man. I could only say he was ordinary, dressed in dark clothes, as anonymous, as unidentifiable as I was myself.

At the corner, I looked back over my shoulder. A small crowd was beginning to gather: voices were raised, a woman cried out. The feeble light from the street lamps made everything murky and hellish, like a scene from a gangster movie. It took several blocks of walking before I began to calm down – everyone I passed looked like a knife-wielding killer, everyone stared at me with loathing and suspicion – and it wasn't until I was walking up Third Avenue, close to home, that it dawned on me that the man in the doorway was dead, I had probably witnessed a murder, and that the scene had made me feel not only shame and fear but the hopelessness I'd just been congratulating myself on not experiencing. In a few seconds on Bleecker Street all the good feelings I had about walking at night – about the city, about life – had been demolished. A kind of terror gripped me. I stopped short, a hard lump in my throat, my heart racing. If that was the world, I wasn't sure I could live in it. If that was the world, my own world was meaningless: why was I writing plays, why was I walking up Third Avenue, or any avenue, going anywhere, doing anything?

I stood there in my desolation, and then I thought of May, in bed in our new apartment, calm in her easy sleep. The street rearranged itself around me, transformed from a barren, ravaged hell into a New York City street at night. Deep blue sky, gray pavement, black road, a tall apartment building, a dry cleaner, a vegetable market with the shutters up. A man and woman came toward me, talking softly. A taxi passed, then a man on a bicycle. A dog skulked along the sidewalk. I took a long breath and continued on my way: up Third to 21st, and down the quiet street to the Alhambra Gardens, where I climbed into bed beside my wife and held her in my arms. Barely awake, she mumbled what sounded like "melody," tucked her head under my chin, and went off again. I held onto her until I could no longer hear the hard beating of my heart, and then I let her go and lay awake beside her for I don't know how long until, toward morning, I must have slept because, soon after, I awoke to hear May singing in the kitchen as she boiled water for coffee.

■■■

Truly, it was a good life. The job was undemanding – mop the hallways, sweep the front steps, water the plants. I had to hang around the building most of the time, but that was okay with me. I had plenty of leisure in which to work, and the play consumed me. May was busy, too, going out on casting calls, practicing scenes with Carlotta, finding out about acting classes. It was summer, and things were slow, but when fall came she wanted to be ready. A lot of plays opened in September, she said, and they were casting now; she had hopes of finding a role in one. "Anything," she said. "The upstairs maid, the nobody who's a friend of the somebody, a person in a crowd scene – I don't care." I was impressed by her ambition, and by the passion that contorted her face. "I'm not proud. I'm not fussy. I'll do *anything*, Robert. I just want to be on the stage."

"You'll make it, May," I said, wishing it was true, wondering how I would console her when she found out it wasn't.

"I know I will," she said, and the passion, I could see, was tempered by a kind of calm belief in herself that, for all its sadness, was even more impressive.

May bought an alarm clock from a woman on the street for ten cents – a miniature white enameled thing with a shrill bell that sliced my dreams open like a razor. On the morning when things changed – we had lived in the apartment for a week – it screamed as usual at seven. May leapt out of bed, instantly awake; she dashed around the apartment, putting on her face, touching up a dress with the iron, cheerfully swearing, gulping coffee, singing along with the radio, while I lay in bed failing to either wake up fully or go back to sleep – trying to come to terms with the fuzzy blankness in my brain.

May stood before me. I could smell her deodorant and her perfume and see the fabric of her summer dress: green circles intercut by pale purplish triangles. "You're tired," she said.

"I'm tired."

"How much sleep did you get?" Without waiting for an answer, she said, "Go back to sleep. Please." She reached over and turned off the radio. "Sleep late for once. Give yourself a break."

I didn't bother to say that I couldn't get back to sleep once I was awake: that the spell, once broken, couldn't be so unlaboriously restored. I had told her many times, but she either forgot or didn't believe me or was incapable of understanding such a concept. She herself slept easily, gladly, instantly, whenever she needed to.

"I'm awake. I feel all right." She gave me her coffee to sip. The coffee was still hot, and it finished the job of waking me up. By the time Carlotta arrived, just past 8:30, I was out of bed, dressed, eating a piece of bread with jelly on it.

May and Carlotta were old friends, best friends. They had memories that went back to second grade, stories I had heard over and over, about the sadistic Sister Elizabeth, and playing doctor with Joey Bogan in Carlotta's basement, and the time May threw up her cotton candy at the State Fair all over Carlotta's patent leather shoes. They had both come to New York to go on the stage – Carlotta first, a year ago – and they were always plotting, trying out new hairdos together, going off arm in arm to whatever came up. It always astonished me that there was so little rivalry between them. I often thought of something said by Verna Quiller, who ran the rooming house on Bedford Street: "Oh boy, wait'll one of those two makes it big and the other doesn't. Won't we see the fur fly then!"

I doubted it, I said to Verna, partly out of loyalty, but partly because I didn't think either of them would ever make it big – a heretical idea I never voiced out loud and hated to say even to myself. Before the two major theatres in Rochester were forced to close, I had seen May and Carlotta in a couple of local productions; both of them were home-town celebrities. In fact, before I ever met her, May had first caught my eye as Kristen the maid in *Miss Julie*, and then as a rather hysterical Masha in *The Three Sisters*. It was her hair and eyes that attracted me, and her vitality – not her acting ability.

"You wait," Verna said, winking at me. We used to drink watery coffee together in the afternoons in her kitchen, usually with a shot of her home-made corn liquor left over from Prohibition; I never told May this, but I used to read Verna bits of my play, and she not only made useful comments but she gave me a couple of my funniest lines.

May had once said to Carlotta, "Poor Verna has designs on Robert. If she quit boozing and lost forty pounds, I'd be a little anxious," and Carlotta had replied: "Yeah, then she'd only have that nose to worry about." Their innocent cattiness was part of their charm: *Look at those ankles. What a face! Ooh, those diabolical eyebrows. Poor girl – doesn't she look just like Peggy Dooling? My God, those lips! Like two wet fish! A face like a pie. Ooh – looks like he's trying to spit those teeth right out.* They made fun of everyone, everything; underneath, as May's Aunt Myra used to say, they were as kind-hearted as Jesus.

Carlotta was thirty, a year older than May. She was dark-skinned, with bluish circles under her eyes, and slender to the point of boniness, with an unexpectedly big, high bosom. She was a stridently, almost comically sexy girl, her hair pulled behind one ear with a jeweled comb, her lips shiny and red. No matter what she said, her husky voice and narrowed eyes made it sound like the buildup to the punchline of a dirty joke. She and her boyfriend, Mickey Kennedy – a huge, handsome guy who didn't seem too bright – were famous for their incredible dancing; their wild, showy tango could stop a roomful of dancers dead. Carlotta loved attention. She gossiped and mimicked people, and told horrible lies and didn't care who believed her. She stole gloves and handbags from department stores. She had a low, seductive laugh that I knew she had perfected, deliberately, over the years, and after a year in New York she had the local accent down perfectly. "Oh yeeah?" she liked to say. "Wot makes ya tink ya so smawt, mistuh? Just because ya live in Noo Yawk City." In spite of her name and her appearance, she was not Spanish; she was a German girl named Carla Silfer, but her stage name was Carlotta Silverado. May's was May Munro; she had been born Mary Kramer. The two of them had sat at the kitchen table all one cold spring day, drinking Aunt Myra's bootlegged gin and thinking up names that would take New York by storm.

"How do we look? Are we divine?"

They struck poses in the doorway. With their faces in shadow, they were just two voluptuous bodies against the light. They didn't look like May and Carlotta; they looked like stars posing for a publicity shot. They were gorgeous. It occurred to me, for the first time, that one or both of them could make it in the theatre after all – not because of their talent but by some fluke, by virtue of glamour and chutzpah and persistence – the passion I had seen in May's face, and that was there in Carlotta's, too – and the idea struck me suddenly dumb.

"Well?"

"You're goddesses."

"Yeeah, weeah da bee's knees, ain't we?"

May kissed me, and I went outside with them and watched them walk up 21st Street together. They were going to a casting call at something called the Marshall Petroff Talent Agency – a contact they had brought from Rochester. They turned at the corner to go uptown – Carlotta so slender and exotic, narrow-hipped, her legs long and skinny and brown, and May blond, shorter, rounder, her sweet backside cupped by her thin summer dress. She had to watch her weight. Secretly, I wished she would get fat. Or fatter, at least. Too fat to be an actress. Secretly – another thing I never said to anyone – I wished she would stay home with me, cooking, sewing things, working with me around the building, making me laugh. And then, as they disappeared up Third, I regretted the wish; I knew that being on the stage was everything to May, and that the days she didn't work were, in a way, days that might as well not exist. And she was a terrible cook.

The goodbye kiss hadn't been a peck; she had put her tongue in my mouth, pressed her hip against me, lingering. It was something she did fairly often, though I wished she wouldn't; it wasn't for me: it was for Carlotta, May flaunting her new husband, how hot I was for her, our happiness together. But the kiss left me weak – especially when I had slept badly – and throbbing with lust I couldn't dispel except by going back to bed and jerking myself off. *A date with Rosy Palms*, Jasper my roommate at Harvard had called it. Sometimes, afterward, I would find myself inexplicably crying: my hand wet, the appalling sound of my own sobs filling the apartment, but other times, newly weary from my sleepless night, possessed by a lassitude I could barely fight off, I would fall back into a dense, heavy sleep.

On that morning, I slept, and was awakened by a knocking at the door. This second waking was much worse than the first. I couldn't open my eyes, couldn't climb out of the dark well. But the knocking didn't stop, and eventually I dragged myself from the bed, pulled on a pair of pants and went to the door, stumbling, unseeing. I peered into the dim hallway. "Mr. Gant."

"I'm wondering about the grass out in the front." Mr. Gant wore a rumpled summer suit and a loosened red tie, and his long pasty face was glum. He glanced behind me into the apartment, at the typewriter and the litter of papers. "That grass needs trimming. And those weeds along the steps ain't going away by themselves. Junk under the bushes. Papers. The windows on the landings. All pretty grimy, look like hell. Floors don't look mopped. I'm depending on you."

The windows? The landings? I had never actually gone up to the other floors since the first day when Mr. Gant showed me around. I had forgotten the upstairs floors would need mopping. I had also forgotten about the little bit of grass; I had, in fact, no memory of being told I had to cut it. But of course I should have known all these things.

"I'll stop by later," Mr. Gant said, with one last unhappy look at my bare feet. "See how it's going."

I had broken out in a sweat. The morning was very hot already. All I could think about was going back to bed, though I was sure that the minute I lay down I would be wide awake. I stood in the kitchenette sipping a glass of water, looking for something to eat. There was a heel of stale bread, no butter, a dish of cold potatoes, a bag of coconut cookies that May liked and I hated. Nothing in the ice box. Our dinner dishes from the night before were still in the sink, and May's underwear soaked in a tin basin on the linoleum countertop – lumps of blue, rose, black. The place looked sordid and cheerless, and I felt deeply ashamed of myself. The job wasn't, after all, a joke – a part in a play. We could be fired. We could be out on the street with nowhere to go but back to Rochester.

I washed my face and drank the dregs of May's coffee with another piece of the stale bread with jam on it. I found a pair of clippers in the furnace room and went out the back door into the small concrete yard. It was littered with papers, bits of newspaper, someone's old brown shoe. The trash cans were overflowing, and I couldn't recall what Mr. Gant had said about garbage pickup. The clippers resisted when I worked them; the blades were rimmed with rust. I stood looking at them a moment, blankly, a bead of perspiration sliding down my back, bemused by the look of that particular brownish-red against the blade's dull gray. Shouldn't there be a lawn mower? If there was, I couldn't find it. Eventually, I walked around to the front and clipped at the grass. There wasn't much area, but it was picky, thankless work, and the sun hit like a lash as I worked. The clippers fought me all the way, and when I was done, instead of looking better, the grass looked worse – thin, parched, with brown patches of dirt between the sparse tufts. Then I started on the weeds.

As I was finishing – shirt off, the sweat pouring down my body – and wondering how so many dandelions could manage to grow in such an inhospitable space, a woman came out the front door and stood watching me. She was tall, middle-aged – overweight in a majestic way, like an opera singer. She wore what looked like long, sweeping robes – something magenta and something poison green: huge bunchy slacks, I saw as she came closer, tied around the ankles, under a flowing tunic that conjured up a word I didn't know I knew: *djellabah.* Her black hair was elaborately braided and twisted on top of her head, her eyebrows were two narrow arcs over kohl-shadowed eyes, her lips and fingernails were brilliant magenta to match her robe. I stopped weeding to stare at her.

She said, "You are Robert Sinclair, I'm told." She suddenly opened her eyes very wide, as if something had startled her, but it was only a trick she had, either a nervous habit or an affectation. She said, "I am Mrs. Amalfi. The sleep specialist." She nodded her head up toward one of the second-floor windows, where there was a discreet sign: *The Sleep Specialist. By Appointment.* I had never seen it before. "I came out to tell you that the garbage collectors will be here tomorrow."

"Ah."

"The trash cans must be brought around and put out by the street. You won't want to miss the garbage collection. We don't have enough trash cans, and if you missed the pickup it would be a disaster." She lowered her voice. "Vermin."

"Oh – yes." I realized that she was decrepitly gorgeous. I wondered if she was a famous person. And her clothes fascinated me: all those layers of cloth on a day when the temperature must be ninety degrees. Her toes peeking out from a pair of sandals were large and splayed, the toenails painted, incredibly, gold. "Thank you, I very much appreciate your telling me."

"Gant won't tell you a thing. Gant will just expect you to know it, and when you don't you'll pay."

"Pay?"

"I don't mean with money. I mean with humiliations of various kinds." She frowned down at the burned-looking grass, as if it were one of them. "With Gant, everything is a struggle for power."

"May I ask you a question?" I had thrown my shirt across the railing, and I reached for it, to wipe the sweat from my face and chest. The smell of my own skin repelled me.

"Of course."

I blurted it out. "Aren't you hot?"

"Not at all. I wear nothing under these garments. The air circulates freely. It's an old desert trick. The nomads in the Sahara wear clothes very much like these. Perhaps not so colorful."

I noticed then that her breasts were two unfettered mounds, the points of their nipples straining against the magenta.

"I see." There was a pause while I looked away, up where her window bore its sign. I couldn't believe I hadn't noticed it before. A man came around the corner, dressed in white. It seemed a long time ago that I had spoken to Orson Price on the front steps, and it was then that I decided that if I did run into him again and he still needed a job, I would offer him one, in earnest. I would beg him.

"Well," said Mrs. Amalfi. "I just wanted to give you that word of warning."

The man walking by wore a bow tie and a jaunty straw hat; he was not Orson Price.

"May I ask you another question?"

"Of course."

"What's a sleep specialist?"

"Do you personally sleep well, Robert?"

It was odd to hear her use my name. "I sleep all right."

She pursed her lips and looked at me as if to assess the truth of this statement. I stared back at her. My sleep troubles were something I didn't like to talk about; I had always been led to believe that the inability to sleep indicated a bad character. *The sleep of the just. Sleep like a baby.* People who couldn't sleep were not just, not innocent.

"I help people who can't sleep," she said after a moment. "So I'd be of no use to you. Be careful about Gant. Don't get on his bad side," she smiled, and did her eye-widening trick again. There was a space the width of a dime between her front teeth. "He would hurt a fly, if you know what I mean. He would take great delight in hurting a fly."

She started back up the steps. I dug out the last dandelion with the point of the clippers and called after her. "Mrs. Amalfi! Ah – to be quite truthful, I do not sleep well."

She turned her massive head, raising her black eyebrows that were like the markings of birds. "I know that," she said. "I can see it in your face." She looked pleased. "I am glad you decided to tell the truth. Don't lie to me, Robert. Lie to Gant, but don't lie to me. Do you understand?"

"Not really. I don't normally lie to anyone."

"No?"

"No."

"I see. A lily among the nettles." Her voice was so even and uninflected that it took me a moment to understand that she was being sarcastic. "You haven't met Hana," she went on.

"Who's Hana?"

Mrs. Amalfi widened her eyes. "How long have you lived in this building? Hana is my daughter, of course."

The sun was beating down on my head. I could feel how red my face was. "No, I haven't met your daughter. I haven't met anyone. I've only been here twelve days. I'm a writer. I stay inside and write. I'm sorry, Mrs. Amalfi, I've got to get out of the sun. This heat is killing me."

She leaned over and put her hand on my arm. Her fuschia-tipped fingers wore half a dozen rings – gold, silver, jeweled. Her palm was pleasantly cool. "Have I been rude? Presumptuous? Intrusive? I'm sorry. We'll talk later," she said. She smiled again. The Wife of Bath had a space between her teeth; traditionally, it was the sign of a lustful nature. "Come and see me. Come for tea some afternoon. Meet Hana. I will show you my animals." She removed her hand and patted her hair. "And we'll talk about your sleep problem."

I put the clippers away. Then I went inside, threw off my clothes, got into the bathtub and stuck my head under the cold water. I was so hot I wanted to die, but of course within minutes I was cool again, and the whole world changed. I soaked in the tub for a while and changed into clean clothes, and then I climbed the stairs to Mrs. Amalfi's apartment and knocked on the door, but there was no answer. I put my ear to the door, heard nothing; with my face against the varnished wood, I could detect a faint vaguely spicy scent that I couldn't identify. I went outside and looked at the sign in the window: *The Sleep Specialist*. It was yellowed and slightly fly-spotted, but the hand-lettering was artistic, and there was a faded painted border of what looked like trailing ivy.

As I headed back to my own door, I remembered the windows on the landings, and I spent the rest of the afternoon cleaning them, and mopping the floors, until I was sweating and exhausted all over again.

TWO

That summer was very hot. Every morning after May left, I got to work before the heat clenched its fist on the city. First I tidied the apartment – made a stab at it, anyway. Then I slopped soapy water over the marble floors and swept the front steps and the walk, and set up the rubber hose and watered the plants and the palms and the boxwood trees if they seemed dry.

It had quickly become obvious that my vision of May working beside me, toiling patiently in an apron with a cloth tied around her head, was a ludicrous one. She had no intention of mopping floors or watering plants. I didn't mind. Whatever I might think of her chances, she had come to New York to be an actress, and there was no denying it was easier to combine the duties of a super with writing a play than with going to auditions.

Not that anything about the job was easy. I performed my tasks in a state of high anxiety. Was I doing enough? What exactly was *clean*? Floors you could eat off of, or just the visible absence of dirt? What did Gant really expect of me? I wished I knew someone else who did this work. I wished I had paid more attention to the buildings in Rochester my father managed. I wished there was a book you could read. *The Successful Super. Ten Steps to Better Building Management*. I had my resentful days when

I wished May were there to help, or at least to make wisecracks and cheer me up.

But all this was tempered by the great joy of the moment when finally, though never without misgivings, I could look around the place and judge it perhaps not clean by some celestial, Gantian standard, but definitely *cleaner*. As far as I could see, it would *do*, as my mother used to say. I could never judge if this was true or not, but as soon as the idea came into my mind – *this will do, it's good enough, I'm done for today* – I found myself unable to mop another square foot. Guiltily, I would put everything away in the basement closet – bucket, mop, rags, Bon Ami and Murphy's Soap – and change out of my filthy, sweaty working clothes. Then I would take a bath. And then I was free to work on my play.

I know I was always smiling as I sat down to my work. At the typewriter, I was no longer the man with the hoe, the clod with the mop. I was in my element there: it must have been like an alcoholic feels who, after a long day of rationalizing or lying to himself or fooling other people, walks into the bar, and there are all his buddies, there's his friend the bartender, and there are those beautiful, blessed bottles on the shelves. I would read over what I'd written the day before, transpose two lines of dialogue, remove a word here, add a word there – and, in minutes, I was gone. Mr. Gant and the Alhambra and my mops and buckets were a lost world, a bad dream: the only reality was on the page before me.

I could work for hours, penciling in and crossing out, deleting whole speeches then putting them back in. I liked to read aloud what I'd done, talking to myself, pacing around the dank little apartment reciting lines in different voices, rewriting them, saying them again. I liked being there alone; I could be as absurd as I wanted. Once, reciting a speech of Oliver's, I laughed to myself until I wept, feeling like a fool, but moved as I had seldom been moved before by the sheer comic beauty of what I had written, the odd power of my words which, it seemed to me, went beyond comedy and reached for some universal human truth, as Barry and Behrman did – my favorite modern playwrights. And as Shakespeare had in the byplay between Lear and his Fool, and in the gravedigger's scene.

On other days I despaired of the whole silly enterprise: what I wrote was drivel, and I was no more kin to Shakespeare than I was to the Queen of Sheba. But I never gave up. The play wouldn't let me go. At least, I told myself, it would soon be over; the end was in sight, the eloquent and witty last lines were calling to me, beckoning me onward like a false-hearted woman leading me down an alley where I knew I shouldn't go. The rest of the play might be pure garbage, but those last lines – two short speeches, Thomasina and Oliver alone together on a darkening stage, ending with Oliver's *bon mot* that pulled the whole thing together, that would release the audience's tension, let loose their laughter and applause – had come to me one afternoon in Rochester, after May and I had made love, and I lay beside her with her head pillowed on my shoulder, listening to her soft breathing, thinking about the void that would take over my life if she ever left me. I almost woke her and forced her to make absurd, extravagant promises, to sign a pact with her blood. Instead, I added wit to the moment's poignancy, I gave it to Oliver and to Thomasina, and I disengaged myself gently from my sleeping wife to write it down in my notebook, laughing to myself and flushed with a kind of ecstasy.

Yes, it was drivel, whole chunks of it were probably hopelessly bad, but I couldn't imagine giving it up. Sometimes, when the typewriter and I had had a particularly painful spell, I would push the play to the back of my mind like an unpleasant memory, trying not to think of all the months and days and hours and foolish optimism I had wasted on it, but it always came

slithering back – or in a fit of masochism and longing I would call
it back: the sick puppy I couldn't abandon. I burned to get it done,
to make something of myself – one of my father's expressions. *I
know you'll make something of yourself, son,* he used to say when I
brought home good report cards. *This will be the making of you,* he
said when I got into Harvard – tears in his eyes. Playwriting
wasn't what he had had in mind, I knew, but it was the thing I
had always, it seemed, known I could do. The only thing. I could
no more have sold real estate like my father than I could have
stayed home and baked pies like my mother.

I let my twenty-fifth birthday go by without a fuss, seeing in
the cards from my mother and my sister, the cake May bought,
the bottle of wine from Carlotta and Mickey, nothing but my
wasted youth passing.

The chores around the place didn't get any easier, and I didn't
get any less incompetent. It wasn't that I lacked common sense, it
was just that I was so ignorant. Raised as the son of a prosperous
businessman, I had never mowed a lawn or hammered a nail. My
father was the kind of man who played golf and went to his club,
not the kind who did woodworking with his son on a Saturday
morning. On Saturday mornings, I pored over my stamp
collection or walked downtown to the library. I had no idea how
to oil the grass clippers; it was Carlotta, finally, who told me what
kind of oil to use and where to buy it. The browning tips of the
palm trees in the lobby were spreading inward no matter how
much I watered them; soon the trees would be dry husks climbing
from the wreckage of their own dead leaves. There were rats in
the cellar, and ancient traps with parts of dead mice in them.
During a torrential rainstorm I discovered that the gutters were
clogged; trying to unclog them from the roof, with a long, hooked
pole I found in the storage room, made me sick with terror, and in
the gutter where it turned a corner I found a small colony of half-
rotted squirrels. Mrs. Kessler on the third floor complained about

a stopped-up bathroom sink, and I hadn't the faintest idea how to cope with it: she had to show me, with a patient little smile, how to use a plunger. She said, "I've lived here fourteen years. Mr. Gant is a personal friend." As for washing the windows, it seemed to be a God-given talent, like perfect pitch, that I surely didn't have; the tall windows streaked and looked murky, and there was a band in the middle of each one that I couldn't reach no matter what sweaty acrobatics I engaged in with the rubber tool I spent seventy cents on at the hardware store.

Mr. Gant made a habit of stopping by every few days to check on the cleanliness of the windows and the height of the grass and the condition of the marble floors. He reminded me of my old history prof, who took gleeful pleasure in springing quizzes on us without warning. I dreaded Gant's visits, his cackling laugh and pointing finger, and I lay awake one whole night wondering whether Mrs. Kessler had told him about the plunger. One afternoon, he announced that in a month or two I would start repainting the hallways. "Let's have a look," he said, and, my heart sinking, I went up the marble stairs behind his shiny gabardine backside that was as wide and flat as an old cushion. For a man twice my age, he was agile, and he never stopped talking (loose banister, stains on the marble, streaked windows). I realized as we climbed that he loved the place, the Alhambra Gardens. I was reminded of Joe McGreevey and his steakhouse, and of that whole world of old men who made a living from tangible things – food, shelter, objects. Mr. Gant and my father would have gotten along fine: Dad with his real estate empire (standing on hopelessly shaky ground, as we discovered when he died) and Gant with his pretty little piece of New York City. They'd have talked rents and zoning and taxes, then gone out for a game of golf. I could easily imagine Gant on the links, his big sagging body striding along, his powerful swing, and the two of them in the clubhouse afterwards, swapping jokes about chorus girls and farmers' daughters.

We went up a cast-iron spiral staircase to the roof to inspect an old leak in the wooden water tower. Except for the raised front that housed a small, useless attic, the roof was a vast bare space enclosed by ornate parapets, and the view was startling: greenish-black treetops, the glittering river, everything precise and clean. A feeling of intense, unfocused gratitude welled up in me. "Ain't it spectacular," Gant said, as if he owned it all. His lips curved into the smug smile of a man who was making money when everyone else was losing it. He spread his arm and his big bony hand in a sweep that embraced sky, clouds, city. "Empire State Building – quarter of a mile high. Chrysler Building. Queens. Brooklyn. The bridges. Seen the bridges at night? Spectacular." His hand dropped, and he shook his head, as if acknowledging the inadequacy of any words, and we gazed out over the river in silence for a strange moment, bound in some sort of communion, like prayer. Then Gant pointed to a puddle at the base of the great silvered tower. "Keep your eye on it," Gant said. "It gets worse, you tell me."

We made our way slowly down through the five floors, inspecting walls and woodwork while Gant detailed exactly what would have to be done. "Hope you can handle the spackling," he would say, looking dubious. Or, touching a bruised piece of woodwork, "Don't know how this happened, you'll probably have to sand it down, maybe fill it in here." I stood with my hands in my pockets, rocking back on my heels, with what I hoped was a fine mixure of concern and insouciance. "Of course," I kept saying. "Yes, I see. Exactly."

"What in hell is spackling?" I asked Carlotta and May the next morning. "What kind of sandpaper do you use on painted woodwork?"

Carlotta pulled a lipstick from her bag. "This is spackling, Robert! Didn't you know? Helena Rubenstein, Spackling Red!" May said I would need that expensive Italian sandpaper, the kind they sold at Tiffany's. The two of them went off arm in arm, laughing. I began spending time browsing at Stein's Hardware on First Avenue.

"You and Mr. Stein are running a regular salon, Robert," Carlotta teased me. "Do all the rising young supers gather to drink coffee and argue about spackling?"

May said, "Isn't Spackling that German philosopher? The one who says that life is meaningless?"

As the month went on, hot and humid, interspersed with occasional days of cold, wet rain, I became uneasily, insecurely familiar with the Alhambra Gardens, the roof and the basement, the hallways on all five floors and several of the twenty apartments, the mysterious workings of sinks and toilets and lighting fixtures. I went several times up the short staircase to the odd space that was the attic: a triangle behind two windows, empty except for dust. I swept it out one cool, cloudy day, and washed the windows as best I could. Looking out, I was face to face with the looming wooden water tower on the building opposite. It was weathered to a brownish silver. A crow sat like an ornament on a finial at the top. It glared at me, then squawked and flew off, making me laugh, and I was startled by the way my voice sounded in that bare room with its sloping walls. I began to recite Oliver's mock declaration to Thomasina on the balcony – the second-act climax of my play. The words sounded just as they were meant to, both profound and comic. The acoustics in the odd little space were remarkable.

I liked that attic room, its spareness and quiet. Our apartment not only seemed to shrink further every day, but was gradually transforming itself, in the grip of a force I couldn't understand, into a surging chaos of laundry strung up to dry, May's omnipresent ironing board, old newspapers, my manuscript in its various stages, stacks of magazines, food going bad in the ice box, and a pervasive stink of mildew. I considered moving my writing desk up to the attic and using the place as a refuge – away from May, if the truth be told. She meant well, of course, but she asked me almost every day when the play would be done so that I could send it out to the names I'd been given – a couple of producers' scouts had seen the pair of one-actors I'd written for the Drama Club at Harvard and given me their cards: she had more faith in those bits of white pasteboard than I did. But even after dark the attic space was still too hot for me to work in, the warm daytime air hanging stubbornly under the roof like the building's hot breath. I thought about offering it to Orson Price if he ever came by again, and I wondered how desperate he was, or if he was desperate at all.

The month of July seemed both endlessly lingering and rapidly passing. *Before much longer,* I kept thinking, *I will have to sand and spackle and paint.* Just as, when I was a boy, the prospect of school starting up again would hang over the perfect summer months like a storm cloud. On my night-time walks, I found himself looking for Orson Price, going over and over our conversation together for clues to where he might be. He had said he was living in the Gramercy Park area – hadn't he? – though he hadn't revealed where he was from originally. His speech had been accentless, unplaceable, something like the speech I myself had learned at Harvard when, with effort, I dropped the flat a's and loose diction I had brought from Rochester. But he had said this was his neighborhood. What did that mean? *I feel at home here,* he had said. *I'll stop by.* He must have gotten work, I thought, that kept him busy. Or maybe he was no longer in the neighborhood after all: *this quiet little corner of the city.* You went where a job took you.

On an afternoon when I had planned to trim the hedge, another rainstorm forced me back inside, and I walked up one flight of the marble stairs and knocked on the door of Mrs. Amalfi's apartment. I waited so long I was sure she must be out. When I was about to give up, the door opened and Mrs. Amalfi gave me her wide-eyed stare for a few seconds before she cried, "Mr. Sinclair! Robert! How lovely to see you!"

"I thought if you weren't busy – "

"Busy! Well, I'm always busy!" Then she smiled, showing her square ivory teeth with their narrow space. "But not too busy for company. It's a pleasure to see you, and I would be delighted if you came in for a cup of tea."

"You're sure – "

"Of course! This is a great treat! Hana!" She turned back to me. "Hana is here," she said in a low voice. "How lucky for you!"

I was wafted inside, where the odor of cooking mixed with a sharp smell like decaying orange peelings, with an edge of some kind of incense. The living room was dark; heavy drapes were drawn across the windows, and a pile of cats dozed on a sofa. Mrs. Amalfi, colors flying, led me through to the kitchen, in back, where rain dashed against two windows looking down on 21st Street. A soup pot simmered on the stove, raising the temperature of the room; it seemed an odd dish for a summer day. On the table two more sprawled cats looked at me with disapproval.

A woman sat at the table, peeling carrots. My first impression was that she was old: she was dressed in shades of brown, with a red and yellow printed scarf wound around her head. When she looked up and I saw her face, I took her for an adolescent. Then I realized she was neither old nor young, perhaps my age or a bit older. She was very small and plain, with a pale face and tiny hands, and she wore steel-rimmed oval eyeglasses. She was, to say the least, nothing like her mother.

"This is Hana, my daughter. And Hana, this is Robert Sinclair. The new super. I told you all about him."

I said, "I can't imagine what you might have said. There's not much to tell."

"To those who look, there is always a great deal to see," Mrs. Amalfi said. "Surely, Robert, as a writer, you must know that." She was at the stove, moving the soup to a back burner, taking a match to light the gas under a kettle of water. Such a prosaic act seemed incongruous with her dangling sleeves and heavy makeup.

Hana put down the carrot-peeler and held out her childish, ringless hand. She squeezed the ends of my fingers. "I'm happy to meet you." Her voice was low and dramatic, as if she were a character in a play – an actress portraying strong emotion barely held in check. I had the impression that she and her mother had been in the middle of an intense conversation. About what, I wondered. Her face was round and smooth, lightly freckled; her smile, which was brief, made her cheeks bunch up like a child's.

There was a fluttering, scuffling sound from the corner by the sink, and I saw four chicken-wire cages stacked together. "The birds," Hana announced in her deep little voice. "Pigeons."

Mrs. Amalfi went over to the cages. "That's Bianca. Quiet down, Bianca. Her beak keeps growing, who knows why, so that she can't eat. Hana has to clip it every few weeks. And this is Juliet, with the broken wing that never healed properly. She can't fly at all. This huge thing is Portia. Can you see how enormous she is? She doesn't fly very well, either. She's some sort of mutation, I suppose. The other birds attack her." Mrs. Amalfi made kissing noises in Portia's direction, and the bird fluttered a wing against the side of its cage. "A giantess among pigeons! And this poor thing is Cordelia." I made out a gray-colored shape, quiet, in the bottom cage, behind a cloth. Mrs. Amalfi opened the little wire door, reached in and stroked it. The bird cooed sweetly, faintly. Mrs. Amalfi sighed. "She's not going to survive."

"You've done your best, Mother," Hana said. She spoke reprovingly, as if it were a tired issue. Hana went to the stove with the carrots and tipped them into the soup pot. She was barely five feet tall, with narrow, sloping shoulders. No wisps of hair escaped from under her scarf, and it was hard to tell if she had any at all. I wondered if she was ill, or if she could be some kind of nun in training.

"But it's so painful to lose even one tiny life." Mrs. Amalfi clucked once more at the cages. "I love my birds. And my dear cats. All strays. All darlings." She rubbed the head of one of the table cats; it lifted its chin, and I could hear it purr. Its back was scraped raw, oozing. "This is Ferdinand. He got out the window and down the fire escape and was mauled by a dog. Didn't you, bad boy? But he's healing. And that's Rosalind. When we found her she had a broken leg, but it has mended beautifully."

I put out a finger, and Rosalind rubbed her head against it, while I looked around the kitchen. It was a very unusual place. There were at least a dozen oil paintings crowded on the walls, all heavy and dark and looking desperately in need of cleaning. On the floor was a Persian carpet, and on the table a dark blue cloth, fringed. The steamy windows were curtained in a gauzy material patterned with gold, and each sill held a forest of green plants. The drinking glass next to the sink was a stemmed goblet with a gold rim. The room smelled strongly of broth and herbs and oranges. In spite of the gas stove, the sink with its plain faucets, the cupboards and table and chairs, this kitchen in 2-B was not kitchenlike at all; the effect was of rich, exotic frivolity.

Mrs. Amalfi fussed with cups and spoons and Hana stirred the soup while I petted each of the cats in turn.

"How many do you have?"

"Cats? Five. At the moment. But please sit down, Robert. And what would you like with your tea?" She set a large teapot on the table before me, with a strainer. "Is there still that cake, Hana?"

The two women watched me eat cake and drink tea – Mrs. Amalfi like some large, bright, sharp-eyed bird, Hana a tiny wren with her tight smile and pale, speckled skin. While I ate, Mrs. Amalfi told me about each cat: where she found it, what the cat's ailment was, how she cured it, and a short sketch of its personality. Ferdinand, who stretched out in front of Hana on the table, was a pleasure-seeking sybarite; Rosalind was a clown, a character; Romeo, who strolled in from the other room, was shy and considerate. I petted them all, tried to ask intelligent questions, laughed at Mrs. Amalfi's anecdotes – conscious, as I so often was, of the impression I was making, wondering if they liked me, if it was really as easy as it seemed to make people like you simply by taking an interest in what they said.

The tea was black and very strong. I finished the cake, which was moist and rich, studded with bits of lemon rind. Hana silently fetched me another piece, and poured more tea, hardly speaking at all. At one point, I asked her about herself. Mrs. Amalfi's head jerked quickly toward her. Hana frowned. "I'm a student. I'm studying nursing."

Her mother's face cleared; she touched Hana's shoulder, smiling. "Yes, Hana will be a nurse," she said, then: "No! Hana is of course already a nurse! It was Hana who set Rosalind's leg, Hana who clips Bianca's beak for her. A magnificent profession, and it's in her blood. Not only am I in my own way a healer, but her grandfather was a doctor, and her great-grandmother was a nurse and a midwife, in the old country."

"Which old country is that?" I asked. "Italy?"

"Heavens, no! I'm Czech. My family came here from Bohemia when I was quite young."

I realized that this might explain her hint of an accent, her slightly eccentric English. "And Amalfi?"

"Amalfi goes back a long way. A long story. A youthful folly."

"And Hana –"

Hana said, "My name is Hana Ribowsky."

"Polish," said Mrs. Amalfi. "Nurse Ribowsky. How does that sound, Hana?"

"It sounds –" There was a pause during which I studied a painting on the wall, of a brass bowl overflowing with fruit: peaches, apricots, pears, and pale green grapes that cascaded over the side. "Fine," Hana finished.

Mrs. Amalfi smiled anxiously first at Hana, then at me, and Hana stared down at the tablecloth.

"Well," I said, and then, more to cover an awkwardness than because I expected anything, I changed the subject. "I don't suppose you know a man named Orson Price. Lives in the neighborhood. Or used to."

Hana raised her head. Mrs. Amalfi said. "Of course I know Orson Price. Yes. I heard a rumor that he was back."

She sounded almost irritable, and didn't volunteer anything further; she turned her head to watch the rain coursing down the window. There was a silence. Down on the street, cars passed, hissing in the wet. One of the pigeons cooed, like a human voice expressing sympathy. Still frowning, Hana petted Ferdinand, who roused himself and began daintily to lick at his paw.

The enigmatic silences were making me anxious. Were my questions too personal? Did they want me to leave? How had this visit gone awry? Were the cats the only acceptable topic? And yet Mrs. Amalfi had seemed so open; Hana had seemed so pleasant.

I persevered. "Do you happen to know how I could get in touch with him?"

When Mrs. Amalfi turned her head toward me, I saw that she hadn't in fact been staring out the window; she had been covertly watching the brooding Hana in the glass. Now, rousing herself, she gave me her attention. "You want to get in touch with Orson Price?"

I couldn't tell if she was incredulous or suspicious or merely curious. I hesitated. "Well – I don't know – I thought I might hire him to do some work," I said. "Some of the more specialized things around the place."

"Here? In this building?"

"It was just a thought I had."

Mrs. Amalfi looked at me thoughtfully for several seconds, then said, "I have no idea where he is." She widened her eyes at me. "You are an intellectual, Robert, I take it. You haven't much interest in the nuts and bolts of superintendenting. Is that a word? Superintendenting?"

Hana came out of her reverie and surprised me with a little laugh. "I doubt it, Mother." She stood up and began busying herself around the kitchen. She turned down the gas and then, with a metallic clatter, she pulled a pot cover from a cupboard and put it over the soup.

"Well, it should be. Yes, an intellectual," Mrs. Amalfi continued. "That, at least, is the impression I am getting. That you are not what is known as a practical man."

"Mother."

"Was that rude? I meant it as a compliment, in fact."

I didn't know what to say. Was I supposed to thank her? "It's true that I'm writing a play," I said, and felt immediately embarrassed. How inadequate it sounded, and presumptuous. I had a longing to be back in my own apartment, at my desk, with the play actually before me, to convince myself of the truth of it. At the same time I felt, suddenly, very weary, and remembered that Mrs. Amalfi was also a sleep specialist, that she treated insomnia. "But that has nothing to do with anything. I don't think writing plays and taking care of a building are incompatible. I'm just rather inexperienced at carpentry and – well, you know the sort of thing. Replacing broken window glass. Plumbing. Dealing with tools."

"Orson Price, you will find, is quite the reverse," Mrs. Amalfi said. Her eyes narrowed. "An eminently practical man. Practical to the core of his being." She sounded vaguely disapproving, as if practicality were a vice.

"He said he might stop by, but he never did."

"That's Orson," Hana said.

"You know him too?"

"Oh, yes." Hana smiled, just barely. "Everyone knows him. This neighborhood is like a small town."

"What about your sleep problem?" Mrs. Amalfi asked.

It was as if she had read my mind, and for a moment it seemed all these things must be connected: Orson Price and my insomnia and the small-town neighborhood. Then I realized that Mrs. Amalfi was simply through with the subject of Orson Price.

"It hasn't gone away, I take it," she said.

"No, it hasn't."

"How long has it been bothering you?"

"Since –" When I thought about it, I realized that the correct answer was: *Since I got married.* But that didn't sound right. And, after all, I'd had periods of mild insomnia all my life. "Several months," I said. "Worse since I came to New York."

"Do you have trouble falling asleep? Or are you waking in the night and lying awake until morning?"

"I can't fall asleep. I get sleepy, lie down, and as soon as I close my eyes I'm consumed with restlessness – not tired at all."

"Not simple anxiety, then." Mrs. Amalfi said, nodding her head. "It's the other kind. The nameless kind. What do you do for it?"

"Nothing. The only cure is to walk."

"You're a night walker?" Mrs. Amalfi looked at me sharply, and it seemed to me that Hana, at the sink, stopped what she was doing to listen.

"You've encountered that before?"

"Oh, my good gracious, yes. The endless journey of the insomniac, the long road that the sleepless travel, the walk to oblivion. It's very common, especially among men. Of course."

"I wasn't aware that other people suffered from it." A surge of strong feeling came over me that I assumed had to be hope until I realized it was disappointment. I pictured ranks of sleepless men walking in the dark, sharing my private night-time city. "And I don't know why I said *suffer*, it's not really accurate. It's not suffering, in fact it's a pleasure, those walks. I see a lot of strange things, things that aren't available to be seen in the daytime. And they calm my brain." I remembered the knifing on Bleecker Street – something I had kept myself from thinking about. "Usually," I added. "And walking helps me with my writing. I don't know how, but it makes my mind into a stage, where my plays can be composed. I'm probably not explaining it very well."

I stopped, aware that I didn't actually want to give up my walks – not for something as dull and paltry as sleep. One must sleep. And yes, I wanted to sleep. But not, perhaps, as much as I wanted to be a night walker.

"What you're saying is that, for many reasons, night walking is rather seductive?"

"Yes. I suppose that's as good a description as any."

Hana turned from the sink to look at me, her round face serious and her green eyes glowing. "I have migraine headaches," she said, and suddenly it was as if we were, in fact, actors in a play: the spotlight on Hana, her big moment. Her mother looked at her expectantly, lips parted. "I see flashing lights," Hana said.

"Colors – very much as I have heard people describe the aurora borealis. I see what to me seem like visions, all in the midst of unbearable pain and nausea and a very frightening feeling of disorientation, of detachment from the ordinary world. It's a terrible thing. There is no cure. Headache powders, aspirin, have no effect. Ice packs, herbal teas, massage. Nothing helps. One can only wait it out. I lose a day or two every time it occurs. I can do nothing but lie in a darkened room, experiencing what I experience, and waiting for it to end. And yet –" Her voice rose, became tense with emotion. "I can't help but feel that if a cure were devised, if a pill could be taken that would end those headaches and all that comes with them forever – well, I would have to think long and hard about whether I would take it. I would miss – certain aspects." She stopped talking as suddenly as she had begun, and blushed. We looked at each other. Clearly, something was wrong with Hana – but none of the usual wrongs, I was sure. Just something a little off, like a radio that wouldn't quite tune in the station. After a moment, she said, more calmly, "I assume that's how you feel about your sleeplessness. Your walks in the night when the world is asleep." She came back to the table and picked up the teapot. "More tea?"

The soliloquy was over. I wanted to applaud. "No, thank you, Hana," I said.

"You're quite sure? How about cake?"

Mrs. Amalfi broke in. "Of course, health considerations are not unimportant. Loss of sleep leads to a lowered resistance to disease. Loss of sleep means a decreased ability to perform simple tasks safely. And of course, despite its good effects on your writing, in the end it makes intellectual labors much more difficult." She reached her plump hand out to a cat, Rosalind this time. "Sleep is exactly what Shakspeare said it was. Nature's soft nurse."

"The best of rest is sleep." I smiled. "And what's the other one? Something about how it knits up the raveled sleeve of care."

"Yes! Such a domestic idea! You can imagine Shakespeare's wife mending his sweater. Or jerkin, or doubloon. Doublet? Whatever they might have called it in those days. But the point is, Robert, that you must have your sleep."

"It's true, it would be good to sleep more." I was, in fact, feeling distinctly drowsy in the warm, scented kitchen. If I just slid under the table to the rug I would fall into a drugged, enchanted slumber. "To sleep normally," I said. "Although, in a way I've gotten used to it, to always being a little deprived. And – Hana?" She was at the sink, her back to the room, her head bent down as if she did heavy labor, though she was only washing our teacups. I imagined her stretched out on a bed with a cold cloth laid across her brow, her teeth bared, her flat chest rising and falling while the aurora borealis flashed and flickered behind her eyelids. "I do most certainly know what you mean about your headaches. It's as if you have an enemy, and one day you see he's your friend."

Hana turned to look at me. "What an odd thing to say! But –" She stared at me briefly, then returned to her washing. She said, "Yes, that's it exactly," and there was another small silence during which the birds in their cages cooed and rustled. Hana held a cup under the tap to rinse it, then glanced toward the window and said, "Look – the rain stopped."

As we watched, the sun came out, back-lighting the rain-glazed tree across the way, placing a band of buttery light across the bright tablecloth. "I'm afraid it's almost time for you to go, Hana," her mother said. I hadn't realized Hana was going anywhere; I had assumed she lived there. It occurred to me as a surprise that she could have another life somewhere, a complete life like anyone's. A Polish husband, maybe, and children, a house of her own.

Feeling in the way, I said, "And I should get back to work," and stood up, but Mrs. Amalfi put her plump fingers on my arm, and I sat down again. "Wait." She took a small packet from a cupboard. "Before bed, make yourself a cup of this, very strong. Fierce! Add milk, but heat the milk on the stove first, so that it will work properly. Do you understand? Everything must be hot, as hot as you can bear." The packet was wrapped in brown paper, tied up with red string. She put it into my hand and closed my fingers around it. "This is very good tea, from Russia. Made from herbs."

"What herbs?"

"Russian herbs. Drink a strong cup of it an hour before you try to fall asleep. And don't walk, even if you're wide awake. You must learn to bring the sleep to you, so you won't have to pursue it. That way you will always have a choice: bring the sleep, or take a night walk. Lie in the darkness with your eyes closed and let the tea bring the sleep."

"And if it doesn't?"

"Ha!" Mrs. Amalfi showed her teeth. "This is just the beginning. This is the first round of ammunition. I have many more guns in my arsenal! I am, after all, a sleep specialist, Robert."

"And I need to pay you for this, don't I? This Russian tea?"

"This part of the treatment is free," she said, with a twinkle in her eyes, as if there was something slightly naughty about it. "Then we'll see. And don't worry. Sleep is precious, but it is also cheap. I won't make a pauper of you."

"Thank you, Mrs. Amalfi." She withdrew her hand from mine, and I stood up again. "And if you should see Orson Price, you'll tell him to stop by?"

"Oh – Orson Price. " Her face became serious; she lifted a ringed hand to her neck. "If you like."

I had no idea if she meant it. Hana stood nearby, smiling at me. I smiled back at her and said, "Good-bye, Hana. I don't mean to keep dwelling on this, I hope you don't mind, but – I was glad to hear what you had to say, about your headaches."

"I hope we'll talk again another time," Hana said, and held out her tiny hand. "Good-bye, Robert."

"Don't forget," Mrs. Amalfi said. "Heat the milk first. And remember what I told you the other day. Lie to Gant."

I went outside for a cigarette. The steps were too wet to sit on, so I walked up and down in front of the building. I was on my second cigarette when Hana came out. She carried a small leather bag. Outside her mother's kitchen, she looked even smaller but strangely more attractive, perhaps because her flamboyant mother wasn't there as contrast. I saw that her legs were slim, well-shaped, and she wore pretty little open-toed shoes, with ribbon ties. I could imagine her in a white nursing costume, a starched hat like a bird perched on her head. *Nature's soft nurse.* I wondered what her hair was like, why she covered it.

"Robert!"

"Just came out for a smoke. It's cooler out. Really very pleasant."

"Yes, it is. It's lovely." To my surprise, she hailed a passing taxicab, raising her arm authoritatively, as if it was something she often did. She smiled at the look on my face. "I don't have far to go. It's a little splurge. Good-bye again, Robert."

The driver sprang out and held the door for her. As she was getting in, she turned to me again. "Orson Price," she said, in her deep, emphatic voice. "If you really want to get in touch with him, you might find him at that big old lodging house up on 25th Street. Do you know where that is? The municipal lodging for men? Down almost to the river. Turn right on 25th, and you'll see it." She looked up at me, and her eyes seemed to glow for a moment, as if she were experiencing the flashing lights of a migraine. Then she got into the cab and waved at me through the window. I watched her bright scarf in the back window until it disappeared around the corner, wondering how I had ever found her plain.

■■■

The next day, the sun shone brightly, but the air had been washed cool by the rain; there had never been a day so fresh. Over her dress, May wore a little sweater, sewn with pearls, that Carlotta had shoplifted for her. I had drunk Mrs. Amalfi's tea the night before; the only effect I noticed was that I had to get out of bed to urinate twice during the night – the second time after I had, at last, fallen asleep at some hour after three-thirty. I was feeling irritable and slightly sick, and after May and Carlotta left I considered whether I should go back to bed or walk up Lexington Avenue to the Armenian restaurant where for ten cents I could have a breakfast roll with unlimited cups of sweet coffee. Instead of doing either, I walked, on an impulse, up Second Avenue to 25th Street and turned down toward the river.

The lodging house was in the so-called Gashouse District – once a famous scene of pestilent tenements and roving gangs, but now just a bleak, crowded warren of streets lined with dismally shabby buildings. The old gas tanks down by the river hulked against the morning sky, which was brilliantly blue after the rain. The place I sought was a vast, prisonlike brick building, almost on the river. I had never walked this way before, and I was unprepared for its size, and for the sign that read: MUNICIPAL LODGING HOUSE and, in slightly smaller letters: FOR HOMELESS AND INDIGENT MEN. I stood in the street staring at it; as I watched, a slow parade of men came out the front door and walked down a pathway to a building like a warehouse on one of the piers, which looked as if it had been converted into a dining room. There must have been hundreds of men shuffling obediently in the direction of breakfast. I looked for one with

Orson's dash, that air of an aristocrat temporarily down on his luck. They all seemed alike, an endless progression of the same gray man in baggy clothes. I stood watching them. Who were they, after all? The only thing that kept me from being one of them, I thought, was my ability to fool Mr. Gant into thinking I was competent. *Don't forget*, Mrs. Amalfi had said. *Lie to Gant.* I realized that if I did ever hire Orson Price to work for me, I would not be able to tell Mr. Gant the truth. Immediately I began to fabricate a story: *This is my cousin Orson – no my cousin Philip – from Rochester – from Buffalo. He's going to be staying with us for a while. He might be helping me out with a few things while he's here –*

I watched the men going toward their breakfasts. *Down on their luck. Down and out.* I thought of my play, which seemed more than ever at that moment like a paltry, pathetic thing, and then of the life I had lived in college, with nothing to worry about but exams and girls. Those years seemed now a golden blur of sunlight dappling the river, the boats gliding under the footbridge, the afternoons lying on the grass with a book or – yes – sleeping, the golden swirl of leaves on the paths of the Yard, the parties at the speakeasy on the Square. I never heard from any of my friends there, not even Jasper, my roommate and best friend for four semesters. He had come up on the train to Rochester for my father's funeral, spoken embarrassed words of condolence at the church, stayed overnight in the spare room, returned to Cambridge the next day, and I never heard from him again. I had a post card that summer from another friend who was traveling in Italy, and a Christmas card from a girl I'd dated freshman year. *Down in the dumps. Down-hearted. Downcast.* The last of the line of men straggled into the building on the pier. I thought, foolishly: *Brothers.* But I was sure Orson Price wasn't among those men, and I found I couldn't bring myself to go in and inquire. With a hollow feeling in my stomach that was more than hunger, I walked up to Baba Neshan's for breakfast.

When I got back, in spite of my tiredness, I sat down at the typewriter. I meant only to look at a few things in the last act, but, as always, my own words drew me in – I was my own best audience in those days – and time leaped onward, marked by an overflowing ashtray and cups of coffee gone cold. Maybe the vision of those gray men drove me on, but whatever the reason, that was the day I finished a rough draft of my play. I typed the last words, typed CURTAIN, composed the sheets into a stack, and began to read it over.

By the time I came to the end of the first act, I knew it was neither poor nor pointless. It wasn't drivel. I must have been mad: it was wonderful, it was pure genius, it would make me famous and rich. It needed revising, but one more rewrite and I'd be done.

It was late afternoon. I couldn't do any more that day, and I couldn't sit still, either. And the hell with the mopping and the grass. I walked down to Union Square, saying over lines from my play in my head – all those clever words, that splendid passion tempered with gaiety, the jokes that had come to me on my walks. I had an immense hunger to see the play produced – to actually see it come to life, Oliver Templeton and Thomasina and Alec made as real as the people I passed on the street: in a curious and magical way, *more* real. *Fish Out of Water* on a marquee, with my name. What a miraculous thing that would be, an impossible wish come true – as if, when I was seven years old and had wished almost daily that my parents would get me a pony, I had returned from school one day to find one eating oats on our front porch.

The sun was angled off the sides of the buildings, and the ragman with his horse and cart was plodding down 17th Street. I walked through Union Square, avoiding the end-of-the-world woman and the "Jesus Saves" couple with their tambourine and their insistent pleas. A crowd was gathered around the old black man with the harmonica; he was playing "Kingdom Coming," and then he began "Juanita." I sat down on a bench, closed my eyes, and listened until he was done. The music calmed me. I realized that I was exhausted, and I threw a nickel in his hat and walked back home.

May was sitting in front of her three-way mirror looking at herself. When I entered she said, "Darling!" to my reflection in the mirror, then turned to face me. She called me *darling* only when she was in an exceptionally good mood: *full of herself*, my mother would say. "You'll never guess."

"You got a part."

"I got a part! Or rather Marshall got me a part. I tried out yesterday, and I went up there this morning and – voilà!" She struck a pose. "May Munro is back on the boards! The New York theatre will never be the same again."

It was incredible, but it was also auspicious, that I finished the play and she was cast on the same day; it was too perfect to be true.

"You really did? You're not fooling me, May?"

"No, I'm not fooling, you big silly husband!" She reached out her arms, and we danced around the apartment, a clumsy improvised tango that left us laughing together on the bed. "I got a part, I got a part, oh Robert, I got a part!" She smiled at me, her lipstick gone and her eyes gleaming. She looked very beautiful.

"You're playing Lady Macbeth with the Royal Shakespeare Company."

"Darling! I'm too young and gorgeous for Lady Macbeth! No. I'm playing Ophelia. Opposite Leslie Howard. Aren't you proud of me? I beat out Gertrude Lawrence for the part."

I kissed her, and she held my head, held my lips against hers, sucked my tongue. I pulled away. "Come on. Tell me."

"Take off your pants."

"May."

She unbuttoned my fly. "I want to gobble you up."

"May. Tell me. Tell me first."

She lay back, but she kept her hands on me. "I'll tell you if you promise we can do it right afterwards."

"May!"

"I'm playing Florence," she said dreamily. " A gangster's floozie in a play called *The Killer Instinct*. Frankie – I'm Frankie's girl. I have six or eight lines, I don't know. I get killed. Onstage. I get to die. I wear a revealing costume. That's all they told me. They wanted a blonde. The director is somebody named George Whitlock. It's a theatre on 33rd Street, the Regent. And Frankie is played by Nathan Kaufman. Nathan Kaufman, Robert! I get to play opposite Nathan Kaufman!"

"Who's Nathan Kaufman?"

She unbuttoned her little sweater embroidered with pearls and pulled her dress over her head. "Who's Nathan Kaufman. I can't believe you're asking me that. Suck my tits. Oh – darling – Robert."

We made love. I sucked her nipples while she brought herself to orgasm with her fingers, and then she knelt over me. I buried my fingers in her hair, heard my own deep shuddering breaths, heard myself cry out. Then she did it to herself again, lying against me with her teeth in my skin. When she was done she fell deeply into a doze, and I lay with her body against me in the greenish bedroom light, my mind blank with tiredness but unable to sleep. I lay there and tried to comprehend it, that May had actually been hired – something I had thought would never happen. I wondered if Carlotta knew.

When she woke up I said, "I'm sorry. I never heard of him. Who's Nathan Kaufman?"

She rolled on her back, stretched her arms toward the ceiling, let them fall. "I don't know who the hell he is. I never heard of him either. It's a stupid dinky part. But I don't care. I'm so excited I could die. Oh Robert! We're in New York! We're really here! This changes everything, doesn't it?" She sat up suddenly and looked at the clock. "I've got to go. There's a pre-rehearsal thing tonight. A meeting. I'm supposed to be there at six."

She leapt out of bed, dashed into the bathroom. I heard the water run, the toilet flush. Then she came out again with lipstick on. She picked up her hair brush and bent her head down and brushed it hard, then stood up and shook her hair into place, a hat made of golden wires.

"Sex is very becoming to you. You look like Carole Lombard."

She looked at the clock. "I guess we don't have time to do it again."

"I sincerely doubt it."

"Just joking."

She came over to the bed where I lay watching her. "Do I look like I've just sucked my husband's thing until he screamed in ecstasy?"

"Yes."

"Good. That's exactly how Frankie's girlfriend is supposed to look."

"Just don't get up to anything with Nathan Kaufman."

She sat on the bed beside me. "You know what my old Uncle Hector always used to say about Aunt Gert."

"You don't have an Uncle Hector. You don't have an Aunt Gert."

"Irrelevant. Know what he used to say?"

"No. I don't. What?"

"Why should I go out for hamburger?" She bent down and licked my penis, sucked the end of it lightly. I could feel her breath on my skin. Then she raised her head, smiling her wicked smile. "When I get filet mignon at home," she whispered.

■ ■ ■

Over the next few days, I typed up a final version of *Fish Out of Water* and mailed it off to the address on the nicer-looking of the two business cards I had: Rex Mason Theatrical Associates, on 43rd Street. "Wonderful, sweetie," May said when I told her. "What lovely timing. Let's get famous together, then we only have to buy champagne once." She was on her way out the door, but she came back to hug me, pretending to pout. "Now maybe you can devote a little time to me instead of to that infernal typewriter."

"I'll walk you to rehearsal."

"What? And have Gant catch you off the premises?" She kissed me lightly. "Hold the fort. Keep the home fires burning."

"Do you love me?"

"Are you kidding? How could I not love the George Bernard Shaw of Second Avenue?"

Our routine was that, if May wasn't home from rehearsal by seven o'clock, I'd find some dinner in the neighborhood. I took Gant's rule pretty seriously, staying around the Alhambra Gardens most mornings and afternoons. If May and I went out together, it was usually only on Saturday nights.

The day I mailed off my play, May hadn't turned up by 7:30. Finishing my play had left me feeling both mournful and bored, as if my adored only child had gone off to school. I couldn't concentrate on what I was reading, and I was too restless to make myself dinner. I went down to a place on Third Avenue for a 25-cent Italian dinner, and I was on my way back when I saw Orson Price coming down the street toward me.

I called out, "Orson!" Immediately, I wished I hadn't seemed so eager; a moment later, I was glad of it. Orson looked distinctly scruffy. He wore a wrinkled summer shirt and a pair of shiny brown pants, too big for him, that looked like he had retrieved them from a trash can. His reddish hair hung down around his collar, and he obviously hadn't shaved in a while. But his smile was sunny enough, and when we shook hands, his grip was firm, as if he wanted to make a point of some kind.

"Well, Robert. I heard you're looking for an assistant."

"Did you? Say, it's good to see you, Orson. How've you been?"

"Not too bad. Getting along." It was so obvious that he wasn't getting along that I almost expected him to burst into laughter, but he didn't. He said, "It's been a pleasant summer, so far. Maybe a bit on the warm side."

I thought of the good dinner I'd just eaten at the Italian café: I was full of ravioli, and I wished I'd run into Orson before it instead of after. I might have bought him a meal. I said, "Well. I'm glad I caught you. Who told you I'm looking for someone?"

"Teresa Amalfi."

"Ah. The sleep specialist."

"Yes. *La spécialiste du sommeil.*"

Interesting that he knew some French. Again I thought of Orson as the young scion of a ruined Gramercy Park family, a man perhaps like myself. I could easily imagine him in tails, lounging against the wall at a dance like the ones I used to go to in Cambridge. I took out a cigarette and offered him one. "How do you know Mrs. A.?" I asked.

"Oh – you know – the neighborhood. She's an old-timer."

"She's a curious woman."

"Yes. She's been around. Had four husbands, that I know of. Amalfi wasn't the last, but it was the name she liked best. Or so I understand. Who knows for sure? Mrs. Amalfi cultivates mystery." Orson took a long drag on his cigarette and exhaled slowly through his nose. Then he looked at me curiously. "So I take it you're one of her patients."

"Her what?" I felt oddly flattered that Mrs. Amalfi and Orson had discussed me. "Oh. The sleep thing. Yes. I suppose I am. She gave me some tea that didn't work."

"She believes in the empirical method. A little of this, a little of that. Nothing works for everybody."

"You have experience with this? You're an insomniac?"

"Oh no. I sleep like a baby. No matter what."

"It's a great gift. Possibly the best gift there is."

"Really? Surely there are better gifts. Intelligence. Talent. Wealth. What else. A happy nature? Beauty?"

"Well – none of those mean anything if you can't get to sleep."

"Mm. *Peut-être*. I wouldn't know." Orson smiled. "I hear you're a walker. You walk at night."

"Yes. I walk when I can't sleep. Which means I walk a lot." I looked closely at Orson, trying to imagine the conversation he must have had with Mrs. Amalfi. *Ah, Robert Sinclair – a complicated young man, an intellectual, not without problems. Really? What kind of problems? He doesn't sleep, he walks the streets at night. Does he now? Yes, all over the city, Lord knows what he sees, what he gets up to. There are depths in that young man, Orson. Yes, I felt that too. I liked him immediately, sensed a kind of brotherhood with him...* And how well did Orson know Mrs. Amalfi? and Hana? Did he sit in that warm kitchen drinking tea with them, petting the cats and eating lemon cake?

I said, "Did you also hear that I like the walking? That it's one aspect of my insomnia that I don't want to relinquish."

Orson frowned. "No, I didn't." He exhaled through his nose, suddenly remote and silent. For a moment, he reminded me oddly of Hana. Then he said, briskly, "But what's this about a job?"

"Oh – I might be able to offer you something if you don't mind working for almost no pay." I had thought this all out, rehearsed it in my head over the last weeks. Now that I was actually saying it, I took intense pleasure in the words, and in the role I was playing: I, who had been poor and jobless until not long ago, was offering someone work. "And I could give you a place to live. A stuffy little attic room, I'm afraid. But it has windows. If you put your bed by the windows, you'd be okay. Plus two dollars a week."

Orson continued to frown. He took a drag from his cigarette and looked at the glowing tip as he exhaled. Then he said, "Well!" and looked at me. We were almost the same height. I may have had an inch or so on him. I was struck again by his pale-blue eyes, the color of one of the pieces in my mother's collection of Venetian glass. "What would you want me to do, exactly?"

I was unprepared for his lack of enthusiasm. I had imagined embarrassing gratitude. "Help me out," I said, surprised into candor. "I'm out of my depth. You know carpentry and that sort of thing. I don't. I'm a writer. I could use help. You know. Cleaning and fixing things, and later in the summer there's some painting to be done around the building. The halls and – well, I don't know exactly. I'm going to need help plastering. Et cetera."

"What about Mr. Gant?"

"Do you know Gant?" Why wouldn't he? Everyone seemed to know everyone. But Orson said no, he didn't. Mrs. Amalfi had told him the name. I wondered suddenly if I'd been stupid: what was to prevent Orson from pulling my job out from under me?

But Orson said he didn't know him. "Gant doesn't care how the work gets done," I said. "As long as it gets done. He knows I'm a playwright, trying to do two things. He thought that was interesting." This was what my roommate Jasper used to call a little gray lie. But I saw Orson slipping away, put off by whatever Mrs. Amalfi had told him about Gant. "He understands the situation."

"And he's a friend of your wife's aunt."

"Yes! Smart of you to remember that."

"I generally remember things. Myra. Right?"

"Yes. An old beau, I think." I actually had no idea, but it seemed good to present Gant as avuncular, fond of us, respectful of family ties.

Orson Price looked at me thoughtfully. When he frowned, his eyes became long triangles. He tugged at his hair, maybe planning the haircut he'd get when I paid him. "I don't know," he said.

"Well, think about it." I looked off down 21st Street, as if I didn't give a damn what he decided. The desire to know what conversation had passed between him and Mrs. Amalfi was almost unbearable. *He's an odd bird, that Robert, the super. Not in any sense a practical man. And he's desperate. I sense that you can get whatever you want out of him.*

Orson finished his cigarette, threw it down and ground it out. "I would do it for three."

I was puzzled at first, and then realized he meant dollars. I said, "All right. Let's give it a try." May would kill me, but I couldn't suppress a huge grin. "Three bucks a week and the attic room."

Orson said, "But, you know –" and paused. "I don't exactly know how to say this, but it might be better if you didn't tell the whole truth to that guy Gant. From what I hear about him. It might look sort of – oh, I don't know. You probably know best. But – do you know what I mean?"

I pretended to consider. I nodded. "Yes, maybe you're right, after all. You'll just be a friend who comes over, and now and then you give me a hand."

"You can even tell him you pay me, to help with the painting or something. But don't tell him too much."

"Yes, OK, fine," I said impatiently.

"Or that I live upstairs."

"Of course. Our secret." I felt slightly trespassed upon, second-guessed, but I also felt giddy with relief. "Let's shake on it." We shook hands yet again, his warm rough palm. "And thanks, Orson."

"You're saving my life," Orson said then.

"Oh, I doubt it." I felt my face grow hot. It overwhelmed me that he had admitted this, that I had thought he was playing games. I felt deeply ashamed of myself. For all my hard luck, and the hard times in general, I had never been homeless or indigent, there had never been a Municipal Lodging House in my life, and never would be. May and I, down to our last seven dollars, had still had family to fall back on; we could always have swallowed our pride, returned to Rochester, and been taken in.

"Believe me, Robert. You don't know the half of it."

I remembered the line of gray men, and I wrung his hand hard, clapped him on the shoulder, and then we walked up Lexington Avenue together. "I'll show you the room. And you'll have to meet May. She should be getting home from rehearsal any minute."

■ ■ ■

Orson and May didn't hit it off. When I brought him to the apartment that first night, May had just come in was sitting at the kitchen table with a cup of coffee and a cigarette. She looked up when we came in. "They changed my lines in the second act. And not for the better. Listen to this. How can I say this crap with any conviction?"

I went over to her and took the script out of her hands. "May, this is Orson Price. He's going to be working for us. You know – I told you. Orson – May Munro, my wife."

She didn't speak for a moment: she was still Florence. "Oh. Yes. Hello. Good." She flashed an absent-minded smile. "I hope Robert told you the job doesn't have a lot of potential. It's mostly helping him keep this place from crumbling out from under us."

"Sounds like heaven on earth to me," Orson said.

"Once in a while you might get to unclog a toilet."

Orson shrugged. "There are worse things."

"Like what?"

He smiled. "I suspect you don't really want to know."

"You probably suspect right," she said, smiling back – a tight, irritable little smile. Her hair was pulled into a snarled knot with an elastic band, and she was still wearing the bright red lipstick she wore to rehearsals. She was stunning. She and Orson stared at each other for a moment, and then she stubbed out her cigarette and reached for the script in my hands. "Robert? Could we – uh – could you help me with this? I have six different readings for these lines, and every one of them is stupid."

Orson went to pick up his belongings, and May and I tackled Florence. "I don't get it, Frankie." Her voice became hard and calculating, her eyes narrowed to blue slits. "How can you do things like this and still live with yourself?" and then she got up and stalked around the room, tearing at her hair. "I don't *get* it, Frankie! How can you do things like *this* and *still* live with yourself?!"

By the time Orson returned May and I were done with Florence for the night: May had thrown the script at the wall and burst into tears. They had ruined the role. It had been bad enough before, but now it was ridiculous. She was a clown, a figure of fun – *a joke*. George hated her, Nathan was jealous of her, the playwright was a moron, she wished she was dead. When Orson rang the bell, she said, "Oh, Robert. Must you?"

"I'll be right back."

I escorted Orson up the five flights to the attic room. He carried his battered canvas bag and a large, awkward paper parcel that he wouldn't let me help him with. I had found a stained horsehair mattress in a vacant apartment and lugged it up there, alternately dragging it and holding it against my chest, sniffing its stink of urine and mildew – that and a rickety wooden chair and a couple of orange crates. The place looked shabby and unaccommodating, but it still had that quiet, waiting quality that gave it, to my mind, a kind of distinction. I wondered if Orson sensed it. The evening was cool, and an aggressive breeze whipped through the two windows. It was not an easy place to live: if there was no wind, the heat and the mosquitoes made the room virtually unbearable, and when the wind blew, it assaulted that cramped space like a hurricane.

"I really do apologize for this place," I said, realizing that I should have cleaned it up better, scrubbed instead of just sweeping; since I'd been there last, the open windows had brought in a film of grit; I could feel it on the floor as I walked over it. "The bathroom, I'm afraid, is all the way down in the basement, you'll have to go down the back stairs by the second-floor fire door. And I forgot to bring you any sheets."

Orson gave me a quizzical look. "You can stop apologizing," he said. Our voices sounded strangely distinct in that acoustically perfect space, as if we really were onstage. "Do me that one favor, Robert, please. I don't care about any of that stuff. I'm going to be fine here. Honestly."

And then he surprised me. He came toward me and put his arms around me: he embraced me, there in that little room with the wind sighing, rattling the windows, then subsiding again. I pulled away in confusion. "Really," I said, but he interrupted me.

"Yes, really, Robert. You have saved me from – from I don't know what. Squalor. Misery. Nothingness. And I thank you for it with all my heart." He smiled. "And I'll stop there, since you're obviously somewhat uncomfortable with gratitude."

"Oh, no." I grinned back – terribly, I knew – and my face was flushed red. When Orson put his arms around me, a memory had come to me – brief, quickly banished – of a night when Jasper and I, after getting drunk on bootlegged gin together in our room at

Adams House, had embraced, had done other things that it pained me to dredge up.

"Not much," Orson said. "You're blushing like a bride. I'm sorry. I don't mean to, but it seems I often make people uncomfortable. It's true, though, Robert. You redeemed me, and I had to say it."

"Well, it's not – it's really not much. Believe me, it's you who are doing me the favor, as I'm sure you'll realize before long." I had to keep talking; I was consumed with embarrassment, and with a kind of manic exultation. I had an almost uncontrollable urge to laugh. "I hope you'll be all right here. If you need anything, let us know. Will you?"

I gave him a master key and the key to the basement. He stood there, still smiling, completely at ease, as if I'd just showed him to his luxurious hotel suite and he was trying to figure out how much to tip me. The light from the bare bulb that hung down from the middle of the room turned his hair flaming red. His teeth were large and square, his mouth pale and pinkish against his tanned face. When his arms were around me I had smelled his body: the curious, indescribable, strangely breadlike essence that was Orson, that had nothing to do with sweat or dirt. "Yes, Robert," he said. "If I need anything, I promise I'll let you know."

When I got down to the first floor I went out to the street and looked up at Orson's windows, glowing golden five stories above me. As I watched, they darkened. Then I went back to May. Her eyes were red, and her hair had come down; she'd been crying again. "I don't know why they're doing this to me. Everything is spoiled."

"Oh, May." When I touched her, her shoulders felt stiff, all bone.

"And now you've put this man in that horrible attic room."

"I need him," I said.

"Oh – need him." She turned away and, for a moment, she reminded me of her hard-faced Aunt Myra. "This'll never work. It can't be so simple."

I wondered about that myself. But another part of me – what I got from my large, cheerful, easygoing father as opposed to my small, stooped, anxious mother – that part said that this is the way life is supposed to be: things are supposed to work out: the pieces of one's life are meant to fall into place with just a little shove here and there, a few small adjustments – maybe the occasional stroke of genius

"Maybe it will, May. It's worth a try. And he's really a very nice fellow," I said, but she wasn't listening. Her face crumpled, and she began to cry in earnest.

"May, what is it? Things were going so well. What's wrong?"

"Oh – nerves. I don't know. It's Florence. It's everything."

I put my hand on her back; it was damp with sweat. "What, May? Tell me."

She looked up at me, red-faced. "I don't know, Robert," she said. "Sometimes I just feel so scared. Everything is changing."

"But a few days ago you were so hopeful and excited."

"A few days makes a big difference sometimes, Robert."

"I thought the changes were for the better, May. Things are happening for us."

"I feel like everything is falling apart."

I was stunned: what had happened? Nothing but good, as far as I could see. I wondered if we were in the same world, May and I, and suddenly I had the frightening sensation that she was right: that if she perceived our world as somehow, bizarrely crumbling, then it was.

"But May, honey, don't you feel that we're both on the verge of success?"

She sighed. "Oh, Robert, you are so sweet."

"I'm not so sweet," I said. "But I'm right. You're just nervous about the part. As soon as you settle down and get it under your belt, it will be really terrific. Okay, let's say the role itself isn't so hot – though I don't think it's as bad as you do – but you're going to be so good that it won't matter. It's a big chance for you. You'll be seen, May. You'll be out there. That's what matters."

"Is that what matters?"

"That's part of what matters."

I found a clean handkerchief in my pocket and handed it to her. Then I went to the sink to get her a glass of cold water. She took it from me and gulped it down like an obedient child. Her hair curled in tendrils at her temples, as it always did in the heat. "You need to sleep," I said, and took the glass from her. I led her to the bed, tucked the sheet around her, turned off the lamp. Through the bedroom's one high window, I could glimpse a small patch of sky, starless and deep blue, bluer than the daytime sky. I pointed to it. "Look, May. It's never really dark in New York, is it? Have you noticed? It's always that velvety blue. I wish you had a dress that color."

"Yes," she said. "It's beautiful." I could feel the tears still on her face when I leaned over to kiss her, and I remembered that when we were first married she had had crying fits – struggles with some nameless malaise. I knew that her family had been poor, her mother had been sick a long time, and died young. Her father drank, I think – he'd been in the war, in France, and had come home a different man. She had hinted a few times at other things that troubled her, even seemed to torture her in some way – too difficult, maybe, to talk about. May liked things to be cheerful, and so I never pressed her for details, even when she wept in my arms. Eventually, her spirits always lifted. But I wondered if she still thought about those things, whatever they were.

She sighed shakily. "You're so kind to me, Robert."

"Do you feel better?"

"No." I could just see her smile. "But I will."

I smoothed her hair off her forehead. She closed her eyes and then, while I watched, she fell asleep – my Queen of the Night. It never failed to astonish me, how speedily she could sink into sleep. It used to frighten me when we were first married, as if I were watching her suddenly die – death was more plausible to me than being on such easy terms with sleep. The dim light from the street gave the bedroom a soft radiance, and I sat beside her for a while watching her face. Her words still hung in the air: *Everything is falling apart.* And yet how could she be so distressed when nothing had happened, and just when everything seemed to be going so well? Her tears were disturbing to me – not because she had wept, but because she hadn't really told me why. At times like this, when she would keep things from me, or talk only vaguely about what bothered her, I always had the feeling she was sparing me. And, in a way, I was grateful to her for that. The future was what we were all about, May and I – not the past. And now, of course, she was casting doubt on that future. But I was pretty sure it was just nerves.

I puttered around the apartment for a while until I felt calmer, trying to put off going to bed until there was at least an outside chance I might be tired enough to sleep. Finally I did lie down, and fell asleep immediately, but I woke at midnight from a dream in which I was with my father on the roof of the Alhambra Gardens; the sky was packed with smoky gray clouds, and the dog Luther was there, panting happily at our feet, wearing his old red collar.

"He's yours now, son," my father said.

We looked down at the dog, but Luther had metamorphosed into something else, it wasn't Luther at all, it was a wild thing, a big catlike creature that took off into the night, to the far side of the roof, where there was just a quick flash of white fur as it leapt over the parapet.

I was hopelessly wide awake. I got up, leaving May asleep, and went out for a walk. The night was warm, almost hot – the heat wave that July was brutal – but as I walked a breeze began to blow off the river, and I felt as if I could go on forever.

I walked over to Lexington and turned north. I found myself thinking about May, pondering what had brought us together, what kept us together. I remembered our early, happier days when, attracted by her bright hair and her teasing jokes, I had slowly gotten to know her at the restaurant. She could always make me laugh – and, God knows, after my father died and I had to drop out of college and my mother became faded and morose, I had needed a light touch, a little humor! I needed May's blatant blonde prettiness, her vivacity, the way she reached out to the world and embraced it. I was the nicest man she'd ever met, she said. Well, I'd met plenty of nice people in my life, I suppose, but never one so alive, so luminous with the love of her own simple existence. I was always amazed and grateful that she had loved me – a bookish, awkward, fumbling sort of person who couldn't begin to match her for liveliness and pluck. But she believed that I'd be famous. I told her about the two short plays of mine that had been performed by the Drama Club – *Oliver at the Ritz* and *Up the Creek* – and she insisted on reading parts of them, saying the lines aloud in her stilted, declamatory way so that they lost all their bite. But she appreciated the comedy: she would mangle one of Oliver's *bon mots*, then double over with helpless laughter. "Robert's a raving genius," she said when she introduced me to Carlotta. "He's going to be the most famous playwright in the world someday."

She claimed she admired me for my talent, but that she had fallen in love with my face, with the way my skin and eyes and hair and nose and mouth, she said, were all of a piece: *inevitable,* was the way she put it. Not that I was so handsome, she told me: it was just that I was *right*. The way I looked clicked into place in her mind like a complicated game that she was always winning. As long as she had me to look at, May said, she was a winner: who but a superior woman would be with such a superior man? And on top of it all, I was a genius.

None of this made much sense to me. Certainly I had had girls in Cambridge. I had been invited to parties, introduced to young women, included in things. I was used to getting along with people and to having a certain kind of girl (intense, mildly intellectual, a bit eccentric, attractive but not really pretty) like me and seek me out. But no one had ever expressed a real interest in me. Often, I would go out with a girl once or twice only to find that she was mysteriously not home when I called back. I got used to having awkward chats with the roommates who made lame excuses for their friends. Sometimes I dated them: the lesser, bonier, drabber girls who would let me kiss them or, occasionally, touch their breasts through their sweaters – but even they didn't seem to mind if I didn't call back. I was charmed by May's looks and her ways, but also by her feelings for me. I had never been called *inevitable* before, never *a raving genius*. May delighted me: she was pretty, she made me laugh, I liked kissing her, we loved each other, we got married.

But, in some fundamental way, I wasn't sure I knew who she was. She was talkative, but she talked mostly about what she observed of the world, and, though she was a shrewd and witty observer, there was nothing behind her funny reconstructions of her day, the vignettes she drew of people she met, that told me who she was besides a smart, brassy blonde who wanted to be an actress, was terrified of pregnancy, and had a wicked eye for the absurd. Why she wanted to act, why the thought of penetration by a man was so upsetting to her, what else went on in her head when she wasn't trying to amuse people, what the details of her life were before she met me, I had very little idea. And yet I knew that I loved her; the presence of May in my life made it worth living: if I hadn't known it before, that became clear to me the night I fled from the murder on Bleecker Street and found what seemed to be a kind of sanctuary back home with May. And I believed that she loved me, and I hoped she hadn't been right when she'd said everything was falling apart.

I crossed over to Madison, west to Broadway, then headed north into Harlem. I liked to walk in Sugar Hill with its mansions and trees, but I liked going over to Lenox, too, where the rich white people pulled up to the clubs in big cars, and to Seventh Avenue, where it was jazzier, seedier, more dangerous, and where once I saw Cab Calloway in his white suit going into the Plantation Club with two blonde women. And once, in front of the Monterey Restaurant, a brown-skinned singer who looked like a goddess was being handed into a taxi, wearing a gardenia in her hair and a dress so silvery, so spangled, that in the darkness lit only by streetlamps all I could see at first was its shine, and had to squint to see the woman inside it. I was always a little afraid in Harlem, though generally I passed through the streets unnoticed. Once a black man in a striped suit, his hat at a rakish angle, danced toward me and said in a belligerent voice, "Hey, man what you lookin' for here tonight?" and another man came up, peeled his friend away, and said, "Don't mind him. He's drunk as a skunk." Another time a fight erupted among a group of men on a corner, and one of them threw a punch at me as I passed, but I ducked and went on quickly, and they didn't bother me.

Now and then a woman would speak to me: I remember a large, imposing one like an African priestess who beckoned to me from the doorway of a church no bigger than our backyard garage in Rochester; painted over the door in gold were the words: I WILL GIVE THEE REST. I was so tired that night, so dopey and sleepless, that I was sorely, sorely tempted. On another evening, it was a beautiful woman in a long dress with straps, her smooth shoulders gleaming in the lamplight. She had bright red lips and diamond clips in her hair, and she said, "Well, ain't you a pretty boy," and when she reached out to touch my arm, I saw her hard muscles and the shadow on her jaw and knew she was a man.

I never went into those clubs. Sometimes, though, the music would erupt into the street, and now, on that sleepless July night, I passed the Cotton Club, with its top-hatted bouncer out front, and then I stood outside the Savoy for a while, listening. No one bothered me. I leaned against a lamp post and watched the crowd go in for the second set. Fletcher Henderson was playing, and all the way out on the street I could hear him blow the place apart with the "King Porter Stomp." Part of me wanted more than anything in the world to go inside, but the truth was I couldn't imagine being there alone, with nobody to dance with. Without a woman, the music – after the first exhilaration of it – became sad, lonely, hopeless. That kind of jazz wasn't something to hear alone: it was music that reached down deep; it was urgent, like sex, and you didn't want to be by yourself when it did that to you. May and I had never been to Harlem together, though we talked about going some night when we had extra money, but as I stood there listening I longed for her so intensely it was as if she had walked out on me and I would never see her again, instead of being back in the apartment fast asleep in our bed. Suddenly, I needed her, and I had one of my absurd premonitions that she wouldn't be there when I returned, that I'd walk into the bedroom and find it empty.

I found a subway and took the A train down to 14th Street and walked home from there. I heard May's soft snore as I let myself into the apartment, and I slipped into bed beside her with gratitude and relief that she was still there – sleeping, inaccessible, but *there*. She didn't stir, and I didn't wake her up, though I lay beside her for a long time, swollen, consumed with wanting her, my eyes wide open, my brain spinning. I WILL GIVE THEE REST: the words came back to me then, like the refrain of a hymn – like a response to May's comment about things falling apart. *Rest*: rest was more than sleep, rest was peace and serenity, and lying beside my wife I felt it was rest that I craved more than anything, rest and peace, but I wasn't sure why it was that, on that night, it seemed so clear to me that those things were missing from my life.

THREE

It took Rex Mason only two days to send my play back with a scrawled note that I read once and burned in the kitchen sink. I re-addressed the package to Samuel Harper, the name on the other business card, and took it right back to the post office. If he returned it, I had no one else.

"Rex Mason must be an idiot," May said. "He'll be so sorry when you're famous, he'll hang himself with his shoelaces."

"Maybe. I'm the one who's sorry now, though."

She looked at me. "You aren't losing faith in yourself, Robert. Are you?"

Everything is falling apart, I thought. Then I kissed her. "Not if you aren't losing faith in me."

"Don't be absurd," she said, frowning. She looked close to tears again.

That was another night of sleeplessness, but on my walk I refused to think about the fate of my play, or about Rex Mason's note, which was like a bad smell in the street that I could only put the window down on. Instead, I began concocting a new play, and by the time I returned home, well after three, it had taken shape in my imagination as if it were something real, tangible – a structure I had built of nuts and bolts and wood instead of nouns and verbs, and I got into bed and slept like the proverbial baby until the alarm shrilled me awake at seven.

■ ■ ■

The Killer Instinct was scheduled to open in September, and, all through that hot July, May was busy with rehearsals. She came home from the theatre each evening in a strange mood – quiet, easily provoked – but she said things were better: a lot of things were stupid but everything about the play was better – even Florence. She was beginning to see that the changes worked, and her role had actually expanded. She took the part, to say the least, seriously. I could see that she was becoming someone else; she was being transformed into *May-as-Florence*. She practiced her wretched lines as if they were indeed Lady Macbeth's and spent long moments in front of her three-way mirror looking at herself. "I need to figure out how to just stand around in a meaningful way," she said. The playwright had done a lot of re-writing, and she now had twelve lines. She was onstage throughout most of the second act and part of the third, until she was killed – shot down along with her boyfriend by a rival gangster in a barroom brawl. Her costume throughout was going to be a tight royal blue dress with a stand-up collar and a slit skirt; she saw sketches of it. She practiced falling, watching herself sink to the floor in various ways. "The audience is going to *mind* when I die," she said. "They're going to *grieve* for a moment or two, and that's the pivot the play is turning on. At least, that's what George says." It sounded good – many of the things she told me that George said about the play sounded convincing and intelligent, and I found to my surprise that in a bemused sort of way I was looking forward to seeing it.

She and I were less close during that time, each of us on our own little road. She was right: things had changed, but not, I still insisted, for the worse. I wouldn't let myself think they had. After all, hadn't we had phenomenal luck? We were, if nothing else, both working, which meant money coming in, and May was actually on the stage again. She wasn't seeing as much of Carlotta; Carlotta was jealous of her success, May said – *Verna was right* – and was all wrapped up in Mickey Kennedy and his plans for getting into the movies out in Hollywood. May had a new friend, a woman named Lois who was stage-managing *The Killer Instinct.* I had met Lois – in fact, she had gotten us comps, somehow, for a revival of *The Barretts of Wimpole Street* with Katharine Cornell – my first New York play since the days I used to come down from Cambridge on the train. It was a wonderful evening, but I didn't take to Lois; she was a short, dark, gabby woman with a monotonous staccato laugh, and she seemed to dote on May; her only topics of conversation, as far as I could see, were her ex-husband, whom she despised, and George, the director, whom she idolized. "I admit she's sort of boring, but she knows everyone," May said. "She's a good person for me to cultivate. She could probably do a lot for you, too, Robert. You ought to be friendlier." Sometimes after rehearsals May went out with Lois and George and a couple named Nancy and Tom that I didn't know, or she'd spend the evenings over at Lois's place near Washington Square, coming home late to cook a cursory dinner or eat a quick meal with me at Neshan's or the Italian place around the corner. There were times when, over dinner, we couldn't think of anything to say to each other unless we had a cocktail or a glass of wine, and we usually couldn't afford a drink. We couldn't seem to work up much interest in sex, either – at least, May couldn't – without alcohol to go with it.

I saw all this as temporary – a period of adjustment. At least she wasn't talking about everything falling apart. As the summer went on, I was glad she had the play to occupy her because the business of superintendenting, thanks to Orson, had unexpectedly become one of the small pleasures in my life.

"It's a funny thing," I said to May. "I'm learning how to do some of these things, and I actually like it."

"You do?" She lowered her head and raised her eyebrows. "Why on earth?"

"It feels good to accomplish something tangible. Not just words on a page."

"So you're giving up the theatre for unclogging toilets?"

"Of course not." I had to smile. "Not that I have much to give up, at this point." I hadn't heard a word from Samuel Harper, and I wondered if the package had been lost in the mail. "I'm just another aspiring playwright in a city where there must be a thousand of us. Ten thousand."

"Your day will come. Meanwhile, if you want to get anywhere in this business, you should be spending your spare time with people like Lois instead of that Orson."

"I like being with Orson," I said. "And the work really is enjoyable, believe it or not."

His very first day on the job, Orson had shown me what would need to be done in the hall, and how to do it. I followed him around the building as I had followed Mr.Gant, but the experience was different, and I realized that Gant must have been trying to frighten me.

"Spackling," Orson said, "is simply filling in these gouges and cracks. It's not difficult. It's like plaster – like mud; you mix it up, trowel it in, smooth it, then let it dry and paint over it. Believe me, there's no trick to it. And it doesn't have to be perfect. Look at this," he said, running his hand over an ancient repair. "Whoever did this didn't know what he was doing. You need to sand it down more than this – see how this has left a bump? We can do better than that."

When we ran into tenants, I introduced Orson as a friend who was visiting me for a while, and who'd be helping with some repairs and redecorating around the place. Old Mrs. Howell up on the fifth floor was coming out her door as we stood there looking at the woodwork; she looked at us, squinting through her glasses. "Why, it's Orson Price."

"What a memory!" Orson grinned and stuck out his hand. "How are you, Mrs. H? How's that puppy of yours?"

Mrs. Howell looked startled, then smiled hesitantly. "Now, you know very well he's not a pup any more," she said, and as if to prove her right a fat bulldog waddled into the hall behind her and gave a short bark. Mrs. Howell and her dog looked remarkably alike. "He's getting deaf, and he's got a touch of arthritis."

"He's still a good-looking animal," Orson said, and seemed as if he might lean over and pet the dog, but decided against it. "He's got such a human face." He grinned at me sideways.

"He's a good dog."

"I'm glad to see him again," Orson said. "And you." He turned to go down the stairs. "Stay well, Mrs. H."

Behind us, we heard her murmur, whether to Orson or to her dog it was impossible to say. "What was all that?" I asked him.

"That? Mrs. Howell? Known her for years," Orson said. "She used to be a real old bitch, but she seems to have mellowed."

"How did you know her?"

"I told you – didn't I? I used to live around here. A while ago." We stopped on the fourth floor, and Orson pointed out a portion of the wall. "Now look at this, around the window. Damp must have gotten in here. We really should replace that bit of molding. Did Gant mention it?"

"He might have. I don't remember."

"Well, I think we ought to take care of it. It's just going to get worse. We need to remove that whole portion – just crowbar it off, it's simple. Then see what's going on behind it. Fix that. And then put this back, but replace the rotten segment. Do you see what I mean?"

I did see. Orson was a natural teacher, and when we completed our tour, I felt better. I was possessed with the feeling that everything would now go smoothly, that life stretched out before me in a sweet and orderly way, predictable but not boring – like a well-made play, I thought to myself. On impulse, a few days later, I invited Orson to eat dinner with me at the Turkish restaurant.   We walked there in the warm early evening. I had pondered for a while about what to wear. I wanted to dress up a little for the occasion, but not to outshine Orson's meager wardrobe. Most of my best clothes had come from my father's closet after he died; my mother had begged me to take whatever I wanted. His clothes fit me pretty well; maybe he was an inch bigger in the waist, but we were about the same height and even wore the same shoe size. At first, though, it had felt wrong, trying on his suits and scrutinizing his ties. My father had been a conservative man who kept things until they wore out, and I could so easily visualize my father in those clothes, see him tying his ties in the mirror – the paisley, the blue and gold stripe, the red knit, the brown silk patterned with miniature horns – snapping one of them through its paces in the morning before he went to work. And the jaunty hats – he must have had a dozen of them – that he bought at Sibley's or Ruston's – only the best for Dad. But I had always been glad I had done what my mother asked. It wasn't only that his clothes were very fine – my father, trim and handsome well into middle age, was a dandy until the day he died – but now I felt good wearing them. My father had been a successful man, a confident man, and buttoning one of his shirts under my chin or putting a leather belt through the loops of a pair of his good linen pants was like putting on a costume. In his clothes, I knew that I became bigger, better looking, more of a personality. For better or for worse, I wasn't a college boy any longer.

I decided, finally, to wear a clean white shirt and an old pair of gray hopsacking pants that were far from new but still presentable. And I put on the red tie. Orson had changed out of his work clothes into the white suit he had worn the night I first saw him; somewhere he had gotten it cleaned and pressed, though there were faint beige stains here and there, especially on the knees, that you could tell were never going to come out. He wore it with panache, though, and as we walked up Lexington Avenue together I felt that the old Orson had truly returned, the French-speaking, down-on-his-luck playboy I had first talked to that day on 21st Street.

When we were seated at a table, I studied his face – the slightly hooked nose, the way the pale eyes sat in their sockets. His face was hawkish but not predatory. It was kind. I liked his face; instinctively, I trusted it. I handed him three dollar bills.

"But I haven't worked a week yet," he said.

"I don't mind paying you a couple of days in advance. And I figure you're probably starting out broke. I know I did."

"Well, thanks, Robert." He frowned down at the dollar bills. "I can't understand why you're being so good to me, but I'm not going to argue. Now I can pay for dinner."

"Nope. Dinner's on me." As I spoke I added up the three dollars I'd given Orson to the dollar dinner was going to cost, and knew I was being more extravagant than I should be, and that May wouldn't like it. "It may not seem like a big deal to you, Orson. You take this stuff for granted – spackling and plaster, and taking off molding and replacing it. A lot of people take it for granted, but I'm not one of them. I was never taught those things. My father was a businessman, and he expected me to be one, too. He was certainly interested in the building trade – it was his livelihood – but only the business side of it, the financial side. He didn't know a damn thing about the nuts and bolts – he probably didn't know a nut from a bolt! And neither did I. Now you've taken away the mystery. I'm still an incompetent – a klutz, as they say. But now I can at least understand what needs to be done, even if I can't do it."

"You can do it. But you don't have to, because I can do it if you can't."

"I'd like to learn."

"Then I'd like to teach you."

We smiled at each other. The waiter came to take our order. The food was obviously no mystery to Orson; he ordered baba ganoush and shish-kebab.

"Was this one of your haunts?" I asked him. "Back in the old days?"

"I used to love this Turkish stuff," Orson said without really answering. "I could eat shish-kebab until it's coming out of my ears. And that sauce they put on the lamb, that yogurt sauce? Have you ever had it?"

We began eating. The scars on the back of Orson's hand gleamed white in the light from the candle. He looked up from his plate and said, "Your father was in real estate?"

"Up in Rochester. Big, successful firm. Signs all over town. Sinclair Properties. He built it up himself after the war. It's gone under now, of course."

"And was that what you were supposed to do? Go into your father's real estate business? I thought you were a writer."

The question made me uncomfortable. I hated to admit that my father's death had been a kind of reprieve for me. My first year of college had been blighted by that very consideration: how I'd break it to my father that I'd rather do almost anything than continue his hard-won real estate empire, and that in fact if I ever did make something of myself it would be as a writer – a profession my father, I had no doubt, thought of as just one rung above a bum. I spent a good deal of time debating with Jasper the possibility of reconciling the selling of houses and office buildings with the writing of plays. I remember being tipsy one night and talking the whole thing over with my date, a girl from Boston University, who said, fiercely, "You've got to be true to who you are," and held me when I made a fool of myself and actually wept boozy tears over the situation. I never called her again.

I said, "It would have been a problem, but he didn't live long enough to have to deal with it. He died four years ago, while I was still in college."

"He would have understood," Orson said.

"I doubt it."

"There's an intensity about you that he would have had to respect."

"What you or I might call intensity he'd probably call stubbornness."

"I think he would have seen that you're obviously going to be successful in your own sphere, Robert. That you've got what it takes."

I had to smile. "Now how on earth can you tell such a thing?"

"It sticks out all over you. How can you explain something like that? It's just there – it's obvious. Don't you feel it yourself?"

I thought about it for a minute and said, "Well – yes, I do." I laughed. "But probably everyone thinks that. Even the world's great losers probably think they're going to make it." I thought about May as Florence, falling this way and then that way to the floor, shot dead. Carlotta with her acting classes. Why was I so sure I wasn't as doomed as they were?

"That's pretty sad, isn't it?" Orson smiled strangely, absently, frowning a little at the same time. I wondered if he considered himself one of the world's great losers. Or did he appreciate the irony of his perhaps appearing that way in his stained suit and shabby shoes, while all the time he knew in his heart that he wasn't a loser but a winner.

"Or maybe you're right," I said. "Maybe it's a different kind of feeling altogether."

"You wouldn't know, would you? Because you're so obviously going to be a success."

"Time will tell, I suppose."

The subject was making me uncomfortable. A part of it seemed missing, something I was supposed to understand and take into consideration. Was Orson comparing himself with me? Was he trying to tell me something about myself? About him? Was he finally showing resentment that I got a job I was unqualified for, and that he felt he should, by rights, have had?

We ate in silence for a minute, and then I pointed to his scars and asked, "Where did those come from?"

Orson looked down at them, surprised, as if he'd never seen them before. "These? A dog bit me. A dog that belonged to a friend of mine back when I was a kid." He laughed. "The dog's name was Roxie, I think. Wait – no, it was Trixie! Nasty little spotted thing." He held out his hand and regarded the scars, almost with admiration. "She did a neat job, the mutt. I bent down to pet her and – bam! Just hung on and wouldn't let go. Now why do I remember that? It was years ago. I was a kid."

"It must have been pretty painful. I'm not surprised you'd remember."

"Blood all over the place. Good thing it wasn't rabid." Orson picked up his fork again and ate a bite of lamb. Then he looked up at me. "But listen, Robert – seriously. I appreciate this dinner. It feels like a celebration."

"Of –?"

"Of our partnership, of course." He smiled; in the low light, his pale blue eyes seemed darker. "We're going to be a great team."

We were eating baba ganoush and lamb, and drinking the sweet minty tea that came with every meal. *Why do I remember that?* Good question. Later that night, lying in bed before sleep, I thought about that conversation, and tried to figure out what bothered me about it, what made me awkward with Orson as we finished our food and walked back to the Alhambra Gardens. Orson went straight up to his cell, yawning. May was home, and we were more companionable than usual; we sat up talking about the play and about whether Carlotta and Mickey would get married and about whether she needed to have her split ends trimmed, and it wasn't until much later that I went over the conversation with Orson in my mind. I remembered what we ate, and I remembered exactly what Orson said, and I knew that what was wrong with the scene was my certainty that Orson was lying to me. The scars hadn't come from a dog's bite. I couldn't imagine where they had really come from – I had assumed some carpentry accident – but I knew I would never find out, and what I wondered as I dropped off to sleep was how horrifying or humiliating or improbable the real truth could possibly be, that he would need to lie, and elaborate, and change the subject with flattery. Or if he did it just for fun.

■ ■ ■

Gradually, as the summer went on, an odd thing began to happen. I began to sleep.

I didn't fall asleep sleep instantly, as May did, and I didn't sleep long hours, but it was better. The reason wasn't hard to find: Orson's presence had removed the anxiety that had been keeping me awake.

I call it *odd* because I continued to have a lot on my mind – worries about Gant, about the three dollars that went to Orson each week, about May. She and I argued about the money – it's true, we were short at the end of each week – and about the risk, which she was more concerned about than I was. "If Gant catches on, I can talk my way out of it," I told her, and I believed that was true. "Orson's my cousin from Ohio. He's helping out. It's not something to get in a dither over. I know Mr. Gant. All he cares about is that the work gets done." As for the three dollars I was paying Orson, I told May he was worth three times that.

All she said was, "He's got you right where he wants you, doesn't he?" And she gave the knowing smirk that never failed to annoy me. She liked to make fun of Orson; she called him the butler. "So what fascinating chores do you and the butler have scheduled for today?" she'd ask. Or, if we ran out of coffee, she'd suggest I send Orson to the market. But every nasty crack she made just made me defend him more, and I knew I was lucky to have him and that the three bucks I paid was a bargain.

I still took my long night walks. On the nights she was home, May fell asleep by ten, and rather than sit up alone reading I would go out and walk for a couple of hours, not to tire myself out but because I had learned to love the way darkness came to the city and pared it down to its essence. The crowds, the noise, the hurry, the squalor, even the smells – of garbage, gasoline, urine, food – all that daytime life fell away and what was left was the huge silver city rising up in the light from the street lamps, a city where I saw the most amazing things – the things that weren't meant to be seen – and where in spite of the dark and the quiet, I always had the sense that life went on, the world was still out there, pulsing behind the dark windows, behind the drawn shades. Even the mannequins in the great, remote stores up on Fifth Avenue, the chic wooden women with their marcelled hair and chiseled chins, seemed to be looking back at me, modestly or boldly, as if even they had a life of their own in the night. I couldn't give all that up, even though sometimes, coming home, I'd have to get on the subway, too sleepy to keep going.

A week or so after the dinner with Orson, walking home around midnight, I saw his light on. I stood there a few minutes looking up at his windows – the two lead-paned yellow squares – and then I went in and climbed the stairs to the attic. When I knocked, Orson opened the door almost immediately, wearing trousers and an undershirt and no shoes, smoking a cigarette, smiling.

"Robert!" He looked past me, to the stairs, and I wondered if he had been expecting someone else.

"I think you ought to ask who it is, Orson. You shouldn't let just anyone in."

"I didn't think it would be just anyone," he said. "I had an idea it might be you. Who else would it have been?"

"Could have been one of your old pals. Mrs. Howell!"

"With her ugly drooling mutt." Orson stood back, swinging the door open. "I'm glad it's you instead. What are you up to? A little noctambulation? Having one of your white nights?"

"I have been out walking, though I'm not really having my white nights so much any more."

"You don't say! What's Mrs. A. giving you now? Opium?"

"It's a kind of natural opium called peace of mind." I grinned. "Getting that plastering done today may be part of it."

"Well, whatever it is, I'm glad to hear it. Come in, Robert. Please."

The place looked very different; it was scrubbed clean, and the mattress on the floor was meticulously made up, with a blanket folded at the foot. Nails in the wall held hangers; I recognized the rumpled white suit. Orson had added a few things: some dishes were stacked inside an orange crate; a shadeless lamp threw a half-circle of light on the wall behind it and a yellow radiance into the room.

I said, "It looks good up here. I like this place. I thought once of using it as a study."

I still had that vision – the plain, peaceful room all to myself. I saw myself at my typewriter in front of the window, and felt a twinge of something so like jealousy that it made me ashamed. I had so much, Orson had so little, and here I was, coveting.

He looked at me with suppressed amusement, as if reading my mind. "Did you come up here to evict me?"

I laughed. "No! I came up to see if there's anything you need."

"What else could I possibly need?"

It was hard to tell if his question was sarcastic or sincere. In a way, he did have everything a rational person could want: light, air, comfort, the spacious feeling that only a top floor gives. I couldn't help contrasting the view from Orson's windows at the top with the one from mine and May's at the bottom. We looked out from our stale, cool airlessness to legs, pigeons, the wheels of bicycles and baby carriages; only from the window by the bed could we see, between two tall buildings, a scrap of sky. Here there was the immense water tower, the expanse of purplish brick across the street with its woven maze of fire escapes, and beyond all of it the backdrop of midnight blue.

"Look," Orson said. There was a small stack of books on the windowsill. "I took fifty cents of my hard-earned wages and went down to Biblo & Tannen's. On Fourth Avenue?"

"I know it well," I said, pleased. "A great bookstore!"

"Best bookstore in New York." Because of the amazing acoustics, our voices were soft but curiously distinct, like voices on a radio with the sound turned down. Orson sounded like a commercial.

"I prefer Stammer's, myself. On the next block. I found a book there that I've been trying to find for years."

"What was that?"

"Oh –" I felt suddenly foolish. "A book about writing plays. Baker's *Dramatic Technique*. Kind of a classic."

Orson smiled. "I'll have to take your word for that. Greek to me. What a city for bookstores, though, isn't it?

I inspected the titles: a dictionary, an anthology of modern poetry, *An American Tragedy*, *The Great Gatsby*.

"My wife's favorite book," I said, holding it up.

"Really? Books about the rich, eh?" He smirked – exactly the look on May's face when she told me I was a fool wasting my money on Orson. "Isn't that a nice edition? Two bits. I got the dictionary for a nickel. And this was a dime." He picked up the book of poems and leafed through it, smiling slightly. "My little extravagance."

I watched Orson's fingers carefully turning the pages, wondering what had happened to other books he might have had – to all his possessions, his clothes, the trappings of his old life, whatever it had been; I wanted to ask him questions, get him to tell me something about himself, but I had a feeling it would be like the Turkish restaurant: Orson would tell me nothing, or lie to me, tell me he had a degree in biological science from Yale, he'd been to the Sorbonne, he'd panned for gold in Peru or been a jazz piano player in Chicago. I wondered how we could ever be friends, and for a moment as I stood by that window I was so downhearted and lonely that I opened the book I was holding and read a line to shut the feeling out. *"There was music from my neighbor's house through the summer nights,"* I read. *"In his blue gardens men and girls came and went like moths among the whisperings and the champagne and the stars."*

Orson looked at me with a smile that could have been mocking. It wasn't hard, after all, to imagine him playing jazz in a bar or striding through the streets of Montmartre. "A romantic image, that's for sure," he said. "Blue gardens. Champagne and stars. Makes you feel kind of–"

He stopped, shrugged, and turned to look out the window. I waited for him to finish, to say something perhaps of what I'd been feeling, but he didn't speak. The breeze lifted his hair, blew it across his forehead, and he raked it with his fingers, pushing it back. I could see that his hair was very fine, silky. Ever since that brotherly embrace on Orson's first night, I had been conscious of his physical presence: the textures of his hair and skin, his distinctive odor. Sometimes, as we worked side by side, and now, as we stood by the window, I had an impulse to touch his hair, or lay my fingers on the scars near his wrist – as if Orson were an animal, or a sculpture in a museum. And yet, despite this, and despite our similarities, I knew that we were very far apart, and I suspected that I failed Orson's test for friendship in some way I was too naive, or dense, or provincial to fathom.

Orson moved away from the window, finally, and said, "But Robert, can I offer you – Well, I guess there's not much I can offer you." He looked around the room. "A seat on the floor? A cigarette butt?"

I laughed. "No – I won't stay. I only stopped in to say hello." The truth was that I had wanted to see the place with Orson in it. "I'm feeling kind of beat, in fact."

"After the day we put in, you ought to," Orson said. "You did a good job on the plastering."

"Did you think so?" I felt inordinately pleased. "I enjoyed it."

"I did, too. I think we work well together. But it was a long day. I'm pretty tired myself." He turned toward the door – still polite, but I could see that he wanted me to leave. I felt let down by this. "I tend to stay up quite late," he said. "I'm lucky. I sleep so soundly I can get by easily on five or six hours. You'll often see my light on your midnight walks. Or won't you be taking them any more? Now that Mrs. Amalfi has you all doped up."

We chuckled. This, then, was the best we could do in terms of being friends: we could have our ritualized little jokes. "I still like to walk," I said. "I like the city at night."

"And writers need solitude, I suppose."

"Maybe. I do get ideas when I walk. Something about the act of walking – moving forward – it gets my brain going. Anyway, I promise I won't bother you every night I venture out."

"As if you could bother me, Robert. I owe you everything!"

"Well –"

I stood at the door, unable not to remember the embrace of the other evening, and as I was about to leave, Orson moved a step toward me and embraced me again, strongly, laying his cheek against mine. And held me for a moment before he pulled back.

"Better get to sleep," he said. "I'll see you tomorrow, Robert. Sweet dreams."

I went down the stairs. Behind me, Orson closed the door quietly. I felt my face burning red, and I thought: *Is that why I went up there?* Two flights down, I had to sit on the marble steps. *Sweet dreams.* Orson's unreadable smile. I hadn't been aware of the heat of the night until now; the sweat was running down my body. I put my head in my hands and remained on the steps for a few moments. Then I went down the rest of the stairs to the dark, cool apartment, washed myself off in the sink, and fell into bed next to May. She was turned away from me, snoring softly. I moved close to the heat of her body, almost but not quite touching her, and my old buddy insomnia settled in, and I lay awake for a long time looking up at the high window, watching the dim brown light from the street turn briefly to gold whenever the headlights of a car went by.

■ ■ ■

Orson and I had evolved a work schedule: after lunch, we would meet up and work together for most of the afternoon, but I used the mornings for writing – I had started the new play – or stopping in at Mrs. Amalfi's, or sitting with a book and a nickel cup of coffee in one of the Village cafés I liked, reading, or writing letters to my mother and my sister. The mornings, it was understood, were mine; Orson was on the premises in case of emergencies. What he actually did in the mornings, I wasn't entirely sure – sometimes, as I headed down Second Avenue or sat at Mrs. Amalfi's kitchen window, I saw him carrying a pail or a toolbox – but the building and the grounds began to look better. He located the lawnmower somewhere, and he knew how to prune the boxwood. The windows sparkled, the wrought iron trim on the front door was shiny black, the marble gleamed. Even the palm trees seemed rejuvenated, putting out new shoots. The whole place had a more cheerful air, and coming up the walk, climbing the stairs, I experienced a comfortable sense of well-being that I used to feel when – in the old days, before everything changed – I went home from college, and my father, who had met me at the station, would fling open the door into the front hall and call, "Here he is, Grace – the conquering hero returns!" – and there would be the gold-framed mirror and the lyre-bottomed table with a vase of flowers on it, and the smells of dinner cooking, and my mother coming in from the kitchen, and Luther wiggling all over and waving his plume of a tail.

The morning after my visit to Orson's room, while I was at my typewriter, Mr. Gant came to the door to tell me that the paint hadn't been delivered yet.

"But no harm," he said. "You're way ahead of schedule as it is."

"I'm looking forward to it," I told him. "To getting everything painted." He had come into the living room, and I could see him examining the place as we stood there. I had never really invited him in, never offered him a cup of coffee. I wasn't sure what the proper etiquette was when your boss stopped in unexpectedly to see if you were on the job. At least the room was relatively neat; I had done a fast, frantic bout of cleaning a couple of days before.

"The painting's the best part, as far as I'm concerned." That was what Orson had said.

"They got a delivery man down at Capitol, but he was out sick or something. I'll give them a call. Should be here tomorrow." Gant peered past me into the bedroom like a cop looking for clues, his eyes raking the place rapidly. I wondered if he really had come about something else: about seeing a stranger clipping the hedge, for instance. *My good old cousin George, he's visiting me from Kansas and he likes to make himself useful...* "So how's your play coming along?" Gant asked me suddenly, turning his gaze from the bedroom back to my typewriter in the corner.

"Very nicely. I've begun a new one, in fact. My first one's done." When he interrupted me, in fact, I had been tapping out a new version of the first scene of what would become *Afternoon Coffee*, but I was so tired I wasn't getting far, and at the back of my mind was the prospect of seeing Orson in a few hours.

"And then what? What happens to it?"

I shrugged. "I have a few contacts. Recommendations. People who have seen my work before and are interested." I couldn't believe I was trying to impress Gant, but I went on. "It's being read now by a very well-known producer," I said, and tried to hold back the dejection that threatened me when I thought of how long Samuel Harper had had it. "My wife is in the theatre, you know. She's an actress. Her new play opens September fifth."

He knitted his brows, and the furrows in his cheeks deepened. "But yours – what's next? Somebody puts it on? Here in New York?"

I laughed. "I hope so. Who knows?"

"Let's assume somebody will," Gant said. "What happens to the job here?"

It took me a couple of seconds to realize he was serious. "Oh – Mr. Gant. I'm perfectly happy to stay on. I mean – it would be extremely unusual if my play became such a success that I wouldn't need this job. I'm not – you know – I'm not Shakespeare. I'm not even Maxwell Anderson!"

"Well, I don't know about any of that, but I'm satisfied with your work here, and I'd be glad if you kept on doing it."

"I appreciate your saying so, Mr. Gant. I'm planning to. You don't need to worry about that. I like it here. I – I love it here!"

"Good." Gant sucked the insides of his cheeks for a minute and nodded. Then he said, "I think I'll go down to Capitol, see them in person about that paint delivery. Should be here tomorrow, next day at the latest." I said that would be swell, and he grinned his big, sloppy grin and left.

I met Orson on the front steps with the news about the paint. "Take the day off," I said. "Go to the beach."

"I might just do that," he said, lighting a cigarette. "Go out to Coney Island and look at the girls."

The night before, lying awake after my visit to his room, full of the memory of that second embrace, his cheek pressed against mine, the oddly pleasant Orson smell, I had tried to prepare myself to say something, ask him (with a laugh) what he meant by it, ask him where he got such freedom, such unself-conscious demonstrativeness, what did it mean, had he traveled in Italy, in Greece, where men embrace freely. The details of those crazy drunken moments with Jasper kept coming into my mind no matter what I did.

But Orson seemed completely normal, and I could see that he had meant nothing by last night's moment of demonstrativeness, nothing beyond gratitude and fellowship. I felt silly for taking it so seriously, for lying awake worrying until dawn. And Gant's words – that he liked me and wanted me to stay on – had elated me. I felt almost giddily light-hearted in spite of my fatigue.

"Have you ever been out to Coney Island? It's an experience you shouldn't miss. How about coming with me?"

"May would love that," I said. "Me ogling girls in bathing suits while she's slaving away at rehearsal. It looks like rain, anyway."

Orson exhaled smoke and said, "I always forget you have one of those exotic creatures, a wife." The smoke curled around his head. "I suppose because I never see her."

"She's busy with this play." I felt apologetic; I had asked May twice if we should invite Orson to dinner some night, and she was horrified at the idea.

"Will she be in yours if it gets produced? I mean, does it have a part for your wife? Something that would – as they say – showcase her talents?"

The idea was shocking: May as Thomasina, or as Babette, the overeducated society girl in my new play. "It's strange," I said. "I never think of my plays with May in them. I can't – I honestly can't imagine writing a part for her."

Orson looked amused; it occurred to me that he often looked amused. "Why not?"

"The kind of parts that suit her are – well, very alien to me," I said, fumbling. "To me as a writer, I mean." The truth was that I didn't think of her as any kind of actress at all – though she was better than she needed to be as poor Florence. "She likes dramatic roles – Strindberg, Ibsen. She's dying to play Nora someday – you know, in *A Doll's House*. I can't think of May as a comedienne."

"You write comedies?"

"Yes, I do."

"Really!"

"Yes. But I try to write comedies that have something to say about – you know – life. That maybe make people think a little bit."

"Now that's interesting. No offence, but I don't think of you as being particularly comic. I mean, no more than the next guy."

"I thought it was almost a cliché that all the really funny men are rather dour individuals." I smiled. "I'm laughing on the inside, Orson."

He gave me a quizzical look. "Really," he said, and frowned. For the first time since I'd met him, I felt I'd achieved some sort of upper hand – who knows why? Before I could reply, Orson changed the subject. "Where do you get your ideas, anyway? You think them up on your walks, I guess. But do they ever come to you in your dreams?"

My dreams. The dream about Luther and my father swam into my head, and one I recalled only vaguely from the night before, just before the alarm clock woke me, about riding a rickety old bicycle through a path in a dark forest, unable to see my way through the thicket of trees. "My dreams are too – well, I'm not sure how to describe them, but no, they don't give me ideas. Mostly, they're just trivial. And not funny, certainly. My aim is to entertain people – make them laugh."

"It's true, I suppose, that dreams do tend to be more terrifying than comical. And maybe an insomniac doesn't sleep enough to dream very much, anyway."

The forest dream was beginning to come back to me: how fearful I had been, and then May was there, clinging to me and whimpering. I said, "I've sometimes thought that's what insomnia is all about."

"What? Not wanting to dream? Resisting?"

"It's one way to avoid nightmares."

"Now there's a novel idea."

"*Perchance to dream,*" I couldn't help quoting, feeling a little foolish. "*Aye, there's the rub.*"

Orson ignored this, and I didn't blame him. *He thinks I'm a pretentious ass*, I said to myself. He stood smoking for a moment in silence. Then he said, as if I hadn't spoken, "Dreams are funny things, aren't they? In a way, I hate the thought of them, how they just wander out of my brain without my permission. All that stuff going on without any say from me. But I read somewhere that if we didn't dream, if we did manage to resist them all the time, we would go crazy. If we didn't let all that stuff out, our brains would just – explode with it."

We stood watching the cars go by. Down on the corner the ragman whipped his horse, shouting hoarsely; then, slowly, the cart moved off. It was late morning, and the sidewalk was mottled with the map of shadows that the trees made, but the sun was unreliable, and as we stood there it disappeared entirely, and a few drops fell. We moved toward the front door. "Damned weather," Orson said. "The radio said there may be a thunderstorm. So much for Coney Island."

"I slept hardly at all last night," I said, then wished I hadn't. But Orson only remarked, "Uh-oh. Sounds like you're due for another visit to *la spécialiste*." He tossed away his cigarette, and we went up the steps. Behind us, the streets became quickly black with rain. Orson grinned as we went inside. "I don't know if she's ever really cured anybody, but some of her concoctions might be interesting."

"I may stop in later and see her." I realized that I very much wanted to do this. I thought with pleasure of Mrs. Amalfi's odd apartment, as if it were a place I had lived, or the home of a relative who was fond of me. "Or now," I said. "Do you want to go up with me, see if she's there? Get a cup of tea?"

My occasional cup of tea with Mrs. Amalfi became one of my great pleasures. She was always glad to see me. Often there was something delicious cooking, but she never seemed to be doing much of anything except fussing over the cats or the pigeons. Once I arrived just as a patient was leaving – a pale, squinting man who hurried by me as if I'd caught him in a shameful act. "Poor lamb," Mrs. Amalfi said when she had closed the door behind him. "His wife left him over two years ago, and I swear he hasn't had a peaceful night since. We're going to try hypnosis."

I think Mrs. Amalfi was disappointed that my insomnia had disappeared on its own, without her intervention, and whenever I stopped in she examined me closely for signs of sleeplessness. "Your eyes are a little bloodshot," she'd say. "Did you have a bad night?" Once she asked me exactly how much I'd slept the night before. When I told her six hours, she said, "Well, my goodness, is it a wonder you look so pale and droopy? Let me give you some of this new tea I've concocted. It doesn't just put you to sleep, it keeps you there."

I took it, of course. When I brought it home, May sniffed it and said, "Isn't this stuff against the law or something?"

"It's only tea," I said, amused.

"Oh yeah?" She held it to my nose. "Smell this."

It was vaguely piney, with an undertone of what it took me a minute to identify as hay, a whiff of the barnyard. "Let's smoke it," May said. When I laughed, she said. "Robert, you're so trusting. You don't know anything about that crazy woman upstairs! She could be smuggling dope from China. She'll get you hooked and you'll be her slave for life."

"I'm your slave for life," I said, but May was already on her way out the door, late for a coffee date with Lois and Nancy.

I introduced May and Mrs. Amalfi, when we all met, once, on the front steps, but I never brought May to the second-floor apartment: I couldn't imagine what the two of them would say to each other. May didn't like mysteries, and Mrs. Amalfi was if nothing else mysterious. Also, May didn't like cats. Mrs. Amalfi, for her part, knew and cared nothing about the theatre. She loved Shakespeare; her Czech father used to read him aloud, she said, to improve his English. But she told me once that she hated seeing the plays performed, it ruined them for her: I imagined her saying this to May, and May's sarcasm in return. The only music Mrs.

Amalfi paid attention to was opera, which she listened to on a radio station that came in so badly the music was almost unrecognizable, but she knew it all by heart anyway, she said. Besides Shakespeare, the only book she seemed to know anything about was a seventeenth-century herbal by someone named Nicholas Culpeper; she displayed a ragged copy of it on a table in the living room as if it were a Bible.

Mrs. Amalfi and I talked easily to each other. She was fascinated by my dreams, no matter how trivial; curing her clients' sleep problems and then listening to their dreams, she said, was like planting a fruit tree for someone and getting delicious pies in return. She liked hearing about the old dog Luther, and she told me endless stories about cats she had owned or heard about, and she repeated odd things she saw in the newspapers. "A mouse has seven hundred heart beats a minute," she told me once. "And it lives less than three years. Whereas an elephant – think of this, Robert! An elephant has thirty heartbeats a minute and often lives for over sixty years. Think of the intensity of that little mouse's life! And then think of the elephant! The slow, placid majesty of it!"

I did find myself thinking of it – of that and other things she told me about: the proper way to make borscht, the changes she had seen in the neighborhood, the pale blue rim around the eye of the mourning dove, ways to calm a panicked animal, the sleep histories of her more memorable clients, the rumors that Gant had been involved in bootlegging, involved with the mob. She explained to me that a cat's purr comes from its brain – what she called its pleasure center – and she told me that her mother had been a gypsy named Marie Zmorsky who could ride a horse bareback and standing up, her red hair flowing down her back.

I often wondered if May was right, if Mrs. Amalfi was perhaps a little crazy. The wild, staring look that would come into her eyes, her dramatic makeup and odd way of dressing, her obsession with sleep and dreaming and Shakespeare and animals, with whom she said she could communicate – all this was certainly eccentric, and when I told May about it, I knew how it all sounded. But when I was with Mrs. Amalfi, despite her ambiguities she seemed just the reverse of mad: sensible, sane, earthbound, full of sometimes enigmatic advice. Once she said to me – very sincerely, leaning forward to put her ringed fingers on my wrist – "Become a sheep, Robert, and you will see the wolf" – but whether her words were meant as advice or caution, I wasn't sure.

I always hoped to run into Hana there again, but I never did, even though I tried to make my visits coincide with when I thought she might turn up. When I asked Mrs. Amalfi how she was, she always said, "Hana is doing beautifully," or "Hana is very well indeed," in a firmly dismissive way, and I didn't pursue it. I thought about her, though, and I was aware that one reason I enjoyed going to Mrs. Amalfi's so much was the chance of seeing Hana.

When I asked Orson if he wanted to go up there with me, he said, "All this talk about sleeping – I think what I'll do is go take a nap."

I went up to the second floor. Out the window, the rain was steady. There was no sound from inside Mrs. Amalfi's apartment, and no smells – nothing cooking. I knocked anyway and was glad to see the door open a crack, then wide.

"Robert. Please," she said. "Come in." Her voice was low and urgent. "I'm so glad to see you. You can't imagine how glad I am to see you."

She didn't look well; her hair was coming down and she wasn't wearing eye make-up, which made her seem older. There was a deep half-moon wrinkle below each of her eyes, and the skin above them drooped down as if the sleep specialist herself had had trouble sleeping.

"How are you, Mrs. Amalfi?"

"I need your help," she said. "I need your help very badly."

"What can I do?"

"It's Hana."

"Hana?"

"Yes. I need you to pick her up. I will give you money for a taxi. I got a telephone call. She is having one of her – you know." She paused. "Her spells. Her headaches. It is so hard for her to function properly. She needs someone to be with her. Will you do it?"

"Of course I'll do it. Tell me where to go."

As always, the place was very warm, the cats were draped over the furniture. The rain by now was lashing at the windows. We went into the kitchen. Mrs. Amalfi sat at the table and wrote on a scrap of paper.

"This is the address," she said, holding it out. The handwriting was large and spiky, beautifully legible. "Downtown, on First Avenue. Do you know the Russian quarter? Where there are restaurants? Shops? You will go to this shop." She reached into the pocket of her voluminous garments and withdrew two dollar bills. She folded the paper around the money and put it into my hand. "Take a taxi, of course. A Yellow Cab. This will be enough money. And bring her right to Bellevue. Do you understand? You know where it is?"

"Bellevue?"

"Bellevue," she said. "Yes. The hospital. Hana lives there."

"Hana lives at Bellevue?" Then I remembered she was a nursing student.

"Yes." She spoke impatiently. "She needs to get back. Take her to the entrance on 30th Street, at First Avenue. And wait there until she goes in. Be sure you see her go through the door. Then take the taxi back here – it's raining. And please – come and tell me that everything happened the way it's supposed to. Go, please.

It's not what I would call urgent, but – well, maybe it is a little urgent. Please, Robert."

I did as she told me. A taxi took me down First Avenue, and I got out at the address she gave me and dashed through the rain to the doorway. It was the kind of shop where May and I saw the Russian dolls that nested inside each other. There were several of them in the window, along with printed shawls and a samovar and some gilt-edged volumes of books in Russian. The door stood open, in spite of the rain. Inside, seated behind a counter, was a woman in a bright scarf tied back the way Hana wore hers. She had tired eyes and bad teeth, and she looked at me expressionlessly, without curiosity.

I said, "I am looking for Hana." I held up my piece of paper. "Is this –"

"Hana. Yes?"

"Yes. Hana." I had no memory of her last name. Something Polish. Or – I wondered – Russian? I recalled only that it began with an R. "Mrs. Amalfi's daughter. I understand that she's here. I've come to pick her up."

There was a bead curtain behind the counter; I heard the beads rattle, and a man peered through. He was large, fat, nearly bald, with a Jimmy Durante nose and almond-shaped eyes that seemed small in his expanse of face. He wore a white shirt that strained over his stomach, and a bow tie. The woman said something to him that I didn't understand. He stared at me, then abruptly disappeared, and after a pause Hana came through the bead curtain. She was wearing a rumpled summer dress; she didn't carry a bag, and she wasn't wearing her eyeglasses. Her hair, escaping from the scarf she wore, appeared to be reddish, and curly. Her face was pinched, her greenish eyes dulled with suffering; she held a cloth to her forehead. I was struck by how petite she was.

"Robert," she said. Her voice was hoarse, huskier than usual. "You're here for me?"

"Your mother said I was to take you to Bellevue."

Hana smiled painfully. "How amazingly good of you."

She turned to the woman behind the counter and said something in Russian, or Polish. The woman didn't speak; she nodded and patted Hana's cheek, kindly. The taxi was waiting; the rain had let up somewhat. Hana didn't appear to notice it. She collapsed in the corner of the seat, her eyes closed. She looked like an old child.

I said to the driver, "Bellevue Hospital."

"Which entrance?"

"First Avenue and 30th Street."

"The Psychiatric Hospital?"

"Oh – I don't really –"

Hana said, faintly, "Yes. Please."

We drove off, crossing over Eighth Street and then speeding up First Avenue. Hana reached out her hand. I took it, touched. I watched her face, waiting for her to open her eyes, but she didn't. Her eyelashes were short and thick, her cheeks faintly freckled. All the way up First Avenue, she gripped my hand, and when the taxi stopped at the hospital, she gave a sigh and let go, and opened the door. I would have followed her out of the taxi, but she said, "No – I'll be all right. Please." Her voice was effortful, a whisper. "This was good of you, Robert. So good of you. You can't know."

She turned and walked up the sidewalk, paying no attention to the rain. She didn't hurry: her steps were slow and measured, her hands stiff at her sides, her fingers spread. I imagined her face: eyes narrowed, teeth set against the pain. A man in a uniform opened the door, and she went in. As she passed through the door, she pulled off her scarf, and her hair – long, auburn, luxuriant – tumbled about her shoulders. She had left the wet cloth in the taxi. I picked it up; it was burning hot.

I let the taxi go and walked back to the Alhambra Gardens in the rain. I hadn't thought to bring an umbrella; I was in shirtsleeves, hatless. As I walked, the rain intensified again, and by the time I reached Mrs. Amalfi's apartment I was wet through. I knocked on her door and she opened it immediately, as if she had been just on the other side. "Robert." I handed her the remainder of the taxi money; she clung to my hand. "That was so quick. I hope nothing went wrong."

"I took her back to Bellevue. I watched her go in. She seemed all right. Still in pain, though."

"Come in. Please. Take off your shoes. Have some hot tea. You're soaking wet! Why did you let the taxi go? You'll catch your death."

In the kitchen, everything was as it always was. A scent of cinnamon came from the oven. I sat at the table dripping water on the floor, petting Juliet and listening to Bianca and Portia and the rest of them cooing from the cages in the corner. Mrs. Amalfi fetched a towel and, surprising me, stood behind me and dried my face and neck with it, and then my hair. It was completely peaceful there, with the rain banging against the windows and this large, strange woman rubbing my head with motherly briskness. I thought with tenderness of Hana's hand in mine in the taxi. When the kettle boiled, Mrs. Amalfi handed me the towel, and I dried off as well as I could. She poured tea into two gold-rimmed cups, and we sat down to tea and a plate of the cookies she took from the oven.

"Now," she said, but she said nothing more, and the silence returned. Absently, she petted the cat for a few moments. I sipped at the hot tea, which was brown and thick and left a sweet aftertaste. The cookies were delicious. I finished one and started another before she spoke again. "You are no doubt wondering," she said. "About Hana."

"Well, yes," I said, and paused. "But I don't want to pry. It's surely none of my business."

Mrs. Amalfi smiled at me. "I sent you out on an uncomfortable errand in the rain, and you performed it beautifully, without a murmur of complaint. It is your business, if you want to hear about it."

"I do, then. Yes. I am – intrigued. But Hana –"

"Yes?"

"She seemed so sad. It wasn't just her headache. Her suffering seemed part of her. I felt it even when I saw her that time here in your kitchen. That she was – full of melancholy." I didn't know what else to say; *melancholy* didn't express what I meant. I remembered the heat of her small hand, and of the cloth she had pressed to her burning forehead. I thought about the shock of her hair set loose from her scarf, the brightness of it even in the dim rainy afternoon. It had changed her utterly. And then she was gone, whisked inside the huge doors. Maybe I meant *tragic*, but it didn't seem right to say it.

"She has much to be melancholy about, Robert. She is very young. Well – young. What is young? To me she is ridiculously young. She is twenty-five."

"That's my age, too."

"Is it?" Mrs. Amalfi's face brightened. "What month?"

"I just had my birthday. In July."

"Ah. Hana was born in January. On the most frigidly cold day! I remember it perfectly, that day."

There was a clap of thunder; the storm had become intense. I hoped it would let up before May came home; I knew she had gone out without her raincoat or umbrella. I drank my tea, while my clothes dripped onto the Persian carpet. Ferdinand sniffed my pant legs suspiciously. Juliet, on the table before me, stretched voluptuously, reaching out with her paws and laying one firmly on my hand.

Mrs. Amalfi smiled. "You and my daughter are the two faces of the year, winter and summer. You are mirrors of each other. Now tell me – no, I won't ask you what day in July. It would be too odd if you were exactly six months apart. This is enough. I like this. I have felt from the beginning that you would be important to us, Robert."

"Important? How?"

"A friend. A true friend."

"I'll try to be," I said.

"Yes, you will. I sense that." She poured more tea from the pot, using a hinged strainer to catch the leaves, and pushed the plate of cookies closer. I began eating a third one. Mrs. Amalfi said, "My daughter has a difficult history," and took a sip of tea. Then she looked at me and did her eye-widening trick. "I will be frank," Mrs. Amalfi said. "For years, she was a prostitute, quite a successful one."

I set down my cup hard, laid the cookie on the saucer. I don't know what I had expected, but surely not what I had just heard. For a moment I could barely take it in. I thought of Hana's burning hand, the avalanche of curls. The birds cooed comfortably, incongruously, in their cages.

"She has now reformed," Mrs. Amalfi continued. "She lives at Bellevue, in the Psychiatric Hospital. She is not studying to be a nurse – not yet. That is more symbolical than true at the moment. She is in a rehabilitation program for women with what they perceive to be her difficulty." I looked at her blankly. "Nymphomania," she said. She seemed completely unembarrassed, merely struggling with ways to say things tactfully. "They call it sexual imbalance. Too much appetite. You understand?" She smiled at me kindly, as she might smile at a child to whom she had to break some bad news. "That was their diagnosis. And – who knows? Maybe there is truth in it. You didn't know Hana in those days. She was quite – quite different." I remembered Hana's sudden stillness when I had confessed to being a night-walker. I tried to imagine her childish body in a skin-tight, low-cut dress like the ones the women in Harlem wore, or the expensive whores I sometimes saw getting into taxis on Park Avenue. "Once she was found by the police on Second Avenue – not far from where you picked her up today, in fact. She was involved with the Russians. She had been stabbed – oh, it's too complicated to explain it. But she nearly died. She was taken by ambulance to Bellevue, and her life was saved. That was five months ago, and she has been there ever since. It's a six-month program. When it is over, she will go to live in an apartment owned by a relative of mine." "Where she can be, to some extent, looked after, if she needs to be." Mrs. Amalfi paused. "At the moment, this is all unclear."

I let out a breath and picked up my teacup again. My hand was trembling, and I had to set the cup down. It rattled against the saucer. "This has affected me," I said, with a little laugh. "I hardly know what to say."

Mrs. Amalfi put her hand on my wrist. "Don't be afraid, Robert. Don't be wishing you had never met us. Hana is a good girl – a good woman. In spite of what you know now. We're good people. The story is much, much longer than the parts I've just told you. Much more complicated. But don't be afraid of us, Hana likes you very much, and so do I. I am more grateful than I can say for your help today. I would have gone myself, but – I thought it would be better if it was a man."

I didn't ask why. I did ask, "Who were those people? The woman behind the counter? And a fat man with the bald head?"

"Iza," she said. "And Tomek. It doesn't matter. They're relatives of one of my husbands – Hana's father."

"And he is –"

"Dead and gone. Long dead, long gone. He died of the 1918 influenza. And not one soul on this earth has ever missed him."

"I'm sorry," I said.

"For what, Robert?"

I spread my hands helplessly. I thought of Hana, bleeding, helpless on the sidewalk: the image was impossible, and yet it had happened. I thought of Orson, and wondered if he had known Hana in her other life. I had a brief, disturbing vision of the two of them together. I thought of Hana, on the streets with men. I thought of the streets at night, the people I saw, the women in Harlem. *A prostitute, quite a successful one*: what did that mean? Successful! I felt young and foolish and inadequate, and I said, with a laugh, "For just about everything," and then I put my head in my hands, and, absurdly, against my will, I began to cry.

Mrs. Amalfi said, "Oh my God, you poor thing, you poor soul. Robert, what have we done to you?"

"No – no, it's not that. I don't know what it is." Mrs. Amalfi handed me the towel and I mopped my eyes with it, laughing at myself, but I couldn't stop the tears from coming. "Maybe it's my wife and me. Things are so different lately, not the way I wanted them to be, it seems like events are just rushing by, and now –"

"Events. What events?"

"Well –" My outburst had surprised me. I couldn't think what I meant: May got a part in a play, Orson came to live upstairs, Hana had been a prostitute, I had gotten caught in the rain and was chilled, May and I never had sex any more, Orson lied to me, Orson embraced me twice. "I don't know what I mean. It's hard to pin it down. Maybe it's just that I finished my play and people are reading it, my fate is in someone else's hands. And it's probably no good anyway. Or maybe it's – ah, I don't know, Mrs. Amalfi." I wiped my eyes on my sleeve and tried to smile. Oddly enough, I felt no embarrassment; I felt better. "Maybe it's the rain," I said. "I'm sorry."

Mrs. Amalfi sat looking at me. "Robert," she said. "Robert, you are a very nice man."

I felt my face flush, though I was shivering in my wet clothes. "I don't know about that," I said, but her words – May's words – touched me. That and what she had said before, about my being a friend, about Hana liking me.

"And your sleep?" she asked, leaning forward. "You're sleeping better?"

"I'm sleeping very well," I said, and added, to be scrupulously truthful, as if I were talking to a doctor, "Usually."

"Really? When – if you'll forgive me for saying so – you seem so troubled. About your wife. Things happening too fast, you said. And you weep! And yet you sleep better. How can that be?"

"I don't know," I said. "I assume it's the relief of having help around the building. You do know that Orson is helping me out, showing me the ropes a little."

"Orson Price?" She was silent a moment. "No, I didn't know that. I haven't seen him."

"I'm surprised."

"He probably stays out of my way."

I remembered that Orson had said he'd heard about the job from her. Teresa Amalfi, he had called her – it was how I had learned her first name. But I didn't mention this. Orson had lied, that was all: lied again.

"He's living right in the building," I said. "There's a room in the attic I'm letting him use. Mr. Gant doesn't exactly know all this, and I'd be grateful if you didn't say anything to him. It's just temporary, just until I get the hang of things."

"I see. Of course. Don't ever tell Gant anything." She looked out the window thoughtfully. "Well. So Orson Price is living upstairs. That's very –" Her voice trailed away. She didn't finish the sentence. *Very interesting, I thought. Very troubling. Very amusing. Very wonderful. Very strange.* "He should be a great help to you, Robert," she resumed after a minute. "Orson is very good at certain things. And yes, I've noticed the geraniums, and the hedge. Other things, too." Her gaze came back to me; she was frowning, but her face cleared, and she got up and went to the window. "It's over now. Come with me. I'm going out to look for birds."

"To look for birds?"

"Yes. There are so often pigeons with injuries after a storm like that. Come – we'll take this towel. And my umbrella." She left the room and came back wearing a cape, with a hat pulled down around her ears. "I know you're wet, but come with me, just for a few minutes, and then you can go right home and have a hot bath. This won't take long. I'll only search these few blocks, maybe between here and the park. If we find a bird, we'll wrap it in this towel and bring it home."

As she talked, I put on my sopping shoes, and then we went down the stairs and out to the street. Everything was washed clean, including the air, which – briefly, suddenly, as we went out the door – smelled sweet, like some kind of flower. Birds were singing, and the sun had not yet come out but the sky was getting lighter. Mrs. Amalfi took my arm. "This way. We'll just go a block or two. You look in the gutter, I'll look on this side. That's where I find them, by the curb, or by the fences."

We walked to Gramercy Park with its lovely old buildings – dark gray, dove gray, red-brown. The trees in the park were the same black as the iron fence; their leaves, dripping, seemed a deeper green. The ragman and his horse, both wearing hats, stood motionless at the corner by Irving Place, and the old horse's worn brown haunches gleamed in that light like fine leather. A small boy came out of a doorway, being pulled by a bony dog on a leash. Just then the sun came out strong, and the scene turned to bronze, to gold. The windows of the stone buildings were lit with it, and where the clouds parted, the sky was pure blue. Mrs.

Amalfi stopped suddenly and looked up at me from under her hat brim. "Ah, Robert," she said, and her eyes were glowing. "Don't you agree that the world is a beautiful place, in spite of everything?"

I said, "Yes, I do." Mrs. Amalfi took off her hat, revealing her elaborate hair-do, a dense mass of black braids laced with gray. I thought of her mother, Marie the red-headed gypsy, with her hair flying, riding a horse bareback.

We saw no injured pigeons. We doubled back over to First Avenue and down as far as 14th Street, and then Mrs. Amalfi said, "That's enough. Sometimes I walk through Union Square, but I'll spare you that today. I feel in my heart, in my bones, that we won't find any poor little birds. I feel that this is a lucky day."

We headed back, and as we crossed 21st Street Mrs. Amalfi stopped dead. A voice said, "Robert!" Orson was standing on the corner, dressed in his white suit, with a white shirt and a tie. "And Mrs. Amalfi," he said. "What do you know."

"Well, Orson." She didn't say anything else for a second or two. We both stood looking at Orson, who seemed either rushed or excited; his hair was tousled, his cheeks pink, as if he'd been running. He didn't look like someone who had been taking a nap. He held out his hand, and Mrs. Amalfi took it briefly, no more than a quick touch. "Here you are back in the old neighborhood," she said. She sounded disapproving.

"My old stomping ground." He smiled. "And you too, I see. Still here."

"The only way I'll leave this place is in a box."

"Not for a long time, then, I hope. And what have you done with Robert? Robert, you look half-drowned."

"He was doing errands for me in the rain."

"Robert is a saint," Orson said, with a wink at me. He stood with his hands in his pockets, jingling change or keys.

"That's quite true," Mrs. Amalfi said. "I don't know what I'd do without Robert."

"And I must say you're looking very well, Mrs. A." He pronounced "Mrs. A." with irony, or as if he was used to calling her something else entirely. "How has everything been going? And how's Hana?"

"Hana is very well," she said. And then she added, surprising me, "In less than a month, she'll be out of there."

Orson raised his eyebrows. "Yes. I had heard." Mrs. Amalfi looked at him sharply, but didn't comment. "Well, that's good news," Orson said. "And then what will she do?"

"That's for Hana to decide," she said brusquely.

"Who better?" Orson asked, his smile widening.

Mrs. Amalfi didn't speak again. There was a short silence, while cars hissed by on the wet pavement. The Greek sandwich man passed us, the ice man behind his mule, two laughing women. Orson turned to look after the women; then he said, "Well – if you really mean it about a day off, Robert, I reckon I'll be on my way again."

"Sure. There's nothing we can do today anyway."

"Then I'll see you tomorrow, I guess. So long, Mrs. A."

He strolled off. Mrs. Amalfi and I climbed the steps to the Alhambra Gardens. "What a thought," she said. "Orson Price up there under the roof."

"You seem to know him well." I wasn't able say what had disturbed me about their short conversation: the sense I'd had before of a play unfolding backstage, secret from the audience. I held the door open, and Mrs. Amalfi went through it.

"Not well," she said, with an amused downturn of her lips. "Definitely not *well*. But certainly for a long time."

"He told me he'd seen you," I said impulsively. "Not long ago, I mean. He told me he heard about the job here from you. From Teresa Amalfi, he said."

"How dare he!" Her eyes blazed. "He told you that? Orson Price is a liar. Orson Price is never – never! – to be trusted, Robert."

"Still," I said. "Someone told him."

"Yes. Someone did."

"Of course I believe you, Mrs. Amalfi. And of course, what does it matter who told him?"

"But you'd like to know who, all the same."

"I would."

She looked at me. She seemed shaken, in the grip of an emotion I could not fathom. "Maybe you wouldn't, Robert."

"What?"

"Or maybe it's nothing. Maybe he just ventured a guess." She seemed to be talking to herself. "Maybe he was hoping you needed someone, and mentioned my name so you'd think better of him."

"Maybe. That makes sense." I smiled at her. "That's it, I'm sure."

Mrs. Amalfi didn't smile back. "There are so many different kinds of lies." She started up the marble stairs, her cape trailing. Then she turned and reached out her hand, and I took it. "Thank you, Robert," she said, and widened her eyes. In the dim light of the hall, her eye make-up looked theatrically tragic; she could have been Lady Macbeth, or Gertrude.

FOUR

The paint was delivered, finally. Orson and I began painting, and for the next few weeks of that summer it was just about all we did. The process was enjoyable: the obliteration of everything that was dingy and old. The paint was pleasantly sharp-smelling, an agreeable ivory color, a shade darker than what had been on the walls and more compatible with the creamy marble floors. Orson and I spread out our drop cloths near to each other but not within comfortable talking distance, so we didn't say much. I didn't tell him I knew he had lied to me about Mrs. Amalfi – simply because I felt the accusation would embarrass us both and serve no useful purpose. I still sometimes thought about that odd night in his room, and the quick, close embrace, but I didn't dwell on it, and the episode moved steadily toward the back of my mind.

What I thought about while we worked was my new play. I began to look forward to getting out there on the ladder in my painting clothes, into the quiet of the Alhambra Garden's marble halls, so that the structure of the play could build itself in my head amid the smells of paint and turpentine and sweat. I took a certain satisfaction in the idea that the hours I spent painting could feed my other life: it was as if Gant were paying me to write plays. Then I'd think about Samuel Harper's long silence, the cruel letter from Rex Mason, and try to think about something else. What was I doing? Writing another play no one would ever produce? But the play always returned, and as the summer went on I made good progress on it.

On Saturday mornings, I used to walk over to Stuyvesant Park and sit on a bench scribbling down bits of dialogue, working things out before I committed them to the typed page, while May washed out her underwear and painted her toenails; she preferred to be alone for these domestic rituals. Saturday nights we sometimes strolled down into the Village together, idly people-watching and stopping for coffee or, if we had a little money left, a cocktail somewhere, or we would sit in a cool, dark movie theatre holding hands. May's Aunt Myra sent her ten dollars for her birthday, and we went to see O'Neill's *Ah, Wilderness*, at the Guild Theatre, and then to supper at the Biltmore. Once or twice we had dinner with Lois at Romany Marie's, a supposedly chic dive that Lois and May loved but I hated, or we met Carlotta and Mickey at Mori's or Chumley's or one of the bars near the river. I still wasn't wild about Lois, though thanks to the hated ex-husband she had plenty of money and usually picked up the check. I was also getting tired of Carlotta and Mickey: Carlotta's shrill silliness was oppressive, and Mickey's only outstanding feature, aside from his dancing and moustachioed good looks, was an ability to wrench off bottle caps with his teeth. But it was a relief in some ways to be with people. Things were livelier, and afterwards, on the way home, May and I had more to talk about.

■ ■ ■

And then, toward the end of August, two things happened. The first was that Carlotta gave a party. She and Mickey Kennedy were staying in an apartment down on West Third Street, upstairs from a noisy night spot called Club Gaucho. They'd borrowed the place from a friend of Mickey's who was away for the summer. May was excited – we didn't go to many parties – and deliberated for a whole week about what to wear. Finally she decided on a dress she said she'd had since high school but that I had always loved: low-cut blue satin that rippled out in a circle from a tightly cinched waist.

"You're beautiful," I said, and she looked in the mirror and said, "Am I really? Do I still look good?"

I could see that she was serious; she wanted an answer. I had never heard May express any doubts about her appearance. But turning thirty had been hard for her. I went over and stood behind her and, hesitantly, put my hands on her breasts. "You have never looked better," I said, and it occurred to me that it was true: she looked radiant.

"Really?"

"Really."

She gripped my hands and pressed them against her breasts, surprising me. I could feel her nipples through the light material. She leaned back against me, and I said, "Let's make love."

"What about the party?"

"We'll get to the party. We'll just get there a little later."

"Oh, Robert –" She drew away from me and looked at her face in the mirror. "I just put my makeup on, sweetie." Her eyes shifted to meet mine. "And I promised Carlotta we'd try to be there early, to help out. She's really nervous about this party, don't ask me why."

It was then that I had my first small moment of panic. It was similar to the feeling I remembered after my father died, that behind the things that seemed to be going on, other things were happening: important, monumental things that I knew nothing of but that would powerfully affect me. In those first few weeks after the funeral, home with my mother in the big house, going through my father's disastrous financial records, I thought back to times like Parents' Weekend my sophomore year, when Mom and Dad drove up to Cambridge and we all had steak dinners in Boston at Locke-Ober's, with two bottles of wine and plenty of brandy after dinner. The next day my father bought me an outrageously expensive carved Meerschaum from the pipe shop on Harvard Square, joking with his arm around my mother about how his son had to learn to be more extravagant, how the girls loved a big spender, *Isn't that right, Grace?* – jokes I was used to, I'd heard them all my life, they went with my father's twenty-dollar hats and cashmere sweaters, his bear hugs and big smile. And all that time, even while he threw money around and made jokes and poured brandy, his world was crumbling.

"May?"

Our eyes met in the mirror. She looked like a doll: red lips, yellow hair, pink cheeks, blue eyes, blue dress. She smiled and said, "Hmm?"

"What's wrong?" I asked her.

She stared at me a moment, then swung around and flung her arms around me. "Nothing is wrong," she said fiercely. "Nothing! Nothing! And when we get home I promise we'll make crazy, wild love until Monday morning!" She pulled back, and I saw that her eyes were wet with tears. "OK? OK, Robert?"

I didn't know what else to say, so I said, "Sure, honey. When we get home." We stood for a moment with our arms around each other, and then May repaired her eye makeup and we walked arm in arm down to the Village. Perhaps I should have been reassured, but it was as if that moment of doubt had been a germ, and now I was infected with it, and I would never be well again.

The party was in full swing when we arrived. The door was open, and as we walked in the first thing we saw was Carlotta with an open bottle of gin. She came toward us, eyes bright, her hair wild. "May! You swore you'd get here early! Where have you two been?"

They embraced – Carlotta already quite drunk, May with a melodramatic cry. "You're looking so stupendous, darling! Isn't she looking stupendous, Robert?"

"Thank you, thank you," Carlotta said, holding out the bottle. "And now let's all get stewed. Come on – catch up with me, girl."

May took the bottle and drank from it. I knew that straight gin invariably made her falling-down drunk, and I could see myself in an hour or two taking May, sick and woozy, home in a cab that we couldn't afford. I could see her swollen with sleep and myself lying awake into the night. I imagined my hands on her body, her oblivious groans as she turned away. She raised the bottle to her lips again – her smooth white throat pulsed once, twice – and then she moved away into the living room, greeting Mickey Kennedy with an elaborate, messy hug as if that little bit of gin had made her drunk already.

I stood there in the hall feeling hopeless. What I wanted to do was leave, slip out and down the stairs and head back through Washington Square Park to Fifth Avenue and – where? What? I didn't know. Take an aimless walk. Go home to the empty apartment. I thought about going up to see Orson, or dropping in on Mrs. Amalfi. But neither picture satisfied me. All I wanted was May. I stayed where I was.

Carlotta went by on her way to answer the doorbell. "You okay, Robert?"

"Yes, I'm okay."

"So mingle," she said. "Drink! Carouse! You look like a death's head, baby." She gave me a tiny, secret smile. "This is a happy occasion, after all."

The apartment was large and crowded, full of people I didn't know. I wandered from room to room by myself, smiling, saying excuse me, pushing my way through, wondering about the people who lived there, whoever they were. They had money: that was clear. They also had gaudy taste in furniture: red drapes, a cut velvet couch, fancy baroque chairs in the dining room. In the kitchen, a skinny black woman was squirting cheesy stuff onto crackers from a metal contraption. When I greeted her, she didn't even look up. In the hallway a cockatoo in an elaborate brass cage chittered at its reflection in a tin mirror.

I went over to a window and pushed aside the drapes. Below me was Sullivan Street, and I stood watching the lights of the cars going by, watching a drunken couple arguing on the corner, watching a taxi disgorge a man who looked a bit like Orson – white suit, reddish hair, something about the set of the shoulders – but he disappeared around the corner to West Third Street before I could see him properly. My first thought had been that maybe Orson had, somehow, been invited to the party, and I felt a surge of relief, that among this alien crowd there would be a friend. Then I realized how improbable that was – almost as improbable as the idea of Orson taking a taxi anywhere. I turned away from the window. I could use a drink.

At the bar, I got myself a gin and lime. Mickey Kennedy came up beside me. A familiar face, smiling. I was actually glad to see him, and I shook his hand with enthusiasm. "What have you been up to lately, Mickey?"

He looked at me oddly, and then he said, "Well, not much, Robert. But that's going to be changing." He grinned, and fiddled with his skinny William Powell moustache. "Carlotta's talking about either getting a little dog – a terrier, I think she said, one of those white fluffy models – or else having a baby. But I think, considering everything, we'd better get the dog."

"Are you two engaged, then?"

I figured maybe their engagement was what the party was about, but Mickey just laughed. "At this point, everything is pretty much up in the air, isn't it?"

I started to answer, though I had no idea what he was talking about, but just then a woman in a sort of feathered headdress came up and took Mickey away. "Excuse us," she said. "I need this darling boy for one tiny minute."

I downed most of my drink and made another. On the phonograph some woman was singing a jazzy version of "Why Do I Love You?" Why indeed. I watched May, who was standing in front of the windows with a man I didn't know, talking in an animated way, drinking. In the dim room, the light from the street lamps darkened her hair to the color of honey. Her blue silk dress was stretched across her breasts, the silky skirt outlining her thighs and her small round belly. I drank one gin quickly and then another slowly, thinking about my hot wife, her eager mouth, her fingers, until I felt myself getting hard and I sat down.

Carlotta came over and stood before me. Her hair was fixed a new way, waved back from her low forehead and caught up behind in a thick, loose chignon that was coming down. She looked top-heavy, all hair and bosom – like a sunflower on her long skinny legs. "Oh, Robert," she said. "It's so nice to see someone I actually like! Where's May? God, I feel like I haven't seen you two in ages. Have you had something to eat? Did you try any of that fishy stuff?"

"I'm not hungry," I said. "I'm waiting to hear what this party's about, Carlotta, and for some reason I'm feeling a little apprehensive."

"Oh – heavens – don't be. It's just a lucky break." She smiled at me uncertainly. I could see that she was not only drunk but nervous. Her eye makeup was smeared, making black shadows beneath each eye.

"What is? What's going on?"

"I just hope May won't hate me."

"Oh, Carlotta, for Pete's sake, May would never hate you."

She knelt before me and laid her hand on my knee. When she bent her head, I could see the part in her hair. It was very white, whiter than her skin; I saw flakes of dandruff. Then she looked up at me with her glassy brown eyes. "You're very sweet, Robert," she said. "Really. You probably have no idea how sweet you are." She tipped forward and kissed me lingeringly on the lips. Her mouth tasted of whiskey and lipstick. "I've wanted to do that for the longest time," she said in a low, seductive voice. I couldn't tell if she was serious or just fooling around. She squeezed my leg above the knee and left her hand there. "But I had to get drunk first."

The music stopped abruptly, and a man I'd never seen before came up to us. "Jesus, Carlotta," he said. "You're loaded." He looked both exasperated and charmed. "Come on, baby, it's time. Come on over here with Mickey."

"Oh Randolph," she said. "I was having such a good time talking to Robert. Do I have to?"

"Do you *have* to? Of course you have to."

She sighed elaborately and stood up, pulling me with her. "Robert, this is Randolph. Mickey's brother. Randolph, Robert Sinclair." She was unsteady on her feet. She stumbled against me, and I could feel her big, hard breasts against my arm; some of the gin in my glass sloshed out. Carlotta grimaced at Randolph. "Do I really, really have to?"

"Since when did you get shy?" He winked at me. "You'll have to excuse Carlotta for a couple of minutes. This is her big moment."

Carlotta went off with Randolph to the other end of the room, where she and Mickey Kennedy climbed up on a low table, Mickey's arm around her, Carlotta swaying a little, smiling woozily.

The room quieted suddenly. "Hear hear!" someone called. "Speech!'

In the relative silence, I could hear Latin music from the nightclub downstairs, the thump of the rhythm section, frantic guitars. I moved toward the wall and stood leaning against it.

There were thirty or forty people at the party, and I wondered who they all were. Someone started to applaud, and several people joined in. Mickey held up one hand, grinning. He was a handsome guy, but there was something untrustworthy about his face, something I had to admit I had never liked. He called out, "Is everybody happy?" and there was more applause, a few catcalls. Then he sobered and said, "This won't take long, folks. Just a little announcement." On the other side of the room, I saw May at the edge of the crowd, on tiptoe, looking over people's heads. I caught her eye. She was frowning, and her hand came up in a tiny three-fingered wave. "I just want to say this. Carlotta and I are going out to California. We're leaving in a couple of weeks – driving out in my new Ford."

There were exclamations, wolf whistles. A woman I knew vaguely but whose name I'd forgotten squeezed my arm and said, "Isn't it just about the most exciting thing you're ever heard?"

Mickey raised his hand again for quiet and went on, "Some of you already know about this, but for those of you who don't – well, we're going out there for a reason."

He paused, and somebody yelled, "Come on, don't be modest, Mick boy!"

Mickey grinned more widely. Beside him, Carlotta drained her glass. Mickey said, "Well, I've got a contract with Paramount, and it looks like I'm going to be some kind of a movie star. We're bound for Hollywood!"

The room broke into cheers. Mickey and Carlotta embraced, kissed, and then Mickey broke away and said, "And this little lady's going to be next! Just wait 'til Hollywood gets a load of this!" Carlotta put her hand on her hip and did a comical little bump and grind. I looked over at May; the expression on her face was part surprise, part anger, and part something else that reminded me of what Verna Quiller had said about the two of them that day over coffee.

The woman next to me said, "Did you hear how it happened? They discovered him on 47th Street! Can you believe it? A talent scout came up to him at Liggett's Drug Store and offered him a screen test. He's just what they were looking for to be in some movie with a new starlet they're grooming to be the next Myrna Loy."

Someone else turned around and said, "What? Is that true?"

"That's what I heard. That's the way it happens! He went over to a place on Sixth Avenue and took the test."

"The screen test."

"Right. He read lines, and they photographed him from every angle, and then they thanked him, and two days later he got a telegram. And now he's on his way to Hollywood! He's my brother-in-law, and I can't even hardly believe it!"

Someone put "You Ought To Be in Pictures" on the phonograph, and people began to dance. May came over to me. "She didn't tell me," she said, her eyes hard. "She's been my best friend since we were kids. We've always done everything together. We've always told each other everything. And now she pulls this stunt."

"I guess they wanted to keep it a secret."

"A secret! It looks like everybody knows but us. She just didn't want to tell me. It's her mean streak coming out. She's had that mean streak since she was nine years old." She took my glass from me and drained it. "Let's leave, Robert. I want to get out of here."

Mickey and Carlotta appeared as we headed for the door. "Say, you two. We've got a rumble seat on that Ford that you'd fit into just right," Mickey said, generous and genial in his new incarnation as the next William Powell. "I'm going to get Carlotta a screen test, first thing I do, and I don't see why I couldn't wangle one for you, May. You two girls would take that town by storm."

May smiled her superior smile. "You seem to forget that I have an opening three weeks from tomorrow night."

Carlotta shrugged. "Later, then. Come out when the play closes. Not that I'm not wishing you a long and happy life as a gun moll. But let's face facts. Times is tough, baby. These things do happen."

May turned and fussed with her hair in the hall mirror. "You know my heart belongs to the theatre, Carlotta."

Carlotta gripped her arm. "You sore at me, May?"

May pulled her arm away. "No, Carlotta I am not *sore* at you, for heaven's sake. You get so childish when you're drunk."

All the way home, May told me a long, rambling story of something Carlotta had done when they were in high school involving a red sweater and a boy named Mike. When we got to the apartment May snapped on the radio and sprawled on the couch, her dress hiked up above her knees. "Oh God, I'm exhausted. This is the limit, Robert."

I sat down beside her and lit a cigarette. "I guess we have to be happy for them, May."

"Oh, I don't care. I don't care a fig what happens any more." She sighed, then sat up straight. "Let's dance," she said suddenly, and pulled me to my feet.

"You're drunk."

"I'm not that drunk. Come on!"

We jigged back and forth to Bing singing "In the Cool Cool Cool of the Evening." I was a rotten dancer, and we were both wobbly by then, but it was wonderful holding her. I inhaled the scent of her hair and her body, and she pressed herself against me. We slowed down, standing there with our arms around each other, swaying back and forth. "It's been a long time since we've done this," I said. "Why is that?"

"Oh, I don't know, Robert." She touched my lips with her finger, tracing around my mouth. "Things have been crazy.

Haven't they? Haven't things been crazy?" She drew away from me, pulled her dress over her head, and stood in the lamplight smiling. She was wearing black panties and a black brassiere and her red sandals, nothing else.

"May –"

She unhooked her bra and dropped it on the floor, then her panties. She licked her lips and waggled her tongue, grinning at me – playing the prostitute, as she did sometimes when we were fooling around. Then she walked backward toward the bedroom on her high heels, beckoning me. I followed her, unbuttoning my shirt as I went, undoing my belt. She kicked off her shoes and lay back on the bed with her legs spread, and touched her breasts as I undressed. I knelt beside her and kissed her lips, her hard pink nipples, the cool smoothness of her neck. "Oh God, May, I've missed you, I've missed this."

She whispered into my ear, "Let's do it right, Robert. I want you inside me."

"Are you sure? Oh, darling, I want you so much."

"Do it to me, Robert. I want you to. I don't care about anything, I just want this."

I rolled on top of her. She locked her legs around me and moaned into my shoulder. I fumbled with my erection, trying to put it inside her, but I went limp against her soft fur. "Oh Jesus," I said. "It's the booze."

"We'll give it a minute," she said softly. "Poor little thing, it's confused."

She caressed me with her fingers, patiently, until I was hard again. But it wasn't the booze: I knew that. It was the strangeness of it. I had never done this, not with May, not with anyone. I had never been inside a woman. Was this what men did, pushed themselves in between a woman's legs? May and I had done it the other way for so long that this seemed wrong, perverse, almost as if she really were a whore, and I was trying to perform some fiendishly unnatural act.

She bent her knees up, stroking herself with one hand, whispering, "Robert, please, I want you to, please do it," and I tried, I tried, but it was no use, and before long we both knew it. I lay beside her in silence, feeling my pulse slow down again and the apartment's dankness cool my skin.

"I'm sorry," I said. She didn't answer, and I realized she was crying. "May?"

"It's all right."

I put out a hand and touched her breast. "Maybe we could –"

"I've lost the mood somehow."

I took my hand away and pulled the blanket over us. Within minutes she was asleep.

■ ■ ■

The second thing was that May was late coming home one night. Finally she burst into the apartment at ten-thirty. She stumbled when she came through the door, and she smelled of whiskey. "I've been getting shit-faced with Nathan," she said.

"Nathan?"

"Nathan Kaufman." I looked at her, puzzled. She had complained at least a dozen times about how Nathan was too snooty to fraternize with the rest of the cast, how she and Lois disliked him. "Yes, Nathan. We found we have something in common after all." She sank down on the bed and pulled off her shoes; then she began to fumble with the buttons of her dress. Finally she got it open, shrugged it off, and sat there in her slip, her arms folded across her stomach, her head drooping and her eyes closed, as if that was all she had to say.

"May? What's going on?"

She looked up at me and laughed – the harsh laugh I recognized as her Aunt Myra's. "Nothing's going on, as a matter of fact. That's it – exactly. The show has been canceled."

"The show?" I asked stupidly. She couldn't be saying what she seemed to be saying. "What show?"

"Oh God, Robert, how can you be so dense! What show do you think? *The Killer Instinct!*" Tears welled up in her eyes. "It's three weeks until opening night. I had my first costume fitting this morning! And this afternoon George came in and told us it's canceled."

"Canceled?"

"Over. The theatre is closing, they can't find another space, and the union refuses to get involved – don't ask me for the details. The whole thing just fell through. George and the producer and the backers decided – oh, I don't want to talk about it any more."

But she did talk about it: the perfidy of the backers, the producer's gutlessness, the stupidity of her role in the first place, the cold-hearted horror that was the New York theatre world. "This is exactly what happened to me in Rochester, Robert. Do you remember when we all got fired when the Lyceum closed? Remember that *Pygmalion* Carlotta was supposed to star in?" She gave a bitter laugh. "And New York was going to be different. Remember how we used to say that? It's all we used to talk about. Broadway. The Great White Way. The Rialto. It'll all be different in New York City. What fools we were."

"It *is* different, May! You know it is. You'll get something else."

She just looked at me, her mouth turned down in disgust, and then she heaved a sigh and said, "I'm beat. I need to go to sleep."

She curled into a ball on the bed, her face pressed into the pillow. I hesitated a moment, then pulled the sheet over her. "I'm sorry, honey," I whispered, and went back out to the dark living room.

I stood by the window. In the light from the street lamp, I could just make out the tufts of grass, the bushes, the sidewalk beyond. At that hour, the street was silent, empty. The roar of the El going by on Third Avenue was muted. I stood there watching as if I expected to see something, but I was just calming my mind, thinking, trying to anticipate what May would be like without Florence the gun moll in her life – how deep her unhappiness would go, what I could do for her, how we would get along without her rehearsal pay: pittance though it was, we had come to depend on it for cigarettes and the occasional night out.

I stood there for a long time, until finally the sound of voices, faint then louder – two men walking down 21st Street, passing, their voices fading off – broke the spell. I turned from the window, thinking I would read for a while until I got sleepy, and that was when I heard, from the bedroom, May's voice raised in something between a scream and a gasp. She came running out of the bedroom and went into the bathroom, slamming the door. From behind it I could hear her sobbing, her voice rising to a hysterical pitch.

I rapped on the door. "May?"

The crying stopped. "I'll be out in a minute. Go away," she said. Her voice was muffled. The toilet flushed, and there was silence, one strangled sob, then water running.

"May? What's wrong? Are you all right?"

"Go away! Go away, Robert!"

I turned toward the bedroom and saw the dark stains on the floor. The bed was crimson with blood, and there was a trail to the bathroom. I had stepped in it.

"May! I'm coming in."

"No," she said, weakly, crying again. "Please don't."

I opened the door. She was sitting on the toilet, bent over, her hands clamped across her stomach, half-panting, half-sobbing. "Go away!" She was wearing only her white slip, which was bloody. A blood-soaked towel was wadded on the floor. Her thighs were striped with red, and on the floor was a shiny puddle like a dish. I thought, for a mad instant, that she had cut her wrists.

"May! What is it?"

She hunched over without speaking, her breath coming fast, and then she clutched at her abdomen with a moan. I saw her wrists: no blood. "Oh, Robert, I – Robert, please –"

"May, what is it? Are you hurt?"

"No!" She raised her head. "No, it's just – it's my monthlies."

"What? Is that all? All this blood?"

.   "It's just a little – out of control. I'm all right, I'll be all right. Robert – *please*. Please leave me."

I crouched in front of her. There was a smell – blood? Did blood smell? She didn't seem to have cut herself. How could I think she would do that? Her face was contorted in pain, the bloody fingers of one hand pressed to her mouth, the other tight against her belly. I felt a wave of nausea, but I tried to stay calm. All right, yes, it was some female thing. Frightening. Painful. Probably not serious. I took a breath and said, "May, try to stay calm. You'll be all right. I'm going to get someone. I won't be long. Just stay where you are. All right? All right, May?"

She made an inhuman, humming noise and then bit her lip, squeezing her eyes shut. I backed out of the bathroom. I considered running down to the hospital by the river, finding a doctor there, but as I climbed the stairs to the lobby I knew the best thing to do would be to get Mrs. Amalfi. She was a healer, she had said she came from a long line of healers. And she was a woman. I knew nothing about the particulars of May's monthly periods, only that she had them. What this hemorrhaging meant, I had no idea. It looked like she was bleeding to death. But she couldn't be bleeding to death. Could she? And pain, she was in pain, certainly. I had no idea what it meant. But Mrs. Amalfi would know.

I banged on the door. I could hear opera music playing softly from inside her apartment. Mrs. Amalfi hadn't been in bed; her daytime self answered the door, wearing her usual billowing robe, pants caught at the ankles, a scarf wrapped around her hair like a headband, fingers full of rings. "Why, Robert! What on earth! Come in, please."

"It's May. She's ill. Can you come? She's bleeding all over the bathroom."

Mrs. Amalfi didn't hesitate. She said, "Yes, of course," and stepped into the hall without another word, closing the door behind her.

I saw that she was barefoot. I felt I should ask, "Do you want to get your shoes –"

We were already halfway down the stairs. "I never wear shoes unless I have to, Robert. Come. Let's hurry."

I could hear May's moans when we got to the door. Mrs. Amalfi went directly to the bathroom, walking with her bare feet through the blood on the floor, and I heard her say, "My God, is it over then?" May made an inarticulate response. Mrs. Amalfi turned to me where I stood in the hallway. "Robert, I want you to leave us alone. This is something between women. You can do no good. Please – go outside. Wait on the steps. Or go to up to my apartment, if you like. Listen to *Rigoletto*. Have a cup of tea."

"But what is it? Is she all right?"

"She's fine. Just leave us alone. Half an hour. I will help her, Robert." I hesitated, but Mrs. Amalfi put her hand on my arm and pushed a little. "Please. It will be easier for her if you aren't here."

I would have liked a drink. At least, I needed a cigarette. I hadn't brought them with me, so I walked down to the cigar store

on the corner. He was just closing up, but he sold me a pack of
Luckies. Then I sat down on the front steps and lit up. I realized I
was shaking, and I took deep breaths until I steadied. I had to
admit to myself that I was glad to turn the situation, whatever it
was, over to Mrs. Amalfi. Maybe the disappointment over the
play's cancellation had brought this on, and it seemed worse only
because it happened when she was in bed. The white sheets, the
white slip. It looked more serious than it was, no doubt. *Women*, I
thought: how heroic and brave they seemed, with their
complicated biologies, their endurance of pain. That sudden
onslaught of blood – how she would have felt it warm on her legs,
how she must have awakened in horror, her stomach cramping. I
had the fleeting, selfish thought: *I'm glad I wasn't in the bed when it
happened.*

I remembered when my sister Joan first started bleeding. A
Saturday morning, my parents and I at breakfast, and Joan
coming downstairs, fear on her face, and my mother hustling her
into the bathroom. There was a big splotch of blood on the back of
her nightgown. She was thirteen, I was about ten. My father saw
my confusion and said, man to man, "It's all right, Robert. It's
what women do. They bleed so they can have babies. Didn't you
know that? Cleans out their systems." Then he winked and put an
arm across my shoulders. "Be glad you were born a man, son." It
seemed a lesser thing, being male – so straightforward, so simple,
no mystery to it. But yes, I was glad. I was still there when my
mother and Joan emerged. My sister was red-eyed and pale, but
she was smiling. She looked proud of herself. "Be nice to her!" my
mother said sternly.

It was considerably more than half an hour when Mrs. Amalfi
emerged. She looked unruffled, her scarf still tied neatly around
her hair, her makeup intact. She touched my shoulder
reassuringly. "She's all right, Robert. She's back in bed, everything

is cleaned up. She is dozing. I went up and got her a small potion."

"The sheets –"

"I left them soaking in the bathtub. And I turned the mattress on the bed. It seemed the best thing to do. There wasn't that much blood, really. I think I took care of everything. I scrubbed what I could. And I found some clean sheets."

"She's all right?"

"Yes. She is perfectly well."

"Mrs. Amalfi – how can I thank you?"

She waved her hand. "She needs to rest. See that she takes things slowly for a few days."

"Can I go in?"

"Of course, of course!"

I stood up and took a last drag on my cigarette. "What – what was it? I mean, what happened?"

Mrs. Amalfi's eyes were like a bird's – alert, wary. "It was just a female problem. One of those things. It happens. But she's all right, I promise you that." She hesitated. "You love her, don't you, Robert?"

"I do," I said, and it was true, but as I spoke I knew it was also true that I didn't want to return to her quite yet. I wasn't ready for it. Maybe I was even frightened of her, or of what she might say: from the depths of my soul, I didn't want to know the details of what had happened to her – the sobbing, the bleeding. If I could have found an excuse to take one of my marathon walks, I would have.

Mrs. Amalfi widened her eyes. "You should go out for a whiskey," she said. "Go down to – what is it, that dark little bar on Irving Place? You've had a difficult evening, Robert. It will help you sleep." She smiled. "Or would you prefer one of my potions instead?"

"No, maybe I'll do that. Go down and have a whiskey. But – can I leave her alone, do you think?"

"Your wife will be all right. She's nearly asleep, she'll be peacefully dreaming by the time you return." Her smile expanded. "Go drink and be among men, Robert. Those uncomplicated creatures. It will do you good."

I laughed at the echo of my father – that, and the giddy relief of not having to return yet to May and the apartment – and Mrs. Amalfi laughed with me. I clasped both her hands. "I don't know what we would have done if you hadn't been there to help."

Her smile faded, and we stood looking at each other. "Frankly, I don't either, Robert. But I owed you a favor, you know."

I walked down Irving Place to Pete's Tavern, a noisy neighborhood bar full of workingmen from the tenements by the river – the Slavs, the Armenians, the Irish. I'd heard that writers hung out there, too, and actors and artists from Gramercy Park. I didn't frequent Pete's. I had gotten to know a few people in the neighborhood – people I could chat with if I ran into them at Stein's Hardware or the Chinese laundry. I looked in at Pete's from time to time, but I never saw a familiar face, and it seemed that everyone in there knew each other. I wasn't the type who could walk into a strange place alone with any confidence. Orson would, I imagined. He'd smile his easy smile and talk to everyone, anyone, and they would be glad he did. As I went through the door into the smoke and noise, I wished I'd gone up and dragged him down there with me. I half expected to see him perched on a bar stool, or holding court in one of the wooden booths against the wall.

Orson wasn't there, of course: it was hard to imagine Orson doing much bar-hopping on his three dollars a week. A few men looked up at me, the bartender nodded, but no one paid me much attention. I stood at the bar and drank a whiskey, quickly, in three gulps, then sipped at another. The whiskey warmed me – I could feel the sweat on my forehead – but it was a good warmth, the kind of warmth that came over me often in the city where I knew almost no one but where the streets, the shops, the bars, the park benches were full of people like me who, somehow, escaped the prison of their lives simply by being there. I liked being in that crowded bar, full of laughter and light. *Life,* I thought.

The two men standing next to me – both burly, bald, foreign – were having an animated discussion in a language I didn't recognize. As I was finishing my second drink, one of them punched me lightly on the arm. "And you, my young friend? What do you think?" His voice was deeply accented, and he was very drunk. "Or don't you speak Polish?" he asked, swaying slightly. I couldn't tell if he was being belligerent or friendly.

"I don't."

"Well. Russian? Do you speak Russian?"

"*Nyet,*" I said. "I don't speak it."

He regarded me for a second with blank blue eyes, and then he burst into laughter. "Ha ha! Is very good. *Nyet,* I do not speak Russian. Very funny!" Unsteadily, he leaned close to me; I could see the big open pores on his nose, his stiff blond eyelashes. "I will say just one more thing, and I will say it for you in English. All is well, my friend." He raised his glass and drained it. "Do you hear what I'm telling you? All is well! You have my word on that."

I emptied my own glass. "*Da,*" I said, which I knew meant either *yes* or *thank you,* and he wrung my hand and said something I didn't understand. Whatever it was, it seemed a good omen. His friend clapped me on the shoulder, and they both stood there beaming at me. I wondered if I was supposed to buy them a drink, but I was out of money, and I was feeling my two whiskeys, and so I smiled and nodded and left.

Back at the apartment, I could see that the bathroom was spotless, cleaner than it had been before the blood. The floor, I knew, had been especially filthy, filmed with dust and spilled powder and toenail clippings. It embarrassed me that Mrs. Amalfi had cleaned our bathroom, changed the sheets, seen my wife naked and bleeding and helped her clean herself. The sheets were soaking in the tub, the water pink, and I knew I would have to wash them out, somehow, in the morning, get the stains out, and then somehow dry them. I sighed, suddenly weary, and then I turned out all the lights and, gingerly, got into bed beside May as quietly as I could. She was asleep, but she awoke abruptly and said, "Oh, Robert, it's you." She wore a clean nightgown, and her hair was combed back, still damp, off her face. She looked older, somehow, and in the dimness she looked very pale. She raised up on her elbows, scrutinizing my face. "Are you okay?"

"Yes. I went down the street and had a couple of drinks."

"You must have been so worried. I'm sorry I was hysterical. It was nothing, and it's over now."

"Yes, I know."

"And she told you I'm all right? Mrs. Amalfi? She explained?"

"More or less."

"I'm sorry I was so –" She gestured, looking helpless. "She was very kind to me."

"Yes, she's a very nice woman," I said. "But now go to sleep." I held her for a moment. She felt frail and boneless. I had a sudden vision of her as an old woman, ill, with me taking care of her. I laid her back down on the bed and tucked the clean sheets around her. I kissed her forehead. She smelled like herself again: like shampoo and soap and, very lightly, of sweat

"I met a guy in this bar, May," I said softly. "And you know what he told me? He said not to worry, all is well. As if he knew me. Isn't that odd? That he would say that to me on this particular night?" The whiskey, May in my arms, the end of the crisis – all this made what I said seem like a truth that had long been hidden from me. Of course: all was well, and how could I have doubted it?

"All is well," I repeated. "Don't you think, May?" But she was asleep in my arms.

■ ■ ■

All was not well, of course, and later when I thought of that peaceful moment when I tucked May in and kissed her I felt ridiculous. Things changed between us completely after that night, as if May's bloody experience in the bathroom were some rite of passage that took her away from me, sent her out into the world on a quest from which I was excluded.

She felt better in a day or two, her color returned along with her languid energy, and she began to be out more nights than she was home. She went drinking with Nathan, with Lois, with God knows who else. Actors. Dancers. Set designers. Second-raters who couldn't find work. When she was home, she lay around the house dozing, reading magazines, polishing her nails, but she spent most afternoons at Lois's place – doing what, I had no idea. Bitching, feeling sorry for themselves. She would go to tryouts, she said. She would look for work. She would do this, do that, do *something* – but not quite yet. She had to recover. She was completely demoralized. It was too hot, anyway. And nothing ever happened in the summer.

I sensed that something had happened to her – something beyond the bleeding episode, beyond the play being canceled – and I began watching her closely to try to comprehend what it could be. She had a habit of staring at nothing, with a look on her face as if she'd just lost her best friend. Well, she had, in a way, but when I asked her if she was still stewing over Carlotta's bad behavior she laughed and said, "Oh, who can stay mad at

Carlotta? No, I'm meeting her tomorrow for lunch at the Automat. Her treat – or so she says."

"Let's hope so," I said, meaning it mostly as a wry comment on Carlotta but also, partly, as a reminder to May that we were hard up.

But she didn't seem to hear me. "I'll tell you something, Robert," she said. "I have this feeling that Hollywood is going to chew Mickey up and turn him into dogfood. I feel bad for them both – they're so full of optimism, making plans. . . ." Her voice trailed away. "Oh yes," she added. "I suppose I'm a bit jealous. But I meant what I said. It's the theatre that's in my blood. I don't give two cents for the movies." She spoke almost absently, as if saying all this was somehow expected of her but her mind was elsewhere. I studied her face – she was gazing at a patch of damp on the wallpaper – and finally she looked at me with a small frozen smile. "Robert, you look so glum. Isn't your new play going well?"

It was the first time she had asked me about it in – how long? Months? "Yes, it is, in fact," I said. "It's coming along nicely."

She cocked her head on one side and looked at me curiously. "You never have what they call writer's block, do you? Never have any trouble getting into it. Shutting out your real life to work on your made-up one."

"No, I don't."

"Well, that's admirable," she said.

We looked at each other silently for a few seconds. "Thank you."

"Not everyone could manage that."

"Probably not."

"Heard from that agent yet? That second guy?"

"May, I would tell you if I'd heard from him! No, I haven't heard a goddam thing, for Christ's sake."

"Just asking. You don't have to swear at me."

Another short silence fell. I looked at her white arm resting on the arm of the couch, her perfect red nails, the way her bright hair fell around her shoulders, and in that brief moment I was sick of May, sick of her moods and her coolness and her secrets. I had a sudden longing to be elsewhere: to be, for example, with Albert and Babette in the hotel room that was the setting for Act One of *Afternoon Coffee*. It was a kind of homesickness, I thought, and the image made me smile.

"What's so comical?"

"Nothing – just a thought."

She shifted impatiently on the couch, crossing her legs, tapping her nails on the upholstery. "Well, don't you want to read me some of it?"

"I don't think so," I said. "It's not really at that stage."

She shrugged. "Have it your way," she said, and went back to looking at the water stain.

"Oh, May," I said, and went over to sit beside her. "Let's not bicker, honey."

She was stiff at first, with the chilly smile, but she warmed up a little and took my hand. "I'm sorry. Were we bickering?"

"We were."

"It's me. I'm in a mood. Pay no attention to me. I imagine it'll all be over soon, anyway."

I didn't know what she was talking about, and I didn't ask. Her cheek was wet when I kissed it.

FIVE

Carlotta and Mickey left early in September. We took them out for a farewell evening: dinner and a bottle of wine at the Palm Room – nearly a week's pay worth of May and Carlotta's boozy, weepy nostalgia, most of which seemed fabricated for the occasion: two actresses miming melancholy, and not very well, and the whole scene complicated by the closing of May's play, which none of us mentioned. I wasn't sorry to see them go. I somehow fancied that May and I would be closer without Carlotta in town.

That wasn't what happened. If anything, May was even more distant as the summer moved into autumn – more wrapped up in her theatre friends and their grievances, though I could see her trying to be kind, trying not to let her preoccupations show. My own life, I felt, was in a kind of limbo. I spent a lot of time with the new play, and there were days when it seemed that it was my play that was real and my life a bunch of people pretending things up on some stage, but it was going very slowly.

Every day I checked the mail, hoping for a letter from Samuel Harper saying he had found a home for *Fish out of Water* on Broadway or some up-and-coming little theatre in the Village. *Don't miss the witty, rollicking comedy by Robert Sinclair that's taking the town by storm.* I knew this was a pipe dream – the equivalent of the once-in-a-lifetime break like Mickey Kennedy's. And yet I lived on my fantasy. I imagined myself going to the mailbox, pulling out the letter and carrying it down to the apartment – no unseemly haste, always expecting rejection – and slitting it open with a kitchen knife. The letter would begin: *Dear Mr. Sinclair, I am pleased to inform you that . . .*

I had a vague idea that, in the treacherous and complex workings of fate, imagining this scene automatically rendered it impossible. And yet I couldn't keep it out of my head. Standing on the top rung of Mr. Gant's rickety wooden ladder, slapping cream-colored paint onto the plaster walls, I would replay it endlessly, and always with hope, though I knew how wafer-thin was the chance that this dream would ever become reality.

This did not, however, keep me from enjoying what I was doing. The painting was going well, the hallways were looking at worst spiffy and at best rather elegant. Orson and I had evolved a wordless, companionable way of working, and I relished those hot mornings, me on my ladder, Orson on his, each of us with his can of paint, his thick brush. From time to time, Orson would call over to me, "So Robert, my lad! What do you think?" And I would reply, "Orson, old fellow! It's going quite swimmingly, don't you agree?" And we would chuckle, and continue. At the moment when our two paintbrushes would meet, when an entire wall, or half a stairwell, had been covered, we would look at each other, occasionally shake hands, and one of us would say, "Enough, wouldn't you say, old man?" Then we would quit – me to work on my play, Orson to clean the brushes and then – well, I never knew what.

Orson was still an enigma to me – a puzzle I would have liked to crack. I tried to get closer to him, still feeling the shreds of that instinctive kinship I'd felt the first day I met him. Occasionally, I invited him down to my cool, closed-in apartment at lunchtime. It pleased me to feed Orson when I could because I knew he must be desperately hard up. He sat at the table across from me in May's chair looking around the place curiously but never commenting. Once I saw him pick up a bottle of May's nail polish, an intense fuschia, from the kitchen table where she had left it, and study it with a funny smile on his face. I couldn't help wondering what he thought of our cozy domestic messes, the glimpse of rumpled covers through the bedroom door, May's high-heeled pumps flung in a corner of the kitchen – if he envied me what I had or was glad to be a bachelor, free of it all, solitary in his garret.

We'd have a quick sandwich and talk about the job, about the state of the country, about people we knew around the neighborhood – who was doing well, who had found work. Someone's furniture was repossessed. The ragman died, and his horse sold for meat. Orson always made sure to ask, politely, how my play was coming along. Occasionally he'd tell me some small anecdote about his own life – nothing really personal, just something an old friend had done, or a tremendous hangover he'd once had, or a train trip he'd taken. These confidences often sounded invented, and I got so that I could see the lie coming, the way you hear a violinist tune his instrument before he plays – something in his tone of voice, the squint to his eyes. The phenomenon was intriguing. I wondered why he bothered with his pointless lies, what he got out of them, but I always wanted to hear more of what he had to say, even if it was false.

On nights when May wasn't home, I sometimes went up to his room, but Orson was out, or maybe asleep; once or twice, I sensed that he was there, that behind the door he was keeping desperately quiet, holding his breath until I went away: I could sense that vacuum, that refusal. The door didn't lock, and I could have turned the knob and gone in, but, though I was tempted to do so, in the end I respected Orson's privacy and just went back down the spiral staircase, wishing I had a friend in New York, wishing I knew some of the men down at Pete's Tavern, or anywhere. I stuck my head in once or twice, hoping to spot my Polish friends, but I never did. I thought sometimes about strolling down to Bedford Street and paying a call on Verna Quiller – big, sloppy Verna with her kind heart and corn liquor. But I knew May would hate that, so I never did. I was thankful I always had the play to turn to.

One evening in September, I caught May before she went out. She was wearing the tarty red-print cotton dress I had never liked, her hair pulled back with combs. As she picked up her purse and slung it over her shoulder, I went to the door and stood there. "May," I said, feeling faintly absurd. We hadn't talked about anything of substance in so long that it seemed artificial.

"What is it, Robert?" she asked wearily. "I'm late as it is."

"I wish you would stay home tonight, so we can talk."

"Talk? Talk about what? Paint and turpentine? Or my failures in the New York theatre world? Or yours?"

I decided to ignore this. "Just talk, May. About anything. I don't care. I never see you."

She looked at me as if I were someone she hardly knew – a man accosting her on the street. I almost expected her to say, "Leave me alone, buster, or I'll call a cop." Instead she sighed impatiently and said, "Oh Robert." But then her face softened. She closed her eyes wearily, opened them again. She touched my arm. "I know," she said. "Yes. We should talk. But not tonight. Please. I'm sorry I've been so –" She waved her hand helplessly. "I know how I've been," she said. "I hope you'll forgive me. I'm guess I'm going through a bad patch."

"But the bad patch has gone on so long."

"I know, I know. What can I say besides I'm sorry?"

"It's just that I miss you."

She looked at me with a reluctant little smile. "You do?"

"I do." I put my arms around her, kissed her hair. She was pliant in my arms, she smelled sweet. I had almost forgotten how lovable she could be. I would have liked to lead her to the bedroom and do what we hadn't done in so long: just thinking of it, of her bending her head and taking me in her mouth, of her soft yellow hair like silk against my skin, I felt the trembling of my erection. She felt it too, and pulled away. I knew I shouldn't force things, and I only kissed her lightly on the cheek and let her go. "Don't be too late. I worry."

"I'll try. I'm going down to Mori's with Nancy and Tom and a few other people. It's kind of an unofficial meeting. We're all trying to figure out what to do next, how to get our lives back on track."

"Good," I said. "I like the sound of that, May."

She was fluffing up her hair in the mirror, taking out the combs and putting them in again, but she turned and looked at me, frowning. "I know you're not crazy about my friends, but do you want to come with me?"

I said no, as I always did, as she knew I would. *That's why she asked*: the words ran through my head, but that knowledge was nothing new. She wanted that part of her life to herself, just as I had the world of my play.

Listening to May's high heels go tapping down 21st Street, I was reminded of that odd night when we tried to do it, tried and failed to get me inside her. Just recalling it made my erection wilt, and I thought instead of her mouth, her tongue, the sweet easiness of our old lovemaking, until it came back and I had to go into the bedroom and masturbate. When I was done, I lay there afterward in a kind of glow, almost as if she had been with me, done it to me herself.

I dozed off. When I woke, my mind was cleared, and I sat down at the kitchen table with *Afternoon Coffee*. I had just begun a draft of Act Two, and it had stopped going well. Lenore, the character based on an eccentric elderly aunt of mine, dead for years, was both too close to her and too vague – a character no one but me could appreciate. It was a small part, but a crucial one, and I worked on Lenore's scene with Albert, where they talk about Babette and Tony, until, when I looked up, the window was dark, I realized I was starving, and the clock said past eleven.

I read over what I had written and decided it would do for the moment. I'd tinker with it tomorrow. I made myself a sandwich and wolfed it down with a glass of milk. Then I went outside. The air was warm and dry, a perfect night. The idea came to me that it might be good not to be home when May got there, not to have it look as if I'd waited up for her, like my father's old dog. Or as if I didn't trust her. Maybe even let her think I had somewhere to go, too – friends to be with. I'll take a walk, I thought. And then I decided, instead, to go up and see if Orson was awake, maybe we could go out somewhere for a beer. We could go to Pete's: my Polish friends might be there and would greet me with laughter and handshakes, and I would buy a round for the four of us.

When I knocked, Orson's voice said, "Hello?"

"It's me, Orson. Robert. I hope I'm not disturbing you."

"No – no. Of course not."

He opened the door. "Hello, old man. Come on in." He was smiling, the lamp was on behind him, and he was stark naked. For a moment he was like a painting – some golden Renaissance thing, the light like a halo.

That image, and his nakedness, made me laugh. "Orson, I hope I'm not interrupting – I mean – if you were asleep –"

"No, no – just trying to stay cool. Come in and sit down while I get dressed."

The room was very warm. I became aware that I stank faintly of sex, my own sex – I hadn't bathed before I left – and I wondered if Orson could smell it. I sat on edge of the bed while

Orson took a pair of trousers – his old white ones – from a hook on the wall. He was standing just outside the circle of lamp light, and his wiry body shone in the dimness. There was a deep tan on his arms and on his neck and face; the rest of him was very pale. I looked at his body, his dangling penis, and then away, studying the pile of books on the windowsill, remembering the moment I had read aloud from *Gatsby*, the exact words I had read, about the music and the moths and the stars. I was aware of Orson stepping into the trousers and then straightening up, buttoning them, fastening a belt. "What are you up to at this hour of the night, Robert?" he asked, moving into the light. "Out for one of your famous midnight hikes?"

I sensed something different about Orson – the slightest clumsiness to his speech, a loose quality in his smile. It occurred to me suddenly that he was a little drunk. I had never seen him tight before, and I was astonished. I changed my mind about offering to buy him a beer. "I'm thinking about taking one. It's a beautiful clear night. But I thought I'd just stop in for a second and say hello before I do."

"I'm glad you did, Robert. Always glad to see you. And especially tonight." He stood before me, shirtless, barefoot, rubbing his hand across his chest and up to his neck. "I've been wanting to ask you something."

"Ask away," I said. I leaned back on the bed, propped on my elbows. I wanted to look at ease because I didn't feel at ease, not at all. Orson seemed very odd – not just drunk but alien, almost menacing. His smile was too bright; when it disappeared his face was too blank. And his coming to the door naked was really more strange than funny; it was almost as if he'd had someone in the room with him who had ducked into a closet when I knocked. But there was no closet. There was no place at all where anyone could hide. I had a sudden mad vision of his guest jumping out the window, or being pushed.

Orson said, "I wondered if we might talk about a pay raise."

"A raise?" I stared at him. "I see. Well."

"You know –" Orson pulled his one chair over to the bed and sat on it, backwards, his arms folded across the top. "I do most of the work around the place. Don't I? And what I don't do I supervise. I've taught you everything you know, Robert."

This was true. It was impossible to dispute. What I did dispute was that it meant Orson should make more money. I had gotten the job, after all. I had talked my way into it, got Gant to hire me, and then I had hired Orson. I remembered my whimsical vision of the Russian dolls. Orson was my employee, and I didn't see why I should give him a raise any more than Gant should give me one. We were doing our jobs.

"What did you have in mind?"

Orson smiled. "I think I should have half of what you get."

I wasn't sure I'd heard right. "Half?"

"Half of your twelve. I think I should get six a week, considering what I do here."

I laughed. "I thought you were going to ask for an extra fifty cents, Orson! At most a dollar. You're asking me to double your salary, which is already a dollar more than I had planned to pay you – not that you haven't been worth it – and to cut mine down by another third." I sat up, taut with anger. "That's ridiculous."

Orson shrugged. "Call it what you like. That's what I want."

"I'm sorry," I said shortly. "It's out of the question."

He sat there looking at me for a long moment, and then he said, finally, "Well, then, I don't know, Robert, old man. I may have to tender my resignation."

Frustration rose up in me. "You're crazy, Orson! You need this job, and I need you. What's the problem? Hasn't everything has been going along pretty smoothly?"

Orson laughed. "Smoothly for you, maybe, Robert. Things have been going beautifully for management, but labor – well, that's what's wrong with this country, isn't it? The old story. The little guy can't get a break."

I stared at him. "Orson – *I'm* the little guy! Are you equating me with Gant? Gant could buy and sell us both with the money he throws away in a week, and you know it. I'm supporting two people on my salary, plus you. And frankly, I don't think I owe you one damned dime more than you're getting."

This was bravado. I knew he had a point. I knew he worked harder than I did. I knew I was dead without him. But I also knew that May and I couldn't have lived on anything less than what I earned. It was hard enough to manage on that nine dollars. I'd begun to think that if May didn't find work soon I'd have to look for a second job. I had run into a guy who claimed that selling soap door to door he made five dollars in just a few days, and I was ready to look into it myself. I could imagine May's wrath if I told her I was giving Orson a raise.

Orson smiled and looked at me a minute. Then he said, "How about a compromise? A dollar raise and the use of your pretty wife a couple of nights a week."

I said, "Orson, you're drunk. I'm going to pretend you didn't say that."

"Then maybe I should say it again, slowly and soberly. How about a dollar raise and the use of your wife –"

I rose up and hit him before he finished. I had done some boxing in college; I wasn't very good, but I knew a few things, and I hadn't forgotten them. My fist caught him square across the mouth, his teeth grazing the back of my hand. He went backwards, falling off the chair, then looked at me from the floor, grinning, his lip bloody. He stood up slowly, righted the chair, touched his lip. "Well, I'll be damned," he said, and laughed. "What a lot of fuss over nothing. What if I told you I've already got the use of your wife? Sweet little blond May. Tight as a keyhole. Not that the extra money wouldn't be nice too."

I barely let him finish. I lunged forward and hit him again, but he was ready for me. He dodged aside, then caught me by the arm with one hand and sank a punch into my gut with the other. It wasn't much of a punch, and I pulled away and hit him again in the jaw.

It was hot and close in that little room, and by this time we were both sweating hard, grunting with the effort. Instinctively, we moved toward the door. Orson continued to smile. His white, bare chest shone with sweat. "Oh, Robert," he said, shaking his head. "Is this the end of a beautiful friendship? Am I going to have to buddy up with Mr. Gant instead? Have a chat with him about this and that?"

I faced him, panting, and felt the threat of tears sting my eyes. "What's wrong with you, Orson? What in hell are you trying to do?"

"You don't believe me, do you? About May? You can't believe that something in your perfect little life is going wrong, can you? Your perfect fucking life." He spread his hands, still grinning his sloppy, drunken grin. "It's the way of the world, old man. The masses rise up, they want more money, they demand their rights, they seize their oppressors' women."

"You're a liar."

"I lie about a lot of things, but I'm not lying about May."

It was his saying her name that convinced me he was telling the truth. He had always referred to her as *your wife* before, as if he could barely remember what her name was; now the way he called her *May*, more than once, intimately, with familiarity, as if he liked saying it, made it easy to imagine him saying it in bed with her – on this filthy old mattress, in this stuffy room.

"You son of a bitch," I said. I went for him again, and we had a brief, clumsy fight. I hit him once more in the jaw, he connected with my left eye – again not very hard but enough to hurt like hell, and to stagger me. Before I could get to him, he punched me again in the stomach, knocking the wind out of me. Then I lit into him, blind to my own pain. I got close and began hitting him – twice, three times. He couldn't summon the strength, or the coordination, to hit me again. Up close, I could smell the whiskey on his breath. We grappled in the doorway – a strange, weak, half-hearted fight – and then I hauled back and, one last time, landed a hard right to the side of his face.

He wobbled and fell, heavily, into the hall and backwards, down the spiral staircase to the marble landing. And lay crumpled at the bottom.

I went down the steps after him. He was unmoving except for a slow slither of blood that seeped from the back of his head, livid red on the white marble. For a few disoriented seconds, I thought of May's blood on the bathroom floor as if this was a puzzle I was supposed to solve. Then I knelt beside Orson.

He lay on his side, his head twisted around so that his eyes, if they had been open, would have looked straight up. He must have hit his head on the sharp projecting side of the bottom step. The cut, or whatever it was, was on the back of his head: all I could see was his still face, the fine auburn hair lank across his forehead, his half-open lips red with blood, blood on his teeth, barely visible. He looked all wrong, too pale, too quiet, with his flat brown nipples, his feet with the pink soles turned up. His grimy white trousers, his cracked leather belt. I could never have imagined that he would be such an inept fighter, such a helpless drunk. It was as if during our crazy fight he had been someone else, a man I didn't know. And yet of course it was Orson: there were the scars across the back of his hand, shining silver against his tan.

I touched his shoulder, thinking: *he's faking, these things do not happen*. The stink of whiskey was very strong. In a low voice, I said, "Orson? Orson? Can you hear me?"

I reached around and put my palm on his naked chest, to feel for a heartbeat against the sparse hairs there. His skin was wet and slippery, and I pulled my hand away with a sudden desire to retch. I panicked then, left him there and ran down the stairs, not knowing where I was going or what to do. I had the idea that I would find Mrs. Amalfi, but when I reached the ground floor and went out the front door to look up at her windows I couldn't see a light. The Sleep Specialist was asleep. Of course. It was after midnight. Nor was there a light in my apartment: did that mean May was home and had gone to bed, or that she hadn't yet come in?

I didn't want to know. My heart was racing, I was burning with energy. I kept walking, automatically, my usual route: down the street and around the corner, and then uptown on Second Avenue. I walked fast, eating up the blocks, looking at the city at night, a tall gray fortress charged with spots of gold. No stars were visible, the moon was just a sliver on the horizon, and the sky was an unnatural mauve color fading out to deep blue over the river somewhere. I felt, suddenly, vividly, a tiny but vital part of it all, one more element in the cityscape, of no more importance – and no less – than a bench, the lights of the skyscrapers ahead of me, the looming skeleton of the El I could glimpse on Third Avenue to the west.

A breeze came up, my skin cooled, and what had just happened – whatever it was – receded as I walked: the words, the fight, the blood. It was a dream, a nightmare, from which the quiet night was waking me. My heartbeat slowed, I calmed down. My thoughts eased away from the encounter with Orson and I tried to focus on Lenore's scene with Albert. It was still giving me trouble, the words wouldn't come, and I had simply skipped it and gone on to the next act, but it was what I always came back to at these odd moments, and I knew I would eventually find the key to it as

I walked, or brushed my teeth, or stood in a store waiting to buy a pint of milk.

At first I was so deep in thought that I paid no attention to anyone else on the street, but as I strode up the avenue I could sense that the few people I met at that late hour – working people on the graveyard shift, the usual dazed-looking vagrants – gave me a wide berth. It finally occurred to me that my shirt was bloody and my left eye was probably turning purple. I ran my fingers through my hair and tucked in my filthy shirt, and tried to compose my face into a pleasant, noncommittal expression. But when I got up into the East 40s, walking in the shadow of Tudor City, I stopped suddenly in the dark. My eye was throbbing, and Albert's dialogue with Lenore turned to ashes in my brain. I looked down at the gutter and saw what looked like the body of a dead rat. A wave of horror went through me. *I've killed a man,* I thought. *I've killed him. He was lying there dead.* I could see the blood, oozing silently across the floor like a snake. I had to turn back. Was I crazy? Where was I going, what did I think I was doing?

I ran the twenty-five blocks back to the Alhambra Gardens, and when I got there I ran up the five flights to the spiral staircase.

Orson was gone. The blood was gone, the floor wiped clean. I touched the side of the metal step where his head must have hit. It was sharp enough, but my finger came away bloodless. I touched the floor. It was not even wet. There was no sound but my own harsh breathing.

I went up the staircase to his room. The door was closed, but it opened when I turned the knob – reluctantly, holding my breath, braced for whatever I might find. The room looked perfectly normal; Orson wasn't in it. Absurdly, I went to the window and looked out. What did I expect? To see Orson hanging by his fingertips from the sill? I saw nothing, of course, but the water tower across the way, and beyond it the stumpy chimneys, the rising moon, the bruised sky. From the river came three hollow blasts from some passing ship – a desolate sound in the darkness.

I leaned my forehead against the dusty window pane, trying to think. There was nothing to think. I had killed Orson. Or I hadn't. He had cleaned himself up and gone away. Or had been taken away. Or was still there, lying in a pool of blood and in my madness and distraction I hadn't seen him. I rushed back to the hall, looked down the staircase. A faint smell of whiskey lingered, my shirt was bloody, and when I touched my eye a tremor of pain beat in my head. But there was no body lying on the floor.

I remembered what Mrs. Amalfi said when we ran into Orson after the rainstorm: *Orson Price is a liar. Orson Price is never to be trusted*

I went downstairs. May's little clock said 1:45 in the morning. May wasn't home. My mind blank, I fell into bed without even taking off my shirt, and was instantly asleep.

■ ■ ■

I awoke at dawn, when a faint light made its way through the low window. For one fragile moment I remembered nothing. I only knew that things were different, wrong – things were bad. I lay there remembering May and her bloody thighs and the blood on the floor, and then I became aware that my head was throbbing, and it all came back to me. *Orson, Orson.* I knew that my eye was blackened, and that May wasn't lying beside me in bed, and that I was in some kind of trouble that would reveal itself in the dreadful course of the day to come.

With difficulty, I hauled my sore body out of bed and used the bathroom. Then I looked in the mirror: there was my haggard face, my swollen left eyelid with its nebula of purple and red, the eye itself a sliver peering out in horror. The other eye looked large and innocent, like a blameless child forced to witness some unspeakable tragedy. My lip was cut, caked with a scab of blood – I didn't remember that happening – and I had a pain in my gut that, I felt, needed hot coffee.

I went into the kitchenette, but there was no coffee. It was while I was looking through the cupboards for it, for something – I thought if I didn't have food, or something to drink, I would keel over – that I noticed how bare the apartment was. At first it didn't register: it was only an absence, a strange sensation of spaciousness in that cramped place. Then I realized that May's bottles of nail polish weren't on the kitchen table where I was always nagging her to get them off. Her pink mules were gone from where she usually kicked them. The bathroom, I now became aware, no longer held her lipsticks and perfume bottles and battery of brushes and powders that were usually strewn across the top of the toilet and on the shelf above the sink. I went to the closet: empty space, a tangle of wire hangers. All May's things were gone and – I took this in slowly, with a feeling of unspeakable strangeness and dread – so were mine. My heavy overcoat was there, way in back, and the gray wool suit I had bought one winter in Cambridge, but my white linen suit was missing, and the shirts that had been my father's. My Panama hat was gone from its hook, my ties from the wooden rack, my alligator belt that had been hanging from a nail. The dresser drawers were empty, and my father's old leather suitcase had disappeared, along with the things I had stored in it: my light wool trousers, a gabardine jacket, the blue sweater my mother had knitted for me when I went off to Harvard. I imagined the suitcase stuffed to bulging, the neatly ironed shirts crammed in any which way, the crease in my linen trousers disappearing in a mass of wrinkles, my ties a snaky mass of silk.

The only other things that were left were the denim overalls I'd bought at Stein's Hardware, the ripped, stained shirts I painted in, a pair of cuff links at the back of a drawer, my shoes and underwear, and the clothes on my back.

Everything else was gone. My wife was gone. The jade cat I'd given her was gone from the mantel, and the photo album from the bookcase. I tried to imagine her packing in a hurry – while I slept? while I was out on my frantic walk? while I was knocking Orson down the stairs? I imagined her taking a last look around – smiling? nervous? in tears? – and deciding she needed to have that cat, those photographs, that record of our meager life together. Was this meant as a final insult? A message? Or had she just, simply, wanted them?

I thought of all those weeks when Orson and I had worked at painting the hallways, each on our ladder, each absorbed in his own thoughts. While I thought about my play, was Orson thinking about my wife? And I pictured him with May – in bed, on a train, in a car, walking down the street in my white suit, my royal blue tie, my straw hat.

I sank into a chair by the kitchen table. My brain wouldn't work right. Too much had happened: more had happened to me in the last twelve hours than in the last twelve weeks. *He took my wife*, I thought stupidly, and then I groaned, put my head in my hands. I thought I might throw up. *He ran away with my wife*: in spite of the motionless body at the foot of the staircase, it sounded like the truth. He ran away with my wife, and, just for spite, he was going to tell Gant about our deal.

I had liked him. I had seen kindness in his face. I wanted to be his friend. *Your perfect little life*, he had said. *Your pretty wife. Tight as a keyhole. May*, he had said. *May.* I thought of how despite his lies and mystery I had seen Orson as a kind of hermit in his attic cave, a saint, a holy man who had come to save me. And May had been my angel, my blonde muse, my partner. They had despised me, the two of them. I was a fool.

I stood up, feeling shaky. The clock said just past six. I went back into the bathroom and brushed my teeth and sponged my face, carefully, with warm water. It woke me up. I spotted a tube of May's lipstick on the floor. When I bent to pick it up, the pain in my head was like a blow. A pair of pink garters was hanging from the doorknob, her Helena Rubenstein bubble bath on the edge of the tub. The sight of these things kindled in me a small, dry patch of anger. I tossed them all into the trash can.

I put on the workshirt with the ripped elbows and headed out the door and up the stairs. In the entrance hall, the heat hit me; sweat rolled down my back, and I could taste it above my cut lip. Already the day was sweltering. I had been going to go out and find some breakfast, but I decided on an impulse to see Mrs. Amalfi instead. I needed comfort more than I needed food. I needed advice, or – well, whatever it was I needed, I knew I was more likely to get it from Mrs. Amalfi than from Baba Neshan's.

As I turned toward the stairway, the front door opened, and Mr. Gant came in, a dark shape against the light. He was wearing his usual suit and suspenders and shiny wing-tips. He was carrying his hat – a natty straw number. He looked ugly and cool and imperturbable, as he always did, and when he saw me he said, "Ah-ha. Robert. Just the man I wanted to see."

My heart sank. I wished I wasn't wearing that particular shirt, and I tried not to think about my black eye, but even aside from such details Gant was the last person on earth I wanted to run into. Still, I managed to smile; my face, I hope, lit up, my eyes twinkled. "Well! Nice to see you so early in the morning, Mr. Gant," I said, trying for a kind of earnest jauntiness. "I'm just off to do the mopping." I made a vague, fatuous gesture. "Morning chores and all that."

Gant barked out a laugh. "The morning chores. That's rich." He shook his head admiringly, as if I'd said something witty. I stared at his yellow teeth, which were faintly marbled with brown stains. "That's really rich, Robert, considering."

"Is something wrong?" I knew the answer, of course: everything was wrong. But how wrong Gant considered things to be was what I needed to know.

"Yes, in fact something *is* wrong, Robert, and I came over so we could have a little talk about it." He pulled a cigarette pack out of his pocket. "Let's go out on the steps where it's cooler."

If anything, it was even hotter outside than it had been in the lobby, but Gant stood there a moment inhaling the air as if he were at the Jersey shore. Then he lit a cigarette. He didn't offer me one. We stood beside each other, staring at the building across the street while he smoked. The Greek sandwich man plodded by, on his way to Neshan's, I knew. I often saw him there. A cart and horse came around the corner, and the horse let out a great steaming turd, never pausing. Down at the end of the street, the pink of the sky over the river got lighter and lighter.

Gant didn't speak. Finally, I couldn't stand it any more. "So what's up, Mr. Gant?" I asked, and as I spoke I knew that all I wanted was to fling myself down somewhere and howl. I knew what was up. My wife was gone, my clothes were gone, and I still didn't know for sure what had happened, whether I had killed a man or simply been the victim of a massive betrayal, or if it was all a mistake, a farce, someone's idea of a joke. But I knew that this scene with Gant was part of the whole thing. Gant probably knew more than I did. Everyone knew more than I did. Because I knew nothing. All that was really clear to me was that the life I had been living was at an end.

"The guy in the attic," Gant said. "Your friend. Living here for nothing. Seems everybody in the damn building knew about it but me."

That was a surprise to me. People knew? Then I thought: how could they not know? Of course they knew! And no one had told.

Before I tried to figure that out, I realized that of course someone had, in fact, probably told. Who?

I didn't say anything and neither did Gant. He just smoked his cigarette for a long quiet moment while I there numbly, clenching my hands together, and when he spoke again his voice was almost kind. "This is an apartment building, Robert. Not a charity ward. When someone lives here, I need to get rent. And when I hire someone to work for me, I expect them to work. I don't expect them to sub-contract it out."

Sub-contract: it was a word I hadn't known until then, and my mind registered it quickly, almost thirstily. It was a good one to know, like *spackling*, *tenpenny nail*, *spirit level*.

Gant cocked his head over at me, holding his cigarette between two thick-nailed fingers. He wore a gold signet ring that looked cheap but probably wasn't. "Are you listening to me, Robert?"

"Yes, Mr. Gant. Yes, I am." *Lie to Gant*, Mrs. Amalfi had said. I searched my mind desperately for a lie to tell but came up with nothing. I waited until a taxi went by, then a dark blue Pontiac, then a pigeon flying low, before I said, "Well, I'm very sorry for everything."

"There's a lot to be sorry for, frankly. Your friend had a master key – am I right? We've had a few thefts. Maybe you didn't know that. I'm going to give you the benefit of the doubt. I'm a friend of your wife's family, after all. But what it comes down to is that I want you out of here by the weekend. Let's say by day after tomorrow."

Gant didn't speak again. We stood there together for maybe another minute. His cigarette smoke made its way toward me through the sluggish air. I closed my eyes and inhaled it. Then, suddenly, Gant checked his watch, clamped his hat over his sparse hair, and went down the steps. He turned toward Third Avenue. I watched him go. He never looked back. He seemed in a hurry – probably off to commit some other act of cruelty before breakfast. Two a day, get them done early.

I went down to my apartment, that dank, melancholy cave, with its dead weight of sadness. It was shabbier than ever in its bareness, in its absence of May and all her things: it seemed unreal, as if I had already left it. I should pack my books, I thought. I should go out and look for work. I should try to find out where May went – get in touch with Lois, or with her other theatre friends. I should buy a newspaper, see what's going on in the world. I should ask around the neighborhood about Orson. I should try the hospitals in the area, see if he'd been admitted.

I sat down on the couch, which smelled strongly of mildew – had it always? As if it mattered. As if anything mattered. I couldn't imagine actually doing anything. All I could see myself doing was sitting dully on the couch until Gant came in and threw me out. I knew that life was full of mysteries, composed largely of things I would never understand. That was what I got out of my walks through the night city. It was what I wrote about in a way, underneath the comedy – or so I hoped. The poetry of life, the dark pulse beneath the surface, the depths we will never sound, no matter how we try.

But when I thought of all the things I didn't know and might never know, my head began to ache. Why had May done this? How could she do it to me, who had loved her and wished her only well? When had it begun with Orson, and why? What had Orson been able to give her that I couldn't? I thought with humiliation of the blood, May's blood: it must have been a pregnancy, I thought suddenly. A miscarriage. Why couldn't I have seen that? I remembered our first night together on Aunt Myra's couch: *I'm so afraid of having a baby*, she had said, and she had shocked me by the way she wanted to make love. And yet Orson had made her pregnant. And then he had goaded me, flaunted May until I had to hit him – as if that was what he had wanted. *Tight as a keyhole.* Had he decided to hate me from that very first meeting, out on the sidewalk? Me in my good gray pants and a job, with a wife waiting inside, and Orson in his scruffy clothes on his way to take his place in that line of hopeless men at the Municipal Lodging House. Or had it come on gradually? And where was he now? Where was May?

And if all this could happen, if my life could be turned around so quickly and so completely and so far out of my understanding, then who was I?

I closed my eyes. To sleep, I thought: that was all I wanted. I needed to sleep for another six hours, six days. I needed to sleep all the sleep I had missed, all the sleep I had walked off all that summer, all the hours I had lain sleepless beside May loving her for her soft body, her jokes, her blonde hair.

But of course there was no sleep left in me – not then. I stood up and, as if in a dream, I began to move around the apartment. I gathered the pages of my manuscript, along with my notebook and some odd bits of paper full of scrawled jottings. I crammed them into the typewriter case along with my typewriter and snapped down the lid. Then I filled a big paper sack with a few personal things – comb and toothbrush and razor, a change of underwear, my clean overalls, and the cufflinks Orson had overlooked: a pair of fourteen-karat gold masks, comedy and tragedy, that had been a birthday gift from Jasper.

When I was packed, I looked around the apartment. There was nothing there I regretted, nothing I needed. The place was almost as impersonal as it had been when we moved in. May's three-way mirror, the dying philodendron plant, the ugly napkin holder she bought at Woolworth's, my heavy suit and the winter overcoat I'd always disliked – I wouldn't be sorry to leave any of that behind.

Only my books. I stood before the maple bookcase, looking at the titles on the spines. *I'll take one*, I thought. I remembered the old desert island game. What would you take? What book? What possession? What girl? What food? I took the book I had always chosen: the big blue complete Shakespeare. I thought of Mr. Greenleaf, my Shakespeare professor freshman year, and of the class when we read parts of *Hamlet* aloud, and how I said to Mr. Greenleaf afterward, "I know this is going to sound a bit pompous and presumptuous, sir, but I just realized I have to write plays." He looked at me thoughtfully and said, "It doesn't sound either of those things to me, Robert. You've definitely got a way with words on the page. I'd be willing to bet you could be darned good at it." I had fallen asleep for weeks afterward with those words in my head. I joined the Drama Club, saw two of my one-actors produced, even began to think about graduate school at Yale – the best program around, Mr. Greenleaf said. Then my father died and I left Harvard and here I was.

I added the Shakespeare to the junk in my bag. There was room for one more, and almost without thinking about it I took a second book and stuffed it in: *The Great Gatsby*. I put on my paint-spattered cap, left the keys to the building on the table, picked up my typewriter in one hand and the bag in the other. Then I went up the stairs and across the marble lobby, past the palms and the metal vines of the newel post, and out the front door.

SIX

I had a total of seven dollars in my pocket, and I needed some breakfast. After the scene with Gant, I couldn't face Mrs. Amalfi: too much like getting beaten up in the playground and going home to my mother to be consoled. I decided to squander fifteen cents on Turkish eggs and rolls at Baba Neshan's and then see about finding work somewhere, but as I was turning in at the door of the restaurant – as Hari the counterman looked up and waved hello at me – it became clear to me that what I had to do was get out of the neighborhood. I couldn't risk encountering Mr. Gant again, and I didn't want to run into Mrs. Amalfi. I didn't want to see any of the Alhambra tenants or old Mr. Stein or the woman who sold apples on the corner every afternoon. I couldn't even bear Hari's friendly good cheer. I gave him an awkward wave and a little smile, as if I'd forgotten something, and went back down the avenue, walking rapidly past my corner and continuing down until I was deep in the heart of the Village. There I stopped at a coffee shop and was charged twenty cents for an overcooked omelet, a piece of burnt toast, and a cup of tepid coffee: not, perhaps, a good omen for the rest of the day.

I finished the food and began to walk. The first thing was to get a job. I was back where I had been when Gant hired us, when I had pounded the sidewalks looking for a job as a waiter – the only practical thing I was qualified to do – and I knew how hard it was to get hired, especially without references. I tried anyway, going into the diners and greasy spoons that were open at that hour serving breakfast; the responses ranged from regretful to rude. I walked over to Fourth Avenue, to the bookstores – I knew books, after all, as well as I knew taking orders and carrying trays – and stopped into Biblo & Tannen's and Stammer's but of course there was no work in places like that. A young woman in Stammer's told me to try Barker's, and a stooped, gray man in Barker's with wire glasses like Teddy Roosevelt's said, "I'm firing here, sonny, not hiring." Then he added, "I hope you won't be offended if I say that I know of a shoe factory that's hiring." The shoe factory was on Greenwich Street. I walked there with a spring in my step, not offended at all but full of hope, in my head a vision of dignified work: operating a mammoth machine, say, that cut soles from leather. But by the time I arrived a chain of silent, shabby men stretched around the corner, being heckled as scabs and blacklegs by a noisy crowd carrying signs. I tried several luncheonettes, a steak house that reminded me of McGreevey's, a couple of drugstores (I'd worked as a soda jerk one summer in high school), and a vegetable stand near Little Italy where the man behind the counter just laughed at me. A man at another bookstore on lower Broadway said, with a sneer, "We don't hire college boys," and at a Tenth Street beer joint with a BARTENDER WANTED sign in the window, the job had just been filled. Not that I knew the first thing about tending bar.

By mid-afternoon, the sun was as hot as stage lights, and the city steamed. Followed by a crowd of kids, the water wagon went by, but the street dried brown within minutes, and the dust was worse than before. Everywhere I looked were bare-armed women in wilted sundresses, shirt-sleeved men fanning themselves with their hats. It seemed that all the kids I saw were crying, all the women were ugly, all the men looked like thugs or winos, all the dogs were mean. Crossing Sixth Avenue, I was nearly hit by a passing taxicab; the driver cursed as he veered around me, and a man on the sidewalk said, "What are you doing, buddy, trying to kill yourself?" My heart pounding, I ducked under the awning of a shoe repair shop. It occurred to me that I was exhausted, and thirsty, and hungry. The omelet had worn off long ago. How long had I been walking? Since early morning – seven hours? Eight? I hadn't dared spend money on the subway; I'd learned just how fast a few bucks could evaporate. My feet were sore, sweat streamed down my back, my typewriter case was heavier with every block I walked.

In Washington Square, I bought a five-cent apple from a boy who looked so beaten I gave him another nickel as a tip. The apple was old and mushy, but I ate it right down to the core and wished I had another. Washington Square, with its vast arch, was a nostalgic place for me. It was the first place I used to go when I took the train down to New York from Cambridge back in my careless college days. Jasper and I liked going to a dive called the Black Cat – now a night club, one of the places May went with her theatre crowd, but then a seedy speakeasy – at the square's south end. An old man we met at the bar told us that the square used to be the place where public hangings were carried out: they would hang people from the trees, and the crowds, he said, were like Fifth Avenue on Easter Sunday. Even now, with no hangings going on, the crowd was thick. The 25-cents-a-head portrait artist, surrounded by his small crowd of gawkers, was idealizing a matronly woman's head in pastels. A sale of some kind was going on over by the arch – craftsmen selling mud-colored bowls and platters – and that drew a throng of people. A woman behind one of the tables caught me staring at her: a rosy-cheeked girl in an artist's smock, with her hair in a braid down her back. *That's the kind of wife I should have had*, I thought, remembering May's high heels and cheap scent. *A real bohemian girl, simple and sweet.* She smiled at me as if she read my mind, holding up a bowl with a metallic glaze that caught the light. I noticed that her hands were graceful, the nails short and unpainted, her wrist circled by one silvery bangle. "You like it?"

I shrugged. "It's beautiful. But I'm flat broke."

She shook her head regretfully and turned to wait on someone else. I stood watching her, but she didn't look my way again, and I decided she was just like May, just as calculating at heart, just as cold.

I had three cigarettes left. I lit one, sat down on a bench, and decided to torture myself by remembering where I had been a year before, when my dreams were undiminished, plausible, glowing, and the world was a place to rejoice in, not to be cynical about. I was making decent money at McGreevey's then, living at my mother's where I had a warm bed and three squares a day, seeing May every chance I got and beginning to talk about marriage. I remembered the night I kissed her in the garden, and how warm her body was, yielding and supple. I remembered the first time we made love, the shock of it, then the happiness. I remembered the day we got married, just before Christmas, and her whisper: "Don't you dare get me a Christmas present, Robert – being your wife is enough for me."

I closed my eyes and let myself relive it all, right up until things began to go wrong. I dozed for a few minutes, just time enough for a brief, mad dream, something about May and me on a bus being pushed and jostled by a crowd of chattering, jabbering women. I couldn't see them, only hear them, and May said, "Don't worry, they're only sparrows." Then I opened my eyes and saw that the sun had moved behind the old brick houses that bordered the park. It must be nearly four o'clock. An elderly man, roaring drunk and filthy, wobbled over and collapsed next to me on the bench, mumbling about how that damned pinko Roosevelt was ruining the country. I stood up: time to leave. I had no idea where to go, but I began to walk.

On the far side of the square, I caught a glimpse of a man in a white suit and a straw hat. By God, it looked like Orson, and I followed him for two blocks before I was sure that it wasn't Orson at all, just another tanned, wiry guy with the same set to his shoulders in a suit like the one I had lost. I told myself that if it had been Orson, this time I really would have killed him. But I didn't know if that was true or not. And I wasn't sure that I hadn't already killed him. With a flash of dread, out of nowhere – perhaps to keep myself from seeing Orson motionless at the bottom of the stairs – the memory came to me of the murder I'd witnessed on Bleecker Street back in June, and with it a spasm of simple fear. What if I ended up with nowhere to go? What if no one would help me and I ended up living on the streets, with everything that entailed? At best, the breadlines, or working as a scab. At worst, I could be beaten, robbed, left for dead in a dark doorway. I could end up like the old man on the bench, muttering and oblivious, stinking to high heaven, begging for dimes. I'd heard that, in some places, vagrancy was punishable by six months on the chain gang.

I had always told myself that, if worse came to worst, I had family, and for a few humble moments I contemplated trading in my six dollars and change for a train ticket to Rochester. The prospect almost made me misty-eyed: the return of the prodigal, the chance to help my old mother make a go of the boarding house, the reunion with my sister and her kids, whom I occasionally missed. They would hug me and cry. I'd move into my old room – or, no, my room was worth two dollars a week. I'd sleep on the couch, or in the tiny maid's room at the end of the hallway, and I would do pretty much what I'd done at the

Alhambra: lawn-mowing, modest chores, small repairs, with plenty of time to write and no Mr. Gant looking over my shoulder.

But I was just play-acting, using up time. I knew I wasn't going back to Rochester. The list of reasons was a mile long, beginning with my absolute conviction that Rochester was a dead end for a playwright and ending with the humiliation of having to confess that either I was a murderer who fled the scene of his crime, or my wife and her lover had not only betrayed me but gotten away with everything I owned. Joan and Bernie would have a good laugh at my expense, but the whole thing would probably kill my mother, and I couldn't shake the feeling that it would mean Orson and May had won, they had beaten me.

The Municipal Lodging House by the river began to seem like an inevitability – preferable, anyway, to a flophouse on the Bowery. Then, as I turned onto Cornelia Street, I thought of Verna Quiller, who had a soft spot for me and who, I was well aware, had never liked May. Someone I could tell my story to – or parts of it – and be assured of the correct response: sarcasm, sympathy, and unquestioning loyalty. Maybe even a drop of booze. *Cocktail hour*, Verna used to say, grinning, and reach under the sink for the bottle she kept there. Suddenly, dropping in on Verna Quiller seemed like the best plan I'd had all day, and I walked the few blocks over to Bedford Street, swallowing my pride on the way.

Verna's rooming house, where May and I had lived for our first month in New York, was a square brick building near the corner of Carmine Street, with a dilapidated Rexall on one side and on the other a tall and ancient slate-roofed house where you could look through the wavery glass in the windows and see elegant carved woodwork, a glossy-leafed fig tree, a marble fireplace with a painting over it of a woman in a bonnet – the home of some politician, one of LaGuardia's boys who, Verna claimed, must be on the take. "You don't live like that on a councilman's salary," she scoffed. And when I suggested that there might be other ways to accumulate money, she just rolled her eyes and said, "I know you're from upstate, kid, but that's no excuse."

Everything looked the same. The brass numbers and kickplate on the front door of the house next door were freshly polished, the seedy drugstore struggled on, Verna's building was as plain and honest as Verna herself. I stood looking at it, choked with emotion. The last time I saw the place was the day May and I carried our suitcases and boxes down the front steps, off to begin our new life.

The doorbell, I knew, had long been disconnected, so I set down my brown bag – ragged and greasy from being carried all day – and knocked, wishing I had bought a bunch of flowers from the woman who sold them in Union Square for a dime. There was no answer, so I knocked again, loudly, and after a minute the door opened a crack: a woman's face.

"Verna?" The face had Verna's big nose, wide mouth, and dark brown eyes like buttons, but it was different, somehow. I couldn't put my finger on what it was until the door opened another three inches and I saw the whole woman: tall, aproned, hair in a bun. An older, thinner version of Verna's face on someone else's body. And yet, for a second, I wasn't sure. It could be Verna minus a few pounds, Verna aged by a difficult summer. "Verna?" I asked again, with a tentative smile.

"Verna's not here," the woman said, and opened the door wide to look me over. Behind her, in the hall, I could see the rickety table and green-shaded lamp I remembered. Verna used to keep a vase of flowers on the table, but there were none now. "You wanting a room?"

"No, not really. I just wondered – well, I just stopped in to see Verna. She's an old friend."

"She's been gone since Saturday."

"Well, I'm sorry I missed her. I held out my hand. "I'm Robert Sinclair. I used to have a room here. And you must be Verna's sister. Dorothy? She talked about you."

The woman softened a little, smiled – a woman in her fifties, careworn, rougher than Verna and without that spark in her eyes. She put her hand limply into mine and I shook it. "Yes, I'm Dorothy Murphy." Her eyes narrowed, but the smile stayed. "What'd she say about me?"

"Not much," I said, though that was a lie. I'd heard all about the husband who hit her, the son who'd gone off to ride the rails, the emergency appendectomy, and plenty more I'd forgotten. "I just remembered the name, and there's a striking resemblance."

"I suppose there is," she said, smoothing her hair. "Though Verna always had a lot more flesh on her. Not at the end, though. She went down hill pretty fast. Wasn't more than a stick."

"Down hill? What do you mean?" Dorothy shrugged, saying nothing. I stammered out, "Are you saying Verna *died*?"

"Like I said, last Saturday." She pronounced it *Sad-dy*. "They took her to the hospital, but she was dead when they got her there. Funeral was yesterday. I been here most of the summer, looking after her."

I couldn't take it in. "But what did she die of? She was fine in June – perfectly healthy."

Her sister gave a snort. "Verna? Verna was sick as a dog all this year. That liver thing." She shook her head disapprovingly, but tears appeared at the corners of her eyes. "She drank too much, to put it to you straight. She got that cirrhosis. But she had a couple other things wrong with her, too. By the end, she had bleeding ulcers and I don't know what-all. Finally, something burst in her stomach. I never did understand it, but the doctor told me she never had a chance."

"Jesus."

"No excuse to take the Lord's name."

"I apologize."

"Ain't me you're going to have to answer to for it."

I flushed; Dorothy wasn't Verna, that was for sure. "I'm sorry. I'm just overwhelmed."

She put her hand on my arm. "That's all right. I shouldn't have lashed out at you, son. You were a friend. I'm sorry I had to tell you." She touched a corner of her eye, stopping a tear. "Verna was a great girl. I'm going to miss her."

"Me, too. I'd hoped to see her again."

She nodded down at my typewriter case. "You on your way out of here?"

"I'm not sure. Might be."

"Wouldn't blame you a bit. I come up from Philly. As far as I'm concerned, you can take this city and shove it right into one of them rivers." She shrugged. "I'm staying here a little while to settle things. Sell this place, I guess. Nobody else to do it. Our brother's out in Washington State, says he'd sooner go to Timbucktoo as come to New York City." She gestured over her shoulder with her chin. "My son's here with me. Weldon. Helping me close it up."

"I see. Well, I'm sorry." I picked up my bag. "I'm really sorry. I wish I'd stopped by sooner. I meant to, all summer, but – I don't know. You know how these things are."

"She was darned sick, anyways. Wouldn't have been the kind of good company you probably remember."

"No, I suppose not," I said, feeling suddenly guilty: all that corn liquor I'd drunk with Verna couldn't have been doing her liver any good.

"You don't need a room, you say?"

"Not really. But – well, I don't know. What are you charging these days?"

She looked at me for a moment with her small dog-brown eyes, frowning, as if she hadn't understood my question. I was about to repeat it when she nodded her head and said, "I'll tell you what. I could use a hand with these windows. I want to get 'em washed." She came out on the step and pointed up. "I'm not going to worry about the back, but these ones facing the street are pretty grimy. I'd like to spruce the place up a bit." She looked me up and down. I knew I must look bad: sweaty and scruffy, in my ratty old clothes, my lip cut and my eye purple. But she nodded again and seemed satisfied. "If you care to do the job for me, I'll give you a bed for the night."

I bargained. "Can I take a bath first? And rest for a while? I've been walking most of the day."

"What are you – some kind of bum?" She said this with a smile, but I could tell she didn't like what I'd said, and I wished I could take it back.

"I lost my job. I was a super in a building up near Gramercy Park, and I got fired, just like that. First thing this morning. Landlord says he's putting his nephew in."

She pursed her lips. "What a nerve. That's what I mean about this city."

"Well, you find people like that everywhere."

"You can think what you like," she said. "I know what I know. People down in Philly, they treat you like a human being." She stood back. "Come on in. If you took care of a building, I guess you know how to wash a window. I'll show you your room – we're out of clean sheets, I'm sorry to say, but I think I got a pillowcase for you. Then you can have a bath, go out and get yourself a bite of dinner. I don't have a thing in the house, to be honest. Then you can get going on the windows. Finish 'em in the morning if it gets too dark. I don't care."

The place still reeked of ancient cooking, toilets, the sweat of a thousand transients. I followed Dorothy upstairs; her legs were white and shapeless, and her skinny behind, in a faded dress, was half the size of Verna's. There was no sign of the son. I wondered if he was the riding-the-rails son or another – I'd forgotten the details. We passed the room May and I had shared – second floor rear, to the right of the staircase – and went up another floor. "I've only got two men staying here just now," said Dorothy. "One long-term, one short. Both of 'em downstairs there. I'll put you up where it's quieter." *And hotter*, I thought, dismissing the thought as ungrateful. But it was sweltering under the roof. "You'll be right next door to Weldon. Don't worry, he doesn't snore. Me, I'm down on the first floor – Verna's old rooms."

She opened the door to a tiny room that contained an iron bedstead with a stained mattress and two nearly-flat ticking pillows. An antiquated wall sconce held one light bulb. The window was closed, and I went over immediately and opened it, which changed nothing. I knew it was a lie about the sheets, but I didn't make an issue of it. All I could think about was collapsing on that bare mattress. "I really appreciate this, Mrs. Murphy."

"Dorothy'll be fine. I've never been crazy about that Murphy part, tell you the truth. Bathroom's down on the second floor. Towels in the cupboard. Just use one, please, and better bring it back up here with you when you're done. And go easy on the hot water."

"I've been dreaming about a cold bath all day."

She smiled again. "You can get to the windows when you're ready. Come and see me, I'll give you some rags. I'll most likely be out back in the kitchen."

I didn't let myself lie down. I went downstairs and turned on the water in the tub, threw off my sweaty clothes and went over to the open window. The air was perfectly still, the sky white-hot, as if it were mid-August instead of almost October. The leaves of the maple tree behind the house next door were turning red; when I left in June they had been fresh and green: during that time Verna had sickened and died.

While the tub was filling, I remembered what I could about Verna. How she had never married because, she said, she never liked any one man more than she liked another. How she loved those mysteries by Rex Stout about the fat detective – what was his name? Nero Wolfe. How she used to imitate Ethel Merman singing "I Get a Kick Out of You." She'd seen *It Happened One Night* four times, was crazy about Clark Gable, the Brooklyn Dodgers, spaghetti and meatballs, gin rickeys. I'd read her part of *Fish Out of Water*, and she helped me with the scene where Oliver meets Thomasina in the park. We'd talked about the theatre, about how to survive in the city, about her childhood up in New Hampshire and mine in Rochester. She liked hearing about my Harvard days. *Tell me more about those rich boys*, she'd say. What else? A vaudeville show she'd seen one time: the world's fastest typist, who could type more than two hundred words a minute without a mistake. She'd pass the typed sheets out to the audience, and if anyone found a mistake she'd give him a dollar, but no one ever did. For her finale, she'd type on a piece of tin to imitate a train, starting out slow, then picking up speed and clattering along the tracks until you thought it was the Broadway Limited coming in. And a boyfriend of Verna's had once taken her to see *La Bohème* at the Metropolitan Opera, and she'd never forgotten it. She hummed a few bars of Musetta's Waltz. Someday, she said, she'd get there again, if it was the last thing she did.

That was all I could think of. It seemed shamefully little.

I got into the tub. After the first shock, the cold water was wonderful. I thought: *I can live, I will survive.* Fleetingly, I wondered where May was, and Orson. I tried to imagine them. May painting her nails and laughing at my naiveté, the ease with which they had fooled me. Orson, the blood caked in his hair, stepping into my clean white trousers. I didn't know how to feel about either one of them. I couldn't seem to summon up hatred.

Puzzlement, hurt pride, a forlorn sense of injustice, a few shreds of anger – that was the best I could do. What I wanted – what I really wanted, more than anything – was to understand what had happened; failing that, I wanted to forget about it. All I'd done this whole long, hot, frustrating day was moon about the past: my college days, my courtship of May, even those drunken afternoons with Verna, God help me. It was time to begin over: I'd start another new life, commencing once again at poor Verna's rooming house.

I lay back in the frigid water and lit up one of my two precious cigarettes. *Act One, Scene One. A dingy bathroom in a New York City rooming house in Greenwich Village. Robert Sinclair is in the tub, his filthy clothes in a heap on the floor. It's clear that Robert is used to better things than this run-down rooming house, but he is stoical and optimistic.* Robert *(singing)*: Roll out the barrel, we'll have a barrel of fun...

My voice died away, and I nearly fell asleep in the tub. I could have stayed there for hours, but I pictured the boarders banging on the door, complaining to Dorothy, Dorothy taking back the bed she had offered, and I got out and washed my sweaty clothes in the same water with the bar of harsh soap that hung from a rope. Then, towel around my middle, I dashed up the stairs.

I met no one. I hung the clothes over the end of the bed, found my overalls and another, cleaner shirt in my bag. The only hat I had was my old cloth cap, and I put it back on. On the wall was a tin mirror, a postcard of the Grand Canyon impaled on a nail, and a picture of a Civil War soldier cut from a magazine and stuck in an old frame. I looked at myself in the mirror and saw with a mild shock that, except for the black eye, my face looked the way it always did. My eye, though a hideous greenish purple, was hardly swollen, my cut lip was almost back to normal, and I wore an expression not of tortured anguish but of pleasant, half-smiling contentment. I was a regular Oliver Templeton, *bon vivant* and man about town. *The magic of a bath,* I thought. *Of a friendly word, a bed, the prospect of a meal.* And tomorrow? The only way to get through today, I decided, was to think about tomorrow tomorrow.

I took the stairs two at a time, and went out to the street. Just not having to carry my packages made me feel better, and though it wasn't any cooler there was a breeze, maybe a promise of better weather to come. I remembered that there was one of those five-cent restaurants nearby on Seventh Avenue. It was still there, a sign in the window saying:

Italian Spaghetti	*5 cts*
Fried Pork Chop	*5 cts*
Chili and Beans	*5 cts*
Denver Sandwich	*5 cts*
Fried Liver and Onions	*5 cts*
Combination Vegetable Plate	*5 cts*
Assorted Pies, Cakes, or Doughnuts	*5 cts*
Coffee, Tea	*5 cts*

MORE INSIDE! COME ON IN!

I got weak in the knees just thinking about the food. Inside, a noisy ceiling fan moved the warm air around. The man behind the counter, fat and cheerful, wore a clean white apron. The waitress was a neat little woman with bright red hair in a snood. There was a glass case full of oozing pies and footed dishes of rice pudding. I sat down at the counter and ordered Italian Spaghetti in honor of Verna. I had no idea if it was any good or not; it was spicy and filling, and when I finished it I ate an order of chili. The counterman grinned. "Bottomless pit you got there, eh?"

"Guess so. I think I'll put a piece of that cherry pie into it, too. And a cup of coffee."

For twenty cents, I was myself again, and I saw that I could return in the morning and have hot cakes and coffee for another two nickels. At this rate – well, I fished my wallet out of my pocket and counted my cash: six ones, a dime, and a fifty-cent piece. It seemed like a fortune, but I didn't know how long it would have to last me. I'd look for work again tomorrow. Maybe Dorothy would find another chore for me and put me up one more night. *Need any toilets unclogged?* I'd ask her. *Walls painted? Any spackling?* I indulged in a fantasy of running Verna's old rooming house. Dorothy could put me in charge, pay me a minimal salary, and take herself back to Philadelphia – that heavenly city of good Samaritans – while I lounged around 46 Bedford Street, changing sheets, cleaning bathtubs, washing the occasional window, working on my play. Occasionally strolling up to the Alhambra Gardens to have tea with Mrs. Amalfi like old times. And if I ran into Gant, the hell with him.

I paid for my meal and bought a new pack of cigarettes and strolled back down Bedford, feeling on top of the world. Or close to it. Not there yet, but on my way. *All is well,* I told myself.

I washed the windows, finishing the last one just after dark. The mosquitos were fierce, and by the time I was done I had several bites. I went back to the kitchen with the bucket and cloths. The kitchen looked different: it was Dorothy's kitchen, not Verna's. The table wasn't littered with newspapers and magazines, there was no stack of unwashed pots on the stove, no jungle of plants on the windowsills, no bags of candy and plates of the creme sandwich cookies Verna loved. The ancient linoleum floor gleamed; the curtains had been washed, all their ruffles fussily ironed. In front of the sink where the linoleum had worn through was a small rag rug, and I would have bet that in the cupboard there were cleaning supplies instead of booze.

"Just leave that stuff there in the sink," Dorothy said. "I'll take care of it."

She had been joined at the table by a blubbery young man who had to be her son: same nose and same eyes, though buried in ridges of fat. His hair was cut short, like a convict's. I got the impression a tense conversation had been going on. Dorothy sat stiffly, lips pursed, as if holding back anger. The son leaned back loutishly in his chair, looking belligerent.

I set the bucket in the sink. "I'm Robert," I said, holding out my hand. "You must be Weldon."

"I must, must I?" he said, and smirked at me. Then he held out his hand and squeezed mine painfully as he shook it, grinning. "Charmed, I'm sure."

I decided to ignore him. "Windows are all done, Dorothy."

"I'll take a look at 'em in the morning," was all she said. Oh well. I hadn't exactly expected her to weep with gratitude. But maybe I was the one who was supposed to do that.

"I guess I'll turn in," I said to no one in particular. "It's been a long day."

"Ta ta, then," Weldon said, with a snicker.

Up in my room, I wondered if I'd be able to sleep. It had been a long day indeed. My wife betrayed me, my friend stole from me, my boss fired me, I was broke, my feet were sore, and I'd just discovered that one of the few people in the world who cared if I lived or died was dead herself. I lay on the bare mattress pondering all this. It was still early, not even eight o'clock, and I could hear voices, laughter, car noises from the street. I was deeply, profoundly exhausted, but fatigue had never guaranteed sleep for me. If I couldn't sleep, I decided, I wouldn't fight it. Not that I'd go out and walk – that was beyond me. No, I'd turn on the light and read some Shakespeare – *Lear* might be appropriate, I thought: a man betrayed, brought lower and lower until – well, Lear died at the end, of course, but he was old, and he did find redemption before the curtain came down. Still, maybe I'd be better off with *As You Like It and* my favorite heroine, the sharp-witted Rosalind. Or I would read *Gatsby* instead, knowing I'd see May as Daisy, myself as a poor, tame version of the pining Gatsby with his hopeless love. The best thing, of course, would have been to get one of Mrs. Amalfi's potions before I fled the Alhambra – none of her sissy tisanes or Russian herbs but the more drastic cures she had often hinted at but never given me. Or Hana, I thought, *Nature's soft nurse.* . . .

Sleep is mysterious, coming and going on its own terms, for its own reasons. I was asleep in minutes, and I slept as soundly and dreamlessly as I ever had in my life.

■ ■ ■

The next morning, after I had washed up, shaved, and combed my hair, I went downstairs. The weather was cooler. I had slept. I had money in my pocket, and I was looking forward to a plate of hotcakes and a cup of coffee. I stuck my head in the kitchen door, hoping to find Dorothy and talk her into letting me stay another night.

She wasn't there, but Weldon was sitting at the table, drinking coffee and watching the door as if he'd been waiting for me. He wore a white undershirt and shiny pants that stretched so tight over his belly and thighs you could see the outline of a massive penis. At the table with him was a very small man with gray hair, a gray moustache and small beard, grayish eyes in a gray face, and what looked like a peddler's pack on the floor beside his chair.

I said to Weldon, "I was looking for your mother."

"She won't be around today. I'm in charge." Weldon set down his cup and glanced up at the clock on the wall. "After seven already," he said. "How time flies. I guess you don't know what time check-out is around here."

"Check-out?"

"That means the time you're supposed to be out of here. You know –" He shrugged, smiling, showing bad teeth, the stink of bad breath drifting across the room. "Check-out."

"Yes, I know what it means, Weldon. I just didn't know there was an official check-out time. As far as I know, there wasn't when Verna was here."

"Yeah, well, Verna's pushing up daisies, isn't she? So, for your information, check-out time is –" He glanced at the clock again. "Twelve minutes past seven."

We looked at each other. "You're kicking me out?"

He shook his head patiently. "Nope. I'm just informing you what time check-out is," he said in a sarcastic Jack Benny voice. "Though maybe a cynical kind of person might say it comes down to the same thing."

A terrible urge to hit him came over me – just to smash my fist into his fat face and feel it crack against his nose. I said, "You little toad. You're lucky I don't bust your damned head in."

Weldon did nothing, said nothing, just looked at me, his face expressionless. The gray man turned his face toward the window, exhibiting an oddly delicate profile. There was a long silence. Then Weldon sighed elaborately and looked at the clock again. "Seven-thirteen. Am I going to have to call the cops?"

I turned on my heel and went up to my room, muttering. All I needed was another fight, another black eye or split lip, another man unconscious on the floor. If it came down to it, I had no idea if I could take him. He looked like a big, unhealthy slob, a fat weakling, but you never knew, and he had more heft, which usually counted for something. *Forget it*, I told myself. *Just get out of here and forget it.*

I collected my typewriter case and my dilapidated paper bag. It was only then that I noticed that my change of clothes, the things I'd washed out in my bath water – work pants, old blue shirt, black socks – were gone from the end of the bed where they had been drying. I looked on the floor, under the bed, in the bathroom. They couldn't have been stolen: who would want such rags? But they were gone, that was for sure. And who but the noxious Weldon would have taken them?

I clattered down the steps: if he wanted a fight, God damn it, I'd give him one. But the kitchen was empty, and when I went out the back door, I couldn't see anyone in the yard, either. I called his name; no one answered. Upstairs again, I opened the door of the room next to where I had slept: Weldon's, Dorothy had said. But it was empty, almost as bare as mine except that there were sheets on the bed. I looked around for something to take as retaliation, but there was nothing except the sheets, and they were rumpled and filthy.

I stood in the hall, breathing deeply, and managed to calm down. I'd get some breakfast, then come back, I decided. But by the time I'd finished my hot cakes, I didn't have the heart for it. The hell with the clothes, the hell with slimy Weldon – and God only knew where Dorothy was. What did they matter, a few rags of old clothes? My bag, at least, was that much lighter.

The morning was definitely cooler. It had rained during the night, and the streets were still wet. I left the five-cent restaurant and looked down Seventh Avenue. There on the corner was the small, gray-haired man I'd seen at the rooming house. I would have avoided him, but he saw me a second after I saw him, and he walked over, bent a little under his pack.

"You were wise not to get into a brawl with him," he said. He had an oddly musical voice, the trace of an accent I couldn't place.

"The man isn't stupid, but he surely is a barbarian. He'd be less impossible if he were stupider."

"What's he to you?" I asked.

"Customer."

"Customer for what?"

"He buys what I sell."

"And what do you sell?"

"I sell what people will buy."

"Such as?"

"Anything. Everything."

I gave up and stuck out my hand. He was nearly a head shorter than I was, and I had to reach down. "I'm Robert Sinclair."

"Gilbert Waldemar," he said. "Gil." His grip was weak. I realized, looking at him, that he must be ill. "What about you, Robert? Anything to sell? Anything you want to buy?"

"Well, I don't know."

"Come over here for a minute."

He led me to the doorway of a boarded-up store and lowered his pack to the sidewalk. It was an ingeniously constructed thing, a wooden support holding a series of fraying leather compartments, each closed with a brass buckle. It looked old enough to have come up the river with Henry Hudson. "Must be heavy," I said.

"It probably is, but I transcended such considerations long ago." He opened one compartment and pulled out an ornate ladies' watch made of white gold. Instead of numerals, there were twelve diamond chips, and in the center, where the hands joined, a small ruby. "Pretty?" He fastened it on his own thin wrist: white skin, stiff black hairs, the fancy gold watch looking ridiculous, like a peacock in a trap. He put his head back and looked at it admiringly. "This is the sort of thing I sell, when I can find it."

"How do you get such stuff?"

"Various ways. Mostly, people entrust it to me." Reluctantly, he removed the watch and put it back into its pocket. He sat down on the sidewalk, took out a pack of cigarettes, and offered me one. I sat beside him, and we lit up – Gil coughing and shaking his head, pounding his chest as he shook out the match. The pavement, through the seat of my overalls, was clammy and damp. I wondered if he should be sitting there, with his cold, or bronchitis, or whatever it was that was wrong with him. It was something, that was certain.

But he stopped coughing after a minute, and caught his breath, then drew deeply on his cigarette and leaned back, eyes half-shut. Close up, he was fine-featured, even handsome, with a thin, elegant nose and a particularly beautiful mouth, full-lipped and firm under his shaggy moustache. He looked to be somewhere in his fifties; the gray hair was misleading – he could have been younger. He was dressed in a rather natty suit that had seen better days, light worsted with a faint stripe in it, and with it he wore a shirt and tie and, unexpectedly, spats.

He looked at me quickly, as if he'd sensed me staring at him, and said, "So. Do you have anything to entrust to me, Robert?"

I had been thinking, and I reached into my bag and took out the cufflinks. "I have these. I figured at some point I'd have to pawn them."

Gil held out his hand, palm up, and I dropped the cufflinks into it. He screwed up his face and peered at them. "Sentimental value?"

"Something like that."

"Gift from a girlfriend?"

I felt my face flush. "Not really."

"Well, in fact, they're very smart. Very fine indeed." He nodded suddenly toward my typewriter case. "And what's in there? Typewriter? Ever think of getting rid of that?"

"Not a chance."

"One of those little Royal portables – right?"

"Remington."

"Yes, I've seen them. I could do well for you."

"No, thanks."

He smiled. "Sentimental value again?"

"I'm a writer," I said, though it sounded absurd. "I couldn't live without my typewriter."

"Another writer on the bum, eh?"

"That doesn't describe it, exactly."

"No?" Gil inhaled, looking at me through narrowed, amused eyes. "Where do you live, Robert?"

"Nowhere right now, but that's not the same as being on the bum."

He seemed to weigh what I'd said, then he shrugged, tossed the cufflinks in the air, caught them and closed his fist around them. "Let me get rid of these for you. I assume you could use a couple of bucks. Say – twenty?"

"You could get me twenty dollars for those?"

"Easily. That's a lot more than you could get at a pawnshop."

"Yes, but then they're gone. Forever."

He shrugged. "Let's say twenty-five."

"You can get twenty-five?"

"I can try."

"Where do you sell such things?

He shrugged. "Lower East Side. The junk market on Second Avenue. These? Maybe a jeweler friend of mine, up in the Fifties."

"You mean – I just hand them over to you?"

"Right. I'll give you a receipt."

"Why should I trust you?"

"Do I look like a thief?"

"Yes, frankly, you do."

He threw back his head and laughed, and in the middle of the laugh he began to cough – worse this time. He fumbled in an inside pocket and found a filthy handkerchief, which he held to his mouth, hacking into it, making noises like some terrible machine coming undone.

I started to stand up. "Can I get you some water or something?"

He waved me back down, handkerchief still held to his mouth. I waited and, gradually, he subsided. When it was over, he looked at the handkerchief, folded it carefully, and put it away again. Then he smiled at me, weakly. "Sorry," he croaked. "You tickled my funnybone."

In the end, I'm not sure how, he took the cuff links, and I took a scribbled note attesting to that fact. Under it was his grandiose signature: Gilbert M. Waldemar, both the M and the W trailing graceful banners that formed a kind of canopy over his name. We agreed to meet at the five-cent restaurant in two days, for breakfast, and he would either give me my money or return the cufflinks.

"I'll tell you what," he said when we parted. "Where are you staying tonight?"

I hesitated, but finally said, "I'm not sure. I have a couple of ideas."

"You might try a place I know – one of the superior flophouses. It's called the Chateau, and it's on Eighth Avenue, near the corner of 33rd Street. If you're there no later than noon, you can usually get a room for twenty cents. It's no palace." He grimaced. "Not even a chateau. Among other drawbacks, the stench can be dreadful. But compared to most places, it's the Plaza Hotel. Just don't hang around in the lobby any longer than you need to. Or the bathrooms. Keep to yourself. Will you remember that?"

I wondered if he lived there himself, but asking seemed to imply that I was interested in the place. "I'll think of it as my last resort. I have a few other ideas."

"Well, if they don't pan out."

"Yeah. Thanks for the tip. And the smoke."

We shook hands again. "I hope you don't think you can sleep in a church," he said. "The cops'll put you out."

"That wasn't one of my ideas," I said, though it had crossed my mind.

"Good. And you might forget about begging for food in restaurants. Most of these places in the village are pretty much bummed out. You'll be lucky if they don't clip you one."

"I have no intention of begging for food."

"All right, then, Robert." He seemed reluctant to leave. We stood there for a moment while he looked at me in a worried way, and then he said, "You'll be fine, I'm sure. And we'll meet again." He shot back his cuff, pretended to consult a wristwatch, grinned again. "Same time, same place, day after tomorrow."

"I'll be there."

I had no idea whether he would be there or not. I expected almost nothing. I had given him the cuff links as a kind of test, I suppose – a test of the world, to see if it was full of Gants and Weldons, or if there was some simple humanity left: some goodness. I had instinctively trusted Gil, but I remembered that I had trusted Orson as well, and Orson was the reason I was trudging up Seventh Avenue in rags and my gold cuff links were in a filthy leather pocket of a peddler going rapidly in the other direction.

As I walked, I planned my strategy. I'd start making the rounds of the employment agencies, or maybe I'd go over to Brooklyn where, I'd always heard, the docks in Red Hook were in constant need of workers. I needed to get out of this part of New York City, where I knew too many people. I didn't fancy meeting up with Lois, for one, or any of the people I'd seen at Carlotta's party. *What a strange fellow that May Munro's husband must be! There he was, the other morning, walking down Seventh Avenue in overalls and a cap!* Or the Alhambra tenants. Or Gant, God knows. And I was haunted by the idea that I might run into Mrs. Amalfi, out searching for wounded pigeons. I didn't know how far afield she went, and every time I turned a corner I imagined her or Hana coming toward me. The humiliation of that meeting – of their kindness, their disappointment in me, their horror at the story of my fight with Orson – would be more than I could stand. I thought: In a couple of days, I'll pay a call. When I get on my feet again.

I set off on my quest, and I spent all that long, damp, chilly day searching for a job that never materialized. I knew of three employment agencies, all on Sixth Avenue, and at all three I waited in long lines before I got inside – two hours at the last one. Incredibly, nearly every man in line was neatly dressed in suit and hat; I was in overalls and faded workshirt, shivering in the cool air. At the first agency, I told the man at the desk I'd been to Harvard, and he gave me a look of such pitying disbelief that I didn't mention it again. The man at the Empire State Agency asked me about my black eye, then about my last job; I wasn't prepared, and I stumbled over answers that I knew sounded false – as indeed they were. It was only the last person I talked to, a white-haired woman at the Atlantic Agency, who said, hesitantly, when I sat down, "You do know that the agencies charge a fee, don't you?"

"Yes, ma'am," I said. "I understand it's taken out of your first paycheck."

"Well – " She produced an unhappy little smile. "That used to be the way it worked. But now we have to ask for the fee up front."

I stared at her. "Up front?"

"Yes. We'll find you a job – or we'll hope to. Who can say? And if it's something you feel you want to pursue, you pay us ten dollars and we send you out to be interviewed."

I stumbled to my feet and through the door, and stood out on the street, breathing hard. I felt as if I'd been punched in the stomach. A man who had emerged behind me asked, "You okay, Mac?"

"They charge a ten-dollar fee!" I sputtered out. "Before they even get you a job. They charge ten dollars just to send you out to apply for it."

"No kidding." he said. "You didn't know that? Where have you been? Listen. I paid them ten bucks for a job that paid three a day. I got the job and I lasted four days before they let everybody go. Made twelve bucks, and it cost me ten plus carfare."

I stared at him. "But you came back."

He looked back at me for a long moment, and then he said, "You're going to learn this for yourself anyway, son, but I'll tell you just the same. You've got to be doing something. That's how you keep your self-respect. You've got to do something. It almost doesn't matter what it is. And even if you know it's not going to get you anything but blisters on your feet."

"There must be a better way!"

"You tell me what it is. I got four kids at home. I come to these places every day."

I bought a pretzel from a cart vendor and sat on the curb to eat it. When I finished, I was no less hungry, and I didn't know what to do next. Buying another pretzel was all I could think of. I sank my head down on my knees. It was surely too late to go over to Brooklyn and check out the docks, or the sugar refinery I'd heard about that was always hiring. Not that I knew how to find them; I wasn't even sure which bridge to go over.

A man going by in a Panama hat made me think of my father. If he could see me now. Is this how you make something of yourself, son? But he had been a sham, too. What had he made of himself but a pile of debts, a house built on sand, a closetful of clothes he shouldn't have squandered money on? And me, his son and only hope, sitting on a curbstone on Sixth Avenue with a black eye and a scruffy cloth cap, carrying a typewriter case and a paper bag with two books in it.

I'd wasted the whole day. I lit a cigarette, wondering how long my pack would last and when I'd ever be able to afford another. Then I walked up the avenue to a cafeteria, ordered a cup of coffee, and took out my wallet. I still had six dollar bills. I still had most of a pack of cigarettes. I had the receipt bearing Gil Waldemar's florid signature. I was out of ideas, but things would look brighter in the morning – provided, of course, I found somewhere to sleep that night.

I sat there until it got crowded and the waitress began to glare at me, and then I walked to another cafeteria. I couldn't face any more coffee. I ordered a bowl of soup and took a handful of oyster crackers, which I consumed slowly, stretching out the time, but by seven I felt I had to move on. I found one more cafeteria, ate a piece of pie and drank two glasses of water, used the bathroom, and when I left there it was almost completely dark. I wandered east and north, crossed over to Fifth Avenue, and walked up to Central Park. I knew people slept in the parks – I'd seen them myself in Union and Stuyvesant Squares – and I figured I could find a place under a bush.

The night was very cool. I plodded through the park, wishing I had some of the woolen clothes I'd left behind at the Alhambra, the things Orson hadn't bothered to steal, including the coat I didn't like. What an idiot I was. Winter was coming. What if I hadn't found a job and a place to stay by the time the cold weather settled in? Something to eat and a place to sleep: that was what it all came down to, that was what life was about. I remembered with a kind of hunger the church I'd seen on my walks through Harlem: I WILL GIVE THEE REST, and the big woman like a priestess. For a second, I was tempted to take myself up there and ring the bell. But I suspected there'd be no rest there for a white man in rags with five dollars and change in his pocket.

An elderly couple came along the path, and the old woman held out her hand, piteously. What the hell. They must have been in their seventies. I dug into my pocket for a couple of nickels. The woman said, "Bless you, mister," her eyes tearing up as if I'd given them ten dollars, and they tottered away. The man was carrying a cardboard box half-full of bottles. I'd heard you could get a nickel a dozen for glass bottles, you could get fifty cents for a hundred pounds of newspapers. Would I be reduced to that, picking through the streets for trash? I had never thought of asking for food at restaurants, but now that I knew it wasn't an option, I felt deprived, dispossessed. There must be so much food in this city going to waste! Why shouldn't I have it as much as the next guy? As much as the rats? I couldn't continue spending nickels and dimes for bowls of soup, pretzels, flimsy meals at the five-cent restaurant. But even as I found myself a secluded spot on the hard ground under a bush, my arms clasped around my typewriter case, I thought to myself: in thirty-six hours, Gil will be there with twenty dollars. I had heard somewhere that a person can survive quite well on fifty cents a day. On twenty dollars I could live for weeks, if I had to.

Sleep came hard, and I saw the quarter-moon come up, sailing above the trees like a luminous boat. As I watched the moon rise, my old life came back to me in a rush, the parts of it that I'd taken for granted. The smell of coffee in the morning. Our tiny bathroom with its water closet that almost always flushed. Those pink cocktails, made of gin and something called Crème Yvette, that May and Carlotta liked to drink at Chumley's. Jack Benny on Sunday nights. Mr. Gant's twelve dollars in its flat brown envelope every Friday. A letter from my sister Joan that started: "Well, Robert, I'm so glad for you. New York seems to be everything you hoped for and more."

Jesus, we were rich! Twelve dollars a week and a roof over our heads. What a paradise it had been. And where had it gone? How had it slipped away so fast?

I don't know what time it was, just after dawn, that a policeman came along and hit the bottoms of my shoes with his nightstick: a searing, unexpected pain. "Come on, there, laddie. Time to get along. Move on, now." I sat up, groggy, stiff with cold, to see his big pink face looking down at me, not unkindly. I sat up, struggled to my feet. The typewriter case was still there, but my bag of junk was nowhere to be seen. "Somebody stole my stuff," I said, looking around wildly. "My bag!"

"Well, I'm sorry for that, son, but nobody said this was a safe place to spend the night. You're lucky they didn't do worse than rob you."

I rubbed my eyes, ran my fingers through my hair. I had been dreaming about Verna's rooming house, about being there with May and seeing the green trees of the yard next door when I lay in bed beside her. That and something else, something elusive and disturbing that I couldn't catch.

The cop kept standing there. "There are places you can go, young fella," he said. "I can direct you to a place that'll give you a bed and a bath and a hot meal."

"No, thanks," I said. I was still half-asleep, trying in my confusion to take in the loss of my books, my underwear, my good safety razor, toothbrush, tin of tooth powder. Could you fail to brush your teeth and still be a civilized person? "I'll be okay. It was just this one night, officer. Things happened."

It seemed to me I was babbling incoherently, but the cop nodded, probably relieved that I wasn't going to ask him for anything. "That's all right, then," he said. "Take care of yourself."

I searched the surrounding area – in a trash barrel, behind trees, under other clumps of bushes – but my bag was nowhere to be found. You'd think they'd at least discard the books, I thought with bitterness. What desperate vagrant wanted a complete Shakespeare and *The Great Gatsby*? Then I thought: *Thank God I gave Gil the cuff links*, and wondered if I was crazy. What did it matter which thief got my only valuable possession?

I looked around for the cop, but he seemed to be gone, so I urinated behind a tree and washed my face and cleaned my teeth as well as I could in the water at the drinking fountain by the 60th Street gate. Then, panicking, I reached into my pocket: my wallet was still there, the money tucked inside. I would be all right.

What I would do, I decided, was go to Brooklyn and try for a job on the docks. But I knew I couldn't carry my typewriter case all day, and if I found a job I couldn't take it with me. And if I had to sleep in another park, I couldn't risk having it stolen.

I sat on a bench for a while, trying not to think about breakfast, trying to make out what to do. A scruffy little man, sockless, in a filthy mismatched suit came down the path, and sang, in an off-key rasp, "Nobody Knows You When You're Down and Out." Then he cackled and said, "Ain't it the truth?" He started to tell me how he'd been in vaudeville, he'd appeared at the Palace Theatre with Eddie Cantor, with Weber and Fields....

I said, "Go peddle it someplace else, buddy," and got up and walked away, down the path to another bench. I counted my money three times. Five dollars and eighty cents. If a person could live on fifty cents a day, I would last eleven or twelve more days. I sat there counting my change, finding myself strangely reluctant to move. The day got brighter – I heard a clock strike seven, then the half-hour. I kept thinking of the vaudeville guy I'd snubbed, and I felt bad that I'd done it. I was tired, my back was stiff, and I had a blister on one heel. I hoped the cop wouldn't come back and find me there. Could they force you to go to flophouses, I wondered, or throw you in jail for hanging around the park too long. I pictured the cop hauling me in for vagrancy only to find I was wanted for something worse, for manslaughter.

The longer I sat there the more plausible this scenario seemed, so I made myself get up, finally, and go down Fifth Avenue, along the park, where the gray apartment houses rose above me in the quiet morning. From time to time a man in a sharp suit emerged from one, usually bowed out by the doorman, and headed down the avenue or over toward the subway station on Lexington. Or the doorman would whistle down a cab. I wondered how you got doorman jobs. I could do that, I thought. Keep intruders out, let residents in, collect packages, ask after people's poodles and children and spouse, wear a stupid-looking coat with epaulets, as if you were the Grand Vizier in a prep-school production of some silly operetta. I looked at the briefcased rich men with dislike, imagining the breakfast they'd just had: two eggs, over easy, Jeeves, please, and a bit of toast? And I'll have two sugars in my coffee. Hello, darling, you're looking lovely this morning. Isn't it a marvelous day?

I turned off Fifth onto a street lined with immaculate townhouses. Halfway down was a particularly grand one, with a frieze of vaguely Greek-looking stone maidens around the front door, holding a banner on which a tortured version of an S was carved. The house was surrounded by a box hedge and a fancy wrought iron fence, waist high. At each corner of the fence was a giant rhododendron, like the ones that sat exactly the same way, guarding the corners, in my mother's front yard in Rochester. *S* for *Sinclair*, I thought, and on an impulse I leaned over, the black curlicues digging into my stomach, and swung my typewriter case across the fence, hiding it among the low branches of one of the rhododendrons. Belatedly, I looked around. I couldn't see a soul. There was no traffic on that part of the street, no one coming down the steps with a briefcase, no doorman or cleaning woman on the way to work. The house looked asleep, no lights visible, silk drapes drawn over the first-floor windows.

I walked quickly back to the corner and strolled down the street again. I passed the building: still no one. The case couldn't be seen from the street, and I was quite sure its black squareness couldn't be seen from the windows either. I stood there a minute agonizing – should I? shouldn't I? – and then, abruptly, I continued down the street, thinking about how someday I would be interviewed in the *Tribune* or the *Times* about the early stages of my career, and I would talk about how *Afternoon Coffee* had once lain under a rhododendron on 53rd Street while I worked on the Brooklyn docks until – until what? Tom Mix rode up on his horse? President Roosevelt declared me a national treasure and set me up in a book-lined study at the White House?

The sun came out as I walked, though the air was still cool, and I ducked into a cafeteria over on Lexington to spend my first fifteen cents of the day on a hot meal: a plate of scrambled eggs, toast with jelly, and a cup of coffee. I knew that if I walked to Brooklyn it would take half the day and I'd be in no condition to work when I got there, so I squandered a nickel on the BMT, feeling as guilty as a kid buying forbidden candy and mentally counting my money the whole way over: five bills, a couple of quarters, one thin dime, and an odd penny I found in my pocket.

I'd crossed the bridges many times during my white nights, but I'd never been to Brooklyn in the daytime, and when I emerged from the subway station I had no idea where I was. I followed the riverfront, asking directions – a long walk through increasingly squalid neighborhoods down to where the huge piers jutted into the East River above New York bay, and the Manhattan skyline to the north was like a distant dream.

I scouted the place out, trying to get my bearings. The stench down there was overpowering, a stew of fish, gasoline, coal, garbage, and sweat. Between the pier sheds, the water was gray and choppy, and the big ships were like cities, swarming with men and belching black smoke into the blue. A rusty rail car ran on a siding along the middle of the street, spewing cinders. I went by a place bearing a hand-painted sign: SEAMAN'S REST, ROOMS 20 CENT, ALL EMENITIES where a man was sprawled across the steps, asleep or passed out. The taverns were open – Teddy's Bar & Grill, the Clam Shack, Bill's Place – and a group of sailors passed me, drunk already, in their dungarees and white caps. Here and there knots of men were gathered around fires inside cut-down oil drums: I saw what looked like a pair of seagulls roasting on a spit. At an inlet was a fleet of small fishing barges, one of them sitting like a miniature house on the sludgy water – curtains at the windows and a ginger cat asleep on the roof in the sun. It was a vision from a lost world, and I stood staring at it until a woman emerged from the cabin and gave me a look, and I continued on, the wind off the water slicing through my clothes.

I trudged around on my sore feet, wishing I were somewhere else, overwhelmed by a distaste for it all and by a violent reluctance to make myself part of it. I was consumed with longing – futile and absurd in that hell of laboring, sweating, drunken humanity – to be myself again, drinking tea in the peace of Mrs. Amalfi's kitchen, or tapping out Act II of *Afternoon Coffee* in my underground apartment. Even my insomnia, my troubles with May, my fight with Orson seemed like scenes from another, better life.

Hesitantly, I joined a crowd that had assembled at one of the piers and asked the man standing next to me what was going on. He spoke in an accent precisely like the one Carlotta used to mimic: *Jewidge*, he said his name was, and I finally figured out it was *George*. At various times during the day, he told me, there was what was known as a shape-up. A ship had come in, they'd put out a call for men, and from the crowd the bosses of the longshoremen crews would select whomever they wanted.

"On the basis of what?" I asked him. He looked at me blankly. "I mean, how do they choose? What makes them hire you?"

George was a tall, droopy-eyed man with a runny nose. He wore three or four flannel shirts, one on top of the other. A miraculous medal hung around his neck. He wiped his nose on his sleeve and shrugged. "Most of the guys they know. If they don't know you, then the tougher you look, the better. The system ain't worth shit. They ought to find a better way. Least, a lot of people seem to think so. Every couple a months, there's a fight, and the bosses bring their goons in to break it up. Then the cops move in and make everything worse. Last time, two guys were carried out of here dead. It's a rum business. Of course, on a good day you can make three bucks, easy. Maybe four." He looked down at my shoes dubiously. "You want to get yourself a good pair of boots."

"I guess it's a little late for that."

"Yeah, well, good luck is all I can say. Uh-oh." George gestured with his chin toward a shirtless man emerging from one of the shacks. "That's Zimmer. From United. He's a tough old bastard. He likes the Norwegians. Always hires Norwegians. And the niggers are next. Hates my guts, don't ask me why."

Zimmer was built like a tank and heavily tattooed. I was near the front of the crowd, and I could see on one bulging bicep a blue dagger dripping red blood. Zimmer carried a clipboard; he took a pencil from behind his ear, wet the pencil between his lips, frowned, and wrote something, laboriously. Then he surveyed the crowd as if we were a cockroach colony, taking his time. When his eyes rested on me, he said, very softly, "Get outta here, kid. Go on back across the river. Don't waste my time."

"I'm looking for work," I said.

"Not here, you ain't."

"Won't you just give me a chance? I'm a hard worker."

He motioned me away with his thumb. "I said get the fuck outta here!"

I moved off to one side, glancing over at George. He didn't meet my gaze, he was looking at Zimmer. Zimmer strutted back and forth like a god, every eye on him. He barely spoke, just jerked his head or barked out a word, and someone in the crowd would detach himself and move to the front. George was right, most of them were big and brown or big and blond, and when he had twelve men out of maybe sixty, Zimmer turned on his heel and marched back to the shed with his clipboard, the muscles rippling under his hairy back, the crowd at his heels. George was the last man chosen, and as he passed me, he said, "Take my advice and get yourself a pair of boots, son."

In a store that catered to sailors I found a pair of thick-soled leather work boots. The shopkeeper was an Armenian with his own incomprehensible accent, and it took him a minute to make me understand that the boots were going to cost me two dollars. Quickly, I unlaced them – not without regret; they were sturdy and warm – and said, "No. Sorry. Mistake. Too much. I don't want them."

He held up one finger and said, "I give them you less. I make one and half."

"One and a half?" I held up one finger straight and one bent. "Is that what you said?"

He nodded impatiently. "Yes! Yes! One and half! And shoes." He pointed to my old tan shoes that I'd had since college.

"My shoes? You want my shoes?"

"Shoes. Yes."

I thought about it. That would bring my small fund of money down to not much more than four dollars. But I wanted the boots more than anything. Four dollars still seemed like plenty of money: as long as I didn't have to pay for lodging – I'd never be able to afford even a dump like the Seamen's Rest – I was getting by on thirty or forty cents a day. And Gil would show up in the morning with the money for my cuff links. Maybe. I felt a rush of my old foolish optimism, and before I could think too much, I said, "One dollar and one quarter," taking the cash from my wallet and showing it to him.

"And shoes."

I gave the guy the money and the shoes, and I knew as soon as I walked out of the store that a pair of cheap boots wasn't going to make a damn bit of difference. Boots or no boots, nobody was going to hire me for any of these jobs. But I'd paid a nickel to get there and laid out the money for a pair of boots and I didn't know what else to do, so I joined a crowd of dockworkers for another shape-up. This time the boss was less polite. "What're you, one of them pansy reporters?" he sneered. "Come down here to spy on us?" He was another huge, bald brute of a guy, and he moved toward me threateningly

"I don't know what you're talking about," I said. "I'm just looking for work."

"Oh, is that right?" He folded his massive arms. "And what kind of work would you be looking for, pal?"

I shrugged. I had no idea how to handle a lout like this except to be honest. "I'll take anything."

"Anything, eh?" He smiled at me – a tight, phony grimace that showed all his misshapen teeth. "Well, I don't think we have any jobs like that. Now get out of here unless you want another black eye."

"Listen, mister, I'm not trying to make trouble, I'm just trying to earn a couple of bucks."

The boss didn't bother to answer, just looked at me like I was dirt and turned away to talk to someone else. I stood there helplessly. I didn't understand where the malevolence was coming from, and why I was such a target. Someone behind me shoved me with his shoulder. "Don't you understand English, kid? The guy said no soap, so get going."

Anger surged up in me. I felt the way I had when Weldon told me it was check-out time, and I turned around, prepared to hit the guy – hit anyone. But he was an emaciated little shrimp, and the look in his eyes was frantic. Compared to him, I was a Goliath – a Zimmer. The competition for these jobs, I realized, could make men crazy, and I turned away without another word.

I walked around the area until my anger passed, avoiding the drunks, trying to banish the urge to go into one of the taverns and have a whiskey. I needed to concentrate on my immediate problem – how to find myself a job – but my mind wandered. I worried about my typewriter case. I worried about the cuff links I'd given Gil Waldemar. I worried about my mother and sister, who would write to me at the Alhambra Gardens and get their letters back marked *Addressee Unknown*. I worried about Mrs. Amalfi, wondering if she knew Gant had fired me and why. And I worried about Orson, wondering for the hundredth time if I'd killed him, if the police were looking for me, if this strange odyssey on the streets would end, somehow, with me behind bars.

I stopped to ask the time of an Italian-looking guy standing next to a pile of bursting crates that looked like they contained cabbages. He pulled out a pocket watch and said it was half past noon. Then he said he'd pay me a buck to help him load the crates onto a rail car. We were about to make a deal when someone yelled to him, "That's enough, Jacko, we've got what we need," and he spread his hands and said, "Sorry, kid, I guess you're too late."

I thanked him and turned away, and he called me back. "How long you been on the bum, son?"

I had to think: it seemed like a week at least, and I was astonished that it had been only three days. "Not long," I said.

He looked at me closely. "Where'd you get that shiner?"

"A fight. Nothing serious."

He had tragic-looking brown eyes, and he stood there looking at me and shaking his head sadly. "I got a son your age," he said with a sigh. "I'd hire you if I could, but it ain't my call. I ain't the boss here."

"That's okay."

"You'll find something," he said. "Don't give up. Here." He reached into his pocket and pulled out a quarter. "Take this and get something to eat."

"No, really," I protested. "I can't."

He took my hand and tried to press the coin into it. "Come on. Take it."

I know my face was flaming red. I'm an educated man, I wanted to say. I'm a playwright. I'm not *on the bum*. "I appreciate it, but honestly – I don't need it. That's the truth. Give it to somebody who does."

He sighed again through his teeth, still shaking his head, and put the money back in his pocket.

The man's kindness gave me hope, and I approached everyone I saw who looked human to ask if they knew of any work. Some men were polite, some were rude, at least half of them just ignored me. I got nowhere with anyone. I stood on the fringes of two more crowds while other men were chosen by the bosses and I was passed over. I went into half a dozen greasy spoons and asked the man behind the counter if he needed help; most of them didn't speak much English, but as far as I could tell none of them needed a goddam thing, least of all me. At one point, when I thought my legs might give out any minute, I spotted a huge terminal where a sign I hadn't seen before read HELP WANTED, but the guy behind the desk gave me a sarcastic smile and said, "You might have had better luck nine or ten hours ago." I stared at him stupidly. "It's almost five o'clock," he said.

"About time for you to be looking for a comfortable park bench for the night."

"Should I come back in the morning?" I asked. Now that I knew the time, I realized I was exhausted.

"Be here at seven. If we're hiring anybody, we're hiring early. But I ain't promising nothing."

Back on the street, the sky was darkening, the air appreciably colder. A man with an accordion stood on a corner near a tavern, his cap on the pavement in front of him. In the cap were three nickels. In a raspy baritone, he sang I song I didn't know:

> *There's fish in the ocean, there's fish in the sea,*
> *But a red-headed woman made a fool out of me,*
> *And it looks like I'm never gonna cease my wandering.*

It seemed the saddest song I'd ever heard, and I tossed a dime into his cap and walked on, hearing his voice behind me like a voice in my own head. I was ready to give up. And yet – what did that mean? How did you give up? Ride the rails to California? Apply for relief? Find a bed in a flophouse with the other derelicts? My money wouldn't last long, and at the city shelters they kicked you out after five nights.

Throw yourself in the river, I thought. That's what it means to give up. I stood at the end of an abandoned pier looking down at the oily water lapping a foot below me. I'd never thought much about death, not as something that could happen to me personally, certainly not something that would happen soon, but it seemed close to me then. The water below me looked like death, and the gulls shrieking as they dove to the river for fish, and the bloated rat that floated by as I watched. Orson lying on the stairs, and May's miscarriage, and my father in his coffin looking like he was carved from wood and painted. What was the point of it all? Why did all these men bother, why did they go through what they went through, every day? Something to eat and a place to sleep. For what?

I bought a bag of fried potatoes and sat for a while on a bench. The thing was not to give up. I tried to concentrate on enjoying the sun on my face, my warm feet, the food's pleasant greasiness. A tavern down the way was raucous with singing, shouting, what sounded at one point like a fight, and I decided that if I hadn't found work by suppertime I'd go in and have a beer. *Life*, I thought, remembering Pete's Tavern. *Something happening.* And maybe someone could give me a tip – if nothing else, about a safe place to sleep. If that failed, I'd walk back over the bridge and sleep again in a park somewhere in Manhattan. Hide myself better. Try to buy a blanket or a jacket cheap from one of the second-hand stalls I'd seen down near the bridge.

Not to give up: that was the thing. *An able-bodied man can always find work if he tries hard enough.* I had said those words myself, plenty of times, in my other life. Lurking around the edges of my sympathy had always been a faint contempt for men begging on street corners or selling apples, men you heard about who couldn't support their families, who stood in breadlines or ran off somewhere or drank themselves to death. *An able-bodied man can always find work.* It was one of the assumptions made by people with jobs, I realized, and at the back of my consciousness something was nagging at me, but every time my brain threatened to settle on it I managed to detour. I knew what it was: it was fear that maybe an able-bodied man can't always find work, no matter how hard he tries. It was the growing certainty that I wasn't going to get taken on as a longshoreman. And I didn't have the clothes to apply for any other kind of job. Orson wasn't dead. Somewhere, no doubt, he was walking around in one of my good suits – a suit in which I'd get hired instantly, I felt, for anything that was going. A newspaper job, an office slot, something that required more brain than muscle – those jobs were out there.

Times were hard, but the city hadn't shut down. People went out their front doors every morning in suits and hats, and ended up in offices, where they worked all day sitting at a desk, and at the end of the week they drew a paycheck. If I could dress the part, there was no reason I couldn't do the same.

The faint shadow of my terror persisted. I needed a new plan. Maybe I should go down to the Lower East Side, I thought, and spend the rest of my money on a second-hand suit, a shirt, a tie, a decent hat. I hadn't tried the sugar refineries yet, and I still had the cards from the employment agencies I'd been to the day before. I could go back. Other men went back, somehow they made it work out, I could do it too. *Clothes make the man*: one of my father's clichés, but some clichés were true. . . .

I tipped my face up to the late afternoon sun, closed my eyes, and instantly dozed off. I was awakened when someone sat heavily beside me. I opened my eyes to see a man who reminded me so much of my father I was briefly disoriented. *Dad? Down on the docks in Brooklyn?*

"Hi there," he said in the New York accent, and I woke up. He wasn't, of course, my father. He was a dapper, middle-aged man in a blue business suit and a dark blue silk tie. "Howard Weller," he said, holding out his hand. "Sorry I disturbed you. You looked so peaceful there, snoring away."

We shook hands. "I'm Robert Sinclair."

He frowned. "Not Robert Sinclair from Cincinnati, is it?"

I had to laugh. "No, sir. Just Robert Sinclair from Rochester, New York."

"Rochester. You don't say." I could see that he was studying my black eye, my paint-spattered cap – trying to figure me out. "Is that your home town? I know it well. I've done a heap of business up in Rochester, and I must say I was always treated fairly there."

For a wild, hopeful moment my mind leapt ahead: Howard Weller was an old friend of my father, he had a thriving – what? –

textile firm, office machinery business, publishing house, what did it matter, he was looking for a clerk, someone to take phone calls and write up orders, someone who could type a little, who could spell things properly, who had a head on his shoulders. *We can't pay much to start, Robert, but I can offer you eighteen a week – let's say twenty, you look like a hard worker . . .*

"Yes, it's a grand little city," he said. "You should be proud to be one of its sons." He leaned back on the bench with a sigh, crossed one leg over the other, and smiled at me. "But now you live in New York?"

"Yes. Since spring."

"A-ha. A newcomer. Welcome to our fair metropolis, Robert. How are you enjoying your stay?"

"I was enjoying it fine until I had a run of bad luck," I said. Might as well get it over with. "Just now I'm looking for work."

He raised his eyebrows. "Sorry to hear that. Want to tell me about it?"

"Well." I took out my pack of Luckies and offered him one. He took it, and produced a monogrammed gold lighter. "There's not much to tell," I said. "I was robbed of just about everything I own except the clothes on my back. And then I lost my job."

"Whew." He shook his head sympathetically. "That's a pretty bad run of luck, for sure. Just proves it can happen to anyone. Even a good-looking, well-spoken lad like yourself." He sat for a minute, smoking, and then he leaned toward me and said, "Be honest with me, Robert. Have you had dinner?"

"I had some fried potatoes a while ago."

Howard Weller jerked his head back with an exclamation of disgust. "Fried potatoes! Is that all? Wouldn't you like a cold beer and a roast beef dinner?"

It was just the kind of thing my father would have said. He even had my dad's modest pot belly, and the tufts of white hair in his ears. It was easy to imagine him on the golf course. "Sure I would, Mr. Weller, but my budget won't stretch that far."

"Well, mine will, darn it! Let me take you to dinner. As a way of saying thank you to the city of Rochester, New York. There's a nice little place just up the street called the Dockside Inn that can provide a pretty good piece of beef. What do you say?"

"I can't let you do that." I could already taste the meat, the gravy, the beer. "You don't know me from Adam."

"I'd like to get to know you, Robert," he said, and he put one hand on my leg, above my knee, and squeezed. "We could get acquainted over dinner, and then maybe go somewhere else. Have ourselves a good time."

At first I didn't understand, and then in a flood of humiliation I did. My face burned. I wasn't even angry: my first reaction was a huge rush of sorrow. "I'm afraid I've given you the wrong impression." Shakily, I stood up and tossed my cigarette away. "I'm sorry."

"Wait! I don't mean anything but what I said, Robert. I'd like to buy you a good dinner. Don't mind me, my boy. I'm a lonely man, and sometimes I get a little – I become –"

"Sure, I understand." I couldn't look him in the eye. "I've got to get going, though. Maybe some other time."

"It's just your company, Robert. Just someone to talk to."

I walked away, conscious of Weller's gaze on me. Suddenly the filth of the place, the stench, the derelict buildings and raucous taverns and wretched groups of drunks – all of it was sickening. I knew I'd probably begun to smell of rotten fish myself, and then I thought: *what in hell does it matter?* Add the stink of desperation to my black eye and two-day stubble and filthy rags. I passed a warehouse where a couple of heavily-muscled men were loading barrels onto a truck.

"Hey, pretty boy," one of them called.

I said, "Leave me the fuck alone."

He jumped back, holding up his hands in mock terror, and I walked on followed by their laughter. Some combination of pity, shock, shame made me blink back tears. The thing was not to give up, I repeated to myself, but it was beginning to seem that the thing was to throw myself in the river.

The walk to the bridge seemed endless, and, by the time I realized I was lost, I was hungry again, my new boots had begun to pinch, and it was as pitch dark as it ever gets in the city. I could see the huge arc of the bridge against the deep blue sky, but I couldn't find the way up to it. I trudged through the streets below the bridge, finding myself on Fulton Street, a horrifying stretch that seemed even worse than the Bowery across the river: a street haunted by blind desperation – men lying on the pavement like corpses, rats scurrying in dark corners, rows of seedy Men Only hotels, the corpse of a cat, a man retching loudly in the gutter, a ravaged woman who raised her skirt to expose her private parts. This was the depths, this was where you went when you gave up.

I turned off, away from the waterfront, and went up a hill to a neighborhood I had walked in once or twice back in my insomniac days, a place of pleasant, tree-lined streets of brownstones and apartment houses. Now I felt almost as unprotected there as I had on Fulton Street among the derelicts and whores. I was dropping with fatigue, my feet were sore and blistered, I was starving. I walked the streets painfully, and the people I passed – folks out walking their dogs, dressed-up couples arm in arm, a uniformed woman pushing an elaborate baby carriage – every one of them looked at me with suspicion and hostility. I kept expecting someone to call a cop and have me arrested for vagrancy. And yet it was all so normal, just an ordinary Thursday night in New York City with people on their way out to dinner, or going home to listen to The Green Hornet, Major Bowes, maybe Bing on the Kraft Music Hall. *That's my life too*, I wanted to say to them. *This isn't me, these last three days aren't who I am. Not long ago I had a wife and an apartment and a job, just like you. I'm Robert Sinclair, and I write plays.*

I write plays.

Suddenly an entrance to the IRT loomed ahead of me, and, without stopping to think, I hurried down the steps as if someone were chasing me. I found a nickel in my pocket, bought a token, and when the train came I slumped into a seat, dripping with sweat, my breath coming fast, my heart beating hard. A woman with a baby moved away to another seat, looking at me with distaste. I didn't care. I didn't care about anything. I needed to go to – oh, Christ, what was it? Fifty-fourth Street? Fifty-third? Where I had flung *Afternoon Coffee* under a rhododendron bush. I must have been crazy. It was all I had in the world, it was my wife, lover, child, self, and I had abandoned it to who knew what atrocity? I closed my eyes and imagined a trash can, a bonfire, a marquee on some Broadway theatre next spring announcing the world premiere of a new play by Joe Schmo, *Afternoon Coffee*, starring Fredric March and Katharine Cornell.

I got off at Broadway and 50th Street, and almost ran the four long blocks to Fifth Avenue and three more to 53rd. Yes, that was it, and there was the fancy house with the finicky hedge, the ornate fence. I stopped before it, out of breath. A light was on over the front door, and the *S* for *Sinclair* was picked out in shadows. It seemed as deserted as it had been that morning, but there were lights on behind the drapes. I imagined a radio playing softly, wine poured, dinner served on plates so thin you could see the butler's fingers through them when he set them down.

I stood there for a long time, wanting to be inside, to be whoever lived there, wanting somebody else's life. Before me in the dark was the rhododendron. No one passed by, no one looked out of the windows. The night had gotten chilly, and I shivered in my old shirt. I knew I couldn't stand there forever, but if I never looked I'd never know for sure. *This might be the last happy moment of your life*, I said to myself. Finally, I shut my eyes and groped through the wrought iron bars of the fence and under the rhododendron. My fingers could just touch the smooth black case.

I had to go around to the gate in order to get it out, and my heart banged in my chest as I slipped the latch and went in, keeping my eyes on the lighted window, imagining a woman in a silk dress looking out – *Doesn't it look cold out there, darling? A good night to be in here with the fire going.* Then a scream, the light spilling out the front door, the shouts, the paddy wagon. *I write plays! I'm not a bum, I'm a playwright.*

But nothing moved. I darted over to the bush, grabbed the case by its handle, dashed out again. I didn't open it until I was half a block away. Everything was just as I had left it – typewriter, play script, notebook – and I closed it up again and bowed my head over it, my cheek against the cold leather. *Thank you thank you thank you*, I thought, and realized I had spoken aloud. I straightened up. All I needed was some chauffeur or yard man finding a bum in rags on his employer's front sidewalk, weeping, mumbling, hugging a typewriter.

I had my play back: my life, in a leather typewriter case. I didn't give a damn about anything else. The docks were behind me, the streets, the long lines of gray men. This was my life, damn it. I was a playwright, not a longshoreman. I hobbled over to Lexington Avenue where I went into a bar and ordered a double whiskey and the blue plate special.

■ ■ ■

I was on Seventh Avenue in the Village by nine the next morning. I hadn't been able to walk far. My feet were swollen and sore, and I was stiff from another night in the park, so I caught an F train and got off a couple of blocks from the five-cent restaurant. I stood in front for a while reading the menu, and then I went in and ordered oatmeal, coffee, and a piece of cherry pie. I ate slowly and had a refill of coffee and managed to kill an hour.

Gil didn't show up. I had lain awake the night before deciding what to do if he did appear with the money (buy some clothes, a pair of decent shoes, a night in a real bed), and if he didn't (head back up to the employment agencies and let them cheat me), knowing deep in my heart that he wouldn't show and that I'd be spending the day footsore and weary and with about as much chance as a French poodle of finding work. Still, every time the door opened I looked for him. At ten o'clock I began to think I'd imagined him, the elfin gray man in spats who somehow wheedled me out of the only thing I owned that could be turned into ready cash. How could I be so naive? And what good would it do to resolve to be stupid no more? And where did I go from here? At this point, I didn't even have the bus fare to Rochester in my pocket.

I left, finally, limping and lugging my typewriter case. At least I had that, and I tried to feel good about it, to bring back the emotion I'd felt the night before at the reunion with my poor play. But everything seemed flat in the hard light of morning. And I was cold: the sky was overcast, a brisk wind had sprung up. Fall was coming. I would have to spend a portion of the pittance I had left on a coat. A coat or a sweater? I debated the question as I walked back up Seventh Avenue and finally decided on a coat: I could wear it to keep warm during the day, and curl up in it in the park at night. It was then, I think, that the reality of who I had become hit me. Playwright or no, I was a man who had to spend most of his time calculating the logistics of eating and sleeping. I was a man among many, homeless and jobless and moneyless. Friendless, too – I could add that. And hopeless.

I sat down on a doorstep, clutching my typewriter case. I was freezing. I needed to head over to the Lower East Side and buy an old coat. The best thing would be to walk there: I'd save a nickel and it wasn't that far. But not quite yet. I sat there a while in a comfortable daze: I had eaten, I was sheltered a little from the cold. Idly, the way I might touch my eye to see how much it hurt, I thought about May, wondered where she was. This was Friday: I'd last seen her Monday night as she went out in her high heels to meet her friends at Mori's. It seemed a long time ago. I thought: in a few weeks I will have forgotten her face, her voice. Even now, as I tried to recall her, she had become indistinct, shadowy, a blonde woman with painted fingernails. And Orson: when I thought of Orson I saw his body lying on the floor, his closed eyes, the dribble of blood; and when that image passed, I remembered his strange, unexpected embrace, his rough cheek, his hands on my shoulders, and suddenly he was so real I had to look up, as if he might suddenly materialize before me.

I left, finally, and continued down Seventh Avenue, then crossed over Houston Street and down to Delancey, where I knew I could find peddlers selling secondhand clothes. It was a long haul. I had wrapped my handkerchief around my blistered heel, and I found that if I walked in a certain way the pain was diminished. In a trash can I found a clean discarded newspaper, all in Chinese, and folded part of it into the front of my shirt and part into the back for warmth. I stepped into a Salvation Army soup kitchen to rest my feet and sat for a while among snoring old men. Breakfast was apparently over, but there was a pile of moldy bread on a table; as I watched a cockroach crawled out from under it. When I got up to leave, one of the men came to and hollered after me, "Hey! Who the hell do you think you are? Get the fuck outta here."

Outside, I paused on the sidewalk, feeling the sharp wind. Was that where I was headed? Would I end up a deranged wino sleeping it off in a soup kitchen? I looked into the window of a shoe repair shop and saw the blurry reflection of my face – *me, Robert*, still myself in spite of the black eye, the stubbled chin. It was a surprisingly reassuring sight. I looked into my own eyes, and the world righted itself for a moment.

And then, quickly, something resembling shame washed over me. *Who did I think I was?* I had been wandering the city feeling sorry for myself for exactly three days. Most of the people I encountered had been poor and desperate for months, years. And I knew that, if I only swallowed my pride, I could go back to Rochester or knock on Mrs. Amalfi's door and find people who would take me in. Three days ago I had recoiled from that particular humiliation with arrogance. Now I wasn't sure how long I could hold out: these three days had taught me, if they had taught me nothing else, that this was a harder life than anything I had imagined, and that it was entirely possible that I would reach some extremity that would force me to ask for help. I looked myself in the eye and told myself I would not starve, I would not die, I would not live out my days as a bum or throw myself in the river. I had resources, I wasn't entirely friendless. But instead of cheering up I became downhearted all over again.

At the first shop I came to on Delancey I bought a Harris tweed coat from a man in a yarmulke. No words were exchanged. I picked it up, tried it on. It had once been a good coat, better than the one I had so blithely abandoned at the Alhambra. Now it was threadbare, buttonless, the pockets ripped. He held up one finger. I put three quarters on my palm and offered them. He shrugged and reached for the coat. I put the quarters back in my pocket and handed him a dollar.

The coat was wonderful. It might not be worth much in January, but in October it was perfect, and I clutched it around me gratefully. But I had two dollar bills and one quarter left, and I felt sick when I thought about it. I went into a cafeteria for a cup of coffee and a roll, and sat down in a daze, wondering what I was doing, was I trying to hit bottom, was that what I really wanted: to humble myself with my mother, my sister, Mrs. Amalfi and Hana.

Or worse: complete degradation. I saw myself going to Gant and begging for another chance. Or knocking on May's friend Lois's door, demanding to know where my wife was.

I had two bills and a dime. By the end of the day I'd have a dollar something.

Defiantly, as if May were sitting across from me, Orson lounging at her side in my blue V-neck sweater and one of my white shirts, I bit into the roll and washed it down with hot coffee. The hell them all. I'd manage somehow. It was still early, there was plenty of time to get out there and pound the pavements: I said that to myself, but it was all hot air and bravado. I knew I had come to the end of something, and that today, or possibly tomorrow, I'd have to give in. And do what? I didn't know, I knew only that it was something that would change me, turn me into a person I didn't want to be.

Then I looked up from my coffee, and there was Gil Waldemar coming in the door.

"Robert!" His eyes were glowing. He came over to my table and set down his pack, rummaging in one of the pockets. "Am I glad I found you."

I couldn't speak. I stared at him. He seemed even smaller than he had two days ago, thinner, sicker, grayer, his princely good looks refined even more down to bone and shadow, but he was smiling, and finally he straightened up and said, "You look like you can use this, Robert." I looked down: there was a ragged twenty-dollar bill on the table in front of me. He laid three ones on top of it and a couple of pieces of silver. "Twenty-three-fifty was all I could get." He heaved a sigh and sank into the chair across from me. "I hope it's all right."

I looked at him in confusion. "What?"

"For the cuff links, Robert. Comedy and tragedy. I sold them for you." Gently, he put a hand over mine. "You remember. I said

I hoped to get twenty-five dollars for them, but this was the best I could do."

I clutched at his hand. "This is mine? This money?"

"Of course. I missed you up on Seventh Avenue. I was late, and I apologize – frankly, I didn't manage to seal this deal until this morning. I was going to go back tomorrow at the same time – that seemed the best thing to do. And then I walk into Vladek's here and you're sitting at a table. Talk about fate!"

I couldn't seem to let go of his hand, which was very thin, very dry and warm. I sat there staring at the cash. "Thank you," I said finally, in a whisper. I wanted to say *You've saved my life*, but I knew that was melodramatic and not even true. I was conscious of wanting to impress him with my extremity, my desperation. And yet in a way it was true – not literally perhaps, but in some profound way I couldn't explain. In my confusion, I said, "Don't I owe you something? Some kind of commission?"

"I wouldn't mind a coffee," he said.

I jumped up. "How about a roll to go with it? Or a sandwich?"

"To tell you the truth, I'd rather have a knish. A fruit knish. Apple? That would be best. But whatever they've got. I have a terrible sweet tooth."

"That's all? Just a knish?"

He didn't answer immediately, just looked up at me, narrowing his eyes. "Your eye is the most amazingly beautiful shade of iridescent green. Like the belly of an exotic fish." Then he added, almost absently, "Yes, Robert, thank you, that's all for now."

When I returned with the food, he was rummaging in his pack again. "I made another good deal yesterday. I sold that watch I showed you. Remember it? That dainty little thing? And I bought this with the money."

It was a gold tiara with three dazzling stones set into it. "Are those real diamonds?"

Gil nodded. "Yep. Not the best, not the most impressive, not the most beautiful diamonds in the world, but it's pretty, isn't it?"

"Sure. It's pretty enough. But – you bought this?"

"Yes. I may sell it again eventually, but for now – well – I like jewels," he said shyly, and then, without warning, he began to cough – his ghastly, wracking cough that sounded like he was about to expire.

"Can I do anything?"

He bent over, one hand in the air, waving me off, while the other pulled a handkerchief out of the pocket of his coat. He pressed the handkerchief to his mouth and coughed into it, muffling the sound, and after a minute he was still. He sat with his eyes closed, and then he opened them and said, as if nothing had happened, "In fact, I love jewels." His voice was hoarse, and he took a sip of coffee. "They are, to put it mildly, my passion. Or one of them." He put away his handkerchief and picked up the tiara, holding it so that it caught the light and sparkled. "Yes, this is a beauty, in its way."

"What are you going to do with it until you decide to sell it? Just admire the damn thing?"

"I have plans for it. Maybe I'll show you later." He took a bite of his pastry, chewing slowly, as if eating was painful. He didn't turn red when he coughed, like most people did: he became a deathly white, and his face still hadn't regained what little color it had had. Except for his eyes, he looked like a dead man. "So," he said. "Here we are again, after all."

"Where are you from, anyway?" I asked on an impulse. "How did you get here?"

He bent down to stash the tiara back in a pocket. "Why do you want to know?"

"Nosy."

He gave me a strange look. "That's all?"

"I guess so."

I felt that I'd disappointed him in some way I couldn't fathom. He fumbled in his bag for a moment or two, and then he straightened up and leaned back in his chair. "I was born in Beaumont, Texas, but I left home when I was fourteen."

I realized that the trace of music I'd heard in his speech was the remains of a Southern accent. "Why was that?"

"Well." He hesitated. "To put it simply, they didn't like who I was. And I suppose I didn't like who they were. These things happen. I made my way along the coast, then went up the river to Baton Rouge, got a job as a houseboy to an old man who missed his slaves. He was good to me. I grew up there. He had a library – you know the kind, all wood paneling and books with leather bindings. He let me read what I wanted. For years, I read nothing but poetry. He didn't care what I did as long as I took care of him. I was with him when he died. He was very old by then, and he died in great pain." He stopped again, looked out toward Delancey Street, and I saw tears in his eyes. "I moved down to New Orleans then. I was still just a kid, not much more than twenty years old, but I knew my way around. I lived in the city for a long time – years – and then I needed a change, and I drifted further south to some of those river towns near the Gulf. I loved it down there. Land of opportunity! You last a year in one of those places, and they'll elect you mayor of the town."

"So why didn't you?"

"Last? The short version is that I got sick and ended up in the county hospital. But a kind of friend of mine was on his way to New York City, and when I was feeling better I hooked up with him and ended up here. This was in 1917. They wouldn't take me for the war effort – said I was too skinny, too small." He smiled. "You must have been a little boy back then, during the war."

"I was about eight years old when we went in."

"That's what I figured. Seven or eight." He seemed to want to say something else, but held it back – just sat there looking at me over his coffee and smiling, as if at a happy memory. Finally, he went on, "So once I got to New York, that was it for me. The only place I wanted to live. I've been here ever since, and I have no plans to ever leave it." His smile widened, but his eyes didn't change. "Unless circumstances force me to, of course."

As if I were waking from a sleep, I became aware as he talked of the life around me: the plump, hairnetted woman behind the counter, the old Jewish man at one table, the young lovers holding hands at another, the fat man with his plate of doughnuts, the schoolmarmy woman with her tea, the people drifting in, sitting down with their coffee or their celery tonic or their Pepsi-Colas, then drifting out again while others took their places. I had a twenty-dollar bill in my pocket, a cup of coffee in front of me, a warm place to rest. My typewriter case was between my knees, and my play was inside it. Under the table, I had eased my boots off. And across it was Gil Waldemar with his gray hair and trim gray whiskers. I felt something in me relax, something that had been stretched tight. *All is well,* I thought, and I leaned forward across the table and said, "I just want you to know, Gil – " It was the first time I'd said his name, and I blushed. "At this point, you're the best friend I've got in the world."

"What do you mean?"

"I mean exactly that. Two days ago I hadn't even met you, and now –" I stopped. What was I saying?

Gil said, "I'm glad to be your friend, Robert, but really – I didn't do much."

"That's not true. You've made everything different, you've saved me from I don't know what." I recalled that Orson had said almost those same words to me that first night up in his room, and I felt my face turning red. "It's not the money, the twenty-two bucks. It's that I believed in you, and you didn't let me down."

He shrugged. "People aren't so terrible. If you give them a chance, they come through most of the time."

"I used to think that was true."

"It's still true, Robert. It's important to remember that. Otherwise, what's the use?"

"That's what I've been asking myself."

Gil broke off a piece of his knish, looked at it, set it down again; he had eaten perhaps two bites and drunk a few sips of coffee. We sat in silence for a minute. Then he smiled over at me kindly. Just seeing his face, the look in his eyes, filled me with an emotion I realized as the kind of simple happiness I hadn't experienced in a long time.

"Come with me," Gil said. "I have a couple of calls to pay, and then maybe I can help you figure out where you are and what you're going to do next. And what makes it all worth it." He put his hand on my arm and looked at me with concern. "Or are you all walked out, Robert?"

His white hand was thin and square on the rough sleeve of my coat, and I wanted to touch it, but I only said, "No, I'm all right. I'll come."

We walked around the Lower East Side while Gil performed financial transactions in two second-hand shops, a pawn shop, and the back room of a Rumanian restaurant. He had two fits of his horrible coughing, one on the street, one in the restaurant in Chinatown where we stopped for some egg rolls for me and tea for Gil. I tried to make him eat, but he wasn't interested. Spending all that time with him, I could see how mortally sick he was. It wasn't just the cough, though that was bad enough; there was also pain: he would press his hands to his chest, his eyes closed, and when he had recovered he was obviously exhausted, and the lines in his face were etched deeper.

After we ate, I insisted on carrying his pack, and after a ridiculous argument (his fatigue, his cough, versus my sore feet) he reluctantly gave in, but he insisted on carrying my typewriter case. By the time we got to Eighth Avenue, it was cold outside, and getting dark; inside, the seedy hotel called the Chateau was drafty, malodorous, and not very clean. The windows were so grimy it was perpetual dusk. In the little lobby, two thuggish young men looked at us with hostility. Gil ignored them. A large black man in a turban lurked behind a desk, peering out at us in the gloom.

"Ah, Mr. Waldemar. I'm glad to see you back safe."

Gil reached into one of his leather pockets and found a greasy packet. "I brought you a couple of egg rolls, Isaac. The vegetarian kind."

"Very kind of you." Isaac showed a row of gleaming white teeth and reached out a hand, his fingers glittering with rings. "Any news on that item you were searching out for me?"

"Maybe next week. But you know I don't promise anything."

"I understand that," Isaac said. "Just want you to know I'm still interested."

"This is my friend Mr. Sinclair. He may be staying with me a while."

Isaac said, "I understand that, too, Mr. Waldemar," and bit into an egg roll.

Gil's room was like an oasis in a desert of squalor: it contained a neatly made-up double bed, a desk, a bookcase in which he kept the complete works of Keats, including his letters, along with a dictionary, a Bible, a couple of poetry anthologies, and Shakespeare's plays in the same edition I had lost in Central Park. There were heavy drapes to keep out the cold and the dust that drifted in even through a closed window from the rail yards down the block. There was a rug on the floor, a pile of pillows, candles, a mirror on the wall in an ornately carved frame.

Gil closed and padlocked the door. "You probably think this place is a snakepit," he said. "But, believe me, I've seen worse."

Then he lit the candles, took a bottle of whiskey from a cupboard, and poured it, neat, into two cut-glass tumblers. My hand trembled when I took it, and I swallowed half the whiskey immediately. Gil refilled my glass, and we sat on the floor drinking, with the pillows at our backs. For the present, he seemed to have revived; he was his ageless, elfin self again. He looked around the room, pleased. "All things considered, it's not a bad life, is it?" he asked.

"It's all very –" I took another drink. The word eluded me.

"Very?"

"Very unusual," I said at last.

He laughed. "What's unusual about it, Robert? The whiskey? The candles? The mousetraps? My taste in furniture?"

I just shook my head. I hadn't slept properly in days, and sleep had dogged me as we trudged around the city; at the Chinese restaurant I could have slipped happily under the table and nodded off on the hard tiles. But now I was alert, my brain racing, heart pounding.

"Being in a flophouse?" Gil persisted. "What?"

I could hardly speak, and when I did my voice was hoarse. "You know."

We looked at each other. "Well, I suppose I do," he said softly. He set down his glass. "Wait. I'll show you something that's really unusual."

He got up and went over to his leather pack where we'd propped it against the wall. He took the tiara out of its pocket and, standing before the mirror, he arranged it on his springy gray hair. When he sat beside me again, his eyes were alive and joyful. "Was I right?" he asked. He posed, his head tilted, the diamonds winking in the candlelight. "Have you ever seen anything like this before, Robert?"

He was completely beautiful, and when he held out his hand, I took it.

SEVEN

We were lovers, and before he became too ill we made love whenever we could. We made love instead of eating, instead of sleeping. We would start to talk and end up back in bed. We would get ready to go out and not get as far as the door. His illness could make him feverish, insatiable; desire energized him and brought spots of color to his cheeks. After we did the things we did he still wasn't spent: he would lie beside me, or with his body stretched across mine, and talk, or listen to me talk, or quote Keats, or hum softly to himself, touching me idly until we were both aroused again.

Sex with Gil was a revelation to me. His gaunt chiseled face, his narrow chest with its nest of black hair, his slender torso and thick sex, his legs as slim as any woman's: I loved it all, every part of him, more than I thought I could love anyone or anything. The things he said to me, the way he made me feel. When I looked back to my life with May, it was like a movie, or a book. I had known pleasure, but never this intimacy, this kind of tie. After making love with Gil, I could no more have leapt out of bed and worked on my play than I could have leapt into the air and flown out the window. All I wanted was to lie there half-asleep with his skin against my skin. I didn't work on the play at all during that time, and when Gil asked me to read it to him I kept putting it off. I cared nothing for imaginary people and their concerns: for the first time in my life, all I wanted was what was real.

Yes, we became lovers, but he was almost more like my brother, or a son, or a father. He was twice my age. He had seen more by the time he was twenty-five than I would see ever. I had known him only a few days. And yet from the first it was as if he'd been in my life as long as my parents, or the old dog Luther. As if there had never been a time when I didn't know him. Gil.

But he was sick, and he was getting sicker. The first time I caught him coughing up blood – something he had tried to keep from me – he held up the handkerchief and, when he got his breath back, quoted Keats: "That drop of blood is my death warrant."

Except that by then it wasn't a drop of blood, it was a gush. After a hemorrhage, I would hold him, cradling him in my arms for warmth, and simply listen to him breathe: the sound of his breathing, ragged at first, then calmer, so nearly normal it could fool you – that was all I cared about. All I wanted was for it to go on. But I knew, we both knew, that a time would come, not too far off, when it would stop.

After the first horror, I suppose I grew used to the blood. Every night I would bring a bucket of cold water from the foul bathroom down the hall and soak that day's handkerchiefs in it, watching the water turn pink. He spent more and more time propped up in bed, wrapped in blankets, and he liked to have me right beside him, talking: before he died, he said, he wanted every detail of my life, from a description of my lost clothes to the names of my nephews in Rochester to May's miscarriage.

"I'll take it with me to the other world," he joked. "I'll take Luther to heaven with me, and the boats on the Charles River, and Mr. McGreevey, and that bastard Gant, and lovely Hana." He smiled at me. "And you, Robert. I'll take you with me forever, wherever I go."

"Don't talk like that," I said at first, and then it sounded so inane I didn't say it any more. He became, paradoxically, much sicker after he met me. "This damned happiness is killing me," he said. His *posthumous existence*, he called those last weeks – Keats again.

But, when he could manage it, he continued to ply his trade. He had strange hectic fits of nervous energy that even sex could not exhaust, and that was when we would take the subway down to the Lower East Side, paying calls – that's how he always put it – on Gil's various contacts: Mr. Silver, the perfectly-named jeweler under the Manhattan Bridge, Weissman the coal merchant on Delancey who claimed to be Emma Goldman's illegitimate son, a mysterious old Gypsy woman named Speranzita who lived in a dirt-floored basement with a dog and a parrot, and – my favorite – a hoarse-voiced, warty, jovial Dickensian man named Hobson whom we always met at the Rumanian restaurant and who shared Gil's love of gems. Those were the ones he dealt with most often, but Gil seemed to know everyone – everyone, at least, who was vaguely seedy, a little peculiar, not quite American but not entirely foreign either, and who (despite appearances that seemed to the contrary) had a solid little sum of money with which to make a deal. Sometimes Gil would sell, sometimes buy, or trade, or just talk about what was being bought and sold and traded and talked about by others. It was an underworld of commerce that had nothing to do with the glitter of Fifth Avenue or even the pushcarts on Orchard Street. It was all about secrecy, obsession, arcane cravings: money was just a by-product.

And yet Gil made plenty of money. Like many of the people we met, he looked poorer than he was. We wore second-hand clothes bought from pushcarts, and lived in a squalid hotel in Hell's Kitchen with roaches and mice, but we had what we needed. We ate our meals in restaurants and drank whiskey. We washed with fragrant white soap from a fancy pharmacy on Sixth Avenue, we had our laundry done by the Chinaman on the corner. We bought cigarettes by the carton. Gil gave money to beggars, slipped quarters to people we chatted with on the street, occasionally bought a pint bottle for the old man who lived in unimaginable squalor in the tiny room next to ours.

And he loved the extravagant gesture. One day soon after I met him, we walked up to a men's store called Keep's on 44th Street where Gil bought us each a soft-collared broadcloth shirt (blue for him, pale yellow for me), and then took us out for *soupe à l'oignon*, frogs' legs, and a bottle of wine at a restaurant called Bonat's. I asked him how much money we had spent that day. He was feeling good; it was one of the days when he didn't even seem sick. He looked at me archly. "I don't know, maybe thirty dollars," he said, and grinned. "Trying to impress a suave guy like you isn't cheap, Robert."

Periodically some other inmate of the Chateau would knock on our door, and he and Gil would have a whispered conversation out in the frigid, urine-stinking hall. "Everybody has something," he would say when he returned. "It's amazing how even in times like these almost no one is truly destitute, truly without some little treasure." And he would hold up a watch, a ring, an old gold coin. Once a pearl necklace he fastened around his neck and once a hideous lamp he said was French and worth good money if he could find the right buyer.

He trusted me without question, keeping his wad of bills in the drawer of his desk and making me take money from it when we needed something. When we went out on our rounds, he would press a five-dollar bill into my hand.

The large bills made me nervous; I wasn't used to such riches. "Were you ever poor?" I asked him.

It made him laugh. "Robert, you astonish me. I've been poor all my life. I'm poor now. Don't you understand that? The poor man is the one who has no home, no security, no future. The poor man lives in the present, like a dog. I have what I earn. That's all."

I didn't want to take money from him; I wanted to go out and find a job, pitch in for the room, pay for food, but he became angry when I talked about these things. "Can't you just stay with me quietly until the end, Robert?" he would say. "Without all this irritable grasping after propriety or self-respect or whatever you call it?" He was always quoting Keats. I didn't catch all the allusions, but when he said, "O for ten years," stroking my cheek as we lay beside each other in bed, I recognized it and knew that when Keats wrote those words he had maybe five years left. Gil, I knew, had much less than that – months, if we were lucky. Weeks, it seemed as November came and the weather turned wintry. It occurred to me one morning that I would probably be with him when he died: I imagined hearing his breath come and go, then silence, and the thought made me colder than the wind off the river ever did.

Once, in bed, he raised himself up on one elbow, looking at me, and quoted:

> *A thing of beauty is a joy forever:*
> *Its loveliness increases; it will never*
> *Pass into nothingness; but still will keep*
> *A bower quiet for us, and a sleep*
> *Full of sweet dreams, and health, and quiet breathing,*

and we tried to be amused, both of us, at the melodrama of his reciting poetry in that candlelit room, intoning it with mock-solemnity, but when he finished we both had tears in our eyes. "*Health, and quiet breathing,*" he repeated, and clutched my hand. "Jesus, Robert, I don't want to die."

"Can't we go to the mountains or something?" I asked. "Isn't that what people do? Or to a warmer climate? Arizona, Gil. Or Florida. This freezing winter can't be good for your lungs. This cold little room."

"Keats went to Italy where it was warm, and he was dead in a matter of months." He held his hand up to the light and we both looked at it. Daily, almost hourly, he seemed to become more fragile: his hand was a flower made of bones. He turned to me and his eyes were anguished. "Don't talk about going anywhere. This is where I live, and all I want is for you to stay with me, Robert. In this room. Just stay with me. Be here when I wake up and when I go to sleep and in between. Listen to me. I saw you in that kitchen, you came in and called Weldon a little toad and the place just lit up." He grinned at me through his tears. "I knew then that you and I belonged together. Don't ask me to explain it, just take my word for it. You know the morning we almost missed each other? When I finally found you at Vladek's? I was like a crazy man, rushing around the streets looking for you. That we met again was a miracle. It was meant to be." He sighed one of his shaky sighs. "Don't leave me, Robert," he said. "You are my thing of beauty. You are my joy forever."

During the hours that we sat together and I talked, he kept up a running commentary. The things I told him animated him the way lust did, and he was as full of ideas and opinions as if we were in a class together, my pallid life a great American novel we were dissecting. Orson, he proposed, had wanted to become me – out of a kind of love, Gil said, and out of envy – and that was why he had stolen my clothes, not to mention my wife. It was obvious that Orson and May had carried on all summer behind my back – an ambiguous and complicated situation for Orson, he said, but probably for May one of those sudden passions, like his for me in Verna's kitchen. Mrs. Amalfi, he suspected, had been the one who cleaned up the blood: there was more between her and Orson than met the eye – couldn't I see that? – and the importance of the blood couldn't be discounted: May's blood, then Orson's, and Mrs. Amalfi was there both times. "So much blood in your life, Robert," Gil said. "Now you have my bloody handkerchiefs to deal with." It meant something, he insisted, the way a poem meant something; if he lived long enough he'd figure out what.

It all sounded like nonsense to me, but I didn't care as long as it amused him. None of it mattered: only Gil mattered. And I had to admit that some of the things he said were plausible. He was especially fascinated with May, who, he said, sensed what I really was, and was repelled, and that was why she didn't want what Gil called "reproductive sex" with me.

I was intrigued. "How could she know? Even I didn't know."

"She was a woman of the world, Robert." He had a way of talking about her as if he had observed her for years. "Compared to May Munro," he said, "you were a puppy, wagging your tail and chasing rabbits and begging for a biscuit."

"That seems to be overdoing it just a bit." Gil's vision of me as a helpless innocent, a lovable naïve Leander, could be exasperating. It was almost as if he were writing his own play, a sort of theatrical *Candide* in which I was preyed upon by a city full of scoundrels and rogues.

He laughed when I told him this; then his face contorted, and he began to cough. It was agony to watch him: his shoulders heaving, the desperate gasps for air, the dry ratcheting noise, and his face getting paler, as if the blood he coughed into his handkerchief was drained directly from his skull. The happiest moments, for me, were when the cough would die away and he would gradually quiet, lying still with his eyes closed and his breath coming softly. I loved just to look at him then – so glad he was there, alive – the way I used to look at May's face as she slept. But looking at Gil filled me with peace.

During that time I spent with Gil at the Chateau, unless he woke up coughing, I slept well every night. "You're a better sleep specialist than Mrs. Amalfi will ever be," I told him drowsily one evening after we had made love. "After this, all I have the energy for is sleep."

"A sleep specialist. What a concept," he said, amused as he always was when I mentioned Mrs. Amalfi whom he considered one of the great absurd comic characters, the equal of Juliet's nurse, or Polonius. Then he said, "Of course, if you think about it, Robert, a sleep specialist was the last thing you needed. You're the real sleep specialist yourself."

"Meaning what?"

"Meaning you and your play-writing, those suave heroes you were in love with. You and your faggot sex with your wife. You and your snuggles with Jasper, your hard-on when Orson put his arms around you in that attic. You never knew who you were, Robert. You've been asleep all your life."

I thought about it. "I suppose that's one way of putting it."

"Those long night-time walks. This was what you were trying to escape. Or maybe this was what you were out there looking for." He reached out a hand and ran it idly down my body. "But Robert," he said softly. "Isn't it better to be awake? I've known who I was since I was a boy, and I know that no matter how long I live I'll never escape it. And you won't either. You're a man who loves men."

"I don't want to escape it," I said, and it was true. I had plunged into my relationship with Gil without guilt or regret. "But sometimes I'm still not sure if this is who I am. How can I know that? All I know right now is that I'm a man who loves you. I can't imagine this with anybody else."

"I can imagine it," he said. "I try not to, but sometimes it's all I can think about, that when I'm gone you'll be with someone else."

We always made love by candlelight, and in the yellow dimness of it his face was the face of a man in an old painting. It was certainly like no living face I had ever seen: his soft beard, his finely molded nose and cheekbones, his strange eyes that were the color of wood-ash, the iris ringed in black – he was like a saint in a medieval altarpiece. I wanted nothing more than to look at his face every day for as long as I lived. "Don't," I said.

"It's all right. It's what has to happen. You'll have a good life, Robert."

"All I want is you."

He said into my ear, "Don't make me cough. You know strong emotion makes me cough." I could hear the smile in his voice. *"In the very temple of delight melancholy has her sovereign shrine.* Or something like that. I may have left out a word or two. But you get the general idea."

I thought the line was an apt description of Gil himself. He was one of the merriest people I knew, but there was always a shadow of sadness in his eyes, as if he were pining for some other life. Whether this had always been there or had come with his illness, I didn't know.

"Say that you love me, Robert."

"I love you."

"Good." He leaned over me to blow out the candle. "Now we can sleep – real, honest-to-God sleep. Not that metaphorical kind you used to go in for."

And then he would doze off, content, repeating one of his litanies: *Mr. Gant was an old capitalist bastard, McGreevey's Steakhouse was on Mortimer Street, May's real name was Mary Kramer, Mrs. Amalfi's cats' names were Rosalind, Horatio, Ferdinand....*

■ ■ ■

I wasn't with him, after all, when he died. He had had a bad morning: he was feverish and in pain, and very weak – almost too weak to sit up. As I had done a dozen times, I asked him if I should get a doctor, or take him in a taxi to Bellevue, where he'd get free nursing. I had visions of doctors in white coats, hovering, with pills and injections. Inevitably, I thought of someone like Hana bringing him back to health. But he waved me away peevishly. "I'll be fine after I eat some breakfast."

I went out to buy us coffee and rolls and thick apricot jam at the diner on the corner, and when I returned he was lying dead, half out of bed, the blood still wet on his face and beard, his flannel pajama top, his hands. His eyes were squeezed shut, his bloody mouth half-open as if he had died in pain, or called for me.

I took the bucket I used to soak his handkerchiefs and brought back warm water from the bathroom. I propped him up on the bed and washed away the blood, closing his lips, smoothing his brow. He must have choked on it, I thought. His lungs filled up with it. He had drowned in his own blood. When he was clean, I kissed his mouth. He was still warm. I had left him alive, irritable, asking for coffee and jam. He could not be dead, and yet I knew he was.

It took me a long time to do anything about it. I stayed with him quietly as he had always asked me to, sitting beside him on the bed and holding his hand until the heat went out of it, and then I went downstairs and told Isaac, and he said I should go over to the 18th precinct station to tell them what had happened because neither of us knew what else to do. I ran there without my coat. The sergeant at the desk made a phone call, and after a while a doctor came and went back to the hotel with me. He pronounced Gil dead, filled out a form, and had him taken away.

I thought there would be money for a small funeral and a burial. I imagined a country cemetery somewhere, a headstone chiseled with the words: *A thing of beauty is a joy forever*. But when

I looked in Gil's pack, I found only a zircon ring and a copper bracelet, both worthless. In the drawer of his desk there was a five-dollar bill. Isaac had obviously gotten there first, and in my daze all I felt was stupid gratitude for the fiver. He had also overlooked a few things wrapped up clumsily in a paper packet on which was written, in Gil's elegant script: *For Robert Sinclair, from Gilbert M. Waldemar with love.* I untied it; my gold cufflinks were inside. I stared at them for a long time, the masks of comedy and tragedy, and then, hardly knowing what I was doing, I put them into my mouth and held them there, tasting the cold metal. He had never sold them. He had kept them for me. After a while, I spit them out and wrapped them up again. Belatedly, I wondered what the *M* stood for: I would never know.

EIGHT

Two days later I was down by the river standing in line at the Municipal Lodging House, four blocks from the Alhambra Gardens. My old neighborhood: it was like a foreign country, the fragment of a dream I had had many nights ago. I no longer cared who saw me or who knew what had happened to me. I felt cleaned out, dead. I carried my typewriter case, and on my back was Gil's pack, its pockets stuffed with my belongings: the clothes he had bought me, my cufflinks, his books. I took them with me only because I couldn't bear to leave them behind. Having possessions again felt like starting over, and yet I had no zest for such a thing.

I had a dollar bill in my pocket, and some change. I joined the line because I didn't want to do anything else, but I didn't want to do that, either. I didn't want to do anything. I stood and listened to the other men talk. I hadn't spoken to a human being since Isaac had hauled his bulk up the stairs and told me I'd have to pay in advance for another week. I looked him in the eye and said, "You know I can't afford this place," and he said, impassive, shaking his huge turbaned head, "Well, then, I'm sorry to say it, Mr. Sinclair, but you'll have to be leaving us." So I left. I spent two days sitting in libraries and cafeterias and Grand Central Station, two nights riding the subway. I ate hot meals, and I gave nickels and dimes to beggars. When my money was almost gone, I remembered the Municipal Lodging House.

It was a frigidly cold and windy afternoon, with a dusting of snow on the ground. I wore my boots and overcoat and a scarf of Gil's and a hat he'd made me buy one day on Delancey Street that he said made me look Spanish. They didn't help much, but I didn't mind. I remembered Gil saying: *I transcended such considerations long ago.* It made me smile. Now he was under the ground – Hart's Island was what the doctor had said, somewhere in the Bronx, the Potter's Field for the city, where the graves are dug by inmates from the prison next door. He was colder than I was, that was for sure. What I tried not to think about was how he had died alone, but I didn't have much else to think about, and so it kept coming back to me.

The line was long, stretching along 25th Street to Second Avenue and around the corner. If I had wanted to turn my head, I could have seen the Alhambra's five stories rising above the shabby little shops. The line moved very slowly. I gathered from the voices around me that it was touch and go on a day like this whether you'd get a bed or not. They took more than two thousand men, apparently, but there were always more in need of a place. You could stay five nights, and so there were men with vouchers who were let in first. After that, no one knew how many beds were available.

We shuffled forward a few paces, and then I felt a hand on my arm. I turned to see Mrs. Amalfi. She was wearing a long black cloak and an elaborate hat, low-brimmed and feathered. The men behind me gaped at her. "Robert," she said. "At last. Come with me. You must be freezing. What is that huge thing on your back? Come."

It was too cold to talk, the wind in our faces. She walked fast, carrying my typewriter case, which made her look oddly prim as she barreled down the street, like a schoolteacher with her bag. I shuffled along numbly beside her. It was a short walk to the Alhambra. The lobby was warm. I couldn't help looking critically at the palm trees, the marble floor, the windows: clean enough. Everything was the same. I had a sudden mad idea that Orson was the new super, living downstairs in my apartment, but Mrs. Amalfi said, "Gant brought a man from one of his other buildings. He does the job, but he's a most unpleasant person – not unlike his employer."

Up in her apartment, Mrs. Amalfi sat me down at the kitchen table, like old times. Under her cape, she wore a loose, flowing lavender tunic. The radiator under the windows hissed, the gauzy curtains billowed a little from the steam. In the corner, the birds were cooing, and one of the cats – Juliet or Romeo – slept on the rug, Horatio on a chair. They barely stirred when I entered.

"They know you," Mrs. Amalfi said.

"Well, that's something," I said. "Because I hardly know myself."

She gave me her sharp look. "You're hungry. Who can think properly when they're hungry? I'll make tea. And there's lemon cake. Or would you like soup?"

I ate everything she put in front of me. Mrs. Amalfi sat and watched me over her tea cup. She said she had looked for me almost daily since I left, and I thought of how she searched for hurt pigeons after a storm. Eventually, she figured, I might end up at the Municipal.

I said, "I always thought if I came back to this part of town I'd be wearing a sharp new suit and take you and Hana out to tea."

She shook her head sadly. "Robert."

"I've been a fool."

"Times are hard," she said. "Foolishness has nothing to do with it." She stood up and went to a cupboard. "What you need is to sleep, Robert. A long, peaceful, healing sleep. And I can see by looking at you that you're so tired you may not be able to sleep without assistance. Here. Hold out your hand." She placed something in my palm: a large white pill like a candy, a pastille, more oval than round.

"What is it?"

"It's the strongest weapon of the Sleep Specialist."

As she spoke, I could feel myself starting to crave it: sleep, silence, dark, nothingness. Surprisingly, the pill was bitter; I swallowed it with the remainder of my tea. "When will it work?"

"Soon." Then a thought struck her. "But maybe you would you like a bath."

I would like a bath, and she ran it for me while I stood in a daze and the cats, one by one, followed us into the bathroom. When the tub was half full, Mrs. Amalfi pushed back her full sleeves and stuck out her hand. "Come. Off with those clothes and get in. Don't be shy."

I hesitated only a moment. Life had become so strange and unlike itself: how much stranger could it be to take off my clothes and get into Mrs. Amalfi's bathtub? I removed my shirt, my shoes, last of all my trousers, letting them fall to the tiled floor, feeling no shame, feeling nothing but a craving for that warm, clean water.

Astonishingly, she intended to bathe me. I gave in and let her scrub me clean, remembering what I hadn't known was still lodged in my head: the sensation of being a very small boy being bathed by my mother, who sang the old songs she'd learned as a girl.

> *Oh my darling Nelly Gray,*
> *They have taken you away,*
> *And I'll never see my darling any more.*

Absurdly, the words came back to me, and I sat there only half awake in the warmth with my mother's voice in my head while Mrs. Amalfi scrubbed my body with a rough cloth –

everything except my privates: she handed me the washcloth and said, "Here. You do the rest." Then she washed my hair and rubbed it dry with a large pink towel, gave me a second towel to dry the rest of me, and led me stark naked down a short corridor to a dimly lit bedroom at the end. There was an elaborate bed with carved wooden posts that ended in pineapples. The wood was very dark mahogany, and the bedcover was shiny and quilted. Mrs. Amalfi removed it, draped it over a chair. Then she turned down the bed: plump pillows, white sheets, lace-bordered pillowcases. The sheets were very soft. I lay down and pulled the covers up, trying not to weep with exhaustion, gratitude, grief. Mrs. Amalfi drew the green shades. The room darkened, the lamp was a pool of amber light.

"There." She stood looking down at me. "How is this, Robert?"

"It's paradise. Thank you, Mrs. Amalfi." My voice broke. "What would I have done without you?"

She didn't speak for a moment, during which I almost dozed off. Then she said, "And yet you didn't come to me in your trouble."

I opened my eyes to see her standing over me in her purple tunic like an angry goddess. "I was too ashamed. I just wanted to hide myself away."

"I heard it all from Gant." She pursed her lips as if she had tasted something rotten. "Or rather, I heard Gant's side of it. You'll tell me yours when you wake up. You'll tell me the truth."

"I'll tell you what happened to me," I said. "I'm not sure what the truth is."

Her stern face frowned down at me. "It hurt me, Robert, when you disappeared without a word. Without a note slipped under my door. Without anything. It hurt me here." She pressed one hand to her heart, her rings flashing. "I know you were deeply disturbed by what happened. I can easily imagine your state of mind. And yet you need to get outside yourself sometimes and think of others. Even in extremity."

"I'm sorry."

She stood there in silence. I felt my eyes closing, sleep coming after me like a wolf. "Well." She sighed. "At least I found you."

I saw her turn out the lamp and move toward the door, I saw the door begin to close, but I was asleep before it clicked behind her.

■ ■ ■

I awoke in stages. First I emerged from dreams to the consciousness of something heavy against my foot, then of a muted noise like a small engine humming. I slipped back into sleep and dreamed I was running with Luther across green grass, and Luther was barking joyfully at pigeons. Then I opened my eyes a crack and saw a band of light on a wall, and a warm presence settled near my cheek. I remembered where I was, and then I slept again. When I woke, I could smell bacon cooking, and I desperately had to empty my bladder.

I dislodged the cat – Rosalind – and got out of bed. I pulled up the shade. There wasn't a cloud in the blue, blue sky over 21st Street, and while I slept snow had fallen, so that the street looked clean, sparkling in the sun, wrapped in white like a present. My first thought was of Gil, asleep forever on an island in the East River. I had a sudden vision of him walking toward me, stooped a little under the pack on his back: Gil and his impish smile. I would mourn him until I died, and yet waking on a sunny day after a good sleep in a warm room, I felt like a million dollars. I had dreamed about Luther and the birds, the factory engine that was Rosalind, a bench by a quiet river where a woman named Gwen I had known in college sat playing the guitar and singing *Oh my darling Nelly Gray*. These dreams seemed all wrong. I should have been dreaming of horrors and lost things, not of sunshine and music and my old dog. For a long time after my father died, I'd had a recurring nightmare about the worst thing I'd ever seen: my father's dead face, rouged, in his pale blue padded coffin. But lying on Mrs. Amalfi's cool sheets, I hadn't dreamed of my father, or of Orson Price, or of Gil. There was no anger or fear in any of my dreams, not even regret, and I didn't understand how this could be.

Forgive me, I thought.

I put my clothes back on, used the bathroom, and, Rosalind at my heels, went down the corridor to the kitchen. Sun poured through the windows, meat sizzled on the stove, the cats crouched patiently on the Oriental rug, the birds rustled in their cages. It was the kind of dream of comfort and warmth I had scarcely let myself imagine during my nights on subways and in parks, even in the cold room at the Chateau where Gil and I slept with our arms around each other to keep warm.

Mrs. Amalfi was there, measuring coffee into the pot. In the light of day – in the midst of her comforts, her care for me, the peculiar ordinariness of bacon and curtains and cats – I understood how wrong I had been not to see her before I left the Alhambra. I hesitated in the doorway, not sure how to approach her. But she spoke first. She put the pot on the stove, turned to me and said, "You look much better. You look almost like that man named Robert who used to be the super here."

"What time is it?"

"Nearly eight o'clock."

"It seems like I slept much longer than that."

Her eyes twinkled. "Eight the next day, Robert. It's Friday morning. You slept for – let me see – something like thirty-two hours. The earth has revolved. Snow has fallen. The milkman has delivered milk, the garbage truck has come and gone. The cats took turns sleeping with you. I hope they didn't disturb you."

I smiled. "Not likely. I feel like Rip Van Winkle." I put up my hand to the four days of whiskers rough against my fingers. "I feel like I've been under an enchantment."

"The world is still here, Robert, just as you left it. Bacon and eggs will bring you back. And good strong coffee."

Mrs. Amalfi cracked eggs into a pan. She was barefoot as usual, her hair hung down in back in a braid, she wore no lipstick; she looked like someone from another country, another time. Her loose tunic was a deep blue, the beads around her neck silvery. I watched her move swiftly around the kitchen, her body strong and mysterious under her garments, wondering absently, as I often had, where she got her money, the carpets, the paintings that crowded the walls, the good food. Had all this come from dispensing sleep potions to insomniacs?

She handed me a cup of coffee, and I took it to the bird corner. There was monstrous Portia, and Bianca whose beak needed cutting. Cordelia had died, but now there was a new pigeon named Beatrix who had part of one red foot missing. The sweet birds. They twittered softly at my approach. Juliet rubbed against my leg. I imagined the regiment of cats coming to the bed in turns during my long sleep, one always cuddled against my body, and I felt blessed, like the privileged son of a noble household.

"Now." Mrs. Amalfi set down a plate of food and motioned me to sit. "Come and eat. And tell me everything."

"I don't know where to begin."

"The day you left. When Gant fired you."

That was the easy part. I sat down and dug into my eggs and bacon, telling her as I ate about Gant's discovery that Orson lived in the attic, the thefts, Gant's early-morning visit to me, his ultimatum, my flight.

Mrs. Amalfi sat across the table from me, sipping furiously at her coffee as I told my tale, her eyes burning with indignation.

"Gant is a terrible man," she said when I was done. "He talked about you as if you were a criminal. He told me you stole things. He told me you deceived him. Of course, I believed none of it."

"I did deceive him. I didn't steal, but Orson did, and I'm the one who gave Orson the key."

Her eyes blazed. "You don't comprehend anything, Robert. Gant is like an old-world despot. With him, it's all about power. You took some of his power away. To a man like Gant that's like a kick in his private parts. It means war. He has to win. You were putty in his hands."

It was the way Gil had described me: Robert the little pet dog who saw nothing while the evil world led him around on a chain. It occurred to me that Mrs. Amalfi must have some private vendetta with Gant. That was why she had advised me to lie to him – because she hated him for some reason I would probably never know. If I had been more honest, told Gant about Orson from the beginning, I might still have my job. Then I knew that was absurd: I couldn't even do my job. He would have fired me and hired Orson.

"I don't give a damn about Gant," I said. "Let Gant have his crummy power. It's the rest of it that weighs on my mind."

"Yes, the rest of it." She got up and poured us both more coffee. "Tell me about your wife, then, Robert. And what has been going on these past two months?"

I told her then about the fight with Orson, the empty apartment, the stolen clothes. The time with Gil had taken away much of the misery of that day: it had become a story, something we talked about as we huddled together in bed – something for Gil to use his wits on and figure out, like one of those games they featured in the newspaper, where clues are provided to a crime and you have to figure out not only who did it but what the crime was. Now I was back at the Alhambra, and it was all real again:

Orson's blood on the floor, May's high heels tapping away, the chill emptiness of the apartment.

"They just disappeared into thin air, the two of them," I said. "Like some cheap magic trick." The memory of it pounded in my brain, and I buried my head in my hands and rubbed my temples with my thumbs. "Like something that you know can't really be happening."

"So. Your wife deceived you," Mrs. Amalfi said. "She deceived you all summer long. She and Orson Price." She spoke his name with such bitterness it surprised me.

"I suppose so," I said. I looked up. "I suppose that's what was happening. But – who knows? There was no ending. It's like a play that hasn't been finished. Like one of my own plays when it's half done, when I'm trying to come up with a final scene that makes sense."

Mrs. Amalfi smiled. "And then you would take one of your long midnight walks, and it all would come clear."

"Yes. It used to seem so easy." Write, walk, return to my sleeping wife, whom I loved.

"Life is not meant to be easy, like a play."

"Is it meant to be a mystery that you can never understand?"

"Sometimes it's just a puzzle. *God writes straight with crooked lines*," Mrs. Amalfi said. "Where does Shakespeare say that?"

My head was beginning to ache – I had slept too long – and I realized that part of what I felt was a deep disappointment: I had somehow expected Mrs. Amalfi to explain it all, not to give me more riddles. "I don't know."

"Well, maybe it's someone else." She waved a hand. "It doesn't matter. We were speaking of your wife. Such a pretty girl, but her nature was not pretty." She raised one finger. "Lilies that fester, Robert, smell far worse than weeds. There! That's Shakespeare!"

"Yes, it is." I had to laugh, but an immense sadness filled me. I could imagine scenes in my plays as vividly as if I were right there – a bystander on the street, a cat on a chair pretending to sleep – and yet the conspiracies of May and Orson, Orson and the master key, Orson and my father's suitcase, refused to take shape in my brain. Still, they had happened. What a stupid waste that summer had been, I thought, our marriage no more real than Oliver's love for Thomasina in *Fish Out of Water*. Less. Much less.

"You've never seen her?" I asked out of a kind of desperation. "Around the neighborhood? Or Orson? I thought I had killed him. I kept expecting the police to come after me."

She snorted. "I haven't seen the pair of them, but I can assure you that Orson is not dead and your wife is not lurking in the neighborhood." She touched her silver beads, as if she were taking an oath on them. "If they were, I would know."

"You weren't the one who cleaned up the blood?"

"Not that time," she said dryly. "Oh, Robert. How can you think such a thing."

"I'm sorry. I don't know what to think. The whole thing is exhausting – trying to figure it out." I smiled lamely. "From now on I'll stick to plays."

"It is without a doubt much simpler than you imagine. You have tortured yourself with this, and it's not worth it. Your wife became infatuated with a strange, cruel, troubled man. They took pleasure in lying to you. That's all it is. Not such an unusual thing. And now they're gone. Someday you may wish to find your wife, get a divorce from her, start over. But for now it's better to forget about them both."

I knew she was right, and that I had to get their images out of my head. Starting over was something else. I had started over with Gil. How many times can you start over? And where would I start? Divorce was something that had never occurred to me, and yet of course at some point it would have to be done. I reminded myself that, no matter what a good breakfast I'd had, no matter how the sun shone through the windows and how sweetly the birds cooed in their cages, I still had a dollar bill and a couple of dimes in my pocket. I still had no job. Gil was still under the ground somewhere in the Bronx.

"I met someone else," I said abruptly.

Mrs. Amalfi widened her eyes. "Someone?"

"Someone who loved me."

She reached across the table to put her hand over mine. "And you loved her, too?"

Him, I wanted to say. It would have given me immense pleasure to say it. But I just nodded.

"Very much?"

For a moment I couldn't say anything. I was flooded, suddenly, by a memory of Gil in the ridiculous tiara: the look in his eyes, his gaunt white face, how beautiful he had been. I took a shaky breath and said, "I adored her."

Mrs. Amalfi squeezed my hand and released it. "I'm glad to hear you say this. This is wonderful, after what you went through. A new love. But – tell me more. I don't mean to pry, but – it didn't last? Or she went away?"

"She died on Sunday morning. She was tubercular, but I didn't expect it so soon."

"Oh, Robert, my poor boy." She put her hand to her mouth, and tears came to her eyes. "I'm so, so sorry. What a terrible thing."

I thought: *Talking about it eases the pain.* In the midst of the chaos in my head, the crazy mix of pronouns, I sat staring at the simplicity of this idea, and with it came a kind of revelation: that I wasn't alone, and Gil wasn't the only person in the world I would ever love. He had told me that, and I had dismissed it, and yet as I sat there with Mrs. Amalfi I knew it was true, and – oddly – it was that knowledge that made me, at last, break down and weep.

NINE

Mrs. Amalfi said that if I didn't let her help me she would throw me out on the street and never speak to me again. I must take my clothes to the laundry, buy myself a decent suit, see a couple of people she knew about possible jobs. I imagined shady errands for the Russians, maybe an apprenticeship to something as bizarre as a sleep specialist. A sonneteer. An ocarina-maker. It was all the same to me. I hadn't yet gotten to the point where I cared what I did. All I wanted was a job, money in my pocket, some kind of life.

My few shirts were filthy, my socks and underwear almost beyond redemption. I said I would gladly accept a small loan for the laundry. After that, we would see.

Mrs. Amalfi and I set out together into the world. The snow was already melting in the sun, and the streets were wet and black. After we dropped off my dirty clothes, I accompanied her to the big market on Second Avenue, where I carried her basket while she filled it with food: a small chicken, some parsley, a turnip, a packet of tea. Then we went around the corner to the pharmacy: aspirin, rose water, and something called Dr. Edwards' Olive Tablets. Then two red apples from the apple man: "Past their prime, but I'll bake them with cinnamon," she said.

It was all familiar and all strange: it was normal life, if there was such a thing. I trotted after Mrs. Amalfi, like the poor dog Gil had said I was, and yet I was not uncontented doing errands with her in the sun. The weather had warmed, and people on the street looked happier than usual. The apple man was all smiles, and when a ragged, half-starved woman I remembered passed us, she was wearing a bright red coat and carrying a grocery bag.

Beyond the market and the pharmacy and the sunshine, I didn't think. What good had thinking ever done me? I would take Mrs. Amalfi's help. Someone would give me a job. And until they did, I would work on *Afternoon Coffee*. I thought about the play with a kind of affectionate guilt, the way I might think about an old friend I'd neglected. I hadn't even looked at it since I retrieved it from under the rhododendron bush.

Back at the Alhambra, we encountered the new super in the lobby. "Ah, Bill," Mrs. Amalfi said, not bothering to hide her disdain. "Are you aware that Mrs. Glass's toilet is still not working?"

He was a little, scowling guy, half-bald, wearing overalls exactly like the ones I'd bought at Stein's. "I'll get to it. I been busy."

"I should think a broken toilet would take precedence over other things."

"It ain't broken, it's just slow." Bill bit off a piece of thumbnail, glaring at Mrs. Amalfi. His face said: *what business is it of yours?*

Mrs. Amalfi rolled her eyes at me. Then she said, "Bill, this is Robert Sinclair, your predecessor. He's gone on to better things."

"Yeah? Good for him." Bill took in my threadbare overcoat, rubbing his thumbnail with his finger. Then his face changed, seemed to brighten. "Wait a minute. You're Sinclair?"

"That's right," I said.

"I've got something for you. Hang on."

We waited while he disappeared down the steps to my old apartment. "He's really not that bad," Mrs. Amalfi said softly. "He does the job. Mrs. Glass is an old pest – remember her? Down the hall from me? Always something. But I do enjoy torturing him a little when I get the chance."

I listened absently. I was imagining Bill living in my apartment: if anything could erase the memory of my pathetic life down there with May, it was the thought of the obnoxious Bill among the things I had once had such a sentimental fondness for. Bill tipping his cigarette into the clasped-hands ashtray, turning on the lamp with the red fringed shade, biting his nails while he listened to Jack Benny on the Motorola. It helped.

He came back with four letters. Three were in my mother's small, worried-looking handwriting, but the return address of the fourth said Harper Theatrical Agency on 43rd Street. I stared at it: dark blue letters, white paper, smudged postmark, my name typed in neat capitals.

Mrs. Amalfi peered over my shoulder. "What is it?"

"I don't know."

I set down the market basket and started to open it, but she gripped my arm firmly. "Not here. Upstairs."

"Mr. Gant told me to hang on to them," Bill said. "In case you ever turned up. Didn't know what else to do."

"Oh – thanks," I said belatedly. I wondered if he expected me to tip him. "That was very good of you."

"Nonsense," said Mrs. Amalfi. "It's part of his job. And you should have given them to me, Bill. From now on, please do so. I'll see that Mr. Sinclair gets them. And don't forget that toilet."

Upstairs, I sat down at the kitchen table and opened the letter, a single page. The date at the top was nearly three weeks old, it was signed with a scrawl, and in between was exactly the letter I used to imagine.

Dear Mr. Sinclair,

I am happy to inform you that I have received an offer for your excellent play, Fish Out of Water, *from the Sheridan Square Theatre Group, who wish to produce it for their spring season. You may have heard of this celebrated troupe, which is headed by Mr. Harold Fitzhugh. Please get in touch with me at your earliest convenience . . .*

I had to read it twice before it sank in. It was like the first time Gil touched me – or maybe when I knew he was going to touch me, and I knew that I wanted him to: in an instant, everything changed.

"My play," I said.

Mrs. Amalfi was stowing the chicken in the icebox, and she straightened up to look at me. "Your play?"

I held up the letter. "They want my play."

She took it from me, holding it away from her face and squinting. "These people are going to put on your play? This Fitzhugh? Is that what this means?"

"I think it does, Mrs. Amalfi."

"Oh Robert, what good news. Mr. Samuel Harper is a saint. A god! You must telephone him – no, go see him – this afternoon. You will go there in your rags, and come back a prince. And we will have champagne for supper. I'll call Hana, and we'll celebrate." She paused, narrowed her eyes. "Now how does it go? *After so long grief, such festivity!* I forget which play. It doesn't matter."

Smiling, she came around the table to envelop me in blue fabric, silvery beads, the scent of cinnamon. I leaned against her. *All will be well*, I thought. Or at least – I'd learned this much – maybe *all* wouldn't be what you could call *well*, but there was an outside chance some things would be somewhat better, at least for a while.

■ ■ ■

I did go there in my rags: specifically, in my one decent pair of pants, an almost-matching jacket Gil had bought for me from a pushcart, and a white shirt with a celluloid collar that had apparently belonged to one of Mrs. Amalfi's husbands. I shaved off my four-day growth and combed my long hair behind my ears. I knew I looked like hell, but there wasn't much I could do about it.

Mrs. Amalfi gazed at me dubiously as I put on my coat and hat. "Maybe they'll see how much you need the money and offer to pay you double."

I walked uptown to Sam Harper's office, on the fifteenth floor of an imposing building at 43ʳᵈ Street and Broadway. Inside the elevator was a bronze bas relief that seemed vaguely Egyptian, and the elevator operator's uniform was dark green trimmed in braid of the same bronze.

The secretary at Harper Theatrical threw me a look when I walked in, but I gave her my name and told her my business, and she asked me cordially enough to sit down. "Mr. Harper is on the phone," she said. "Transatlantic," she added. If she wanted to impress me, she succeeded. "But as soon as he's off I'll tell him you're here."

After a few minutes, she spoke into the intercom, and Sam Harper came bounding out of his office, hand extended. "Robert Sinclair! Am I glad to see you! I didn't know when the hell you were going to ever get in touch with me. I was about ready to get them to start dragging the God-damned Hudson River. What took you so long?"

I didn't know what to say, but I didn't seem to need to say much of anything. Sam Harper was plump, dapper, cigar-smoking, and noisy; if I'd put a theatrical agent in a play, I wouldn't have dared make him so predictable. He wrung my hand, introduced me to everyone in his office, and said he hadn't seen such a God-damned good play in he didn't know how long. Funny? The God-damned thing had him in stitches. His secretary kissed me on the cheek. Sam produced a bottle of Seagram's from the bottom drawer of his desk, poured some into two not quite clean highball glasses, and we drank to the success of *Fish Out of Water*.

Sam made some phone calls and arranged for me to meet Hal Fitzhugh and Van Kalman, his partner, on Monday afternoon, when they would give me, he said, an advance check of two hundred dollars, out of which I would give Sam Harper his percentage. I signed a contract with him. I would sign another one, he said, with Sheridan Square. They wanted to begin casting and rehearsals as soon as possible for an opening late in March. Before I left, he asked, "Haven't you got another suit?"

"It's at the cleaner's."

Sam grinned. "Get it out. You're a sharp-looking guy, Robert, and you ought to dress better than this."

"Next time you see me, I will."

"Good man!" He poured us each another shot.

I took the A train down to 14th Street, and walked from there to the Sheridan Square Theatre – a yellow brick building with three sets of double doors opening on the street. I imagined the audience streaming out after seeing *Fish Out of Water*, chattering, happy, excited. The marquee advertised a Noel Cowardish play called *The High Life* that had just opened. I had read a favorable review of it in one of the discarded newspapers I used to pick up, and I forced myself to remember in detail how I had found the paper in a trash can near the Chateau, stuck it in my pocket, took it out to read at an Automat on Tenth Avenue while Gil conducted some business with a guy named Lou Vance. I had read the review in a state of gloom; all those superlatives had put me in a bad mood for the rest of the day.

Now I walked back and forth in front of the theatre a few times, feeling much too pleased with myself. I had less than a dollar in my pocket. I was wearing a shirt that went out of style in 1918, and my only friends in the world were an old woman and a bunch of cats. Sam Harper was probably a con man. Hal Fitzhugh would change his mind over the weekend, and I'd be like May, betrayed by the New York theatre world. I'd end up painting samovars in the back of a shop on First Avenue. And yet there I was, pacing the sidewalk and grinning like a maniac. People stared at me, probably thinking I was a Trotskyite anarchist.

I went into a bar and spent my last dollar on a double shot of good bourbon with a beer chaser. By the time I got back to Mrs. Amalfi's, I was half loaded. Hana was there. I hadn't seen her since I had carried her to Bellevue, and I was astonished at the change in her. Her wavy hair was loose, hanging to her shoulders; she wore pinkish lipstick and dangling earrings and a silky brown dress, very short. She had started nursing school, and she told me about some of her courses. I told them both about Sam Harper and his cigars. We drank champagne and ate a candlelit meal of roast chicken and potatoes that reminded me of my mother's Sunday dinners except that the gravy was spicy and had raisins in it, and when we were done Mrs. Amalfi pulled a dusty bottle of plum brandy out of a cupboard. Sometime after that I had to put my head down on the table. I had meant to borrow some money and check into a hotel, but the last thing I remember was Mrs. Amalfi tucking me again into the big mahogany bed and Hana leaning over to kiss me on the forehead.

■ ■ ■

And so I became a playwright. I got myself a room at the Hotel Brevoort, on Fifth Avenue at Eighth Street. I had often passed it, and liked the look of the place; it was cheap and rather grand, with a nice bar downstairs, and was only a short walk from the Sheridan Square Theatre. I began spending a good deal of my time at the theatre with Hal Fitzhugh and Van Kalman and the cast. Officially, I was making myself available in case they needed re-writes, but mostly I just liked to be there, and they didn't seem to mind. When I wasn't at the theatre, I was working on *Afternoon Coffee*, on which Hal had an option. And one memorable afternoon I was interviewed, over drinks at the Biltmore Hotel, by a woman from the *Times* who was doing an article on promising new playwrights.

I always made time to have dinner with Mrs. Amalfi and Hana once a week or so – often enough that the Alhambra meant that warm, scented apartment on the second floor, the affectionate cats and the exotic food and Hana with her little steel glasses, instead of Bill's dank basement apartment or the sick memory of the attic room and the spiral staircase. I went home to Rochester for Christmas, but I spent New Year's Eve at the Alhambra with Mrs. Amalfi and Hana, and we put on paper hats and opened the windows at midnight to hear the sound of bells and see the crowds passing on the street below, blowing horns. Sam Harper had sent me a bottle of Dom Perignon with a card that read, "Happy 1935! This is your year!" and we opened it at midnight and got pleasantly tight. "A better year for everyone, let's hope," Mrs. Amalfi said, raising her glass, and Hana kissed me chastely on the cheek.

It started to become clear to me that evening that – I was never sure how to put this – Hana was being given to me by her mother, like a gift.

Mrs. Amalfi had always been full of praise for her daughter, but now she tended to comment on Hana's physical perfections.

She would reach across the table to touch Hana's hair and say, "Such soft, abundant hair. Isn't it extraordinary?" Once, she had Hana remove her glasses and exclaimed, "There! Did you ever see such eyes?" Like a horse dealer. After dinner, she would sometimes go out of the room, leaving me with Hana on the living room sofa, saying as she went, "Hana, tell Robert about that amazing cat you saw in the alley." Or that movie she had seen. Or the beggar on 14th Street who sang whole arias in Italian, better than Caruso.

Hana would endure all this patiently, with a tiny smile, occasionally glancing at me sideways with a look I couldn't read, and, obediently, in her lovely, slightly theatrical way, she would tell me about the cat or the movie or the tenor on the street. I pictured Mrs. Amalfi in the kitchen, cooing to the birds, counting the minutes, torn between wanting Hana and me to be alone, and wondering how we were getting on.

Hana and I always got on fine, and after I grasped the situation, once I had accepted it as a reality and not just fanciful imaginings on my part, I began to see the humor in it. But it made me feel bad, too. I wished I had told Mrs. Amalfi the truth about Gil when I had the chance, and I hoped Hana wasn't counting on me.

It was on an unseasonably warm February night, that Mrs. Amalfi said, when we had finished dinner, "Why don't you walk Hana home, Robert? Such a lovely evening. And it's not so far out of your way."

I expected Hana to object, but she lowered her eyes demurely, waiting for my reply.

"Your place is on First Avenue?" I asked. "I'd be glad to walk you down, Hana." She looked up at me and smiled. Her cheeks were very pink.

"Tell Robert about your apartment," Mrs. Amalfi said. "She lives just two doors down from Iza and Tomek, Robert. In a building owned by Tomek's father. A very droll man, something like Will Rogers, but more rapacious." I tried to imagine this. "He has known Hana since she was a baby, however, and so she pays a very small rent. And they are there if she needs them."

"I only have one room, but it's a big room," Hana said. "The walls are painted the color of unhealthy flesh, and I don't have much furniture, and there's a cockroach or two, of course, and the bathroom is – well, not very nice. And I have no bathtub."

"She bathes in the kitchen sink," Mrs. Amalfi murmured, raising her eyebrows, as if she wanted me to picture this.

"But the windows look out on a back garden where there were flowers all summer," Hana went on, her voice becoming husky. I glanced at Mrs. Amalfi and saw she was looking at Hana with approval. "Peonies," Hana went on. "And, I think, dahlias and something like daisies, all in shades of red and pink. It's all very passionate, somehow, all that pulsing color. And there's a carpet of green grass, and in the middle of it all a fountain where the birds come to drink."

"In its own way, a paradise," I said, smiling, and she smiled back, agreeing.

Mrs. Amalfi beamed at us. "You both have that gift," she said. "Of finding the good, always finding the good. Are you aware that you do that, Robert?"

"I don't know. I never thought about it." I thought about it then, because it sounded like a positive trait, a compliment – and I know that was how she meant it. But it occurred to me that it was just that quality – and yes, I did have it, I knew, though Gil might have called it my puppyish side – that had allowed May to have an affair with Orson under my nose, and to run away with him. "It doesn't sound like such a great thing," I said. "It sounds like fooling yourself."

"But you're an artist, Robert," Hana said. "I think it must be more like freeing yourself."

"Freeing myself?"

"From the burdens of real life." She leaned toward me, and the candlelight gleamed in her spectacles. "So that you can live in the plays. So that you can live in those other worlds you've created, and make them real."

"And what about you?" I asked her. "Do you think it's true that you seek out the good in things? To see the birds and the peonies instead of the roaches?"

"Yes, I think I do. That's my nature, Robert. But I'm not an artist."

"Surely you are, Hana, in your way!" Mrs. Amalfi said. "An artist of the spirit, of the soul."

"Oh, Mother," she said, and laughed. "That's much too grandiose. I think it's just that I'm a very, very simple little person."

We finished our coffee and had a small glass of Mrs. Amalfi's brandy, and then Hana and I got our coats and set off across 21st Street to First Avenue.

It was a short walk, and pleasant. The hour wasn't late; the streets teemed with people. I was reminded of my night walks. When I had dropped Hana off, I decided, I would walk, as I hadn't really done in months – go back up First Avenue, maybe, all the way to Yorkville, and then catch the subway home at 86th Street.

We came to the shop where I had retrieved Hana in the rain; her door was in the same block, between a Ukrainian meat market and a pharmacy marked APTEKA. She fumbled in her bag for her key and said, "You don't have to kiss me, Robert. When my mother asks me if you did, I'll tell her yes."

I stared at her. "You mean it's not my imagination?"

She laughed gently. "Far from it. She wants us to get married."

"How do you know?"

"How do you think? She told me. I'm surprised she didn't tell you! My mother, for all her mysterious ways, is nothing if not direct when it comes to the basics."

"*Speak what we feel, not what we ought to say,*" I quoted.

"Is that Shakespeare?"

"Yes. One of your mother's. I think it's out of context, but it's probably good advice all the same. In moderation."

"It's not advice I always take, Robert." To my surprise, Hana put her arms around me and buried her face in my shoulder. "What I haven't told her is that I prefer women."

At first I wasn't sure I'd heard her right, she spoke so softly. "You mean you –"

"I mean I prefer women." She raised her head and regarded me shyly. "As lovers." She stopped and took a breath. "I have had men lovers, Robert. But now –" She shrugged. "Do you understand? I've finally admitted to myself that I would rather go with women."

I was shocked, and stunned, and something else that was harder to put my finger on. We stood in the doorway embracing, the top of her head against my chin. The life of the city bustled around us: the honk of a car horn, the faint scent of cooked meat from a restaurant called Odessa, the low hum of traffic and, from somewhere nearby, a burst of dance music. But it was as if the two of us were inside a small, silent room that was suddenly full of light, where everything was perfectly clear. Hana went with women. Hana preferred women.

She raised her head and we looked at each other and then, like children, we began to laugh. "Dear Robert," Hana said, her face creased by the broadness of her grin. She stood on tiptoe to kiss me lightly on the cheek. "I thought you should know."

■ ■ ■

After that night, Hana and I spent much of our time together. I went with her to bars where she danced with women and, after a time, I found bars where men could dance with men, but I wasn't ready for very much, I was still mourning Gil, and in those days nothing was as important to me as my friendship with Hana, the hours I spent with her, meeting her after her classes to go to dinner or see a movie, or just to talk in some bar or slouched on chairs in my living room. I sat with her during her migraines, putting cold cloths on her head. She found me the apartment I moved into that fall, where I would live for the next forty years: three big rooms on Jane Street, with windows looking down at the river. I helped her study for her exams, asking her questions from her textbooks or quizzing her about anatomy from a chart.

I knew Hana hadn't told her mother about her lesbianism. I don't know what Mrs. Amalfi thought our relationship was, or if she still had illusions about our getting married. Whatever Hana might have said to her, if anything, I didn't know, but it seemed to have been the right thing to say because it was clear that seeing Hana and me together was deeply satisfying to her.

My play progressed pretty much on schedule and was due to open at the end of March. I was working on *Afternoon Coffee*, but the rehearsals for *Fish Out of Water* drew me like an addiction, and every day I'd find myself walking over to Bleecker Street. It was the most exhilarating experience I'd ever had, seeing what Hal and the actors did with my play, the way the world I had made out of mere words became, day by day, flesh and blood, pain and joy, jokes and a few tears, and a man with an apron over his tuxedo, all I had imagined it to be on those late-night walks of mine. It was so good I couldn't imagine it getting better, and then, as I watched, it got better, and better again.

I had good success with my plays – or nearly always; I suppose I would have to call *What We Remember* a flop, relatively speaking – but nothing ever equaled the experience of watching

Fish Out of Water come to life in that plain little playhouse in the Village. I always associate that play with Hana, because our friendship progressed along with my play, and those two things made my life became rich and satisfying in ways I could never have imagined.

Then, one day early in March, Hana rang my doorbell – her two quick, special rings. I wondered why she wasn't at school; second semester had just begun. It was the middle of the afternoon and it was only by chance that I was home. I'd been out late, slept late, and didn't plan to make it to rehearsal that day. I buzzed her in, and when I opened the door I knew instantly that something was dreadfully wrong, and I wondered if it was an especially bad headache, her face was so full of pain.

"My mother, Robert." She came in, tracking snow on the rug, not bothering to remove her coat and hat. She held her gloves in one hand. "I had to come and tell you in person. She's dead. Bill found her in the hallway. She must have been on her way home from the market. The basket had spilled all over the floor. Broken eggs, and a sack of sugar, a bottle of vinegar." Tears ran down her face as she told me all this. I took her in my arms. "What will happen to the cats?" she asked, weeping. "And the birds. And what will I do without my mother, Robert?"

Mrs. Amalfi was cremated on a damp day with the smell of spring in the air. The crematorium was full of people. I recognized Iza and Tomek, and a girlfriend of Hana's named Bella, and a couple of women from the Alhambra Gardens. A man I had never seen before – a relative, Hana told me later – spoke briefly, about Mrs. Amalfi's kind heart and her gift for healing, and everyone cried. Then he repeated it in Russian, or Czech, or he said something else, I had no idea, but everyone cried again. The congregation sang two songs, one in English about flying away like a bird from this life of woe and strife, and one in Russian, about I didn't know what, but it was very sad.

I would have liked to speak, if only to say, "She was so alive. I can't believe she's dead." But I was too shy, and no one knew me. Hana took the urn – so small, it was hard to believe it could hold an entire woman – and then she and I and Bella and a middle-aged couple named Paul and Anna – cousins of Hana's – went to a bar around the corner and got very drunk.

Hana put me up that night. It seemed a long way to my apartment, under the circumstances. The day before, along with a carpet and a few other things, we had set up Mrs. Amalfi's big pineapple-post bed in Hana's big room, and Hana arranged a pile of blankets on the floor for me beside it. I couldn't sleep, of course. I was cold, in just my underwear, and I was probably too drunk, though I felt sober enough as I lay in the darkness with Rosalind and Horatio at my feet. Ferdinand slept on the bed with Hana; Romeo and Juliet, the twins, were at my apartment, along with the birds in their cages. I thought Hana was asleep, but after a while she said, softly, "Robert?"

"I'm awake."

"I thought you might be."

"We need one of your mother's potions."

"Oh, those – her crazy herbs and tonics." She laughed. "I doubt they ever put anyone to sleep."

"They worked on me, once or twice," I said. "She had her ways."

"Oh, I know she did." We were quiet a moment, and then she said again, "Robert?"

"Yes."

"I want you to know something. I mean, there's something I want to tell you. Now that my mother is dead. Something she didn't want you to know."

"Then maybe you shouldn't tell me, Hana."

"No. I should. It was something she was ashamed of, but she didn't need to be. And it would be good, I think, for you to know it."

I trusted her: if she said it was true, I believed her. But I felt sick to my stomach, suddenly, in a way that had nothing to do with what I had drunk. I hesitated, and then I said, "All right, then. Tell me."

"Robert – don't I ever remind you of anyone?"

"You mean your looks?"

"Yes."

I thought for a moment. "Sometimes," I said. "But I can never think who. It's something that used to strike me, but I don't notice it so much any more, now that I know you better. Why? Who are you supposed to remind me of?"

"My half-brother, Orson. I think we look somewhat alike."

We turned on the light, then, and I wrapped myself in a blanket and got up on the bed, my back against the foot board. We faced each other while she talked, Ferdinand draped over our legs. Orson was Mrs. Amalfi's son by her first husband, Harry Price. Harry died in 1905, when Orson was a toddler. Harry had been an importer – rugs, fabrics, antiquities – and he left Mrs. Amalfi a well-off woman. Soon after that, she married Ribowsky, Hana's father – she never let more than a year go between husbands, Hana said – and Hana was born six years later.

"Wasn't it obvious?" Hana asked. "Didn't you see it?"

"I see it now," I said. "And maybe I saw it then, but didn't recognize it." The biggest resemblance, I realized, was the way I had been drawn to both of them. "It's your hair, of course, though his was straight and yours is curly. And maybe around the mouth. You're built the same way, too, I suppose. I mean, you're both very small-boned. Small hands, small feet."

"We look like our grandmother, my mother's mother."

"Marie the gypsy bareback rider?"

Hana smiled. "Is that what she told you? Well, it's mostly true. Yes, we take after Marie. It's not obvious, but it's there."

"Why didn't your mother tell me all this? It would have explained so much." I remembered the day we ran into Orson in the rain, how he had called her "Mrs. A." with that wry twist in his voice. "All she said was that she had known him a long time."

Hana spoke fiercely, leaning forward. "She would never have told you, Robert! She was so ashamed of him, she would have rather died than let you know he was her son." She sat back again against her pillow, sighed, ran her hand over Ferdinand's fur. "My mother and Orson have been estranged for a long time now," she went on. "They never reconciled. I wondered if he'd be at the service today. But – well, even if he's still in town, he most likely doesn't even know she died. I wish I had a way of telling him, but even if I did find him, he'd probably just try to get her money, or some of her things. He always loved those Persian carpets. And my mother told me probably two dozen times that Orson was never, ever to have anything of hers, not a teacup, not a pot or a pan."

"Would he take it hard? Her death?"

"He worshiped her," Hana said. "He didn't want to – Orson didn't want to love anyone, and mainly he succeeded. But he did love our mother. He was devastated when she disowned him. That's what she did, you know. Formally. In her most dramatic way, Robert. She told him never to darken her door again, or words to that effect. She cursed him."

"Hana – *why?*"

She didn't answer right away. She peered down at me, her face young and rather blank without her glasses. "Because of what he did, the kind of life he preferred to lead. Orson is an adventurer, a con man, a thief, an opportunist. He's thirty-two years old, and he's been all over the world, and he's never done an honest day's work."

"That's not true," I said. "He worked for me, and he worked hard."

"Well, either you had an amazing effect on him – or –" She shrugged. "He wanted something from you."

I squeezed my eyes shut and put my head down on my knees. With my eyes shut, I felt drunk again, and slightly sick, so I opened them. Hana was looking at me with sympathy. "I'm sorry."

"I was such an idiot. Slapping paint on the walls, thinking I was happy, while Orson calmly went ahead and ruined my life."

I knew this was an overstatement, and so did Hana. She reached over and squeezed my foot through the blanket. "He took a lot, Robert, but he didn't take everything. And, if it's any consolation, please don't think you were his only victim. He made dozens of enemies, all his life. But he had guts, I'll say that for him. He had pride. I was amazed when he showed up in the old neighborhood. Down on his luck, too. Most unlike Orson. Mother was waiting for him to ask her for money, but he never did."

"He found me instead."

Hana sighed. "He did." She reached over to the nightstand and got her spectacles and put them on. She offered me a cigarette and put the ashtray halfway between us on the bedclothes. Oddly, in her glasses, she looked more like Orson, maybe because they gave the rest of her features more definition. Her squared-off jawline was like his, and her pointed chin, her small white teeth. As I stared at her, I could see that she looked uncannily like him, and then when she turned her head a little, she didn't so much.

"How did you feel about him, Hana? Were you ever close to him?"

I watched her inhale and exhale and tap off her ashes. She was a beginning smoker, and she held her cigarette awkwardly, between thumb and forefinger. "Well, that's complicated."

"Tell me."

"Orson and I were in business together for a while. He was my pimp."

"Hana!" I lurched forward, and Ferdinand, disturbed, jumped down. I leaned back again, breathing deeply to calm myself. I didn't want to hear any more, and yet, of course, I had to hear whatever she wished to tell me. "Hana. What are you saying?"

"You didn't know about me?"

"I knew something. I knew why you were in Bellevue."

"Ah, yes. Bellevue. Where I did my penance." She snorted, half a laugh. "Where they turned me into a normal woman."

"But Orson, Hana. You can't mean what you just said!"

She put her head against the pillow and closed her eyes. "He knew these wealthy men. How he knew them, I don't know, but Orson always knew everyone, especially people who could be useful to him. These were bankers. Businessmen. Men who came through the crash with more money than ever. Men who lived on Park Avenue and had expensive wives and expensive cars and shirts from Sulka and diamond rings from Tiffany's – the elegant kind of diamond ring, not at all vulgar."

"How many?"

"Men? Oh, three – four, if you count the last one, but that didn't work out so well."

"Hana – why? I mean, why *any*? Why did you do this?"

"I made a great deal of money. They were kind to me, mostly, until the end. The last one was a Russian who had made a fortune in the diamond district. He was as crooked as a cane, Robert. And one night a gang of thugs attacked him with knives – not far from here, just around the corner. They killed him, and they nearly killed me." She took a puff from her cigarette and blew it out thoughtfully. "That's when I was sent to Bellevue."

"I don't understand. I mean, I still don't understand why you did it."

"I let Orson talk me into it. And – how can I explain this? I was always small and thin, flat-chested. I looked like a child. Orson introduced me to the first one, and he liked me. His name was Morton. He liked the way I looked. He bought me little dresses, and – well, he didn't ask that much of me." She tapped the ashes off her cigarette, let out a long sigh. "It wasn't so bad. I was very young, and I knew nothing about anything. It was a way of educating myself."

"How despicable of him."

"Orson?"

"Yes – Orson."

"Oh, Robert." She smiled. "I loved my brother. For years he was my best friend – even after – " She stopped and shook her head, but her smile remained. "He could be wonderful. You know that – don't you? He was funny and entertaining and kind, and in his own peculiar way he took care of me. Our childhood was so chaotic, Robert. We both lost our fathers when we were young, and my mother's life was always tumultuous. We loved her so much, but she gave us no stability. In one way, she was like Orson – an adventuress. When I was nine, she sailed to Paris with some man, and I had to live with a friend of hers in a tenement down on Rivington Street – a wonderful, colorful woman, a painter, but there were rats on the staircase when I went in. I'd have to scream and stamp my feet to chase them away before I went upstairs. And Orson lived for a while with an uncle of ours in a flophouse on the Bowery. You can't imagine what all this was like." She paused. "But Orson?" she said. "Yes. He was despicable. He made money from it, too, of course. From those men. More than I did."

"I can hardly take this in."

"I know. It's horrible. It's all so sordid. My family is –" She gestured with her cigarette. "Hopeless. Everyone's crazy. Someday I'll tell you about some of those people you saw at the service today. Unbelievable."

I remembered Orson's scars, his pointless lies, the way he taunted me before I hit him. Orson the liar, the thief, the pimp. I should hate him, too. If we were characters in a play, I would despise him, I would hunt him down and make him pay. Or would I? A play that was truer to life would be more complicated. Or was it just that life, life itself, was more complicated? Whatever I had been drawn to in Orson – that warmth, that familiarity, that mysterious sense of kinship – had been pushed aside by all I had learned, but it hadn't been wiped out. I was ashamed of this, I saw it as a weakness, but I knew it was true and wouldn't change.

"Hana – do you really not know where Orson is?"

She stubbed out her cigarette. "No, I don't. I didn't communicate with him while I was in Bellevue. I'd had enough of Orson for a while, frankly. He and my mother had their big blow-up, and he left town, I know that. Then I saw him once or twice after I got out, around the neighborhood. I told him you were looking for him, and after that I'd see him now and then, and we'd talk for a few minutes. But I had no idea he was plotting against you. Or that he was fooling around with your wife."

"He haunts me, Hana. I thought I'd killed him."

"Well, you didn't. If there's anyone in this whole mess who doesn't need to feel guilty, Robert, it's you, so please stop."

Hana was silent for a moment. Then she reached over and turned out the light. The room was plunged into darkness. Ferdinand leapt back to the bed and settled himself. "Sleep there, why don't you?" she said. "I like to know I can reach over and squeeze your foot in the night."

We curled up beside each other, head to foot, the cat between us, and, eventually, we slept.

■ ■ ■

Not long after that, Hana and I went to see a movie called *The Woman in Red*, a courtroom drama starring Barbara Stanwyck – one of our favorites. There was a flashback scene, late in the movie, set in a restaurant, during which a cigarette girl in tights and a low-cut blouse comes to the table where Stanwyck is dining with Gene Raymond. They're deep in conversation. The girl holds out her tray, saying, "Cigarettes?" and they wave her off, Stanwyck looking imperious, Raymond obviously appreciating the cleavage.

"Hana!" I gripped her arm. "Hana, I think that was May!"

"Who? What?"

"The cigarette girl. It was May!"

We sat forward in our seats. The cigarette girl had moved away, but I caught a glimpse of her again, in the background, when the camera pulled back and panned around the restaurant. Then she was gone. I thought it was May, but I wasn't sure, it had been so quick, such a shock. I found I had tears in my eyes, and an odd laughter was bubbling up inside me. How strange, I thought, to see her huge on the screen, in black and white, with that smile, and the breasts I had caressed so often tumbling out of her costume.

She didn't appear again. When the movie was over, Hana suggested we sit through it once more, so I could make sure. She said she was curious. We stretched our legs, went downstairs with the crowd and bought boxes of popcorn, watched the newsreel, the cartoon, and then the film began again. This time I was ready. I watched her walk up to the table, offer her tray, say, "Cigarettes?" in the cooing, seductive voice I remembered. I watched her move away, and then I watched her in the longer shot, stopping at another table, smiling.

Hana asked, "Well?"

"Definitely."

She looked into my face. From the screen, ominous music swelled, crescendoed. "Are you okay?"

I was okay. "It's good to know," I said.

We got our coats and left. It was late, and cold out. Hana took my arm as we went down 42nd Street to the subway. "It didn't take her long," she said. "But of course, she's awfully pretty. I think it must be very good to be in a movie with Barbara Stanwyck, even if you're just the cigarette girl. I wonder if Barbara ever talked to her. If they became friends. Wouldn't that be something?"

"Yeah, that would be something."

Hana smiled at me. "Would you mind, Robert? If she became a success?"

I laughed. "That's not likely." It was what I had always believed, but now I had to reconsider. She had looked good up there on the screen. She had one of those faces that, as they say, the camera loves. Face and body, husky voice, blonde hair. For the moment that she was there, offering cigarettes, I had to admit it: the screen lit up. "Well, maybe it is. Who knows?"

"And if she did become a star? Really. I want to know. Would you mind? How bitter are you against her, exactly?"

There was a bar on the corner, and we ducked inside and found a table. I ordered drinks for us both before I answered her – Hana's usual Pink Lady, a scotch on the rocks for me – and then I looked at Hana across the table. I thought how much I loved her. I could always count on her, she was always Hana. A very simple little person, just as she had described herself. What did it matter that she was a lesbian, a former prostitute, Orson's sister, and that I was – well, whatever I was. I reached over and tucked back a loose strand of her curly hair. "I hope May becomes rich and famous. The idol of millions. A film goddess."

"Do you really?"

"Yes. I'm not bitter. I'm a little bemused, I suppose. I don't know if I was ever angry at May, not really. I'd be happy for her if she became a star. In a funny kind of way, I'd be proud of her. It's what she always wanted – to act, to be noticed. I've got what I wanted, Hana. I can't begrudge it to her."

"Maybe you'll write about it someday."

"Maybe."

I had a feeling I wouldn't, though. My plays come from somewhere inside, or from far outside. I couldn't imagine writing about my own life – that secret middle ground, that dark and private kingdom that, no matter what its dramas, would always seem like a lesser place.

Hana took a sip of her drink and then leaned across the table, chuckling. "She really milked it for all it was worth, didn't she?" She lowered her voice to her dramatic, husky contralto, cupped her breasts and lifted them in her little sweater. "Cigarettes?"

We laughed, and finished our drinks. Then we went down to the Village, to our favorite Polish restaurant on St. Mark's Place, for a late supper of pirojski and bigos and beer. The place was full of people, a few of whom we knew, and we were invited to join a large table of noisy vodka-drinkers. That was the night Hana met Della Lyons, the dancer, who would be such a force in both our lives, and I met Arthur Maloff, who would be my friend for many years, and who would introduce me to the sunlit pleasures of Mexico.

It was quite a year, 1935. *Fish Out of Water* opened and, as Byron once said, I woke up to find myself famous. And, by the end of that year, May the cigarette girl had become May Munro, the movie star, with a lead role in *Lover, Come Back*. And at Christmastime, Hana and Della were married – unofficially, of course – at a funny little ceremony in my apartment on Jane Street, with Arthur playing carols on the piano, while Mrs. Amalfi's birds made contented noises in their cages and Romeo and Juliet wove around our ankles, purring, as if no better life could be imagined.

■ ■ ■

One warm summer night, on my way home, I stopped into the Brevoort for a drink. The place was filling up, but there were seats at the bar, and I took one and ordered a cold beer. I sipped it thankfully, thinking of nothing, enjoying the frosted glass, the metallic coldness of the drink, the soft whirr of the ceiling fans. I associated the Brevoort, inevitably, with those first heady days of my new life, when I took a room there and sat at the bar in a daze, eating chips and drinking scotch and telling everyone who spoke to me that my play was in production. Just walking through the door into its brown-and-gold interior brought that all back, and made me happy.

I exchanged a few words with the bartender, Walter, who always remembered me. Then, as I sat there drinking, I had the unsettling sensation of being watched, and I raised my head and glanced into the mirror behind the bar. Framed between two whiskey bottles, and looking at me quizzically, was Orson Price, three seats down. Our eyes met. He grinned, hesitantly at first, then broadly, and got up to sit beside me.

"Robert Sinclair," he said. "Well, what do you know."

"Orson."

We didn't shake hands. For an odd, giddy moment I thought I should hit him, knock him off his stool. "It's good to see you, Robert. You may not want to say the same to me, but –" He broke into a laugh. "I'll be damned. It's a strange world, isn't it?" He was wearing a lightweight tan suit, a pale blue shirt open at the neck, a silk tie hanging loose. A straw hat lay on the bar beside his drink – some kind of whiskey, neat – and he had grown a small, trimmed moustache. He looked the way I had never seen him but often imagined him in some previous, *luxe*, privileged life: the real Orson, expensively tailored, at his ease in a Fifth Avenue hotel bar.

"It's been – what? – two years?" Orson said. "That crazy summer." As if he were drinking to the memory of it, he raised his glass. I saw the scars on his hand, like pearls, and I could see now that his chin and jaw were amazingly like Hana's. I marveled at my failure to notice the resemblance before.

I swallowed some beer. "It seems longer ago than that."

"Does it? Maybe it does. She kicked me out, you know."

"Really."

"She took up with that Kennedy guy for a while. Mickey. You knew him – right? Dropped me cold." He shrugged and lit a cigarette, talking around the smoke. "It wasn't exactly a surprise. I saw it coming. She wasn't interested in anybody who wasn't in the business. That's the way it is out there. It's another planet, Robert. You can't imagine. Quite an experience. I made some good contacts, though. It wasn't what I could call a wasted trip." He held out the pack, and I took a cigarette. "You know she's done pretty well for herself, don't you?"

"I'm aware of her career, yes."

"Must have been a surprise to you. I remember you didn't think much of her talent."

Had I told him that? I couldn't remember. "You said it yourself, Orson – it's a strange world."

"Understatement of the year."

We sat for a minute or two, smoking in silence. I thought of all the questions I'd wanted to ask him, the little mysteries I used to long to know the answers to: I couldn't articulate any of them. I couldn't even take satisfaction in the fact that May had dumped him. The shock of seeing him was insignificant, meaningless, like having a tooth pulled under gas. What was Orson to me now? Or May? Or – what was he telling me? Mickey Kennedy and Carlotta – what had happened to those people? And did he know his mother had died?

He finished his whiskey and signaled to Walter for another. I remembered the smell of booze when we fought in that airless attic room, and I wondered if he had a drinking problem. When he had the glass in front of him, he turned to me and said, "Well, Robert, you look like you've made out okay yourself. Still writing plays?"

"Yes, I'm still writing," I said.

For a while, my name had been hard to avoid. It was astonishing, if it was true, that he hadn't come across news of my career in a newspaper or magazine. I was reluctant, somehow, to tell him about the success of *Fish Out of Water*, or the new play opening in the fall – as if they were my children, and he was a known molester.

Perhaps sensing this, he persisted. "Having any luck?"

"Some."

He waited, and when I didn't volunteer more he said, "Well, I'm glad to hear it. I always knew you'd land on your feet. Didn't I say that?"

"You did."

"It's nice to be right."

He looked genuinely pleased, and I had to struggle to remember that he had hated me – hadn't he? Hated and resented me, been jealous of what I had that he lacked. *Your perfect little life.* Or had I been wrong about that, as I'd been wrong about so much?

He took a slug of his drink, and then he launched into a rambling story about his own activities, a business that failed, he said, and a new business he was a partner in, something to do with public relations for a new soft drink company. He did a lot of traveling, had spent time in Chicago, but now he moved back and forth between there and New York. As he talked, I had the familiar feeling that I was listening to a string of lies, or at best half-truths. But he was as easy to listen to as ever, and he was, like all good liars, the master of the small, entertaining detail: the drunken business lunch, the manager of the Chicago plant who looked like Wallace Beery, the airplane flight from Los Angeles with its lecherous stewardess. Trixie the dog, I thought, looking at his scars. Or was it Roxie? Orson was undeniably prosperous, confident, comfortable in his stylish clothes – as debonair as old Oliver Templeton himself. But maybe this was the demeanor of a pimp, a con man. Who knew how he was really making his money? I thought protectively of Hana, and knew I would not tell her about this encounter.

Orson talked on, while Walter behind the bar polished glasses and cut up lemons, and in the mirror I watched the evening crowds passing by the window outside. People left the bar, and other people came in – no one I knew – and a woman at a table kept singing snatches of "I Got Rhythm," snapping her fingers, imitating Mildred Bailey. I began to feel foolish, sitting there submissively. I should challenge him, I thought. I should express some outrage. He was, after all, a thief, a pimp, a liar; he had stolen my wife and caused me to lose my job. But what I was remembering was how well we had worked together, those long, companionable mornings on the ladder and Orson's quietly patient instruction in the fine arts of plaster and wood. The funny thing was that, when I thought back to those days, I could remember Orson perfectly – his tanned, muscular arms, the level gaze of his light blue eyes, his easy way with tools – but myself, what I thought and felt, why I did what I did, I could hardly recall.

> *I got starlight,*
> *I got sweet dreams....*

I knew exactly what I felt, though, as I sat there sipping my beer and listening to Orson's stories: I felt sad, as if someone had died, and I wasn't sorry when, after a while, he broke off in the middle of a sentence to consult his watch. "I've probably bent your ear long enough, Robert. And I really should push off."

Again I had the feeling this was part of an act, that he nowhere to go, and though I knew it was absurd I had a mental image of Orson leaving the Brevoort and heading for the Municipal Lodging House.

He unfolded a ten from a silver money clip and laid it on the counter. "I'll take care of this."

"Thanks."

"Don't mention it," he said, and then, to Walter, "Keep the change, old sport."

A sneaking fondness for him came over me, suddenly – the old feeling. *He could be wonderful*, Hana had said, in spite of everything. Orson with his stories and his extravagant gestures, his scars, his handsome tanned face and the new, rather dashing moustache. No – not the Lodging House, I decided. He would be off to meet May, to take her dancing at the St. Regis, or the Empire Room at the Waldorf, and they would chuckle over my gullibility all over again. The idea amused me, improbable though it was, and I almost hoped it was the truth. Then my own detachment amused me even more. I thought that maybe I would tell Hana after all. *I ran into Orson*, I would say, *and he was just – Orson.*

"Jesus, it was good to see you, Robert." Orson slid off his stool. "You're looking good, you know." He fingered my lapel. "Nice jacket. And I don't think you got that tie at Woolworth's. But then you always did have good taste in clothes – I can testify to that." He grinned, showing his square teeth. "No offence."

I shrugged, and he jabbed me with his elbow, playfully. "Oh come on, Robert. Don't you see the humor in the situation? For God's sake, can't I get a chuckle out of you?"

"I'm laughing on the inside, Orson," I said.

"That's right. I'd forgotten." He tipped his head back and drained his glass. "Hell of a thing, in this city, to run into you like this. Among the faceless millions." He stuck out his hand, and I shook it. "Maybe we'll meet again."

"Who knows?"

His smile faded, and he said, abruptly, "You don't miss her."

Oddly, it was a statement rather than a question, but I answered it. "No."

He kept hold of my hand. For a moment, I thought he was going to embrace me, as he used to, and I had a vivid recollection of his wiry body, and his peculiar, yeasty odor, like bread. *I ran into Orson, and he was just Orson,* I would say, and in some sense that would be a lie. He and I stared at each other for a moment, and then he let go of my hand and walked the length of the bar to the door. He was a little unsteady on his feet. At the door he turned and looked as if he might come back and say something more, but he didn't. He went out the door onto Fifth Avenue and turned toward Eighth Street. Except in dreams, I never saw him again.

EPILOGUE

San Miguel de Allende, Mexico
1990

"Is that you, Darnell?"

"Yes, sir, it's me, all right."

"How was the cantina?"

I see your white smile in the dark. "It was the way it always is, Mr. Sinclair."

"You were gone a little longer than usual."

"I know it, Mr. Sinclair. I apologize for that. I'm here now."

Your voice, Darnell, calms me like a cool cloth on my forehead. A snifter of Hennessy's. The scent of our lime tree in blossom. The candles have burned low. The moon has risen over the tops of the roofs. It's been peaceful here in the warm breeze, and that music coming from somewhere, those guitars. Don't push me inside just yet, Darnell. Sit a while. Sit here with me.

"Something I need to say, Mr. Sinclair, and I don't know just how to do it."

"Sit down, Darnell." The moonlight glows on your face, on your skin that's as smooth and brown as fine wood. Your face is an ancient carving – but so young, Darnell. So young. "Have another cigar, why don't you? And pour yourself a little of that cognac."

"That might help."

"That's what I thought. And then – well, Darnell – *speak what you feel, not what you ought to say.*"

"That's what I want to do, Mr. Sinclair. But I hope you won't take it wrong."

"Let's have it, then." When I reach out for you, my old white hand, all spotted and knotty with veins, is the ugliest thing I've ever seen. I have to turn my head away.

"It's hard for me, Mr. Sinclair. I've been with you a long time – came down here with you from New York because I'd never had such good job. You've been mighty kind to me all these years. But what I want to say is that I'm going to have to be leaving you."

I knew the day would come. But I thought it would be I who would be leaving, going off to the undiscovered country, from whose bourne no traveller returns. It's odd how Shakespeare keeps coming back to me. The way Gil Waldemar used to quote Keats toward the end. Gil, who choked on his own blood. How will I die, exactly? How will this thing take me? I always thought you would be with me, Darnell. But in the end, we die alone anyway, don't we? Like Gil. Like Mrs. Amalfi with her groceries.

"The truth of it is, I've met someone over at the cantina. Been seeing him for some months now. And we're going to go away together, Mr. Sinclair. What we want is to travel to Paris to live for a while. He's got some money saved, and so do I, and it's what we've both always wanted to do. It was a coincidence, you know. How that was a dream for both of us. So we were thinking of taking off, maybe in the fall. Maybe sooner, if you could find someone to take my place."

Those are more words than I've ever heard you put together all at once, Darnell. And there's a lot in them. You're telling me the story of your life, you're telling me your dreams. I'm seeing you and this man at the cantina, confessing your dreams to each other. I'm seeing his eyes on your smooth skin, your arms, your hairless chest where your shirt is open at the neck, and your lips like fruit.

"Well, Darnell. I'm at a loss for words."

"I know, Mr. Sinclair. It's a sudden thing. I know that. I didn't know what you would say."

"What's his name?"

"His name?"

"Your friend. What's he called?"

"Diego. That's Spanish for James. You probably knew that already, Mr. Sinclair. I call him Jim sometimes."

"Diego. A very beautiful name. Is he a good man?"

"He's a very good man."

"Then I'm happy for you Darnell. I hate to see you go, but you have to do these things when you're young."

"That's what we thought, Mr. Sinclair. That's what we said, just tonight."

And then you left the cantina and slipped off together somewhere, maybe he has a room nearby, maybe you never went to the cantina at all but went directly to his bed. I remember when I used to meet Rennie Knox like that, those nights at that bar on West 4th Street, near Christopher. What was it called? And those arguments afterward with Arthur.

"He's a musician, Mr. Sinclair. Plays the guitar, plays keyboard. I don't speak much Spanish, you know, but Jim speaks pretty good English. We figure we'll learn some French when we get to Paris."

"Yes. You will, Darnell, I'm sure."

Arthur's still alive, but he's in a home, Hana told me. Alzheimer's. And Rennie died long ago from an overdose. Who else? My poor sister Joanie. Della Lyons last year after they took her breasts off. Van Kalman and his new young wife in that plane crash. Yvonne just after the revival of *The Monkey Tree* in London, dropped dead in the street. Mickey Kennedy, I saw that in the paper last summer. And Ophelia, my last cat – dear old Ophelia, the little gray cloud....

Ah, Darnell – how does it go? *Precious friends hid in death's dateless night.* And now May Munro. Hard to imagine her dead. May with her dreams, her blonde hair. Her ambition. You could see her burning with it, Darnell. If you want something badly enough you can overcome anything, even lack of talent, even a cheap and stunted soul. There. That tells you something, doesn't it? I used to think I wasn't angry with May for what she did, but the anger is there now – right there, simmering away. Maybe now that she's dead. Or maybe now that I'm dead.

And Orson Price. I wonder what happened to Orson. His hair would be white now, most likely. He'd still be thin, though. Lean and muscular. The skin would be loose on his arms, and he'd have hands like mine, Darnell. But he'd still look good. He'd look like Hana, maybe, my lovely Hana with her sharp little face.

May and Orson. Well, between the two of them, I grew up. I can't think of that boy I used to be without chagrin – how could anyone be so dense, so ignorant – so *green*? And yet I have a great fondness for him. That was the last summer of his existence, and what he left behind was just a younger version of who I am now.

"Would you like to go inside now, Mr. Sinclair?"

"Maybe I should, Darnell. It's just a little chilly out here."

How strange, really, to be so old. You can't imagine it until you're in the midst of it. To be old, sick, helpless, to give over everything to the young. You won't need to wait until fall, Darnell, you and your Diego. I won't last 'til midsummer, I don't think, and Dr. Mendoza agrees with me, though he won't say so.

You push this heavy chair so easily, Darnell, hoist me up over the little step. Always gentle, always there. Another thing about being old. You're always having to be grateful. Always having to think you're lucky things aren't any worse. Glad when you wake up in the morning, sun pouring through the window, and think: *one more day – they've let me have one more day.*

Ah, take it, Darnell, take this world, take this life, with its sweetness, its lime flowers. But stay with me until I'm gone.

It's in my will that my money will go to Joanie's boys, my nephews. Grown men now, with their own troubled families. But they don't need my money. They've got plenty – more than they deserve, it seems to me. I'll leave it to you, Darnell. What a surprise it will be. Like Gil and those cuff links – comedy and tragedy – when I found them wrapped in paper with my name on it. You'll be sorry when I die, I know, but then you'll have the money, and I don't fool myself – it will help you stop grieving for me. But you won't forget me, either. Comedy and tragedy, Darnell. I'll call Mateo Diaz in the morning, get him over here with his secretary and her little laptop computer, make it legal.

"You ready now, Mr. Sinclair?"

"Yes, Darnell, I am."

"You seem tired tonight."

Tired. Yes, I'm tired. But there are worse things than tiredness, God knows. Your voice is like music, like honey, like the scent of a flowering tree. It fills me with – well, I can't call it happiness, I'm too old for that, but something resembling happiness. Something I remember that's almost as good. Maybe better.

But I'm rambling now. Take me to bed, Darnell, lay me down with your strong arms, your warm brown hands, and make me sleep.

Make me sleep.